Some Hidden Force
Drew Them to One Another....

Suddenly she was all emotion, all feeling. There was something so right in the look that passed between them—so intimate and caring—that she could not deny the sensations stirring within her.

Their lips fused and their hands joined and clasped tightly. He drew her against him, and she was so close she could feel the powerful beating of his heart. After several minutes, Alex slowly pulled away, brushing her parted lips with his as he tried to speak.

"Maggie . . ." he whispered, "will you stay?"

Her palm in his hair, she guided his lips back to hers. . . .

Dear Reader:

We trust you will enjoy this Richard Gallen romance. We plan to bring you more of the best in both contemporary and historical romantic fiction with four exciting new titles each month.

We'd like your help.

We value your suggestions and opinions. They will help us to publish the kind of romances you want to read. Please send us your comments, or just let us know which Richard Gallen romances you have especially enjoyed. Write to the address below. We're looking forward to hearing from you!

Happy reading!

Judy Sullivan
Richard Gallen Books
8-10 West 36th St.
New York, N.Y. 10018

Roman Candles

SOFI O'BRYAN

PUBLISHED BY RICHARD GALLEN BOOKS
Distributed by POCKET BOOKS

Also published by RICHARD GALLEN BOOKS

Waters of Eden
 by Katherine Kent

An Elegant Affair
 by Kathleen Morris

A Dream of Fire
 by Drusilla Campbell

This novel is a work of fiction. Names, characters, places and incidents are either the product of the author's imagination or are used fictitiously, and any resemblance to actual persons, living or dead, events or locales is entirely coincidental.

A RICHARD GALLEN BOOKS *Original* publication

Distributed by
POCKET BOOKS, a Simon & Schuster division of
GULF & WESTERN CORPORATION
1230 Avenue of the Americas, New York, N.Y. 10020

Copyright © 1981 by Sofi O'Bryan

All rights reserved, including the right to reproduce
this book or portions thereof in any form whatsoever.
For information address Pocket Books, 1230 Avenue
of the Americas, New York, N.Y. 10020

ISBN: 0-671-43470-5

First Pocket Books printing August, 1981

10 9 8 7 6 5 4 3 2 1

RICHARD GALLEN and colophon are trademarks
of Simon & Schuster and Richard Gallen & Co., Inc.

Printed in the U.S.A.

Roman Candles

Chapter 1

Maggie Reardon was smiling as she climbed into the cab on Vanderbilt Avenue. Carefully, she put a cardboard box beside her on the seat as she gave the driver the East Seventy-seventh Street address.

"Any particular way you'd like to go?" The cab driver was young, hungry and fishing to find out if she were an out-of-towner, unfamiliar with New York City. After all, he'd picked her up at Grand Central Station. If she were vague, she knew, he'd drive her crosstown and then back to the East Side. But she couldn't blame him today; she was much too happy, much too mellow and much too eager to be with Craig. Weddings did that to her. Her cousin's wedding in Wilton, Connecticut, had been exactly right for her—the flowers, the music, the church, the family and the enormous wedding cake with two tiny figures speared to the top tier.

"Take the Drive, it's faster," she told the driver, settling back in her seat.

Craig would be waiting for her, surprised, of course, that she had come back so soon. He didn't expect her until late this evening, and now it was barely ten A.M. He'd be pleased. She'd give him the slice of wedding cake. He'd smile, his brown eyes would light up, and he'd laugh and say something silly like, "Maggie, how like you, wedding cake!" And she'd laugh, and they'd reach out for each other quickly because she'd been away for two days. She had missed him, really missed him!

Maybe it was the wedding, or her parents, still happily married after all these years and able to communicate with each other with just a glance. It gave substance and reason to her life to know they were there, people like her mother and father and her cousin Martha too—getting married, buying little Cape Cod houses, having children, paying taxes, going to church on Sunday. She felt warmed by the stability of their lives. Still, she had her own—she was eager to return to Craig and the life that was hers now.

"Do you want to scream, or should I ravish you and then let you scream?" he'd said to her the first time they'd met in a stalled elevator in the building where Maggie worked as a research editor for *Shout,* the monthly magazine whose motto boasted, "You Are There With Us." It was an amalgam of fast-breaking news stories with longer, in-depth series on social, cultural, political and economic issues around the globe. She loved her job, and that day she wasn't aware that the man in the elevator with her was Craig Hastings, the son of the publisher. All she knew was that he was teasing her.

She stared at him out of clear, hazel eyes in an oval-shaped face outlined by soft, auburn hair that curled its own way and fell just short of her chinline. He didn't exactly look the part of a ravisher in his gray, pin-striped suit, white shirt and narrow, black silk tie. But when he smiled, she could almost see him in jeans and a sweatshirt, that shock of brown hair flying in the wind, dashing around a soccer field. A preppie gone legit, as she and her best friend Ellen Townsend said about boys who became men, boys who left college campuses to become instant chameleons, changing quickly to suit their immediate needs and circumstances. In her four years at Skidmore, Maggie had met dozens like him, and she felt very comfortable with Craig.

"I don't scream easily, and as for being ravished by you—no thanks, I'm not interested," she'd said to him that day.

He'd laughed. "I like you. You work here, of course."

"Of course, doesn't everyone?" she had smiled. "Do you?" She felt so stupid afterwards, not knowing who he was. But, then, why should she? Craig Hastings was a golden boy.

ROMAN CANDLES

He flitted in and out of the empire his father had built and didn't spend too much time getting to know the hired help.

"Sort of," he'd answered, a wide grin spreading across his face.

"What kind of sort of?" she had started to ask, when the elevator jolted, ascended a few feet, stopped, then started to descend again. Jostled by the jerky elevator, Maggie somehow found herself in Craig's arms, being held close, the smell of his shaving lotion pungent in her nostrils.

"Before we die, may I say I love you?" he'd teased, and his mouth came down on hers so suddenly that she practically went limp in his arms. It was a passionate, heart-stopping kiss, and so unexpected that she allowed herself to stay in his embrace longer than she felt she ought to. When the elevator came to a halt on the tenth floor, he started to get out.

"I'll be seeing you." He smiled. "What did you say your name was?"

"I didn't." She glared at him then, not wanting him to think he'd unnerved her with that kiss.

He kept the door open with both hands, holding it steady in place. "I'm Craig Hastings, who are you?"

"Maggie . . . Reardon." He let the door go, the elevator continued its ascent, and Maggie was in love. That's how she told it to her roommate Ellen two weeks later, after Craig had called, and she'd gone out with him five nights in a row and found out he was the son of the publisher.

It is obligatory—and corny—to be young and in love in September in New York. They did everything, the horse-and-buggy rides in Central Park, great fish dinners at a place Craig loved on Fulton Street, the ferry to the Statue of Liberty, wild nights at Friday's, feeling sorry for all the singles. And, finally and inevitably, there was the night at Craig's apartment when, after a bottle of Dom Perignon, he said, "Stay . . . don't go home tonight."

"No, of course not," she'd murmured.

It was as natural and as right as that. His lovemaking that first time was abrupt and urgent, as though having found her, he had to establish priorities. And then they made love slowly and quietly, his hands trailing lines of fire across her firm breasts, cupping her flat belly, moving downward at her urging, and then moving over and around her again, engulfing her, mesmerizing her.

ROMAN CANDLES

"I knew the day we got caught in that elevator that I was going to ravish you!" he whispered.

"Like in novels?" She giggled.

"Like this." His mouth clamped down on hers, his tongue snaked into her willing mouth, touching, arousing her again.

They talked about college. He'd gone to Dartmouth.

"I should have known, a wild Indian," she teased. "I spent a weekend fighting for my honor on that campus."

"Did you lose?"

"You'll never know," she'd taunted him.

He wanted to know all about her. Her parents in Wilton, Connecticut, her younger brother, her first job as a reporter for a Hartford newspaper.

"The great white hope of journalism," she'd laughed. "I learned. There was this crusty old newspaperman—they're all crusty when they're old, aren't they? He was twice-divorced, sour, but good. He did badger me, but for good reasons. Know what he did one day? Right there in the city room? He came over, stood at my desk, glared down at me and yelled in a booming voice: 'Do you have a period on your typewriter?' Dummy that I was, I looked down and said yes. And then, he barked: 'Use it!'"

"Damned good advice."

"Yes. I was still doing college papers. You know—long, flowery sentences."

"And then you came to New York. I hear all ambitious little girls do."

"I came to New York and I got a job on a trade paper that folded after three months, and my poor father had to subsidize me until I got the job at *Shout*."

"Like it?"

"Love it. For now. But I really want to write. I've done some fillers, nothing earth-shaking. I did regular columns at my previous jobs but, I'm well aware, you move up, you have to start back at scratch. Mostly I do research now. But I have to write."

"What?"

"I'm going to write on important subjects like . . . people, women, politics. That's why I like working at *Shout* now. Some of the exposé-type pieces really get to me."

"Name one."

"That series on illegal aliens; I think that was very powerful."

"Alex Parisi," Craig grinned. "Friend of mine."

"He's good."

"The best. We're sending him back to Rome in a little while. He did a hell of a job on the Aldo Moro news when it broke—the kidnapping, execution, the whole bit. Alex likes that sort of thing. He's always looking for a revolution to happen. Terrorists should be right up his alley. He'll be our European connection."

"I'd like a job like that."

"You're my New York connection. I like you right here," Craig had murmured. And again they'd made love, and again it was almost like the first time, exploring, exciting, insatiably passionate.

Then one night she met Alex. She and Craig were having dinner at Piccolo Mondo on First Avenue. Maggie adored the northern Italian food Craig had introduced her to and was digging into her *linguini alle vongole,* dipping hunks of crusty bread into the white clam sauce, when Alex stopped by their table. She looked up, felt sauce dribbling down her chin, and laughed as she acknowledged the introduction.

"Sorry, I love to eat," she grinned at Alex.

"Sit. Have some wine," Craig insisted.

"Thanks, just for a minute," he said, sitting between them. "I'm meeting someone."

Maggie thought she'd never met such an angry young man. There was a tenseness about him that belied the athletic, broad-shouldered look and casual, dark brown hair falling across his forehead. He had almost black eyes and a square chin that somehow invited a punch. His metal-framed glasses kept sliding down his prominent nose. He stared at Maggie, then at Craig, as though trying to put together jigsaw puzzle pieces that didn't fit.

"The hotshot writer you admire," Craig told Maggie. "Your number-one fan, Alex. She likes what you do."

"So do I," Alex said.

"Umm, modest too," Maggie retorted.

"I don't believe in the word," he said bluntly. "If you can do something well, do it and take the kudos. My father's credo."

"What was he? A politician?" Maggie asked.

"He's a writer. Writes nature stuff, books on conservation."

"An ecologist."

"Hardly." Alex laughed, and when he did, the tenseness went out of his face. He wasn't so much handsome as he was ruggedly male. Maggie could almost detect the little boy he'd been long ago behind this façade of the tough investigative reporter. "No, I'm afraid dad doesn't have the necessary degrees to qualify as such. He was drafted in World War Two when he was barely eighteen, and by the time he got back, college seemed an unrealistic goal. Mostly he wanted to wake people up to the beauty of the earth they were destroying."

"Off the soapbox, Parisi, this isn't college anymore," Craig cut in. "How's the Italy thing shaping up?"

"Good. I ought to be cutting out soon. I'll make Rome my base for a while, see what develops."

"Got anything special lined up?" Craig asked.

"Lots of things have to jell, it's all in the thinking stage now. Me talking to me."

"Sort of one-sided, isn't it?" Maggie couldn't stop herself from interjecting.

"Try it sometime." He looked directly into her eyes, challenging her. "You learn a lot about yourself."

Before Maggie could answer, Alex's dinner companion showed up. It was an older man. Maggie had simply assumed it would be a woman. But, then again, Alex looked like the kind of man a woman would have to run to keep up with. Personally, she wasn't sure it would be worth it.

Alex thanked Craig for the wine, nodded to Maggie and walked away.

"Is he always so angry?" she asked Craig.

"Well, he's a good guy, just running too hard, let's put it that way."

"You're not."

"Why should I run when I've got what I want right here?" He reached over and took her hand in his, holding it tight. "Now, how about it? Have you eaten enough? I want to make love to you."

"Umm, right here?"

"Could be a first."

ROMAN CANDLES

"Silly."

"Let's go." His eyes blazed into hers, and shivers of anticipation raced deliciously up her spine.

Gradually—so easily she wasn't aware of it herself—she began staying over at Craig's apartment more frequently. She even left some of her clothes there, and Craig had given her a key for the times when they planned to meet at his place but he had to be late. She began playing house. She bought real food for his refrigerator, pushing aside the bottles of Bass ale and Dom Perignon he seemed to live on and adding cheeses, eggs, orange juice and some steaks in the freezer. Craig had noticed, but hadn't particularly liked it.

"I enjoy eating out," he said cryptically.

She'd been hurt, so she soft-pedaled the homemaker image after that.

One weekend, she went to Wilton to visit her parents on her mother's birthday. Her mother asked if there were anyone special in her life—her mother always wanted to know those things.

She found herself talking about Craig Hastings too Oh, not telling everything, but still gushing like a schoolgirl.

"Do I hear wedding bells?" her mother prodded her.

"Mother! Don't push!" She realized she sounded abrupt.

"Speaking of which—wedding bells, I mean—you'll be getting an invitation to your Cousin Martha's wedding. I hope you can make it."

"Uh-oh, another wedding present. Too many cousins in this family, mom," Maggie groaned. "What'll I get? And keep it reasonable, okay?"

She hadn't promised to attend the wedding because she wasn't sure what Craig might have planned for that weekend. Although she kept her days and evenings open, he wasn't always available for her. Not like in the beginning.

"The old man wants me to work up some kind of diversification thing, lots of meetings and crap like that."

"You're a bloated big shot," she'd teased.

"Something like that."

One night she waited in his apartment until after ten. Hungry, she'd made herself a dry cheese sandwich, washed it

7

down with a beer, and had fallen asleep on the couch. She awoke some time in the early morning hours, stiff and chilled. She staggered toward the bedroom, suddenly fearful that Craig had been in an accident or a mugging. The apartment was empty; the bedside clock read 3:45 A.M. Frantic, she'd paced the floor like a nervous cop on a Harlem beat. She'd put on a pot of coffee eventually, undressed, and decided to take a bath to calm herself. She was drying off when she heard his key in the door. It was nearly seven in the morning.

She'd rushed toward him, the towel covering her nakedness. "Are you all right? What happened? Damn it, Craig, I've been worried about you!"

He'd frowned. "What for? And why are you here?"

"I was waiting for you." She slammed a fist into his chest. "Last night—don't you remember? We were going to meet here for dinner."

"Oh, Christ." He slapped a hand to his forehead. "I forgot. The thing is, I got caught up in this business talk with the old man, and then mother insisted that I stay and eat, and then I fell asleep. . . . Sorry, baby, really sorry."

"You could have called," she'd said in a small voice, not quite sure he was telling her the truth, but also not sure it was her prerogative to quiz him.

"Sure. It'll never happen again. Promise. Hey, you look cute. I think I'll ravish you."

"Fool." She wrapped her arms around him, letting the towel fall to the carpet. "I was so damned scared. And then I fell asleep. And I never did get dinner!"

"Always hungry! But you're not scared now, are you?" he'd murmured in her ear, hands sliding slowly down her nakedness, teasing her breasts, smiling broadly when her nipples hardened under his fingertips. She could feel his excitement throbbing against her, and she began to melt. "How much time do we have? Will you get fired if you're late?" he asked, picking her up, carrying her to the bedroom, and then laughing at the idea that she could be fired.

"That's all right. I'll tell my supervisor I was late because I was in bed doing terrible things with the boss's son." She was reaching eagerly to help him undress, sliding onto the empty bed and putting her arms up to receive him. So right, so natural, she thought. She forgot that she'd been angry with him for hours.

She was two hours late for work that day. Mabel Weeks, her supervisor, had frowned and walked over to her desk with some folders when she saw her walk in.

"Glad to have you with us," she'd said. A stern woman in her fifties, she was a powerhouse around the office and knew everything and everyone. Mabel was a shrewd, hard-working woman who was widowed and had raised two sons on her own. She had been with the magazine since its inception. "See what you can dig up for us on this."

"What is it?" Maggie had asked, taking the folder, wondering if Mabel Weeks had ever known real passion in her life, wondering if her lips, still tingling from Craig's kisses, betrayed her with what she had been doing so recently. But Mrs. Weeks didn't seem to have anything on her mind except work.

"Children, servicemen's follies."

"Is that going to be the title of the piece?" Maggie asked.

"I don't know yet. Right now we need statistics, lots of them. Like how many GIs there were in the European theater and in the Pacific during World War Two and the particulars on war brides. I think there were restrictions on so-called alliances between servicemen and locals; company commanders had to give permission and there was always a long wait before a marriage was okayed. That sort of thing. We need all of those facts and more. We can move up to Korea and Vietnam later if we need it, but for now let's concentrate on Europe. See what you can come up with. Our servicemen undoubtedly left thousands of offspring all over the world."

Maggie had shivered when Mabel had said that. She'd never really thought of it that way but, of course, wars were hell, as Sherman had observed, and not just for the men who fought them but also for all the innocent people, the women and children involved.

"This will take some digging," Maggie said, as she glanced through the folder.

"So?"

"Who's going to write it? I mean when I've finished the research."

"No one's been assigned yet, came out of yesterday's

editorial conference. Let's see what you can come up with, and we'll pass it along to the editorial board at one of their next meetings."

Maggie began her research with fervor. She made calls to Family Service, to the U.N. missions, to the Washington Chief of Staff of Army Personnel; she spent several days at the main branch of the public library at Forty-second Street; she called adoption agencies, and was still at her research on the Friday afternoon before the weekend of her cousin's wedding.

"I have to go," she told Craig.

"Sure. I understand."

"I want to," she had surprised herself by saying.

"Enjoy."

"Want to come?"

"God, no. I hate ceremonies, especially in other people's families. You go alone."

"Will you miss me?"

"What do you think?"

"I think . . . you'll survive." She wanted to hear him say he'd miss her. She would miss him.

But she loved the wedding, as it turned out. And it had been more than fun. It had been a refreshing renewal of old faiths and mores, and she had pleased her parents by attending. She honestly liked pleasing them, she mused, back in Manhattan, as the cab pulled up in front of Craig's building. No anxiety, no pressing need for total approval, just the delight of seeing the love in their faces. One day soon she wanted to take Craig to Wilton to meet her parents. Oh, not one of those acceptance kind of meetings, just nice people meeting a very special guy.

She forgot her parents and the wedding and everything about the weekend as she punched the elevator button, holding the carton with the cake close to her. They'd have champagne with the wedding cake, toast the absent bride and bridegroom, and then . . . and then, of course, they'd drift toward the bedroom and maybe spend the day there, eating caviar on stoned-wheat crackers, sipping more champagne, exploring their bodies all over again after this short time away from one another.

She decided, as she walked out of the elevator, not to awaken Craig this early. She'd use her key to let herself in and take the cake and champagne to him in bed. She was as quiet as she could be, turning the key in the lock, pushing the door open, moving in softly. A glance at the coffee table made her frown. An empty wine bottle, glasses, some dishes. Craig was no messier than usual, she supposed. She put down the box, went toward the bedroom, and peered in. She saw a mound of covers with Craig's head falling sideways off the pillow, just as he always slept. Then her heart thumped, stopped, and raced on. There was another head on the second pillow, a blonde head with hair in disarray and a naked shoulder peeking out of the sheet.

Maggie had no idea how long she stood there taking in the scene. Tacky. The word began to pound in her brain. Unaccountably, she didn't even feel betrayed at the moment. Tacky, tacky, that's what it was. She backed out of the bedroom, took one last look around the apartment that she knew as well as her own, and then fled, leaving the wedding cake on the coffee table.

Chapter 2

She rushed out of his apartment more in rage than shock, back to the street and into another cab. She went to her apartment half-hoping Ellen wouldn't be in, that she'd be off somewhere with Stan. As luck had it, though, Ellen was in bed, asleep, when Maggie came in.

She went to their tiny kitchenette, plugged in the coffeepot, and stood near the sink, staring at the drainboard as though it were a Broadway marquee. It hurt, dammit, it hurt. Maybe it was just her pride for the moment, but the scene had cheapened her too. And her relationship with Craig. She had thought—no, *expected*—that theirs was such a close relationship there hadn't been a need for a third person. What now, Maggie Reardon? Act noble and forget the scene? Be a woman of today and say, aw, shucks, Craig, I know how these things can happen, let's just forget it and pick up where we left off. . . .

She couldn't do that. It wasn't in her to accept deceit. Again, the pattern of her life asserted itself. Once a thing was ended, she discarded it quickly with as few postmortems as possible. Actually, she knew herself well enough to realize that having seen Craig in bed with that woman, she would keep the image emblazoned in her mind forever. She couldn't go to bed with Craig now any more than she could fly. It was over, *finito*, *kaput*. Like that, in one little moment on a

Sunday so bright with promise. And it still hurt. She leaned into the sink.

"Hi!" Ellen, sleepy, her tousled blonde hair awry, stood in the doorway. "I thought I smelled coffee."

"Have some." Maggie, glad of something to do, poured coffee into mugs and handed one to Ellen.

"What are you doing back so soon? I thought you weren't coming home until tonight."

"Oh, Christ, don't tell me Stan is . . . ?"

Ellen shook her head, walked into the living room and curled up in a chair. "No, he left a while ago, has to spend Sunday with the family in New Jersey. So, how was the wedding?"

"Great, you know, here comes the bride, God help her hide." Maggie tried to laugh.

"That much fun, huh?" They'd been together since college and Ellen always knew when her roommate was trying to be tough and stoic. "So, after the wedding, what happened?"

"Oh, I decided to come back early, and then I thought I'd surprise Craig with some wedding cake and all, since the spirit had so moved me. I let myself into his apartment and tiptoed into the bedroom. . . ."

"Uh-oh, who's that sleeping in my bed!"

"You got it. She had to be a blonde too. I mean, why is it always a blonde?"

"I'll ignore that comment. What happened?"

"This isn't a goddam soap opera, Ellen! I left!"

"He didn't see you, hear you?"

"I didn't stick around to find out," she said. "Christ, I feel so . . . used!"

"I know what you mean," Ellen murmured, and then suddenly she began to giggle. "You mean you actually . . . he was in bed and didn't hear you?"

Maggie began to laugh. "In bed, in the buff, both of them. And they didn't . . . they didn't even hear. . . ." The laughter burst out of her in a raucous guffaw that was very close to a sob.

Ellen stood up, looking slightly embarrassed. "I've got to get a move on, I'm meeting Geraldine for lunch later. Hey, want to come along?"

"No thanks. I've got some work to do." Maggie waved

aimlessly toward the coffee table where her work folders were piled, where she'd tossed them before going to Wilton.

"I'll shower fast," Ellen promised.

"Take your time."

She was tense until Ellen left. Then she hurried into the shower, tearing her clothes off and tossing them on her bed. Surprisingly, after squeezing out a few tears in the shower, she didn't really cry. Always in college, when things got too much for her, she'd rush into the shower, turn it on full force and wail into the spray.

She wandered back into the living room, wrapped in a blue chenille robe, and curled up on the couch. She felt so tired. Like someone had suddenly pulled the plug on her, she was drained. Her anger had left her, and now she was simply confused. About Craig, about herself, about herself and men, about that scene in his bedroom. Obviously, he hadn't expected her to return to New York so soon. He'd met someone who attracted him, and he'd taken her to bed. Did that infringe on their relationship in any meaningful way? Neither one had a stamp on the other. That she thought she'd loved him—or still loved him—was *her* problem. She put her head back, trying to slow down her thinking.

Tacky. It really was. Well, what else could she have done? What if she'd become outraged, dragged the girl out of Craig's bed, denounced him as a stinker? God! That brought a smile to her face. Like a replay from a thirties movie. So, her pride had been damaged. She had believed that she was the only one in Craig's life. Not that he'd told her in so many words, but she'd wanted to think it.

Her eyes fell on the folders on the coffee table. She should get her notes together to hand in to Mabel Weeks. It was difficult to keep her mind on her work. Her thoughts kept edging away, going back to Craig. Wait, he didn't even know she'd been in his apartment this morning. Well, he'd have to know by now. When he found the wedding cake, he'd understand that she'd left it there. When would that be? After he woke up, padded into the kitchen and made coffee, then went back to the bedroom, the way she and Craig often had, to make love once more? She closed her eyes, feeling the ache deep in her gut. Damn, it had been so good, waking up, turning, the first shock of surprise that someone else was in bed with her, and then reaching out ... touching ... stroking ... sighing. ...

"Gotta brush my teeth," Craig always said. "Christ, I hate it when people in movies wake up and kiss without washing out their mouths!"

They brushed their teeth together, turning to kiss through each other's foamy lips, then they would run back to bed and fall in with mouths tingling of toothpaste, bodies warming to eager thrusts, and always the long time afterwards when they stayed, spent and limp, sated with passion.

The ringing phone startled Maggie out of her reverie. She dropped a folder, scattering papers all over the braided rug she and Ellen had bought to cover the worn wood floor. She hesitated. Craig! It had to be. He'd found the cake, realized she had been in the apartment. So what now? Call Maggie and apologize, say an old friend from out of town paid a surprise visit and stayed over?

She let the phone ring. She wasn't in the mood to talk to him. Not now, maybe not ever again. She sulked and hated herself for sulking. It was all so unnecessary. She ought to pick up the phone, talk to Craig, dismiss him from her mind and her life and forget the entire experience. Be like his friend Alex Parisi. There was a cool customer, driven by inner career demons, totally unconcerned about what others thought or did.

The phone rang again, and again a half-hour later. After a few hours, Maggie put aside her work and made herself some scrambled eggs and bacon. *Funny. Habits die hard. If I'm broken-hearted, how can I be hungry?* she wondered. *Except I'm always hungry—happy, sad, silly, hungry.* She ate heartily, washing it all down with two cups of coffee. She wanted something else to eat when she was finished. Scrounging around in the kitchen cabinet, she found a package of chocolate, cream-filled cookies and ate half of them.

"Maggie, my girl," she said out loud, "you are going to be a fat old lady one day." She walked into the bathroom again, took off her robe, closed the door and stared at her thin, lithe body in the full-length mirror. A body, she thought, not unlike millions of other bodies. What is it that makes people fall in love, anyway? Is it chemistry? Or is love just a state of mind? Does there come a time in life when the mind says: now, it is time to fall in love, pick one or the other, copulate, propagate. Is it nature taking its course? Just one more spin on the wheel of life?

She stepped into the shower again, as though wishing to wash away the last few hours. When she was finished, she felt invigorated; she could start again. She pulled on her robe and returned to the livingroom couch to tackle the papers on the coffee table.

Seen through a prism, it occurred to her, everything looks tacky. Even a wedding. How barbaric! The bride in virginal white presented by a doting father to the groom so that their union can be consummated on some motel bed that night! The corny toasts, the tapping of spoons on glasses, "The groom kisses the bride, the bride kisses the groom. . . ."

But it's right for some people, her heart told her. For most people. The corniness and the blandness and the tackiness is so right and so real. It changes over the years—deepens or mellows or something, like it had for her parents. *Do you have a better solution, Maggie Reardon?* she asked herself.

She jumped. Someone was leaning on the doorbell. Not Ellen—she'd use her key. It had to be Craig. She pondered a moment. She could let him lean on it until he got tired and went away, but what was the point in that? She'd have to see him and talk with him sooner or later. And this was much better than meeting him in the office with nosy people around.

Tightening the belt on her robe, she went to the hallway, buzzed the downstairs door, opened the apartment door, and waited. He stomped up the flight of stairs, glaring at her as he walked past her into the room. He had the carton with the wedding cake under one arm.

"Yours, I presume." He dumped it on her coffee table.

"Yes, Doctor Livingston," she quipped.

"No cracks, Maggie. Why in hell didn't you call?"

She shrugged. "Didn't think I had to. I wanted to surprise you. Some surprise."

"Cut the crap. What do you want me to say? I'm sorry? Okay, I'm sorry. It didn't mean a damned thing. I went out, got a bit crocked, met this chick. . . ."

"Hey, you don't have to spell it out for me," Maggie cut in. "It's okay, really."

A smile creased his face. He came toward her. "You know something? You're some kind of girl. I knew it the first day we met in that elevator. Christ, all the way over here, trying to call you earlier, I kept thinking it was a lousy thing for you to walk in on."

"Forget it, I said. Uninvited guests expect to be unwelcome."

"What's that supposed to mean?"

"Craig," she turned back to him, "why don't we just drop it? You're sorry, I'm sorry, the world hasn't stopped. I've got a headache, so why don't you just go away now?"

"Just like that?"

"Is there another way?"

"I get it. You *are* sore, you're going to make it hard on me, right?"

"Wrong. I'm not sore. Hurt maybe. Feeling stupid for sure. Feeling the whole thing was unnecessary. But I'm not sore."

"I accept that. Now, if you're really not sore, put something on and let's go out and have a nice meal," he said.

He made a move toward her. He actually put an arm out to try to draw her toward him. She ducked away.

"You amaze me, Craig. Are you really that insensitive?"

"What are you talking about? I apologized, didn't I? Don't make a federal case out of this, Maggie. Come on, grow up. Let's go sit over a bottle of wine and some spaghetti and forget it ever happened."

"No thanks. I don't want to go anywhere with you. Not now, maybe. . . ."

"Jesus, you *are* mad. I thought you were a cool lady, a sophisticated woman."

"Craig, will you get the hell out of here before I say something I'll regret? If I haven't gotten through to you by now, I never will. Just go!"

"I guess I didn't know you at all."

"Have you tried lately?" she snapped.

"I'm trying now to understand why you're throwing away a perfectly good relationship because of one mishap."

"You son-of-a-bitch." Maggie said it quietly.

"Aw, that's not a nice thing to say." Craig grinned, albeit in an embarrassed way. "Maggie, I swear, it was one of those things. It happened. I was out with people, and I met this girl. We got to drinking, and she wound up in my apartment."

"In your bed, you mean."

ROMAN CANDLES

"It was nothing! Hey, come off it. Since when have you been appointed my keeper?"

Maggie flinched. She had that coming to her. How naïve could she be? She had no right to come down so hard on Craig just because she'd been shattered by the scene in his apartment and he thought it was nothing. They were different people with different perspectives on life. She ought to have called from Wilton, or even Grand Central. But now, oddly enough, it didn't really matter to her. She just wanted him out—out of her apartment, out of her life.

"Look, it wasn't my fault! It just happened!"

"I know. You told me. You're sorry, I'm sorry, and I'm sick and tired of talking about it. Get out, Craig, right now, split. That's all there is left to do."

"Like hell." He came toward her, grabbed her, pulled her hard against him, and forced her head up so that his mouth found hers in a savage kiss. She kicked out, getting him in the shin. He let go and backed off, glaring at her.

"Jesus," he growled. "You really mean it."

"Try me." She glared back, her hands balled in fists at her sides.

He moved quickly to the door, opened it, threw her a backward glance, then stomped off slamming the door. Maggie slowly relaxed her fists, stumbled to the couch and sat down. She was shaking, livid. How dare he think he could walk in on her, apologize and have her fall into his arms? He couldn't be that callous—or could he? Had she seen only the rich and handsome Craig Hastings and not the real man under the façade—a spoiled, egocentric, hedonistic male?

She sat there for a long time, until shadows darkened the room and she began to doze off. She didn't feel like working anymore. She didn't want to read or watch television. She even wished Ellen would come home. She needed to talk to someone.

After a while, she went to the phone and dialed her parents' home. Her mother came on the line.

"Hi, honey, have a good trip back?" Her mother sounded secure, warm, loving, as always.

"Umm, just wanted to tell you I had a good time at the wedding."

"Glad you came. It was nice, wasn't it? Everyone was happy to see you. Family kept asking when it'd be your turn."

"Mom!"

"I know! I know! You have your career, but it wouldn't hurt to add a man to it."

"I'll advertise, mom."

"Oh?"

Before her mother could get into anything personal, she cut the conversation short. "Gotta run, but I just wanted to say I enjoyed the weekend and seeing you and dad, not that that's something new."

"We feel the same, honey. Come again soon."

She hung up feeling warmed and soothed and loved. She had that. No one could take that away from her.

Chapter 3

Monday morning, Maggie decided to walk to the office. It was a long hike from Eighty-fourth Street to the *Shout* offices at Madison and Forty-eighth, but she needed to get some of the kinks out of her mind. She hadn't slept very well the previous night, and this morning she was determined not to think about Craig. She would concentrate on her work.

She didn't kid herself that it would be easy. Craig had become an important part of her life in the short time he'd been in it. And the end of a love affair was a time of desolation. Already, she felt rootless. She wouldn't be talking with Craig on the phone today or making plans to meet him tonight or going to his apartment. . . . A thought occurred to her. She'd have to go and take back her clothes. And she still had the key to his place. Damn! What was wrong with her? There was no reason this man—or any other, for that matter—should be able to get to her this way and distract her from what was really important, her work. After all, their relationship had not exactly been deep, or even caring. A lot of good food, good sex, good laughs, but surely nothing to cling to. Probably just Ellen's influence, and her cousin Martha's. She'd let the wedding-bell thing go to her head, briefly. But now, she vowed, it would be work and only work.

She had her job; she liked it a lot. She was deeply involved in her research now. The war-baby problem—now there was a real problem, something to be really concerned about. All those kids sired by American servicemen overseas and left with their unwed mothers. All those lonely, fatherless. . . . She stopped herself and laughed aloud. *Boy, Maggie, when you start feeling sorry for yourself,* she thought, *you sure spread your neuroses around.* Some of those kids probably grew up happy and well-adjusted, in spite of everything.

She was pleasantly tired when she got to the office at 8:45. She stopped at the coffee shop downstairs for coffee and Danish, picked up a paper, and walked into the elevator. Then she knew why she'd come in early this morning. Because she wanted no more elevator encounters with Craig. Not today, and hopefully not for a few days, until she got her emotional bearings. Later, she'd be able to handle it on a strictly business basis.

The office setup was austere and stark—no glamorous glass-and-chrome for Peter Hastings' *Shout*. The reception area was small and contained a desk, a couch, two chairs and a table piled with magazines. The walls were covered with framed back issues of *Shout*. Down the hall from the reception area was a line of cubicles where individual editors sat at cramped desks with one extra chair and, if they were lucky, a window looking out on an airshaft. Mabel Weeks' office was the largest one, at the end of the narrow corridor. Maggie was sitting at her desk, sipping coffee and glancing through the *Times*, when Mabel walked by.

"Early today, aren't you?" she said, somewhat surprised.

"You know me, the eager-beaver type," Maggie smiled.

"Got anything on that baby stuff yet?"

Maggie pointed to her folders. "A lot of good starts; I'll have more in a couple of days."

"Come in around nine-fifteen. I want to go over what you have so far. I'm meeting Jennings at ten, and I want to give him some idea where we're heading."

She walked away before Maggie could answer. Maggie began putting her notes together and sketched out a general outline. She stuffed everything into her folder, gulped down the last of her coffee, tossed the paper cup in the wastebasket and glanced at her watch. She waited a few moments, and then walked into Mabel's office.

Mabel was on the phone, but she waved Maggie to a chair and indicated she'd only be a few minutes. Her no-nonsense manner evidently got through to whoever was on the other end of the line, because in no time she put down the receiver and asked Maggie, "So. What've you got?"

"Lots of notes on lots of subjects. I've contacted a group called ALMA—Adoptees Liberty Movement Association. The acronym means 'nourishing' in Latin, like alma mater, you know? Anyway, this group is less than ten years old, got started when a woman advertised in the *Times* in March, Nineteen seventy-one, asking other adoptees to get in touch with her for mutual assistance in finding their natural parents. So far, they've had success in helping adoptees search and find biological parents all over the country. They're setting up computer databanks around the world for adoptees. Most important, they're pushing for legislation that will make all sealed court records available to anyone trying to find his or her natural parents."

"I've read about them—good outfit."

"I also met with a Mrs. Ledman, at Family Service. She told me nothing much has changed in the adoption picture, i.e., an adoptee still needs a court order to enable the service to begin a search for biological parents. They charge a nominal fee, about two hundred-fifty dollars, which doesn't begin to cover expenses, legal costs, etc. They try to contact natural parents and feel them out, ask how they'd react to meeting the child they gave away at birth. A large number of these parents don't want to get involved. It would compromise their lives to open up old wounds."

"I can understand that." Mabel nodded. "That's something to think about. Can't just barge into people's lives, can we?"

"No. But my feeling is, it's better to know than to wonder. That's why ALMA was formed. They told me they feel it's their birthright—it's a missing part of their identity and they're entitled to it. Mrs. Ledman, the Family Service woman, also told me something else that was interesting. In almost all cases, the man or woman institutes the search for a parent when he or she reaches some sort of a crises in life."

"Crisis?"

"Yes, life-crisis, like marriage or having a child. Naturally, that's the time you begin to worry about genes, inherited diseases, possibility of incest, that sort of thing. Maybe I should have called it a milestone. Like when a teenager is about to go away to college and becomes more aware of his or her background. There was a girl in my dorm at Skidmore; as a matter of fact, I've been thinking about her lately. Her being adopted gave her real problems, and she didn't really know how to deal with them. She was desperate to find her biological parents, and was always talking about them—you know, were they rich, did they have some sort of musical or artistic talent? It was kind of unfinished business for her that needed to be settled."

"I can understand that part," Mabel agreed, "even though genius can spring up out of a gutter. What else?"

"At the library, I looked through a December, Nineteen forty-five, issue of *Life* magazine. The title of this article was 'War Babies'. . . ."

"War babies, I like that," Mabel cut in.

"There was a haunting picture of babies bunched together on a blanket. God, it really got me! The copy dealt with a couple in a small French village, who took it upon themselves to form their own private charity after World War Two to care for unmarried mothers. The babies were placed with neighboring farmers, with the government chipping in fifteen hundred francs a month, about twelve dollars and fifty cents. They had no aid from the American government or the Red Cross. Just these babies. A nameless American soldier said he hoped to return to Europe to claim his illegitimate son one day."

"Good. This is the kind of story I think Jennings will go for," Mabel said. "Obviously, there were servicemen who knew they had left children all over Europe. Some of them had to feel something about their ties."

"Yes, but there's no official record. I mean, no one took down statistics saying, hey, the Americans racked up fifty illegitimate babies this month. I got some more material from an article in *Time*, September, Nineteen forty-five. Like the European countries, our government did nothing about this problem. It was there, but apparently they felt there wasn't anything they could do about it. Servicemen could talk to the chaplain, arrange for a marriage if possible, acknowledge paternity or, as in most cases, just split. I called at least half a dozen army offices in Washington and they all said the same thing—they never did and still don't keep track of offspring of American servicemen. What a soldier does on his time with a woman is his business, not the army's.

ROMAN CANDLES

"Norway was the only country in all of Europe that looked the problem square in the face. There were nine thousand children born of Norwegian mothers and German fathers during the Nazi occupation. The kids' origin was purposely obscured in order to protect them against Norwegian resentment toward their parents. They proposed, uh," Maggie looked down at her notes, "a special war-baby law changing the children's names and providing for their adoption by Norwegian families."

"How about Italy?"

"Well, Italy is a very family-oriented country, and the people resist government programs, especially in family matters. Even today, when a girl gets into trouble, the family forms ranks around her and takes care of the problem themselves."

"Hmm . . . I was just thinking about Alex Parisi. He's been in Rome and is going back there soon, you know, and undoubtedly we'd get more cooperation from his contacts in Italy than we would in Korea or Vietnam. We have a couple of people elsewhere in Europe, but Alex is so good . . . and Italy would be a great place to do this sort of piece."

Maggie's heart started thumping. "So Alex is going to write it?"

"Right now I don't know if anyone is going to pursue this further. It's up to editorial to decide to go with it or not, depending on how well they like the research. Tell you what, type up something I can pass along to them, everything you've told me, whatever else you can get between now and Thursday morning's editorial board meeting."

Maggie stood up and grinned. "I'll go over to ALMA, how about that? I'll interview anyone who'll give me some new clues. Maybe Italian government agencies, foster-care centers. . . ."

Mabel smiled at her. "Good, Maggie, I see you enjoyed your research on this one."

"Very much." She hesitated, then went on, "You know that picture in *Life*, all those babies bunched together on that blanket—I can't get it out of my mind. I mean, where are they today? Do they even know their fathers were GIs? And how has it affected them? How do they feel about their fathers? Their mothers? Their split nationality? Like the adopted girl in our dorm I mentioned. It was an obsession with her, trying to find her natural parents, and I remember it created a big problem with her adoptive parents, who had raised her, sent her to college, the whole bit. At the time, I really didn't understand, but since doing this research, it's gotten to me. I'd sure like to be writing the story," she blurted out.

The older woman looked at her shrewdly. "You haven't done that much here yet, Maggie."

"No, but that doesn't mean I couldn't do it if I had a chance. My credentials from my other jobs should tell you that."

"Pretty confident, aren't you?"

"Eager." Maggie grinned. "So? Can't shoot me for aiming for it, can you?"

"Not at all. Everyone deserves that one big break. You too. Hang in there—if it's not this story, it'll be another one."

"Mabel, I did do that off-Broadway review stuff when they were stuck for someone, remember?"

Mabel nodded. "And the filler on jogging. I know, Maggie, you probably could do a job on this, but right now it's just an idea. I don't even know if it'll go. Just calm down and get back to work."

In the next couple of days, Maggie felt as though she were in limbo. She called the ALMA office and made an appointment to see a Mrs. Sloan and had a long talk with the president of Foster Parents Plan in Warwich, Rhode Island. She skimmed dozens of books on World War II looking for leads and never finding enough concrete material on children of American GIs trying to find their fathers. Luckily, ALMA had anticipated most of her needs, and when she arrived on Wednesday morning, Mrs. Sloan was waiting with an armload of printed information. She was a small, delicate woman in her early sixties, with a neat cap of pure white hair and an elegant manner that went with her tailored navy wool suit and silk print blouse.

"I understand you're doing a piece on Italian war babies, Miss Reardon," she said, after offering Maggie a cup of coffee.

"I'd like any help you can give me, you know, start me thinking in a variety of directions, since we want an entire series on the subject. If you know anything about children born to American servicemen in Italy, I'd be really grateful. There's a possibility I might be going to Rome to work on this." There wasn't any possibility, but Maggie never missed a chance to make herself seem more credible in an interview if she could.

"I must say I'm delighted the problem is finally getting the kind of public attention it deserves." Mrs. Sloan sighed. "When we first started here, a lot of people were very hostile. Many still are. Biological parents often don't want a reconciliation with the past, particularly if their child was born under—" she paused to select the right word—*difficult* circumstances.

"If a child wants to find his or her birth parents, all there is to go on, generally, is an adoptive birth certificate with the date and place of birth on it. Adoption agencies, orphanages, they've all been involved in a blatant subterfuge, covering up information that should be given to any adopted child—or any natural parent, for that matter. Then there are the corrupt doctors and lawyers making thousands in the black-market baby business—well, I won't even go into that! The search for real records is often a fruitless job. Doors slam in your face and people look at you as if you were asking for privileged C.I.A. information or something. What ALMA is doing right now is trying to get a legal judgment on a state and federal level about the unconstitutionality of sealed records, you see. Now, that's in America. As for Italy, well, we haven't really extended our efforts that far yet, but it's an interesting place to start."

"I'm glad you said that. How do you mean—interesting?"

"Well, a Mediterranean, family-oriented nation, where Americans came in and had quite an influence during the war. Interesting, but very hard, Miss Reardon. I wish I could give you more encouragement, but you're talking about digging into records that go back thirty-five to forty years. And, of course, I'm sure the army doesn't want anything to do with their soldiers' foreign affairs." Mrs. Sloan grinned at her own pun. "In a sense, your work might be easier in a more recent war, in Vietnam, say; but, then, the political situation. . . ." She gave a short laugh. "What am I saying? Things are pretty hot in Rome now too, if I recall correctly from the papers."

"So I've heard," Maggie nodded, collecting her things.

"Well, in that case, I suppose I better just read through what you've given me and maybe, if I have questions, I can call you."

"Naturally." The two women got up and Mrs. Sloan walked Maggie back to the reception area.

"There's just one thing to keep in mind, Miss Reardon. Something I always mention to people getting involved with the problems and rights of adoptees. A lot of folks will try to stop you from doing what you're doing. You have to be prepared for some hard feelings and a lot of dead ends. Remember, you are dealing with very personal and very emotional issues. Never try to wrench details from people who would rather keep it all buried. And by the same token, don't try to force information on people who are happier without it. Try not to tread on too many toes. If you can be discreet and considerate, I'm sure you will do fine."

"Thank you. I'll remember that."

"And best of luck. I look forward to reading your series."

Feeling less than cheered, Maggie started back across Fifty-seventh Street. She stopped at a coffee shop a block from the office and sat at the counter, flipping through the ALMA literature. The waitress handed her a menu and, as she looked up to order, she noticed Alex Parisi several stools away from her, lost in thought, scribbling away furiously in his notebook.

"Oh, hello," she said, moving over to sit next to him. He really was a very interesting-looking man, she thought suddenly. He didn't have that scrubbed, preppie look that Craig had, but he seemed to be surrounded by an intense, involved aura that made him very attractive. She decided he seemed sure of himself, and his poise carried him beyond the sloppy chinos with the ink stains around the pockets. The flaps of his beige corduroy jacket were tucked in, as if he were always reaching into his pockets for a pad or pen and couldn't be bothered to pull them back out just for appearances' sake.

"Hi." He was preoccupied, but he ceased writing long enough to gaze at her with those incredible dark eyes of his that penetrated her thoughts and sized up her character in one glance.

"Maggie, isn't it? We met when you and Hastings were having dinner?"

ROMAN CANDLES

"Right. So, what do you recommend on *this* menu?" She was hungry again, as usual, but for a change her appetite wasn't the only thing on her mind.

"Have a western omelet," he suggested. "Only thing that won't give you the repeats."

"I guess you come here often." She laughed.

"I like to live dangerously." He shrugged, turning back to his notes.

"When are you going to Rome?" she asked him after she'd ordered and he'd been served his omelet, a large, bright yellow concoction flecked with bits of green, pink and white.

"Couple of days."

"What are you working on?" God, but the man was taciturn, she thought.

"High terror in high places." She looked blank. "I'm going to interview a couple, Italian royalty, and do a piece on how their lives have been affected by the threats of the various terrorist groups in Italy. I met them when I was doing the Aldo Moro series, and they agreed to sit still and talk to me before flying off to Monte Carlo or wherever rich people go for the winter. Count and Countess Sciarra, you know, Roman society people, party-givers and goers. He owns lots of Frascati vineyards outside Rome. I want to find out whether they've gotten used to terrorism, and how they see the political and economic climate, their own futures, business, Common Market, etc. What are you up to?" He didn't sound very interested.

"I'm . . . well, I'm just in the midst of the research for a story, actually. As a matter of fact, if Jennings decides to let me write it, I'll be in Rome too."

"Oh, yeah? What's the piece on?"

"War babies. The kids born—"

"Oh, that one. I thought that was mine." He shook his head, surprise and annoyance registering on his face. "That was my idea in the first place, dammit. My uncle was an army doctor when Eisenhower liberated Italy. He took some great photos of Italian orphans in Anzio after his platoon landed on the beach in forty-four, and it always made me wonder whenever I looked at them. Well, that's editorial meetings for you. They go in with your thoughts; they come out an hour later with their plans. Okay, so good luck with it. If you get to *la bella città*, look me up. I'll buy you some pasta."

ROMAN CANDLES

With that, he threw a couple of bills on the counter and abandoned his half-eaten omelet.

"Hey," Maggie said, more than a little embarrassed. "I didn't know. And you probably will get the assignment. Horning in on another reporter's territory is not my idea of getting a job."

"Listen, no sweat. Don't worry, I have a lot more on my mind right now than Italian kids without fathers. By the way, how's Hastings?"

"He's. . . ." She stopped herself, not wanting to say too much. "Well, frankly, I don't know. I haven't seen him in a while."

"Really?" He gave her another X-ray stare, then turned and walked out of the restaurant.

Damn, Maggie thought as she paid her bill and started back to the office, why did he have to bring up Craig? She still missed him, if only because he had become a very nice habit. She felt too loose without an attachment. Since Ellen was usually with Stan, she came home to an empty apartment now, ate something quick and easy and not terribly palatable, washed her hair, did her nails and wondered where she was going next. After a week and a half of that, she was going stir-crazy looking at the walls, so she took a deep breath, dressed herself up, and went out to a singles bar that looked reasonably prepossessing a few blocks away from the apartment.

She was pleased to see that the atmosphere was not quite as bad as she'd feared. Some of these places smacked of aggressive women and hostile men, staring each other down, daring each other to make the first move. But Quibbles seemed nice enough, and after half an hour and a glass of white wine, she felt relaxed enough to engage in a little light conversation with the two guys on the stools next to her. When one of them came on pretty heavy an hour later, she decided she wasn't interested, and felt perfectly comfortable walking out alone.

Ellen fixed her up with a couple of blind dates after that, but neither of the men was her type. One was a dull-as-dishwater accountant who kept stressing the importance of her starting a money-market fund, and the other was an out-of-work actor who was far more interested in himself than in Maggie.

ROMAN CANDLES

So, she went back to her evenings alone. It was all right to have the time to herself. At least it gave her the time to finish the presentation on the baby article. Alex Parisi be damned, she was going to fight to the death to get this one. She handed her material to Mabel, feeling pretty pleased with herself, and sat back to wait.

Thursday morning, Maggie was asked to do some research on the No-Nukes movement and write a capsule filler for a longer article. She was out doing interviews all day, and didn't get back to her desk until after two. Mabel had left a note on her typewriter. It said, "See me."

She walked into Mabel's office and waited for her to get off the phone. Her heart was thudding. Trying not to think about her presentation to the editorial board that morning, she sat down. Maybe it had bombed—weeks of work down the tubes. Mabel hung up at last and grinned.

"They loved it!" she said. "You did a fine job, Maggie. They especially liked the fact that war babies happen to be an international problem. Hell, that could cover a lot of markets!"

"Then they're going to do it?"

"Looks that way. A whole series."

"Who?"

"Didn't get into it too much, but they agreed with me that Italy was a convenient place to research it. Alex's name was mentioned. Jennings thought it would be something he could dig into."

"But isn't he up to his ears in all this terrorism and political stuff?"

"Sure. So, you'll be delighted to know, I brought that up and suggested that *Shout* might think about assigning a woman to do the series. At least to get it off the ground."

"And?"

Mabel wasn't smiling now. "I hope I'm not putting myself out on a limb, Maggie. I mentioned that the logical person to do it would be the researcher."

"Oh, God!" Maggie thought she would suffocate, her heart was tripping so hard.

"Now hold on. You know how these things run. They'll take it under consideration."

"Is there anything I can do?"

"Nothing. Sit tight. Let them think about it. You know,

when I was starting out on a paper in Moline, Illinois, someone gave me a break, let me write a slew of articles on postwar education. Up to that time I'd been pumping out little society gems like 'Miss Gwen Madison today was betrothed to' . . . you get the picture."

"Thanks." Maggie's voice was husky as she got up and went to the door. She knew if she stuck around much longer she'd be blubbering, and that would blow the whole picture of young, intelligent writer.

The next few days were agony. She tried talking about it to Ellen.

"I know I'm acting stupid. I mean, Christ, why would they give me the assignment? They've got all kinds of people on the magazine. . . ."

"So? You've got Mabel Weeks pitching for you, that's a big plus."

"Sure. But is it enough?"

"How about Craig?"

"Craig? What about him?"

"Listen, my girl, and you shall hear, how people get ahead in politics, business, society, whatever. They use their contacts. Why haven't you asked him to pitch for you?"

"You know damned well why not! I'm not seeing him anymore."

"On a business level, dummy! You've got a right."

Maggie's face brightened. "It's a thought. But, I don't know. . . ."

"Do it," Ellen insisted.

She turned it over in her mind a thousand times. God knows, Ellen had a point, but she really couldn't see herself phoning her ex-lover and coolly asking for a ticket to the moon. Or, at least, that was the way she saw it. Why couldn't she be objective about him? Enough time had passed for her feelings to sort themselves out. Only they hadn't.

Regardless of how much she hated what he'd done to her, his cavalier attitude about sleeping around, she had to admit that her chemical attraction for the guy was still strong. Would she give that away if she saw him again? Would she be unable to act like an eager-beaver reporter, determined as hell to get her story?

On the other hand, what better way to get the big chance?

ROMAN CANDLES

He was the son of the publisher. That's clout. Even though he was management, not editorial, his putting in a good word for her could just cinch the assignment. So that was all she had to do. Get over the anxiety and go get the job. She would talk to Craig; Craig would talk to Andrew Jennings, the editor-in-chief; Jennings would go to the editorial board and say, this is the only reporter who can handle the series. And, poof, Maggie's on a plane to Rome.

Steady, girl, she told herself. *One step, then the next. Just swallow your pride and your neuroses and go see Craig.*

She chewed on the notion until it was all she could think about. She spent a weekend doing laundry, buying groceries, checking over her clothes, but always with that hope in the back of her mind that it would work out. That she would make it work. This was the absolute perfect time to be plunging into a new project, preferably away from the office and New York. The change would clear her mind of her personal dilemma and might be just what she needed to hone her research and writing skills. And it would undoubtedly help her to get ahead at *Shout* if she did a bang-up job. She knew her future potential there was promising. From a magazine that had started out twelve years earlier with an almost entirely male staff, it now boasted a large proportion of females, many in executive and managerial positions.

On Sunday night, she decided. She would call Craig the next morning and see him in his office. It might not be a comfortable meeting, but all she had to do was state her case and get out. She could return his apartment key while she was at it, and ask him to mail her clothes to her. A grand finale; it made her smile as she went over the scene in her mind.

She called Craig's secretary early Monday morning and requested an apointment. The secretary told her he had a few moments at ten o'clock, then he had a meeting, and later in the day he was flying to the Coast on business.

She had dressed carefully that morning in a navy flannel blazer with brass buttons, a Black Watch plaid skirt with a thin navy self-belt, and a heather-gray cowl-neck sweater. Simple gold studs in her ears and a gold chain around her neck completed the outfit. She had washed her hair the night before and brushed it back from her face that morning in a soft, chin-length aureole that enhanced her hazel eyes. It had occurred to her that she was taking pains with her clothes in

ROMAN CANDLES

order to disguise her anxiety. She hoped she looked fresh and competent. Appearances meant everything in a business meeting. She wanted to appear to be just what she was—a serious and eager writer. The one for the job.

Craig met her halfway across his office when she came in. He reached out and tried to pull her into his arms.

"Jesus, it's good to see you, Maggie. I've missed you like anything."

Gently, she disengaged herself and walked toward the chair facing his desk. "This is business, Craig."

"Oh? You sound very dramatic. What is it? A raise? A promotion . . . ?"

"Not exactly. You may recall I mentioned the research I was doing." Quickly, she told him about some of her findings and the editorial board's okay of the project. "The series could easily be set in Rome since . . . well, Mabel Weeks thought Asia would be too difficult and there were many illegitimate children in Italy as a result of the American occupation."

"So? What's the problem? Alex Parisi can handle it while he's working on his other stuff."

"I want to do it."

"You?" He looked at her, incredulous.

"Yes. I'm very up on the research. I know what I want to find, how I can write it and I can bring a woman's point of view to a subject that most directly concerns women."

Craig walked around the desk, sat down and leaned back in his chair. "Ah-ha, so now we come to the nitty-gritty. You're going to pull that woman crap on me to land an assignment. Equal rights and all that, but give the woman the edge. You're a minority, right? I'm disappointed in you, Maggie. Or are you just running away from me? From us?"

She was so angry she had to clutch her hands together to keep from socking him. To think that his macho pride would twist her request around and turn it into a woman's whim!

"Craig, let's get one thing straight. There is no 'us'. Whatever us there was is over. In fact, I have the key to your apartment here. And I left some clothes there. I'd appreciate it if you could mail them back to me."

Maggie reached into her bag and put the key on his desk. Craig looked at it for a moment but did not reach for it.

ROMAN CANDLES

"I can't believe you called off a good thing because of one stupid incident," he said.

"I didn't come here to discuss that. All I want is a professional favor."

"I'm glad. Shows you're not sore at me anymore. You're not, are you, Maggie? You've cooled off?"

"Certainly. I'm not childish or vindictive. Frankly, I don't give a damn anymore. I thought I could ask you to talk to Jennings and put in a good word for me. As a friend. If I were sore at you, Craig, would I be here now?"

"How the hell do I know? You made it pretty clear that morning what you thought of me."

She smiled. "Well, let's put it this way—I wasn't so much sore as disappointed. In you, in me, in us. Can we drop this, Craig? Just tell me whether you'll help me. Let's not make this a personal combat mission."

"Quid pro quo, Maggie?"

"Hardly. You don't owe me anything."

"Hell, you're using me."

"Sure. But why not? I can do a good job, and I need someone to help me prove it: you. Our personal relationship shouldn't enter into it."

He laughed and she recognized the absurdity of her remark at once. Of course she was here because of their personal involvement. She felt terribly stupid and gauche.

"What if you get this job and fall flat on your face?" he asked.

"I suppose you'd like that."

"Hell no, like you said, business is business, that's why the editorial board will want to make damned sure if the magazine spends money to send someone off on an assignment, we'll get what we pay for."

"I understand. All the more reason for me not to flop, to do a fantastic job, don't you think? I not only have to prove I can do it for the sake of the magazine, but for myself as well."

"You're good with words, I'll grant you that. And good in other ways." He got up from his chair and came around the desk. Maggie moved quickly, getting up and starting for the door. He caught her arm and she turned, staring him down.

"Will you help me?"

He frowned. "I'll think about it."

"That's all?"

"What do you want me to do? Say you've got the assignment? I'm not the whole magazine. I said I'd think about it."

"Thanks."

He reached for her so fast that she didn't have a chance to escape. He pulled her up against his chest, and his face came down toward hers. She went slack in his arms like a dead weight, glaring up into his eyes. He held her a second longer, his face red with anger.

"Damn you, Maggie, it's not over for us yet, you better believe that."

He let her go so abruptly that she stumbled against the door. Then, without another word, she walked out and got into the waiting elevator. She leaned against the wall, suddenly feeling very shaky. Now that she'd gone ahead and asked Craig for his help, she wasn't sure it had been the right thing to do. But, what the hell, it was done. The meek and the mild, Maggie decided, did not exactly inherit assignments abroad or seats on big boards in business. Boldness and aggressiveness were the code words of the day, after all.

That evening, she told Ellen about her coup.

"I'm not going to let myself feel bad about going to Craig. I'd do anything to get this assignment. I won't get anywhere sitting back and waiting for things to happen to me. I've got to get out there and make my own opportunities."

"Hmm, a tough cookie," Ellen teased.

"Is that what I am?"

"Aren't you? You really crave this job, so you're going after it tooth and nail."

"Why not? It's not just an assignment, it's the bottom rung of a huge ladder. This can be a giant step up. Yes, I want it. I can taste it."

"Then stop sweating and forget it for now. Put it out of your mind. It'll happen if it's meant to. I don't want to work at the bank forever, Maggie. I believe in Fate these days. Personally, I'm beginning to think I might be destined for a little house in Jersey with Stan and three kids. That would be very special for me."

"Then I hope it happens, Ellen. I really do."

"Oh, it will," Ellen said firmly.

Maggie was always a little embarrassed by these conversa-

ROMAN CANDLES

tions. Ellen was so sure, so fixed in her goals, that it was hard for her to imagine someone else doing life differently. Maggie was greedy: she wanted both worlds, the career and the special guy too, the way Ellen had Stan. Since the most recent man in her life hadn't worked out, she could concentrate on her career. But that didn't mean she had ruled out the other half for good.

In the next few days, Maggie tried not to raise her hopes too high about the job. She was dying to ask Mabel if she'd heard anything, but she restrained herself. When Mabel found out, she'd tell her. The days meshed into one another. She talked with her mother and told her she'd be home for Thanksgiving since Aunt Tessie was coming up from Florida. And, one day, she began working on an updated résumé. It seemed like the right time to think about a new job, something more challenging, something really different.

Still, she wished for the assignment. She wished for it when she woke up and when she went to bed at night. It was an all-consuming passion now, and every day that passed, she continued to hope.

On Tuesday morning, Mabel came back from a private meeting with Jennings, went straight to Maggie's office, leaned over her desk and said, "You must have a friend upstairs. Jennings wants to talk to you. Go get it, Maggie!"

Maggie gulped and stared hard at the other woman. She felt like her heart would flip into her throat. She couldn't speak.

"Go on, he's waiting for you," Mabel urged.

Andrew Jennings was an intimidating, Lincolnesque type, who demanded the best and usually got it. He grilled Maggie unmercifully from the moment she walked into his office.

"What makes you think you're qualified to write this series?"

"I know the story better than anyone else who'd be starting in fresh. I've spent a great deal of time researching it."

"Anyone can work from notes."

"I want to do it." She stared him down. She would not be afraid of this man. He was just a person; he had had to start somewhere too.

"Alex Parisi is in Rome. He could do it for us."

"I admire Mr. Parisi, but his specialty is hard news. He

can't do everything, especially not this. My expertise is in human-interest pieces. Well, not for *Shout*, yet, of course—I haven't been here that long. But I'd be happy to send up tear sheets of my work for my former employers. I always got the assignments on divorce and child-rearing at the Hartford paper, and I've done a lot of psychology-type fillers, too. And there's something else—another reason I feel I'm perfect for this job. I'm a woman; I can bring a special empathy and sympathy to the series. So, may I send up those tear sheets?"

"That won't be necessary. All right. The assignment is yours." He paused and gave her a stern look. "You have some very powerful friends behind you, but I'm going to tell you the truth, Miss Reardon. I don't think you have the background or the experience to do this. I would be hesitant about assigning you one major piece in New York City, let alone a series that involves hard research in a foreign country. However," he got up from his desk and walked around it to lean on one edge, "I've been overruled. My powers only go so far in this organization, and if the big boss says he wants pablum instead of pasta, that's what he'll get."

She met his gaze without flinching. If he thought she'd apologize for using her contacts, he was wrong. "I'm aware I have support from upstairs," she said evenly, "but I disagree about being unqualified, Mr. Jennings. I hope to prove you wrong."

"I hope so too. Believe me. Now, let's set down some ground-rules. You'll leave the first week in December, and I'll allow you five weeks maximum to dig up what you need. I want regular reports—you can cable them in. I'd like to run two or three pieces, but of course that will depend on how much you're able to get. *Shout* likes the personal angle, remember. I don't want a lot of dead-weight generalization and philosophizing. We'll start the promo whenever you let me know the number of articles this subject can carry, but I'd like to lead off with a teaser piece in the February issue. If you can manage it. That means we need finished copy by December twenty-fourth."

"You'll have it," she said confidently.

"I wish you luck." He held out his hand. "And don't hesitate to ask Alex to help you. He's a top reporter and writer—you'll need him. I'd prefer it, as a matter of fact, if

ROMAN CANDLES

you'd collaborate. You stick with the woman's angle; Alex will handle the hard-core World War Two stuff."

Not on your tintype, Maggie thought, but she just nodded and left the room. She'd sweated off five pounds waiting for this assignment, she'd gone to Craig even though she hated the thought of using him, she'd put all her efforts into the research. Now she was going to pull it together.

In the time between her interview with Jennings and the moment she stepped on a TWA plane for Rome, Maggie found no time to relax. She hardly had any time to get excited. She had to buy some clothes and pack, spend her lunch hours with a special tutor at Berlitz, paid for by the magazine, in order to pick up a little conversational Italian. She spent an afternoon with Sammy Falco in accounting, where he explained that he was transferring three thousand American dollars to the Manufacturers Hanover Trust Company on the Via Bissolati in Rome in her name. It would be safer for her to handle her finances that way, rather than to carry along a lot of money, so they'd cable her regular salary the same way. She went to Rockefeller Center to apply for an emergency, rush passport. The company travel agent booked her on a TWA flight and cabled a *pensione* to make a reservation for her.

Somehow she still found time to run up to Wilton for Thanksgiving dinner with her family, who seemed even more excited than she was, if that was possible. She laughed off her mother's warnings about drinking the water and going out with Italian men. Finally, on her way back to New York in the train the next morning, she decided to call Craig to thank him.

"Hey," he said lightly, "you did it. Bearded Jennings right in his den. Listen, sweetie. Don't eat too much pasta, okay? I love ya just the way you are."

The day before Maggie left, Ellen took her out to lunch. Mabel was supposed to go with them, but she was in bed with a bad flu, so she called Maggie that morning to wish her well.

"And call me if you want to," she insisted. "That's what supervisors are for. To stay home and mind the fort."

At noon, Ellen picked her up and they walked over to Moran's. Ellen toasted her with a glass of white wine. "I hate you, of course," she confessed, "but I'm glad you got what you wanted, girl! Knock 'em dead, especially that other reporter, Alex what's-his-name?"

Alex was the last person Maggie had on her mind before her hectic departure. Her brain whirled with the thought: I'm going to Europe! She felt a little funny celebrating, since what she really wanted was someone special to share the feelings with, but, privately, she was delirious with excitement. Her first trip abroad—something she'd anticipated for years. Her parents had promised to send her after college, but, somehow, there just hadn't been enough money. And Maggie's savings since she'd started working were hardly enough to pay her round-trip airfare and meals. But here she was on an all-expenses-paid professional trip—not a mere vacation but, perhaps, the start of a really substantial career.

There was so much to do before she left, she finally threw up her hands and decided she'd have to live without getting it all done. She and Ellen came to an agreement about the apartment, Maggie offering to pay something toward the rent while she was away. Ellen smiled mischievously and assured her that she had a temporary roommate in mind; he'd already promised.

At last there was nothing else for Maggie to do but take a taxi to Kennedy airport late one Wednesday evening.

Chapter 4

It was raining in Rome. As the plane came in for a landing at Fiumicino airport, Maggie peered out of the window and, seeing the mist against the glass, she felt vaguely apprehensive. She'd been thinking about the assignment all through the flight, and she had to admit she was worried. But there was no going back now. She'd put up a big front; now she had to deliver. She began to think about Alex Parisi. She hoped his nose wasn't out of joint because she was coming to do a piece that logically should have been his. She'd be suitably grateful for whatever time he spent orienting her in Rome, buy him a dinner, and emphasize the fact that she could manage very well on her own. If, she thought to herself nervously, if she could just make herself understood. She'd pored over the English-Italian dictionary she'd brought with her until her eyeballs burned. And when the pilot announced that they would be landing within twenty minutes, she'd begun to panic.

"Please keep your seatbelts fastened until the aircraft has come to a complete stop," the voice boomed over the loudspeaker.

No one paid much attention. There was the usual flurry of pulling out hand luggage from under seats and craning necks for a sight of the airport. The woman sitting next to Maggie turned to her and smiled.

ROMAN CANDLES

"Here we are in Rome! I guess we don't say goodbye now, we say *arrivederci.*"

"Sounds right to me," Maggie smiled. At least she knew "hello" and "goodbye", but the Berlitz course hadn't taken her too far beyond the basics. Luckily, Italians spoke with their hands a lot, she thought. "Have a wonderful time in Italy," she said to her seatmate.

The woman was with a group of tourists who were now exuberantly embarking en masse. Maggie envied them. They knew exactly where they were going while she, as Craig had put it, might be going off to fall flat on her face. No matter what he thought, she was here to do a job, and the worst that could happen was that she wouldn't live up to her own expectations. After which, she could always slit her throat, she thought grimly. Well, perhaps a nap would fix her mood. She hadn't slept much on the plane and was looking forward to a real bed in her *pensione,* where she could collapse quietly for a while. And then, to work.

The plane finally eased to a stop and the seatbelt sign went off. Maggie followed the line of passengers directly onto the field to the minibus parked nearby. She got on and stood, clutching a pole, as the bus began to wind its way past hand trucks and smaller aircraft toward the main terminal. She pulled the lapels of her raincoat together against the chill air. She hadn't expected December in Rome to be so cold, but it looked like she was going to need the lining she had in her suitcase.

Someone bumped her pouch purse, and she shied away quickly. Her mother had also warned her about pickpockets.

She had chosen light gray-flannel slacks with a faded rose turtleneck sweater for the trip and had packed her trusty gray wool blazer with the brass buttons that thankfully went with just about everything she owned. The tourists around her were mostly older women with dyed hair, many of them wearing what Maggie called "spongy" pants suits. Well, she might not be a fashionplate but, at least, she didn't look like one of them. Not yet, anyway.

She walked into the terminal and followed the signs to the luggage carousel. A young couple stood beside her, arms around each other, nuzzling like newborn puppies.

"Honeymooners," someone at Maggie's elbow muttered. She turned to an elderly, gray-haired woman with reading

ROMAN CANDLES

glasses strung on a chain around her neck. "Been carrying on like that since we left Kennedy. You should have seen them when the lights went out after supper!"

Unaccountably, Maggie felt her throat constrict Craig's face, his smile, floated through her mind, and she had to force herself to turn off the image. Goddammit, he was just another handsome man, right? Craig was another world, another time. Anyway, he sure wasn't the honeymoon type. And maybe she wasn't either. Right now, she was the consummate professional.

She went over toward the carousel, having spotted one of her bags. She retrieved it, then grabbed a trolley before three German businessmen could beat her to it, and put the bag on it. Then she waited for her other bag and her typewriter, pushing and shoving with the rest of the tourists. Maggie glanced up at the signs in English, Italian, French and German, and began to follow the arrows to the immigration booth, where she waited on a short line before handing her passport to a young man in a glassed-in booth. He stamped her passport and returned it to her. Again, she followed the line toward customs control.

As soon as she finished with customs, she pushed her trolley toward a roped-off area. Then she saw him. Alex Parisi. For God's sake, what was he doing here? How did he know she was coming? Oddly enough, although he had never seemed friendly, she felt a sudden rush of relief, even though he wasn't smiling and did seem a bit grim. Looking exactly like an aging Ph.D. candidate in his army jacket and jeans with that shock of brown hair falling into his eyes. At least he was a familiar face.

He saw her then and waved. She smiled back, giving an extra push to the trolley. When she reached the exit, he held the gate open for her, pulled the trolley aside and looked down at her.

"Hi! Welcome to Rome," he said.

"Thanks. You don't know how good your face looks in this crowd. Although I can't for the life of me figure out what brought you to Fiumicino except ESP."

"Nope. Hastings. He called and told me to pick you up. Said you were the type to get lost in a supermarket, so it might be a good idea to play nursemaid for a while."

Maggie drew in her breath sharply. "Well, he's wrong. I

can look after myself just fine, thank you. So you don't have to...."

"Got my orders, ma'am."

He busied himself taking over the trolley from her, indicating that she was to follow him. She trotted along beside him, trying not to glance sideways at his leanness. He was taller than she remembered, his demeanor more serious. Undoubtedly, he resented having her foisted on him this way, and she was determined to set him straight about that. She had no intention of being a burden, certainly not his.

The milling crowds forestalled any conversation. They made their way through the terminal and walked out to a wide sidewalk with a circular drive, where buses and cars streamed endlessly in and out. Maggie wasn't a small-town girl, but Rome gridlock made New York rush-hour traffic seem like Sunday afternoon.

"My car's out in a parking lot." He glanced at her. "Think you can manage one of these?"

She reached for her typewriter case. "Sure, let's go."

He nodded approvingly, hoisted a small bag under one arm and picked up the other two. She followed behind as they dodged traffic and made their way across a wide bus zone toward the parking lot. His car was a small Fiat that looked insubstantial enough to be blown off the road with one good gust of wind.

"I rent this, company pays," he grinned. "It's the only way to get around Rome, you'll see."

He stuffed her luggage in the backseat while she wedged herself into the tiny passenger seat. He got in the car and then gave all his attention to making his way out of the airport traffic and onto the *autostrada*. Maggie felt a sharp thrill course through her when she saw her first sign that said *Roma*. She was here, she had done it. Rome. And all that waited for her here.

In no time at all, they had left the airport behind, and Alex was clipping along a wide highway at a perilously fast speed. Maggie sighed and sat back to take in the view.

"How long will it take us to get into the city?"

"It's actually eighteen miles—thirty kilometers—to Rome from this airport, but once we hit traffic, we'll be slowed down. You have a hotel?"

"*Pensione.* The travel guy said someone or other had

stayed there on a business trip and it had running water and no fleas. That sounded good to me." She dug into her purse and brought out a notebook. "It's Pensione Trinità dei Monti. He said it was near the Spanish Steps."

"Should have picked Trastevere. Much more interesting district. How long do you intend to stay?"

Did he mean he hoped she wouldn't stay too long, or was he really interested? "I guess until I get my story. Jennings gave me five weeks." She hesitated. "About that, Alex, I hope you don't mind that I'm here?"

"Why should I mind?"

"Because you have a right to think you ought to be writing this. You came up with the idea."

"I'm pretty busy, can't do everything. Anyhow, no one has a patent on ideas, and there's plenty more where that one came from. How's Hastings?"

She was startled for a moment. Why would he ask about Craig in the same breath as her assignment?

"Fine, I guess. I haven't seen him in a while." There, that ought to tell him something, but she'd be damned if she was going to explain her relationship with Craig to this man. "Anyway, about my being here. . . ."

"Stop with the *mea culpa* stuff, will you?" he snapped. "Do you speak any Italian?"

"I just had a Berlitz quickie and not much of that. I've been trying to study words and phrases I'll need to get around. Frankly, I don't think I absorbed a lot of the crash course. I guess I'll pick it up as I go along, with some cramming at night."

"You have to live the language before you can speak it well, but don't sweat it. Lots of people speak English here. Very trendy to sprinkle Americanisms through your speech in some circles. You'll probably do fine, once you learn to get around by yourself."

Maggie tensed again. The man was so infuriating! Why did he keep implying she was incapable of navigating foreign waters alone?

"Alex, what are those trees up on that hill," she said, changing the subject, "I don't think I've ever seen anything like them."

"Umbrella pines, you see them all over Italy. Vegetation stays pretty green around here even in December. They don't get a hard winter in Rome, rain this month but hardly ever snow. They tell me it snowed a few years back, and all of Rome came to a halt."

"Like good old New York."

"Like good old New York. How are things back home?"

"Good." She wasn't sure what he was really asking. He had a subtle way of inflecting his words so that they seemed to mean several things at once.

"Tell me, this assignment, how did you get involved in it?" he asked bluntly.

Then he *was* upset. Well, she'd just be up-front about it. "I started with a great deal of research. Eventually, I began to feel the story in my bones, you know what I mean?"

"Not a personal involvement, someone you know personally?"

"No, I never knew a war baby. But I don't think that counts for much. You never knew a terrorist before you did that Moro thing, right? By the way, I really enjoyed the series—learned a lot from it. That was a fantastic job, Alex."

"The story was there, terrorist guerrilla-warfare is news. *Shout* needed someone to be on the spot reporting. So, it was me." He maneuvered the car from one lane to another. "About that," he continued casually, "I think you should know the problem still exists. It's still kind of touch and go in Italy, especially in the big cities."

"What are you telling me, exactly?"

"That there are daily incidents, and you'll have to be careful. We'll talk about that later. If you don't mind a word of advice, it's best not to get too personally involved in a story. It can color the facts of your article—distort it completely sometimes. Example: I've met with the count and countess, talked to them a lot, but I don't stay over for dinner, if you get my drift."

They had reached the outskirts of Rome. Maggie sat up, entranced by the ancient brick buildings and the narrow winding streets she glimpsed. The traffic got denser with each block, and Alex slowed down. She smiled to herself, seeing the unfamiliar traffic signals: *Alt* for stop, *Avanti* for go.

"I think I'm going to fall in love with Rome," she said softly.

He laughed. "You don't know what you're suggesting,

ROMAN CANDLES

lady. The Eternal City gets under your skin in spite of its pollution, traffic and terrorists. I didn't see much of it the first time I was here, but now I intend to see as much of it as I can. There's something about this place, the Pantheon, the Colosseum, the Forum, the fountains, the churches—it's like walking into a time warp."

"Sounds great. I'm really anxious to get started."

"Oh, by the way, I have someone for you to meet. A friend of mine—met him the first time I was in Rome. His name is Pippo Geraldi, he's a tour guide, speaks excellent English. He went to the American college here in Rome. A little bit of a playboy, but, then, so is every other Roman male. Nothing to worry about. If he grabs your ass, don't take it seriously . . . just laugh it off. Unless you're interested, that is. I'll introduce you to him as soon as I can arrange it. You'll have to meet Gabriella Sciarra too, a good friend of mine. She works for some big fashion designer and speaks English. You need all the contacts you can get."

"Thanks, I know I will." She wondered whether Gabriella might be more than just a friend. But why not? Alex Parisi was really something; lots of women would consider him a catch.

She was intoxicated with everything she saw out the dirty car window. By the time they arrived at her *pensione,* she had a mental list of all the sights she wanted to jam in on her free time, if she had any. The antiquity of this city was simply awesome. Alex zoomed into a parking spot that looked as though it wouldn't accomodate a motorcycle and they both got out to inspect her new digs.

It was a small, rather drab hotel, with a carved wood-paneled lobby and worn armchairs placed in a circle by the hanging newspaper rack. Alex asked the middle-aged man behind the desk about a reservation for Miss Reardon. The man took a puff of his foul-smelling cigarette and opened the large ledger on the counter. He flipped through a few pages and frowned. He put his glasses on and went through it again, dropping ashes over everything.

"Che ne so io." He shrugged despondently. *"È riservato lo sabato, signore. Mi dispiace molto. Non c' è una prenotazione questa sera."*

The man shook his head. "I am sorry," he said in heavily-accented English.

ROMAN CANDLES

Alex turned to Maggie. "Great work in the home office. He says you're due to come in Saturday, not today."

Maggie made a face. "Tell him I must have a room!"

The man was adamant. They had not made a mistake, Miss Reardon had made the mistake. They had no room for her for the next two nights.

"Damn" Alex muttered under his breath. "All right, it's all right, nothing you can do about this foul-up."

"So, now what? I suppose I should find a hotel."

"Look, we're not far from my apartment. Why don't I take you there for now, and we can talk about this later, when I get back."

"I can't do that, Alex! I've put you out already."

"Have a better solution?"

"I can hire a taxi and sort of scout around."

"Too expensive," he said bluntly. "Come on, this is the simplest way."

Maggie was as embarrassed as she was annoyed. She was off to a bad start. The last thing in the world she wanted after stealing a plum story right from under Alex's nose was to tag along after him. She tried to focus her anger at the agent who'd messed up, but she was just as furious with herself. And her fuzzy head from the lack of sleep and jet lag didn't help either.

As they sped through the crowded neighborhood, she caught glimpses of exotic street names on each corner and stared at the narrow alleys and red brick buildings huddling into each other. She saw an ancient crone, clad all in black, lugging two string bags in each hand. She saw kids playing what she assumed was a Roman version of stickball. She felt the tempo of the city all around her as they drove on. Finally, Alex pulled into a small street and jammed his car into a space.

"I got this apartment through a guy at UPI here in Rome who was reassigned to Beirut. It's a great section, Parioli, loaded with atmosphere and great for students and foreigners who want to spend some real time here. I prefer the apartment to a *pensione* because of the kitchen and private bathroom. By the way, I trust you don't mind running down the hall for a bath—it's easier on the pocketbook than an apartment, and I know Peter Hastings appreciates our penny-pinching. How else would he keep the company going? Let's take your stuff upstairs. Can't leave it in the car—it'd get ripped off."

Maggie picked up her overnight case and typewriter and followed Alex into a red-brick house with wide, worn steps out front. A small tree leaned precariously into the windows from the narrow courtyard between the street and the house.

Alex led her into a square vestibule with worn terrazzo floors and stairs leading to the upper floors. In a niche in the wall, she noticed a four-foot-tall statue of St. Jude prominently displayed. Alex caught her glance.

"The landlady's patron saint. The saint of lost causes! Hey, there are hundreds of churches in Rome, enough saints to go around for everyone." He chuckled. "We're on the third floor, no elevator."

"We?" she murmured, but Alex was already loping up the steps ahead of her. There were two apartments on the third floor, with doors facing each other. Alex unlocked the one on the right on the staircase and ushered her into a fair-sized room painted bright yellow, with windows facing the front. A daybed sat against one wall, a rickety table was pushed up to the window with two chairs on either side. A bookcase stuffed with books and magazines and a chipped marble coffee table on a wrought-iron base completed the furnishings. There was a faded blue rug of indeterminate age on the gray terrazzo floor. Alex walked to a door on the other side of the room and waved.

"The kitchen, or *la cucina*. Might as well start your lessons now, eh? Point of fact, I had to buy the kitchen cabinets from my erstwhile friend. He had to buy them from the tenant before him." He grinned at her astonishment and gave an Italian shrug. *"Ma, che fa?* That's the Roman custom. You buy your own cabinets and hang them up. When you move out, you take them with you or sell them to another lucky tenant. Come on, the bedroom is here."

He walked across the kitchen and pushed open another door.

"A railroad flat," Maggie laughed.

"Sort of."

The bedroom was small. There was a double bed pushed up against one wall, an armoire huddled next to a tall dresser, and not much else. Alex retreated, and she followed him back to the living room. He opened another door.

"The situation," he said.

"Wild set-up," she commented, glancing into the bathroom, which came equipped with tub, shower, toilet, sink, plus a bidet and a window high up on one wall. "What do you mean, situation?"

"Gabriella calls it that." There was a warmth to his voice when he mentioned her name. "Well, why not? Just another euphemism for the same thing." He wheeled around and walked back to the living room. He went to the far wall and touched a large knob imbedded in the plaster. A Murphy bed slowly descended, and Maggie howled with glee.

"This place is a gem!"

"It's a real find, don't I know it. I can put up six people, if two sleep on the floor. Good for, well . . ." he stopped and gave her one of those extraordinary looks of his, ". . . times when you never know who might show up. Look," he said, his voice taking on a practical tone, "I have an appointment right now. I can't take you around and it doesn't seem too smart for you to lug your stuff from place to place. You stay here until Saturday. Relax, make yourself comfortable. Take a bath, whatever. There's food in the fridge. I'll run down and get the other bag, then I'll be off." He started down the stairs to his car.

It suddenly seemed like a very sensible idea. The jet lag was really getting to her, and she could have killed for a shower. She went to pick up her overnight case and then she heard someone at the door, which Alex had left slightly ajar. An elderly man with a fringe of white hair, wearing a long brown sweater, was standing there, nodding and speaking to her in rapid Italian. She just couldn't begin to follow him; her mind went blank. He motioned toward the living room, and she looked around at her bags. Oh, Lord, he was trying to tell her she couldn't move in here with Alex!

"No . . . I'm not staying, just visiting. . . ." She waved her hands madly.

Sì." He walked in, went to the radiator and fiddled with the knob on the floor. He was just checking the heat. She laughed nervously.

"Sì, caliente," she said. *Good, Maggie, just great.* Caliente

is Spanish. The man gave her a little bow and left the room, and in a second, Alex was back with her suitcase.

"What did my landlord want? I saw him on the stairs," he explained.

"Something about the radiator; I don't know. I guess he was checking me out."

"He keeps this place too damned hot anyway," Alex complained. "Well, like I said, make yourself at home. I shouldn't be more than a couple of hours. We'll have dinner."

"Thanks Alex, really. I really appreciate this. I hate to impose on you, but. . . ."

"Stop apologizing, hang loose," he said.

"Will do. But I still owe you."

"In that case. . . ." He came across the room swiftly and caught her by surprise. His arms snaked out and drew her up against the hardness of his body, and she felt herself go limp as his mouth came down on hers in a hungry kiss. He had the warmest mouth—it was as if his body emanated heat, or he was running a fever. She could not have been more taken aback if he'd jumped out the window. She stayed in his arms a moment too long, and after a while, he released her.

"That wasn't necessary," she said, trying to re-establish their previous businesslike rapport.

"Sure it was. Italian custom—always kiss when you say hello and goodbye, and I didn't do that at the airport. See you later, *ciao.*"

He was gone, clattering down the stairs noisily before she could say anything. She wished she could get a handle on Alex Parisi—she'd never met anyone like him. At the airport he'd been positively rude about being expected to babysit for her, and then he had warmed to her excitement about Rome. He'd been patient about her hotel problem and seemed genuinely disinterested about her having nabbed his story. That kiss was totally unnecessary. If he was baiting her because of Craig, he was wasting his time. She was grateful to have a place to stay, that was all. He didn't get special favors just because they'd been thrown together for a few nights. Regardless of how attractive she found him.

That settled in her mind, she felt oddly reprieved. She was hungry, even though she'd wolfed down all the plastic plane food, so she wandered into the kitchen where she found a bottle of Chianti and a loaf of bread on the counter. There were black olives, cheese, milk and eggs in the refrigerator. She sliced some bread, poured a glass of milk and munched on olives and cheese. She made a mental note to go grocery shopping for Alex when she went out to explore his neighborhood.

When she was full, she put things away and went back into the living room, fatigue suddenly washing over her. She let it hit her, and kept walking into the bedroom, kicking off her shoes as she went. Then she stripped down to her underwear. Her clothes were grubby, and she felt too exhausted to unpack. She slipped under the sheet and was asleep immediately. Jet lag had won.

She awoke with a start. Someone was in the room with her. She opened her eyes and was momentarily disoriented. She sat up in bed, her heart pounding.

"Who is it?" she demanded. She could just barely make out a form on the other side of the room. The Roman shutters, which kept the sun out in the summer and heat in in the winter, made the room very dark. The only light filtering into the bedroom came from a lamp in the living room.

"It's me, take it easy. Did I wake you?" Alex came toward the bed. "I was going to get some pants out of the closet, that's all."

"You scared me silly. I was dead asleep." She realized he was staring at her filmy bra and she yanked the sheet up to cover herself.

"Sorry." He was grinning, she could hear it in his voice. "I'll get my pants and get out."

"What time is it?"

"About seven P.M."

She groaned. "Oh, fine. I didn't mean to sleep so long. I thought I'd go look for a hotel after dinner."

"Forget it. I told you you can stay here."

"I don't like putting you out."

"Stop acting like a sixteen-year-old virgin. You're safe with me, Maggie. I'll sleep in the other room. But if it's going to bother you that much, I'll call Pippo and go bunk with him."

"Don't be ridiculous. You've twisted my arm. I'd be delighted to stay." Well, there was no getting around it; she'd have to accept his hospitality and like it. But her mind reeled with all she had to do, and so far she'd slept a whole afternoon away. Tomorrow she'd go to the bank and change some dollars into lire, gather her notes and begin to make contacts.

"May I bother you for one of my bags? The middle-sized one, please. I'd get up, but I haven't got much on."

He laughed, the first real laugh she'd heard him utter. "The lady is being modest, when I've just offered to share my room and board. Don't growl, Maggie, I'll get the bag. After you've dressed, we can go get something to eat."

"Only if I pay!" she yelled at his back.

"I wouldn't have it any other way," he called back. A second later, he came back, dumped her bag on the floor and left.

She took out a short kimono and wrapped it around her slender frame, then pulled out a gray wool pleated skirt and a turquoise georgette blouse with an ascot tie at the neck. With as much dignity as she could muster, she stalked into the living room, went past him and dove into the bathroom for a shower.

"I'm taking you to a great place on the other side of town," he called in when she was standing naked on the mat drying herself off. She had a funny feeling, talking to him without any clothes on.

"Tell me about it."

"It's called Amborata d'Abruzzi, a real *ristorante tipico Romano*, as they say. White-washed walls, white tableclothes, discreet waiters and great food."

"Sounds marvelous," she yelled back, tying the belt of her robe securely. She raced back to the bedroom and dressed quickly. When she came out, she noticed that Alex had only changed his pants. He was still wearing that awful army jacket.

"Are you going . . . I mean, am I dressed right?" she asked, trying not to stare at his less-than-formal wear.

"Sure, sure. This place is very casual. You'll like it."

The ambiance of the restaurant made her imbibe too much and she began to unwind. Alex ordered. They had an ievable *antipasto*, which included marinated mushrooms, salami, artichoke hearts, and a succulent dish of pork and mustard greens. They washed it down with more wine.

"I could eat like this every day," she sighed.

"You'd get fat."

"Nope. I can eat day and night, and I never gain a pound."

"Lucky. You'll be the envy of most Italian women, who have to watch their pasta intake."

"I love it here," she proclaimed, just a bit high from the wine and the atmosphere and the fact that she felt incredibly drawn to Alex. "I just feel right here."

"Good. And at least you've got a bed. I promise, I won't charge much rent," he teased.

"Look, I'm not staying. I told you. . . ."

"Honest, the rates and service are much better at my place than at the Trinità dei Monti. Why don't you stay?"

"Oh, cool it, Alex. You've made your obligatory pass, now we can be colleagues. Let's keep this friendly and professional, all right?"

"Whew!" He sat back and stared at her over his wineglass. "You can relax, Betty Businesswoman. I would not dream of anything more intimate with you than a quiet little rendezvous at the office copying machine. People with connections in high places are never taken advantage of—don't worry."

"Alex. . . ." she began, but he cut her off.

"Now. I suppose you've got your maps of Rome, you can familiarize yourself with districts that way. The Piazza del Popolo is more or less the center of the city, this leads to a wide boulevard called Via del Corso, which has a lot of good shops and so forth. You can walk to the Via Veneto from there, that's right near your *pensione*. Walking might be a good idea until you get used to public transportation. Buses are fast and inexpensive, about forty cents a shot. Taxis are another story, you have to call for one or else find a taxi stand. Remember, if you make that call, it'll be an extra charge of a hundred lire on your tab. There are two undergrounds, subways. Termine EUR and Termine Cristofore Colombo. Not exactly the IRT, but they do the job."

"That's wonderful. You're a walking tour guide. Look, you didn't have to bite my head off. I really would like to be your friend." He was silent and wouldn't look at her. "Well, in that case, I'd be grateful for your advice too. I assume sleuthing out a story here is quite different from doing it in New York?"

"About five times as tough. Seven times. Any idea how you'll get started?"

She sighed. "Truth? No. Back at the office, it seemed so easy, with all my facts and figures. Now I need people, interviews. All those guys dumped here to fight a war that wasn't theirs, it's no wonder they had to search out some diversion. It boggles the mind."

"What's your theme? Why don't you start with one clear focus? Like the title. What will you call the series?"

"I'm not sure. Well, the theme is those innocent babies born because of a war."

"That's it then. Innocents."

Maggie stared into space for a moment, and then a smile lit up her face. "The Innocents. Of course, what a marvelous title!"

"It's okay."

"Alex, thanks. You're really good."

"I know. Now you get to do the hard part: the legwork."

"Tell me, how did you start the Aldo Moro kidnapping and execution pieces? Where did you go for your first contacts?"

He looked away for a minute. Then he turned back to her. "I began with the UPI guys, press services, the embassy for background material and government people I could contact. Then I . . . stumbled onto some other sources, let's put it that way. A friend introduced me to a friend of a friend of his. After a while, he trusted me and he talked. He even clued me into the night they were going to bust up Via Negroli in Milan. That's when they caught Corrado Alunni, one of the ringleaders, the one they said was responsible for getting Moro in the first place. I have to warn you," he went on, "nothing much has changed since that time—if anything it's gotten worse. People walk carefully everywhere, and you'd better learn to do the same. There are little incidents every day, some of them never reported. A grenade goes off here, a bombing there."

"Who's behind all this? The Red Brigades?"

Alex shrugged and lit up a thin black cigar. "Terrorism, or whatever you want to call it, is as Italian as pasta. Supposedly, it all started with a couple of idealistic college kids back in the sixties who called themselves Marxists . . . political naïves, is what I call them." He paused as smoke half-clouded his face for a moment.

"Oh?"

"Sure. They were dumb. But it goes back a lot further. The Italians are anarchists at heart. They haven't been able to decide on a government since Garibaldi united the two kingdoms. It's Italian nature to overthrow the status quo. And these days, it's not just the Red Brigades. It's Fascists, and it's free-lancers, kids, anyone, kidnapping for money, snatching purses, ripping jewelry off women as they shop. When you walk around, you see bars on windows where there never had to be any before."

"You're scaring the hell out of me, Alex." She glared at him and took another mouthful of veal and peppers.

"Good. I want you to be scared. Then you won't do anything stupid and get hurt." He looked at her closely. "Sorry you're here?"

She wasn't sure whether he was concerned or just testing her.

"Of course not! I can take care of myself. I've lived in New York City."

"Multiply that by ten and you've got conditions here today," he said grimly. "So, what else do you have in mind to write about?"

"Well, I need one specific case, one person who could give me a personal viewpoint. What he or she feels about having an American soldier daddy, what's it's like to be born out of wedlock in Italy and to live your life wondering whether you can connect up all the dots. Whether you have the guts to put the pieces together."

Alex's voice was suddenly harsh. "Why should anyone spill all this private data to you? What's in it for them?"

"Wait a minute. Something like this can be an opportunity to open a door, change more than one life for the better."

He snorted. "Or for the worse. You're talking like an American, an idealistic, naïve child. We're dealing with people of a different culture here. I think that's been our basic fault throughout the years, the whole problem of our foreign policy. We try to Americanize them, and it can't be done. For example, Italian people are family-oriented and very Catholic, never mind that the men have a mistress or two on the side. The women often fool around too, if they think they can get away with it. But underlying it all is a kind of strict morality. A girl gets into trouble, the family comes to her aid. And I mean completely. It had to be even more so during the war."

"You're telling me it won't work," she snapped. "That it's pointless for me to try to get this story."

"I'm telling you to be prepared for some hard knocks. You're not going to waltz into a strange country and buttonhole a dozen people who say they are illegitimate offspring of American servicemen and that they're dying to tell you about it!"

Anger washed over her, and she felt her face flush. Damn the man, he didn't give her credit for being any kind of reporter. She'd never given up on a story, and she wouldn't start now.

"I intend to write this if I have to probe clear into the Vatican."

"Okay. I was just preparing you for the worst, as is my custom. I guess you can start by seeing someone at the embassy. Nice bunch of people there, especially the press attaché, Dick Ord, a friend of mine."

"Thanks. I appreciate the intro. I'll take it from there—don't worry, I'm not going to ask to talk to your underground terrorist moles."

He threw back his head and laughed. "Although I wouldn't be surprised if a couple of them had ghosts in their family closets. Hey, you know, you'll do all right here—you're pretty savvy."

"Thanks."

"I saw my friend Pippo this afternoon. I told him about you, and he said he'd be very happy to show you around. You'll like him—he's handsome, bombastic and full of tidbits about the city. Why don't I ask Pippo and Gabriella to stop by for some wine and cheese tomorrow night? That all right with you?"

"Sure, great. So, what do we do next?"

"Why don't you tell me all about your life and I'll tell you all about mine?"

She looked up, startled. He was giving her that look again, and she felt her cheeks turn red.

"Well, I'm New England born and bred. My father's a schoolteacher—was—he's retired. My mother's my best friend, except for my roommate Ellen, who's going to marry Stan. I've got one brother who's fourteen, a late-in-life baby, and I adore him. I'm pretty conventional: Skidmore B.A., newspaper gofer, magazine researcher. And writer to the wee hours of the night, ever since I was seven."

"Sounds comfortable. No traumas, disappointments in love, arrest records?"

She laughed. "No. Well, one of the above."

He nodded. "And when you get to know me better. . . . Now, I'll tell you about me. I've got a big Italian family—I'm the oldest of eight. Mama always had a pot of gravy bubbling on the stove until the day she died, that was when I was fifteen. Heart attack. You know, she was what cardiologists call a real Type A, always too busy looking after us to bother eating or sleeping, never thought about her health. Papa was a florist before he turned writer, self-taught. He had his own nursery, raised trees from saplings, exotic flowers from seed. Then, when mama died, he sold the business and sat down at his typewriter to try to convince people they ought to care about the earth they lived on. I went to Berkeley, stayed on for an M.A. in international economics and was just about to become a perennial student when I started churning out articles about the revolts on campus. *Shout* offered me my first fulltime job because of them." He chuckled. "Do you know I was twenty-five before I knew what nine-to-five meant? And twenty-six when I told them I'd quit if I couldn't go traveling and make my own hours."

His face had softened as he spoke about his parents, and she realized that Alex Parisi was probably a man with a great deal of love in him. He just did a good job covering it up.

"Interesting."

"Glad you think so. You do want dessert, don't you? A girl with an appetite like yours never turns down dessert."

"Well, I have heard about those *tartuffos* in the Piazza Navona. I've had a fantasy about eating one for years. Can we go?"

"Sure. In a minute. Let's just sit for a while. You have to learn not to rush, Maggie. Look around you. Do you see the Italians rushing? They're sitting back enjoying their espresso and conversation as civilized people ought to."

"I know. I'm just a barbarian from Connecticut. And a forward, aggressive woman. Remember, I'm paying this check." She dug into her purse. "Will they accept American dollars? I'll go change money tomorrow."

ROMAN CANDLES

"Money is money in any language." And when she put down two twenty dollar bills, the waiter took them without hesitation.

They left the restaurant, took a ride in his car, walked for a while and sat in the Piazza Navona, savoring the fountain and the sweet chocolate dessert. An hour later, they started back to Alex's apartment.

"I'll be busy tomorrow morning, but in the afternoon I can introduce you to some possible contacts. Look over any New York leads you want to try to follow up here. Has anyone ever told you your eyes look like pea soup with turnips? All those yellow flecks."

There it was again: he was being kind, helpful, almost flirtatious, as though he were happy to take her under his wing, and have her around for a while.

The apartment was steamy when they walked in. The landlord, unlike most Europeans, evidently felt that the hotter it was, the better. So they went around throwing open the shutters and opening windows. The cool moonlight poured in, tinting everything with a blue-white glow.

Alex went into the bedroom and took out some clothes. "In case you're sleeping when I leave in the morning. There's coffee, bread for toast and eggs if you like. Help yourself."

"Thanks, I'll be up early. Got to get going."

He offered her the bathroom first and she hurried through her business and got out quickly. She said goodnight to Alex, went into the bedroom and closed the door. She heard him moving around for a while, and then all was quiet. It was comforting to know he was there, much nicer than being in a strange hotel room in Rome by herself. She slept soundly.

Chapter 5

Despite her intention to get an early start, it was past eleven when Maggie was finally able to bring herself to face the day. She sat up in bed groggily and hugged her knees, absorbing the insulating silence and wondering just where she would begin. *A shower first,* she thought, *then I'll start worrying about the rest of the next five weeks.*

Forcing herself out of the warm sheets, Maggie stood up and stretched. The room was dark—she'd just fall back to sleep if she didn't have some kind of stimulus to prod her. She threw open the shutters and cranked them all the way up, bathing herself in the bright midmorning rays. Encouraged by the sun, Maggie quickly pulled her nightgown over her head and, squatting naked next to her open suitcase on the floor, she rummaged for her faithful old blue chenille bathrobe.

Pulling the belt tight around her, Maggie stumbled barefoot through the empty living room, heading for the bathroom. Alex must have left in a hurry to make his morning appointment. The daybed was unmade, and a half-full coffee cup was still sitting on the kitchen table. Yawning and still groggy, Maggie went into the bathroom, glanced at her sleepy image in the mirror and dropped her bathrobe to her ankles. She turned on the hot-water faucet full force and stood outside the tub, waiting for the frigid blast to get warmer. Rubbing the goosebumps on her arms, she frowned as she

ROMAN CANDLES

recalled Mabel Weeks's warning about the reliability of Italian bathrooms and heating systems. At least there was a bidet—she'd always wanted to try one. Very practical invention, she thought, examining it like some piece of Roman statuary while she waited for the hot water.

Resigned to the fact that lukewarm was the best she would get, Maggie plunged into the shower and quickly worked up a rich shampoo lather, scrubbing away the hours of an international flight and heavy jet lag. She washed hastily and rinsed off just before the water turned ice cold again.

Stepping out of the shower dripping wet, Maggie grabbed a towel to wipe herself off. She rubbed it briskly into her scalp, then peered into the mirror through wet, shaggy-dog bangs.

"Boy, what a beaut," she murmued to herself.

Suddenly, she heard the apartment door open and close.

"Alex?" she yelled.

"Yeah. It's me," he yelled back.

"Hi," she said, peeking through the partly-open bathroom door, her hair still an unruly mass of damp ringlets.

"You just get up?" he asked.

"Yup. Guess I overslept." She didn't like having him see her like this. It wasn't the image she wanted to project, not exactly the hardworking reporter personified. Oh, well, he probably had his bad days too.

"Jet lag really is a pain. I hear astronauts get chronic jet lag. They say the only thing that'll straighten them out after a trip is sex."

Maggie chose not to respond and made believe she hadn't heard him. Just being cute for her benefit, she decided. Or maybe he didn't mean anything by it—some people she knew threw the word "sex" into the conversation any time they could, whether it was pertinent or not.

After brushing her teeth, Maggie emerged from the bathroom and scurried through the living room toward the bedroom.

"I'll be dressed in a minute," she said to Alex, who was reading through some of his notes at his shaky, makeshift desk.

"Did you have breakfast yet?"

"No," she called from the bedroom as she was stepping into her panties.

"I'll heat up some coffee for you, okay?"

ROMAN CANDLES

"Please—thanks."

After puzzling over her wrinkled wardrobe, she pulled out a plain white broadcloth, buttondown shirt and a wraparound blue corduroy skirt. A little dull for Rome, she thought, maybe I'll take a day off at some point and do something about the clothing problem. She tied a blue and red print scarf around her neck, slipped into her gray blazer and hunted under the bed for her penny loafers. One thing she was determined not to do was get sore feet from clumping around the cobblestone streets of Rome in high heels.

When Maggie entered the kitchen, Alex was sitting at the table with his notebook spread open before him. Immediately, she again felt that she was imposing upon his routine. But when he looked up, pushing his glasses up on his head, and smiled warmly at her as he sat before two steaming cups of coffee and a plate of circular, pretzel-like biscuits, Maggie's apprehensions melted.

"Hey, you're looking pretty good for someone who just flew in from New York."

"Thanks, but I still feel a bit logy."

"Don't worry about it. After you drink some of this, you'll be racing around in fast-forward."

"What is it?" Maggie asked, sniffing the heady aroma steaming up at her from her cup.

"Camerounian coffee," he explained, "the closest thing in Rome I've found to our back-home brew. I thought about smuggling in coffee from the States, but I couldn't figure out a good way to hide a month's supply in my underwear. Anyway, this Camerounian stuff tastes okay. The only problem is that it's got so much caffeine in it, you're speeding all day long. It's a nice change from espresso once in a while, though."

"Hmm," she murmured, tentatively sipping the hot liquid. "Not bad. Very strong, the way I like it. What are these? Bagels?" she asked, picking up one of the biscuits.

"*Taralli*. Sort of like dried-up doughnuts. They have fennel seeds in them. Gives them a nice, tangy flavor. Be careful, though, they're really hard."

Maggie picked one up, examined it, then rapped it on the table and looked up at Alex with mock skepticism. She put it in her mouth and carefully bit down, suddenly surprised by the loud crunch that it made. She took a sip of coffee to wash

ROMAN CANDLES

it down and then continued to gnaw on her *tarallo,* obviously enjoying it.

"I like them," she announced with crumbs falling from the corners of her mouth. "Too bad they're so hard."

"Why?"

"Because if they were softer, I'd be able to eat more of them faster," she giggled.

"You really *are* a bottomless pit. Hastings should have warned me you might eat me out of house and home."

Why was he continually harping on her former relationship? "Alex," she said, putting down her cup, "do me a favor. Forget about whatever Craig might have told you about me. We are not a couple, and he needn't feel obligated to have you look after me, okay?"

"Sounds like there's some lingering hard feelings there."

"Not at all. I'm here to get a story, that's all. Please don't assume that this is a paid vacation for the boss's kid's girlfriend—that just isn't so. As far as I'm concerned, Craig Hastings is one of the employers, and I'm just another employee."

"Well, I guess that clears that up. Consider Hastings a closed subject. I won't bring him up again. Now, what've you got on your itinerary for today?"

"I was hoping to get to the Manufacturers Hanover on Via Bissolati first and change some money, open my account—things like that."

"Good, we'll go after you finish breakfast."

"Oh, hey, Alex. You must have your own work to do. Please don't feel that you have to chauffeur me around Rome."

"Sure, I have lots to do. But one, *Shout* sends my salary to Manufacturers Hanover too, and I have to go get some cash myself. And two, I've set aside this afternoon to show you around, get you acquainted with the town. Better take me while I'm available. I may be off any time following a lead in the north after tomorrow."

"Okay. Thanks, Alex, really. I'm going to cool it with the independent woman bit and calm down."

"Good. Remember what I told you last night about Rome's easy pace."

"Right. I'll keep that in mind."

"After we go to the bank, I thought I'd take you over to the

ROMAN CANDLES

American embassy to meet Dick Ord, the press attaché. He's a good man to know. I'm sure he'll be able to give you a few hints as to where to start."

"Great. I could use some concrete leads." Maggie took another *tarallo* as Alex gulped his coffee and glanced back down at his notes.

"So what's this story you're doing in the north?" Maggie asked, breaking the silence.

Alex's expression changed abruptly. He looked dead serious as he stared into her eyes. "As I told you last night, I'm working on a profile of wealthy Italians who have to live under the constant threat of terrorist violence. Most of the terrorist groups like the Red Brigades and the Prima Linea are concentrated around Genoa, Bologna and Milan, so many of my leads start up there."

"Interesting. Why didn't Jennings just station you up there, then?"

He took a deep breath and looked away. "What is this, an interview?"

"Jeez, Alex, I just asked a question."

"Yes, well, it so happens that now their prime targets—the rich industrialists and the government officials—have gotten wise to their tactics and are protecting themselves. Specially-trained bodyguards, you know, the works. So the terrorists have moved on and turned their attentions to the wealthy Italian royalty in Florence, Venice and Rome. Maggie, I really don't want to tell you much more about my story. Believe me, the less you know, the better off you'll be. These terrorists are driven fanatics. They're nasty, brutal and ruthless when they don't get their own way."

She shook her head and put her cup down. "Okay, I don't intend to get in their way."

"Sometimes you can't help it. They have a facility for coming and finding whomever they want. Or they just take whoever happens to be available. Married women have stopped even wearing their wedding rings for fear some thug with vaseline on his hand is going to reach out and slide the ring right off them on the street. But, of course, that's gentle treatment—that's your average, everyday mugger—that's not one of the organized groups.

"Recently, the wife of a certain automobile executive was kidnapped by one of the right-wing Fascist groups. They demanded over two million dollars for her life. When the executive said their demand was too high, he received a box in the mail containing all his wife's hair. They made their demand again and warned him to stop 'fooling around.' He pleaded with them to be more reasonable and lower their ransom price. The next day in the mail, he received his wife's finger with her wedding ring on it. Enough said?"

Maggie shuddered. "More than enough, thanks. I don't think I'm curious anymore," she murmured, wincing.

"Finish your coffee. If we want to see Dick today, we better get over to the bank. That may take a while."

"Anytime you're ready," Maggie agreed, taking another *tarallo* for the road when Alex wasn't looking.

"Signor Parisi, good to see you again." The gray-haired, impeccably-dressed bank manager rose from his desk to greet them, encasing Alex's muscular hand in both of his. His crisp, gray, pin-striped suit and starched French cuffs were the antithesis of Alex's battered Army jacket and open-collared shirt.

"Maggie Reardon—Gaetano Alecandri. Gaetano—Maggie. She's here on assignment from *Shout*, too."

"Please, sit. Tell me what I can do for you." Signor Alecandri waited until Maggie and Alex had seated themselves before carefully pulling at his neatly-pressed pant legs and drawing up his chair close to his desk as he sat. He positioned his elbows on the blotter and began to stroke his trim, steel-gray mustache with his thumbnail, prepared to listen. Now this was a real Continental character, Maggie mused. They just had something—an air about them—that she'd never seen in an American male, at least not a heterosexual American male. The Italian men walked around like they always expected someone was about to take a picture of them. There was this air of pride mingled with a kind of charming conceit that was attractive in its own way—perhaps for its foreignness, if nothing else.

"Well," Alex began, crossing his legs and folding his hands over his stomach, "the magazine has forwarded money for Maggie's expenses. She'd like to get some lire today."

"Of course, of course." The banker threw up his hands like Aladdin's genie, as if Alex's request was his command. "Just a few formalities, Miss . . . ?"

ROMAN CANDLES

"Reardon . . . Maggie, please."

"Maggie, yes. If your journalistic abilities are as potent as your charming beauty, you are sure to be a Nobel Laureate some day." He tilted his head, confirming his statement with the gesture. "Excuse me for a moment. I must get the proper forms."

"Christ, what a character!" Alex exhaled after Alecandri had disappeared into a back room.

"He *is!* He's wonderful. And when was the last time you got this kind of treatment from a New York bank?" Maggie was a bit disappointed with his snide attitude. Evidently, the charm of the man was lost on Alex.

"Wait till you get in line for a teller. You'll eat those words."

"I don't think so." Maggie had to keep herself from getting testy. Alex seemed to have the knack of putting her on edge. Before she could start an argument, though, the banker was back.

"Now, Maggie," he bowed his head to indicate his hesitation about using her first name, "if you will fill out these two cards and this form, I will make you a rich woman very soon."

Maggie proceeded to fill out the form with Alex looking on to translate the questions for her. Signor Alecandri busied himself with other forms. pretending not to hear their conversation.

"They'll send you checks in a couple of days if the mailmen don't go on strike."

Maggie scowled at his cynicism. He seemed determined to pull her away from her enchantment with Rome, no matter how he accomplished it.

"You can use my address if you like. It's probably safer for mail deliveries."

"No thanks, Alex. I'm sure my *pensione* can handle a letter or two for me." Her tone was brusque.

"Fine with me. It was just an offer."

"Respectfully declined."

"No problem. Forget I said it."

"I will." She finished filling out her forms in silence. When she handed them over to the banker, he raised his eyebrows in practised surprise and quickly examined them.

"Excellent, excellent. Your expense money has been cleared, and everything is in order. I have made out a bank

ROMAN CANDLES

draft for two hundred thousand lire for you until you receive your checks. Just sign this and take it to one of the tellers." He reached over and put his hand over Maggie's. "Remember, Maggie, if I can help you with anything while you are here in Rome, anything at all, please know that I am here waiting for you." He smiled warmly and his eyes caressed hers.

Maggie blushed despite herself. Bankers, in her experience, had never made the chore of getting and receiving money quite so seductive. "Thanks a lot, Gaetano. *Ciao.*" She nodded, withdrawing her hand from his, as Alex stood up and waited for Maggie to lead the way toward the tellers' windows.

Gaetano smiled and watched them until they were positioned in line, then returned to the work on his desk.

Maggie soon found that the bank manager's delicious charm was simply the calm before the mad storm at the tellers' windows. The lines of people—if one could call them lines—were loosely arranged, snaking haphazardly all over the bank lobby. There was a great deal of jostling for position and shifting of eyes searching for a faster teller.

"Now we come to the truth about Italian banks," Alex said to Maggie as they stood waiting. "What came before was just a cover. See, Italians hate to stand in line, and they'll do anything to get ahead of you. Hang on, you'll see." His smug confidence about his prediction annoyed Maggie, and she hoped that they'd be whisked through the line just to prove him wrong. Suddenly, a frantic voice broke out of the general hubbub of the bank customers.

"Scusi, scusi!" A young man in his early twenties, clutching a leather shoulder bag, was trying to push his way to the front of the line. "Please let me go ahead. My wife is in the hospital and the babies are home all alone. I can't leave them for long. *Per favore—signori, signore!"* His pleas were met with grumbles and sneers. Then a woman in another line shouted at him in Italian and a great uproar began. The line of people harshly shoved the young man aside, ignoring his requests. Resigned at last, he shrugged and quietly went to the end of the line.

"What was that all about?" Maggie asked, puzzled by the momentary anarchy.

"That's exactly what I was talking about. The guy thought

he could get ahead by telling them a good story. Italians are generally suspicious, but there was a fair chance that they would have believed him and let him go ahead. Unfortunately for him, that woman in the other line lives in his apartment building, and she informed the crowd that he had no children and that his wife is fooling around with another man. So, he had to get in line and wait like everyone else."

"And this kind of stuff happens all the time?"

"Sure. If they haven't left the *bambini* home without a sitter, then mama is dying in Salerno and they have to take the train down and see her before she kicks the bucket. I know I must sound cynical and jaded to you, but that's just the way things are in Rome. I only hope we can get out of here in time to make it over to the embassy and catch Dick before he leaves for the day."

At a quarter to three, Maggie and Alex were racing up the front steps of the American embassy on the Via Veneto. At the door, they were confronted with a uniformed marine wearing a chrome-plated combat helmet.

"May I help you?" the marine said emotionlessly.

"Yes," Alex told him, pausing to catch his breath. "We have an appointment with Mr. Ord. Alex Parisi and Maggie Reardon, tell him."

"Just a second, sir." The marine took a step back and reached for a phone on the wall. "Betsy, please," he intoned into the receiver. After a few seconds, he spoke again. "A Miss Reardon and a Mr. Parisi to see Mr. Ord . . . right." He replaced the receiver in its cradle with a military snap and stepped forward again.

"Go right ahead. Second floor, last door on the left."

"He tells me that every goddam time I come here," Alex complained to Maggie under his breath as they walked past.

"Thank you," Maggie said to the marine, trying to get a peek at his hidden eyes under the helmet as she walked by him.

Climbing the stairs two at a time, Alex hurried on ahead of Maggie, who hung back to admire the huge mural on the wall next to the staircase, depicting a fairy-tale Italian landscape. She could almost taste the heady red wine suggested by the deep magenta glow emanating from the hills on the mural's horizon. When she could finally tear herself away from the magnificent spectacle, she looked up to find that Alex had disappeared.

She reached the second floor hurriedly and spotted him all the way down the hall.

"This way, Maggie," he whispered loudly. "Dick's about to leave for an appointment, but at least you'll get to meet him."

"Coming," she said breathlessly, practically running down the corridor.

Alex held the glass door open for Maggie. She noticed the gold and black lettering on the glass pane—Richard W. Ord, Press Attaché. Sitting behind her desk in the antechamber was a woman who seemed to be about Maggie's age. She was very angular, with broad shoulders that supported a neat, long face capped with a henna-red chignon, from which wisps of hair escaped at every angle. She had an oval face with sad, hazel eyes that told the world she'd seen a lot and accepted it all. Her face was open and caring—the kind you suspected you could tell your troubles to. The nameplate on the edge of her desk read: Elisabeth Farrell—Administrative Assistant.

"Hi," the woman beamed up at Maggie, "I'm Betsy. You must be the new American in town, Maggie Reardon."

"I see my reputation has preceded me," Maggie said good-naturedly, sensing the genuine friendliness of Betsy's manner.

"Watch out, Betsy," Alex interjected. "This one may be trouble."

"Alex!" Maggie shot him a dirty look. Did he think he was being cute?

"Behave yourself, Mr. Parisi," Betsy quipped. "You're on U.S. government property. You don't want me to have Sergeant Sanchez come up here and arrest you for disorderly conduct, do you?"

"No ma'am," Alex said with a smirk, and then they all laughed. Betsy had skillfully averted an awkward situation.

Just then, the door to the press attaché's office opened and a tall, lean man walked out. He was prematurely bald, with a fringe of longish, sandy hair and tiny, sparkling eyes that crinkled up when he smiled. He looked more like an Olympic track coach than a government official, Maggie thought.

"Is this a party? Am I invited?" He looked from Betsy to Alex to Maggie with a big grin on his face.

ROMAN CANDLES

"Dick, this is Maggie Reardon. Maggie, Dick Ord and Betsy Farrell—but you two've already met, kind of."

"Pleased to meet you, Dick. And let me thank you, Betsy, for curbing my colleague."

"Think nothing of it. But I must admit, things are getting out of hand when we State Department folks have to protect Americans from other Americans overseas." Betsy squinted and screwed up her mouth at Alex in mock disgust.

"It's the company he keeps, Maggie," Dick added. "Alex hangs around with terrorists—what do you expect?"

"All right, all of you, I'm outnumbered," Alex complained. "Give a guy a break!"

"Poor soul." Betsy shook her head in dismay.

"I'm going to have to run," Dick cut in, "but I'd like to talk to you some more, Maggie. Alex has told me a little about your series. Maybe I could give you a few leads. Why don't you come in later this week and we'll talk. How about Monday?" He flipped out his pocket date book and glanced through it. "Around eleven-thirty, okay?"

"Great."

"So I'm off now. I'll be back after four in case anybody wants me, Betsy. Maggie, I'll see you on Monday. And, Alex, try to stay out of trouble, will you? We run a nice quiet embassy here, so don't start giving American journalists a bad name."

"Wouldn't think of it, Dick," he chuckled.

"So long now," the attaché called, as he started down the corridor.

"A real card, that Mr. Ord," Alex laughed. "They wouldn't put up with this kind of laxity in Washington, you know. Good thing you're stationed here, Betsy, the way you two carry on."

"Yeah, I think so too. The food's certainly better. But I do get homesick, sometimes."

"Where are you from originally?" Maggie asked.

"Danbury, Connecticut."

"You're kidding! I'm from Wilton. My grandparents used to live in Danbury."

"Hey, we're practically cousins. We'll have to have lunch before you leave."

"I'd love to. How about Monday, after I see Dick?"

"It's a date. And, Alex, you're not invited."

71

ROMAN CANDLES

"Don't worry about me. I'll be lunching with my thug friends on Monday."

Betsy laughed, and Maggie threw him a sidelong glance. This morning, he'd nearly scared her to death with the implications of being connected to terrorists, and here he was making a big joke of it. The guy was so mercurial—one way with her, another way in public.

"Well, Maggie, I think we'd better let Betsy get back to work," he said, starting for the door.

"Yes, of course. I'm looking forward to Monday, Betsy."

"Me too. Take care now."

"I like her; she seems nice," Maggie murmured to Alex as they strolled back down the corridor.

"Betsy? Yeah, she's a good egg."

"Where to now?"

"Well, I think we should pick up some wine and cheese for tonight, then head back for Parioli. You must still be recovering from jet lag and all. You can take a nap if you want."

"I think that's a great idea. Don't want to look like a dishrag when Pippo and Gabriella show up."

"Okay, let's go." Alex took her by the arm and whisked her down the stairs and out the door to his car.

At 8:30 that evening, Maggie was busy cutting wedges of cheese and arranging them on a platter between carefully-placed black olives and rolled slices of *prosciutto*. Since she had slept through the late afternoon and early evening, having awakened just an hour ago, she was famished. For every piece of cheese she cut, she took another for immediate consumption, then complemented it with some of the cured ham and an olive. She poked around the cupboard for some more *taralli*, but when she couldn't find any, she settled for a crusty heel of bread. As she gnawed on the hard bread, she wondered whether it was possible to call out for pizza in Italy.

She hoped she was properly dressed for this event. Europeans were supposed to be so uptight about correct manners and clothes. Of course, Alex didn't seem to care about his wardrobe, so she could only look more appropriate than he. In her sweater-dress, a long, lean tube of mauve wool with a big cowl collar and self-belt, she looked thinner than ever. She was still trying to get used to having heels on again—

these black pumps were a full three inches taller than her loafers.

Alex had just gotten out of the shower and was dressing in the bedroom. Maggie was working on the cheese when he emerged from the other room and came into the kitchen to check on her progress. He had shed his wrinkled shirt and beige cords for a pair of gray wool trousers, a navy turtleneck, and a herringbone sport jacket. He still had on his scuffed cowboy boots—a small protest to the formality of the evening, she assumed. Still, Maggie had to admit to herself that he was quite something, all dressed up. Then she wondered whether his dramatic change in appearance was for Gabriella's benefit.

"Hey! Leave a couple for the guests!" he exclaimed with mock annoyance when he spotted the saucer full of olive pits.

"Don't worry; there's plenty."

But before he could object, the doorbell buzzed downstairs. "That's them, I bet," he said, heading for the door to greet his guests.

Hearing their voices in the hallway, Maggie suddenly felt a few slight butterflies in her stomach, not quite knowing what to expect. As soon as she heard that they were in the living room, Maggie grabbed the platter, took a deep breath and walked into the next room, ready for anything. She entered the room and saw Alex leading Gabriella to the couch. She was a gorgeous, dark-haired beauty, with high cheekbones, huge, cool eyes and a figure any woman would kill for. Alex held her wrist and shoulder with a tenderness that Maggie hadn't thought him capable of, and the expression on his face was extremely caring, very involved.

"Oh, Maggie." He looked up abruptly. "This is Gabriella Sciarra."

"Hello."

"How do you do, Maggie." Gabriella scanned Maggie's face and body with a cold, imperious look.

Maggie could not ever remember seeing anyone dressed quite the way this woman was dressed. She was a fashion photograph come to life, but, then, of course, she was built like a model and could probably carry off the most extreme outfits. She had to be 5'8", maybe 5'11" with the black, spiked heels she had on, and as she shrugged off her huge silver fox fur coat and threw it over a chair, Maggie marveled at her thin figure that was miraculously amplified with absolutely fantastic curves.

She had on a tight black crepe skirt with a tasteful slit up the right side, which was the perfect dark accent for her raspberry silk jacket and camisole with a gray leaf-print so subtle it was scarcely noticeable. The camisole, with tiny spaghetti straps holding it up, was low-cut and closed with a series of covered buttons leading to the gathered waist. The jacket over it had a Chinese collar and tucks at the top of the long, slim sleeves that gave a slight puff to the shoulders. Gabriella had on small diamond-cluster earrings, the stones arranged in a perfect triangle, and was wearing a single diamond on a gold chain around her neck. She gave off a wonderful musky scent—Bal à Versailles—Maggie remembered it from a rich old friend of her mother's. It was a perfume Maggie would never dream of trying. She imagined Gabriella sprayed her drawers and closets with the stuff—the heady mist around her now pervaded Alex's living room.

"Sit down, both of you," Alex said cordially. "Let me get you some wine." He ran into the kitchen, and Maggie suddenly dreaded being alone with this imposing beauty, though she didn't know exactly why.

"I've only been here a day and a half," Maggie said, decided that she would have to be the one to break the ice, "and already I'm madly in love with Rome."

"How nice," the other woman said flatly.

"Yes." Maggie chose to ignore her unfriendliness and forge on. "You must consider yourself lucky to live here."

"Lucky? What do you mean lucky?"

Maggie silently begged for Alex's return, knowing that she and Gabriella would never be able to carry on a conversation by themselves. "You know—fortunate—to be here . . . in Rome . . . all the time."

"I still don't know what you mean," Gabriella shot back, whisking strands of hair away from the sides of her face. "This is just a city, after all."

"What don't you understand?" Alex asked, returning from the kitchen with a tray with four juice glasses and a liter of Bardolino on it.

"She says I am lucky, Alex. For what reason am I lucky?" She said "lucky" as if it were a dirty word. Maggie just wanted to walk out of the room. She couldn't fathom the woman's hostility—it seemed clear she was purposely being dense. Her English was fine—it wasn't that she didn't understand the word. It was more like she wanted to make Maggie look foolish.

"Rome is not so good for the Romans anymore," Gabriella declared, almost defiantly, exchanging quick glances with Alex.

Fortunately, the doorbell rang, interrupting what would have been a long and embarrassing silence.

"That's Pippo," Alex proclaimed, bolting from his seat.

Gabriella lit a cigarette, glaring at Maggie as she did so. Maggie sat stolidly, figuring her best tactic would be to remain silent, at least until there were other people around. Why lay herself open for any more unpleasantness? She certainly couldn't tell Gabriella off the way she wanted to, because it seemed apparent that there was something going on between this woman and Alex. She couldn't afford to insult her host and colleague's . . . well, whatever she was to him. However, it bothered her that she just felt so incompetent in this situation.

"Gabriella, Maggie, this is Pippo Geraldi," Alex announced gaily, trying to lighten the pall that Gabriella had cast.

Pippo was a slender, sweet-looking fellow in his early thirties. He had dark, droopy eyes like a hound dog's, which complemented his trim mustache and short black hair that was meticulously brushed straight back. His clothes were very stylish—pleated pants of a subtle ivory color, an ecru silk shirt open halfway down his chest, and a loose-fitting, double-breasted sportcoat of a nubby-textured, clay-gray material. He stood in the doorway smiling at the two women, clutching his oxblood leather handbag, an accessory favored by most Italian men, Maggie had discovered. Straight-backed, he strode forward, took Maggie's hand and kissed her cheek.

"*Piacere*," he said, in a soft, lilting voice. "Welcome to Roma."

Maggie blushed. "Thank you, Pippo."

Gently drawing his hand away from Maggie's, Pippo turned to Gabriella. "Signorina Sciarra, it is a pleasure to meet you. I have heard so much about you and your parents." He did not take Gabriella's hand as he had Maggie's, but held his out instead, waiting for Gabriella to accept it.

"Hello," Gabriella murmured, barely touching his fingertips, as if they were not particularly interesting to her. She looked away, though he looked directly into her face.

"Sit down, Pippo," Alex broke in, "let me pour you some wine."

"*Grazie, grazie,* Alex." Pippo pulled up a director's chair next to Maggie, though there was room on the couch next to Gabriella. Perhaps, Maggie mused, he was reserving it for Alex.

"So, Maggie," Pippo chirped, "you are here on vacation?"

"No, business. I write for *Shout,* too."

"Ah, a *giornalista!* How wonderful! Do you write political stories? You are America's Oriana Fallaci, I am sure."

"No, not quite," Maggie laughed. "I'm doing a story on war babies, the illegitimate children of American soldiers. We . . . I call them 'the innocents'."

"How interesting!" Pippo rubbed his chin, stoking his curiosity.

"Yes. I'm hoping to meet a grown-up innocent from World War Two and interview him. Perhaps even help him find his father in American if he'd like."

"What makes you think one of these . . . these *bastardi* will want to talk to you?" Gabriella cut in unexpectedly. "Why should they want to find their fathers?"

"Well, I don't really know . . . that's why I'm here . . . to find out." Again, Maggie was at a loss as to how to respond to Gabriella. Her antagonism seemed to materialize out of thin air.

"I do not think your idea is so good. I would not buy your magazine for that." She glared at Maggie again.

"It wasn't my idea originally. It was Alex's," Maggie shot back.

"Oh?" Gabriella said, raising one eyebrow, looking to Alex for confirmation. He nodded his agreement and Gabriella shifted her gaze to the coffee table. "I still do not like the subject. People should not interfere with other people's lives."

"On the contrary," Pippo protested, "I think this is a fascinating topic, one that deserves to be exposed. Excellent idea, Alex. Tell me more about it."

"I think a good reporter shouldn't discuss his subject too much." Alex threw a mischievous look at Maggie. "It wears out the material."

"Right," Maggie chimed in, eager to drop the matter of her work.

Gabriella sighed, looking bored, and Alex placed his hand over hers. "How's your work going, Gabriella?" Before she could respond, Alex answered for her.

"She's the hub of fashion in Rome," he explained to Maggie and Pippo. "Aldo Amarone wouldn't be able to put out a new line each season if he didn't have Gabriella. She arranges the shows, the publicity, she's his première model—am I right?" He stopped and looked at her, trying to prod her into congeniality with his nervous chatter.

"Yes," she concurred. "I wear the clothes for him, the ones the private customers may choose. But that—" she pointed at the enormous silver fox coat lying across the room, "that is a favor for Carla Fendi. I must return it to her tomorrow." She reached up and touched her upper lip, smoothing it carefully. "I do some writing myself," she told Maggie. "Fashion publicity, you know, not the sort of thing you would be interested in. Not—" she paused for effect, "not *journalism*."

"Well, I think," Pippo jumped in, "a good *giornalista* needs background. She does not waste her time in Rome only working. Maggie, you must allow me to show you the city. I am a professional tour guide, and I know this city better than anyone. Please, do me the honor. I will give you my personal tour."

"Oh, really, no. You're awfully kind, but...."

"I am better when you get to know me better."

"You sure have a way with words, I can see that."

"But you will come with me, no?"

"Well, I don't know. I have so much to do yet. Tomorrow I have to move into my *pensione* and then...."

"That reminds me, Maggie," Alex interjected. "I have an appointment tomorrow morning, and I'm not sure when I'll be back, so I don't think I can move you in till Sunday."

"No, that's okay. I'll take the stuff over in a cab." Maggie shrugged.

"No problem," Pippo announced. "I will help you move. Noon I will be free. I will come then. Is that all right?"

"Uh ... well, okay, yes, I guess so...." Maggie felt

slightly strange imposing on a total stranger—particularly one so over-eager to please.

"Thanks, Pippo, you're a saint," Alex chuckled.

"By the way, Alex," Pippo said, leaning forward, "how is *your* work coming? This week are you chasing the *Fascisti* or the Red Brigades?"

Alex frowned and glanced quickly over at Gabriella. "Like I said, Pippo, a good reporter doesn't wear out his topic with conversation."

By ten o'clock, Pippo and Gabriella both said they had to leave, and Maggie was anxious to get to bed. The evening had been rather strained, and adjusting to so much at once had probably exhausted her. Alex went downstairs with the guests to see them out and to lock the front door. When he walked into the kitchen a few minutes later, Maggie was standing by the sink, rinsing out the glasses.

"So what did you think of my Roman friends?" he asked off-handedly, popping a piece of leftover cheese into his mouth.

"They're very nice, really. That Pippo is some character."

"He certainly is. A real playboy. I've heard he's actually rich, but he works as a tour guide just to meet women."

"I can believe it. Gabriella didn't seem to enjoy herself, though. Was something wrong?"

"No, she's just moody, that's all."

Maggie wanted to ask whether Gabriella was perhaps slightly jealous because another woman was encroaching on her territory by staying with Alex, but she decided not to. It seemed to her that there had to be more than moodiness behind her oddly sullen, sometimes hostile behavior. But if Alex sensed that his hospitality might cause friction between him and Gabriella, then why hadn't he just suggested that Maggie stay in a hotel for the two nights before the *pensione* was available? Well, she figured, that was his problem.

Suddenly, she felt a pair of arms encircle her waist. Alex was standing behind her, taking the platter from her hands and running it under the faucet. "Let me do that; you must be tired." He leaned closer, pressing her against the sink, his face in her hair.

"Alex . . . !"

"What?"

"What are you doing?"

"Washing the dishes."

"Alex, I . . . you. . . ." She felt the way she had when he'd planted that kiss on her mouth the previous day. He was the strangest man; she was confused and flustered by his abrupt advances.

"Sorry." He stepped back from her. "I realize I'm not being very professional. Didn't mean to do that."

"Look, Alex," Maggie began, nervously wiping her hands on a dish towel. "I figured you and . . . I mean. . . ."

"No, no, let's just forget it, okay?"

"Okay, all right . . . I'm going to bed now. Goodnight."

"Goodnight. I apologize for being so crass."

"Hey, it's nothing—forget it, Alex."

But Maggie couldn't forget it. She lay awake until past midnight wondering about Alex's intentions and the nature of his relationship with Gabriella. There was evidently something between them stronger than friendship. Yet, why would he come on to a virtual stranger, just because she happened to be staying under his roof, right when his girlfriend—or whatever Gabriella was to him—had been around? Had he embraced Maggie because he really was attracted to her and liked her, or because things were less than perfect between himself and Gabriella? Maggie stared at the ceiling, wondering why she always found it so impossible to fathom what was going on inside a man's head—especially when she was interested in the man.

If fatigue had not overcome her, she would have been up all night, mulling over her mixed emotions.

Chapter 6

Maggie was sitting on her large suitcase on the curb in front of Alex's apartment building. Her foot was propped up on her typewriter case, and her flight bag was on the ground nearby next to her other suitcase. The noonday winter sun was so bright, Maggie had to put on her huge, Jackie O dark glasses to keep out the glare. She'd dressed that morning for the move, pulling on the one pair of jeans she'd taken with her to Europe. She had on a blue Lacoste T-shirt and had thrown on a blue cardigan under the gray blazer.

At twenty past noon, a fire-engine red Alfa Romeo roared around the corner, disturbing the serenity of the neighborhood, and pulled up in front of Maggie, stopping short about a yard from her feet. It was Pippo, wearing a white cashmere sweater, a butternut-colored leather jacket and tight cords.

"Maggie, please, forgive me," Pippo leapt out of the car with a flourish. "The traffic was . . . how you say? All these *ingorghi,* uh, turtlenecks . . . no, bottlenecks!" He laughed at his mistake. "You have been waiting all this time."

"Only a few minutes, Pippo, really. Don't apologize. You're doing *me* the favor."

"You American women are so wonderful! You think . . . fair and square, I think you call it. Not like Italian women. They only know how to complain and eat and make the babies. Italian women are *mucce* . . . cows!"

"You don't mean that!"

"Yes, truly, I love American women, rich American women. You see this bag?" He indicated his leather handbag. "Very expensive. Rich American woman buy this for me at Gucci. I love it!"

Did he mean he loved the bag, or he loved being taken care of? Probably both, Maggie surmised. She wanted to drop the topic of American women, afraid where it might lead. She wondered as she examined Pippo's tiny sportscar, who might have bought him such an expensive item. "Pippo, I don't think we can fit all my things in your car. It's only a two-seater."

"Don't worry, *cara*. I am marvelous engineer—I will make it fit." He opened the miniscule trunk and wedged the flight bag and typewriter in over the spare tire. Maggie winced as he slammed the trunk down repeatedly, forcing it to close. *Whatever you do, don't damage the typewriter,* she prayed.

Then Pippo grabbed the large suitcase, opened the passenger door, moved the seat forward and started to work the heavy object into the small space behind the seats. He pulled the other case in on top of it and pushed and shoved, tipping the suitcases one way, then another, until he finally managed to cram them in. Maggie would have found his efforts hilarious if it hadn't been her luggage he was pummeling.

"Now," Pippo announced proudly, "we go."

Staring at the vehicle skeptically, Maggie bent down and wedged her body into the cramped passenger seat, her suitcases bumping her head as she sat back. The dashboard crunched her knees into an unusual position. "Okay," she sighed, "let's go."

A harrowing race into the city from Parioli—complete with hairpin turns, dangerous jockeying for position in lanes and violent curses yelled back and forth between cars—brought Maggie and Pippo to the Pensione Trinità dei Monti. Grateful to be out of the car at last, Maggie stretched her back and legs as Pippo began to remove the luggage like a comic dentist extracting stubborn teeth.

The ornate rococo façades of the cream-colored travertine buildings on the Via Gregoriana provided a unique background for the numerous *crèches* set up along the street in anticipation of the holiday season. To Maggie, the humble manger scenes seemed incongruous with the extraordinary architecture and modern, pollution-laden bustle of Rome. Everywhere you turned there was another fountain or another ancient, crumbling monument. When you were least expecting it, you would look up and see a carved face or an array of birds and animals in bas-relief. The grayish marble fountains streaked with green from the endless flow of the waters seemed absolutely right to her—an apt complement to the squat stone buildings. She gazed up and down the street, scanning the buildings, wondering about her future in Rome.

"You know, Maggie," Pippo said, straining to pull the large suitcase out of the car, "it is good that you will be here at Trinità dei Monti. Here you will write great things."

"Kind of you to say so." She smiled wryly. "Hope you're right."

"Oh, yes, I am! Many great artists have lived in this neighborhood. Scarlatti, the painter Reynolds, the fine Russian novelist Gogol. See on the buildings, the stone plaques? Each one honors the great person who lived there once. Your *pensione* soon will have to make a Maggie Reardon plaque."

"Yeah, sure." She smiled.

Having locked the car, Pippo stood by the curb, trying to figure out how to carry the suitcases, flight bag and typewriter all together.

"Let me take something," she offered, still fearing for her typewriter.

"No, no, Maggie. *Impossibile!*"

"Pippo, I insist. You know how we American women are." And before he could object again, she snatched the typewriter and flight bag.

Pippo shrugged and lifted the two suitcases. It was fortunate that Maggie had taken some of the luggage, for it soon became evident that his slender physique could just about manage what he was carrying—and not very well at that.

Maggie could see that his masculine pride had been dealt a heavy blow by her luggage. Although she was eager to forge on ahead to see more of her new neighborhood, she forced herself to hang back behind him. She didn't want to offend him further by not letting him lead the way. After all, he had made it clear, in his amusing way, that he was the tour guide—and the man.

The *pensione* was around the corner, and as they turned it, she heard Pippo sigh, looking up at the flight of steps before him. Sensing the problem, Maggie climbed the steps ahead of him, hoping to find a bellhop to help him with the suitcases. But before she even got into the lobby, the same man she and Alex had met here two days earlier whisked past her. He stood on the top step with his hands in his baggy black suitcoat, puffing furiously on a cigarette, scowling down at Pippo, as if he were annoyed that such a person would even dare to carry luggage so badly at his *pensione*.

He yelled something in Italian, then descended the stairs, fluttering his hands to shoo Pippo away. Pippo spat back something that sounded like a curse, gesturing with his shoulders. The man grabbed the handle of the larger suitcase, but Pippo would not relinquish his grip, so together they dragged it up the stairs, fighting each other all the way. Maggie tried to intervene, but they were deaf to her words. Growling at each other like angry dogs, they scampered to the front desk, where they unloaded the suitcases. Then the manager walked behind the counter and smiled cordially at Maggie, as if miraculously transformed from a crank into a respectable *hotelier*. The expression on Pippo's face was that of a small child who has just been told he can't stay up past his bedtime.

"May I help you?" the manager purred at her in perfect English. Odd, Maggie remembered he hadn't been able to manage one phrase the other day. Perhaps now that she was about to become a resident, he felt he had no choice but to speak in her language.

"Ah, yes." Maggie was astonished by this sudden transformation. She looked over at Pippo, but he was staring out the door, sulking. "Yes, I have a reservation. My name is Maggie Reardon. You remember, we came the other day . . . ?"

"Yes, Miss Reardon, we've been expecting you. Your room is all ready for you. Number thirty-four. On the third floor, on the right." He reached behind him and took a key off a large, gridded board, bristling with hooks for the room keys. "You will find the bathroom at the very end of the hall. We serve breakfast in the dining room every morning between seven and ten o'clock.

"My name is Ugo. If you need anything, please let me know. I hope you enjoy your stay in Rome, *signorina*." Punctiliously, he marched around the desk, lifted the suitcases, and took them to the gilt-cage elevator to the left of the desk. He placed the suitcases in the waiting elevator and then held it open for Maggie.

Seeing that Pippo did not like being out-charmed, Maggie picked up her typewriter, put her free arm in his and let him escort her. Pippo walked slowly, almost haughtily, into the elevator.

The manager ignored him, however, and pressed the button for the third floor, then closed the door. He smiled and nodded pleasantly to Maggie as they ascended, evidently satisfied with his performance.

The third floor had bright mustard-yellow, stucco walls with chocolate-brown painted woodwork. Maggie held the elevator as Pippo carried the luggage out one piece at a time, not rushing, and not even glancing at the manager. Maggie discovered that the big suitcase slid easily on the marble floor, so she began pushing it down the hall before Pippo tried to prove his pathetic strength again.

The door to Room 34 was open. A crisp set of sheets were pulled up on the bed, and a long, tubelike roll lay below the headboard where the pillows should have been. The window that looked out on a platoon of gargoyles on the building across the street was half-open, to air the place out. The room was simply furnished—a single bed, a plain maple nighttable, a well-worn armchair, wardrobe, stand-up dresser, desk, straight-backed chair. Maggie fixated on the small brass lamp on the desk. It suddenly felt very right to her. It was the kind of lamp beside which one could do serious work. Maggie let her imagination fly, envisioning this room as her version of the fabled Parisian garrets that the great American writers of the Lost Generation worked in. This was where she would write a great piece of journalism, a series that would undoubtedly launch her career and, realizing this, she immediately felt anxious, eager to start writing. Her sense of urgency seemed to fill the room with electricity.

Maggie ran to the window and gazed down at the pedestrians on the street. She fantasized one of them looking up and announcing his illegitimacy. Then she would swoop down and interview him before returning to the brass lamp and her typewriter—to create. Well, no, it wouldn't happen exactly like that. But still, she felt inspired.

"It's perfect, Pippo, just perfect."

"Your manager downstairs, he is not so perfect."

"Pippo, I'm starving. Let me take you to lunch to thank you for your help. Please."

He was obviously glad to hear that she appreciated his efforts, and she was happy to see that his wounded ego healed so quickly.

"Come," he smiled boyishly. "I know a very special place nearby on the Piazza del Popolo. *Magnifico!*"

Dal Borghese faces the Piazza del Popolo at the end of the Via Ripetta, and according to Pippo, it served the best pasta in the world.

"This is a fantastic restaurant, Maggie. Everything is good here." Pippo punctuated his recommendation by kissing his closed fingertips demonstrably, then tossing the ephemeral kiss to the heavens.

The room was large, with sedate wood paneling and brass fixtures everywhere. The waiters were rotund, serious men with bald heads and little clipped mustaches. Maggie suspected they might all be brothers. Covered by a perfectly-ironed and starched white tablecloth, their table was placed next to a window that looked out on the piazza. An unlit candle in a mesh-covered jar was their centerpiece.

"If you do not mind," Pippo said, looking down at the menu with a knowing air, "I would suggest you start with *quattre paste,* a sampling of four of their best pastas. I guarantee that you have never had pasta like this before."

"Sounds great." Maggie was almost salivating.

"Then have *pollo con carciofi,* chicken with artichokes. And for dessert, we'll have the house specialty, *mostarda di frutta,* a big bowl of spicy preserved fruits. Is that okay?"

"*Bellissimo,* Pippo!" Maggie kissed her fingertips, imitating Pippo's gesture, and settled back to enjoy her meal.

When Maggie eventually tumbled out of Dal Borghese, there was a dreamy look on her face. "That was wonderful, Pippo."

"See! I tell you I know all the best things in Rome. Soon you will agree."

"Okay," she nodded, acquiescing to his insistence to show her everything. "Tell me, why is this called the Piazza del Popolo? Was this a grand meeting place of the proletariat?"

ROMAN CANDLES

"No, no, nothing that admirable," he sighed. "The piazza is named for the citizens who were made to contribute money for the building of the church by the priests. It is said that this church—Santa Maria del Popolo—was built over the Emperor Nero's grave in order to trap his mischievous ghost. Some say he still runs around in there, but he cannot get out."

"That's fascinating." Maggie's eyes widened as they strolled by Santa Maria del Popolo on their way back to her *pensione*.

"Stories, just stories." He passed the tale off matter-of-factly.

"Really, you are a marvelous guide," she said earnestly. "You really do it because you love it—you know, it's not just a job for you. I feel the same about my work. It's hard to get started when I begin on a story, but it's exciting, like I know the whole thing will jell if I just give it time and put my mind to it. And I can see you give the same energy to showing people your city—making it meaningful for them, you know."

"Then you will let me show you Roma?"

Maggie smiled warmly at him, confident that she had made a friend. "Of course, Pippo. But not today. I'd like to go back to my room and unpack, maybe make some notes and just be alone for a while."

"All right, but I promise to show you everything when you are off New York time and on Roman time. We shall start tomorrow, how is that? I will be leading a tour at the Vatican tomorrow. You find me at Saint Peter's, at the front of the basilica around one o'clock, and then your tour will begin."

"It's a date."

When Maggie got back to her room, the first thing she did before unpacking was to set up her portable typewriter on the desk next to the brass lamp. She sat before it, staring at the keys, positioning it just right for the moment when it would have to endure the onslaught of her prose. It played in her mind like a movie: the open notebook under the lamp on her left, crumpled pieces of paper on the floor, a pencil clenched in her teeth and only a yellow Italian moon, peering over spires and rotundas, privy to her work.

Then she pictured her finished pieces laid out in the magazine with bold, modern-print headlines, striking graphics and photographs. She imagined hers as the cover story, announced by two side-by-side photos—a grainy black-and-white shot of a watery-eyed, emaciated war baby and a color portrait of a good-looking Italian man, who was that same war baby today. He would be staring into the camera with accusing hawk eyes. As she began to unpack her clothes, mindlessly hanging them in the wardrobe, she saw her imaginary issue of *Shout* on newsstands, in supermarkets and drugstores, in subscribers' mailboxes. Pushing the empty luggage under the bed, Maggie continued to dwell on the thousands of magazines with her feature that would be distributed across the USA, throughout the western hemisphere! It was better than counting sheep. She didn't mean to take a nap, but as she sprawled out on the bed fully clothed, she soon drifted off to sleep. There was a satisfied grin on her face as her breathing became deep and regular.

A knock at the door woke Maggie immediately. For a moment she didn't know where she was, not yet familiar with her surroundings. The knocking increased to a soft pounding. Maggie lifted her heavy head and looked toward the window. It was dark out. Then she glanced at her wristwatch, squinting and tilting it to focus in the dim light. Seven forty-five.

"Just a second," she muttered. She dragged herself up and trudged to the door with slow steps.

"Yes, yes, I'm coming," she told the pounding stranger, who refused to let up.

In the middle of a gaping yawn, she grabbed the doorknob and swung the door ajar. "Alex!" her puffy eyes struggled to open.

"I figured you'd be asleep again. Jet lag can be a bitch, but too much sleep can make it worse. I thought it would be nice to wake you up." He stood in the doorway like Gene Kelly in *An American in Paris,* leaning against the doorjamb with an impish grin on his face.

"Alex, what the hell are you doing here?" As soon as she said it, she frowned, knowing that she didn't mean it the way it sounded.

"I came to see how you were doing, your new digs, etc. If you want me to get lost. . . ."

"No, no. I just woke up and I'm still a little out of it." She went to the desk and turned on the brass lamp. "Have a seat." Maggie indicated the worn armchair by the window.

"Thanks. Well, you look like you're all set up and ready to roll. Not exactly the Ritz, huh? You should have stayed at my place." He seemed so nonchalant, Maggie couldn't figure out whether he was making her an offer or not. "Would have made them happy back at the office, saving them the cost of the room. You won't reconsider, will you?" He gave her that sexy grin of his again.

"No, Alex, I like it here. And I need to have my own space to write. You know how it is."

"Yeah, yeah. I know how it is." He took off his glasses and cleaned them on his unbuttoned shirt cuff.

There was an awkward moment of silence. Realizing that she must look like a wrinkled mess, Maggie made a futile attempt to smooth her disheveled hair, running her fingers through it haphazardly as he watched her with a small, amused smile on his face.

"By the way," Alex suddenly blurted out. "I got a telegram from Hastings today." He dug down into the side pocket of his army jacket and produced the rumpled telegram. Unfolding it, he pushed his glasses down to the end of his nose. "He says that I should make sure you stay out of trouble." He looked up over his glasses, checking for a reaction.

Maggie's lips were pursed. She was itching to say something vile, but she controlled herself. "Craig doesn't have to worry about me any more than he has to worry about you," she said slowly. "I can take care of myself very well. And if by any slim chance he told you to look after his woman, let me set the record straight. That was all in the past, what there was of it. Whatever delusions Craig has about me and him are his problem, not mine. And I'm sorry he had to bother you with it." She wanted to punch something.

Alex sat poised with the telegram on his lap, still looking at her over his glasses. "That's what I thought," he said calmly, crumpling up the message and tossing it into the wastebasket by the desk.

Maggie glared at him from the shadows. What was he up to? Suddenly, she felt that she had been laid bare before him. Now he knew all about her and Craig, but his relationship with Gabriella was still a mystery to her. She was vulnerable for having her personal entanglement out in the open—or whatever you'd call it at this stage—personal unraveling, maybe.

"How about dinner?" His face brightened as he suddenly changed the subject. "I know you must be hungry."

But even that remark rubbed her the wrong way. What right did he have knowing such details about her? Of course, it was true, she'd made no attempt to cover up her voracious appetite, so she had no right to be angry. She softened slightly and pushed her hair out of her eyes.

"Oh, I don't know, Alex. . . ."

"Come on. I can hear your stomach coming down the tracks like a freight train."

"Okay." She shot him a dirty look. "But I have to change and freshen up. Wait for me in the lobby. I'll be down in fifteen minutes."

"Okee-doke."

She imagined that smirk on his face again as he closed the door behind him. He was very attractive, she couldn't deny that, but why did he insist on being so vague, so. . . . It was hard to describe what she felt about him. Certainly she was grateful for all his help and hospitality, but wouldn't anybody do what he'd done for a colleague, especially far from home as they were? Well, maybe not. But what about his flirting and that kiss? What was all that for? He wasn't so flirtatious when Gabriella was around, was he? Despite Alex's cloak of serious professionalism and dedication, Maggie couldn't help comparing him to Craig.

She looked at her rumpled bed, and a picture formed in her mind—that blonde and Craig in bed together. She never wanted to find herself in that sort of situation again—and, she vowed, she would not let herself in for anything that might be emotionally damaging. Was Alex capable of the same kind of callousness? *God,* she thought, *we can't live with them and we can't live without them.* Then she smiled to herself. *Cliché, Maggie—you're a better writer than that.*

She went to the wardrobe and considered what she should wear. Vetoing her nicer, more dressy dresses, she decided that she wouldn't give Alex any undue encouragement. She picked out a pair of brown wool slacks and threw on her red turtleneck, which she covered with a bulky, beige Shetland pullover with red forget-me-not flowers on the yoke.

ROMAN CANDLES

Examining herself in the full-length mirror on the inside of the wardrobe door, she was satisfied with her appearance. Comfortable and protected by her big sweater that hid her figure, she was ready for dinner and shop talk with a fellow reporter.

"See that fountain in the middle? The one with the four figures?" Alex pointed with one hand as he drove around the Piazza Navona. "That's Bernini's famous Four Rivers. I don't know who did the other two, but it wasn't Bernini. I think he did the plans for them and someone else executed them, or something. The Four Rivers is supposed to be one of his best fountains. Frankly, they all look pretty much alike to me. But Gabriella tells me this one is special."

"Hmm," Maggie murmured, picturing the romantic, midnight circumstances under which Gabriella would have given Alex a lecture on Bernini fountains.

"Unfortunately, I'm a real barbarian when it comes to great art, so I forget all the good stories and fine details about the stuff."

Immediately, Maggie recalled Pippo's story about Nero's ghost in Santa Maria del Popolo. She couldn't help comparing Pippo's Continental charm with Alex's vacillating manner—first frank, then evasive.

"Where are we going?" Maggie asked, with deliberate evenness in her voice despite her continuing terror of racing through Roman traffic. It didn't seem to matter what time it was, there were always maniacs intent on running you off the road.

"A place called Carmelo, near the Pantheon. They feature Sicilian cooking. I guess I like it because their food is similar to what I remember my mother feeding me."

Maggie sat silently, wondering why Alex would take her to a restaurant that was obviously very special to him. If they were in New York, they would go someplace like The Palm or Pen and Pencil to discuss office politics over scotch and steaks. He didn't seem like the type who went in for intimate little hideaways in the Village. He was such a goddam mystery, and she was becoming upset with herself for getting so obsessed with him.

"What luck!" he declared, pulling into a surprisingly large

parking space on Via della Rosetta, right in front of the restaurant.

They got out of the tiny blue Fiat, and Alex came up from behind Maggie, jovially escorting her into Carmelo. "You're going to love this place," he confided with a wink, oblivious to her brooding mood.

But as soon as she was in the door, Maggie's defenses dropped. The light was warm and glowing, and a friendly bustle of clattering dishes, tinkling silverware, shouts from the kitchen and laughter mingled in the air with a hundred savory aromas. Bulbs of garlic strung together, wicker baskets, old hats and a variety of household utensils hung from the low ceiling. This felt more like a house party or a big family reunion than a restaurant.

A short, overweight waitress spotted Alex and shouted a greeting to him across the room. She held up two fingers and raised her eyebrows questioningly. Alex nodded, and the waitress pointed toward a back room.

Maggie and Alex worked their way over to an empty table and sat down. Immediately, a busboy came over and plopped down two stout juice glasses and a wicker-covered bottle of Chianti.

Alex smiled and nodded with satisfaction. "They know me here. And they know what I like. Try some of this." He poured her a glass of the deep red vintage. "There are hundreds of great wines in Italy, but I think Sicilian Chianti is the best with food."

He lifted his glass and gestured for her to do the same, encouraging her like an old Italian papa gleefully offering her his own homemade stock. Maggie was dazzled and pleased by this new, charming aspect of Alex. His brown eyes glistened, and his face glowed like an American hybrid of Marcello Mastroianni and Santa Claus. He paused for a moment with his glass held in the air before him. Maggie sensed that he was holding back a special toast he was dying to utter.

"Yes?" she asked, smiling.

"*Salute!*" he said finally, with a soft grin.

"*Salute,*" she nodded back, feeling her heart open to this enigmatic man.

"Now, would you like me to order? I've been thinking about this meal all day."

ROMAN CANDLES

"You should know what's good here. Just keep in mind that I'm starved."

"You're always starved," he said incredulously.

"I know," she declared proudly.

"Christ, every time I eat with Gabriella, she just picks at her food like a bird."

"Oh." Maggie looked down, the mention of Gabriella's name suddenly spoiling the moment.

Alex sensed his blunder and tried to repair the damage. "I mean, she models sometimes, you know, she works for this big designer. Always on a diet; always complaining about it."

"I see." She wouldn't look at him. "Nice that she gets to wear those fabulous clothes."

"Is something wrong, Maggie?" He seemed concerned.

"Alex, I don't want to be played with. You have Gabriella, and I have no intention of being the other woman."

"Whoa, girl. You're jumping to some wrong conclusions. Gabriella and I are not lovers, just friends. Really, she's not my type. Furthermore, Gabriella thinks of only one man, someone she's been grieving over for months. She was engaged to a very wealthy Milanese industrialist. Because he was constantly threatened by terrorists, they had this regular system where his bodyguards drove him to her palazzo in his specially-built Mercedes with the bullet-proof glass, you know. Gabriella would wait by the window until the car pulled up and her fiancé rolled down his window and waved his handkerchief. One night, he came by as planned, but as he started to wave, three grenades were rolled under the car from different directions. The Red Brigades proudly took the credit."

"Christ!" Maggie breathed.

"Gabriella is still mourning, and determined to nail the killers. See, we met when I was doing the Aldo Moro story. She thought I could find the killers for her. She still hounds me all the time for new leads, names, places, you know. But I haven't got a clue. I wouldn't know where to start if I did want to help her. Still, I haven't got the heart to send her away, and she has been useful in introducing me to people. It's all very sad, and I feel sorry for her."

"God, Alex, I didn't . . . I feel so awful for what I was thinking. I'm really sorry."

"Hey, it's okay. I realize Gabriella comes off a little proprietary, but that's just the way she is. You can read a lot into her manner, but I guarantee that most of your feelings are unfounded. Just a poor little rich girl, that's all."

"Oh, right, she's royalty, isn't she?"

"Uh-huh. Her parents are the Count and Countess Sciarra. I've interviewed them for my article. They're always on the society pages, always seen here and there and at the best places—like they're living in a fishbowl. It's no wonder Gabriella acts like a princess sometimes."

"Not a very happy one. A fiancé dying is bad enough, but actually seeing it happen. . . ." Maggie shivered.

"Yeah, a real tragedy. But do me a favor. Don't ever mention to her that I told you all this. She values her privacy above everything else. She'd have a real fit if she thought her personal affairs were the topic of our dinner conversations."

"Of course, Alex, I understand."

"Good. Now, I think I was about to suggest some dishes before we got sidetracked. Have some more wine."

She smiled, still acutely embarrassed, but taking his cue to change the subject. It was hard for her to imagine what that poor woman might have gone through. Under the same circumstances, Maggie was sure she herself wouldn't exactly be the life of the party. Gabriella's moodiness was more than understandable—it was like a self-constructed defense.

"First, we'll start with lasagna for our appetizer. . . ."

"Lasagna! That's a main course."

"Not in Italy. And wait till you taste *this* lasagna. It's light and fluffy and stands up like a layer cake, a torte."

"My mouth is watering. What's the main course?"

"*Zuppa di pesce,* Italian bouillabaisse."

"I can't stand it. Order, quick!"

"You got it!"

Maggie sat slumped in the passenger seat, her head tilted back on the headrest, a contented grin on her face, as Alex maneuvered the Fiat through the intricate winding streets around the Pantheon.

"I think I have died and gone to heaven."

"Oh, yeah. Wait'll you've been here a week."

"Don't burst my bubble yet," she protested.

ROMAN CANDLES

"How about a nightcap? Got to revive the ghost. Sambucca and espresso."

"Sure. Where to?"

"My place."

Suddenly, Maggie tightened up. "That's kind of far, isn't it?"

"Ten minutes at night when the traffic is lighter," he said confidently.

"Okay. Why not?" She decided not to offend him by saying no. After all the terrible things she had thought about him, she felt she had to make it up to him. Anyway, she could always use his help and advice, and Alex was unquestionably a good friend to have in a strange town.

She nestled back in the seat and watched the buildings, fountains, churches and lights of the city whiz by. Soon the old ornate architecture of *vecchia Roma* evolved into the modern, squared-off structures of Parioli. Alex brought the car to an abrupt halt, and together they drifted, sleepy-eyed, up to his apartment. When Alex unlocked the door and swung it open, Maggie suddenly found herself feeling that she had come home. His apartment was still more familiar to her than her room at the *pensione*.

"I'll make the espresso," she announced casually, not wanting Alex to make a fuss for her.

She pulled her sweater over her head, pushed up her sleeves, and busied herself with filling the espresso pot. She carefully ground the black beans, then spooned the grounds into the basket and screwed the top onto the little pot. Setting the pot on the stove, she lit the burner and turned down the flame so the coffee would not boil over.

Out of the corner of her eye, she noticed Alex standing in the doorway of the kitchen, looking at her. Apparently, he had been there the whole time, watching her in silence. He had a tentative but tender half-smile on his face, and his hair had flopped over onto his forehead, giving him that careless, boyish look he sometimes had.

Maggie froze, her thoughts whirling, her hand still on the knob of the stove. He moved toward her, his eyes never leaving hers.

"Maggie . . . I don't want you to . . . misunderstand me." He put his hand over hers, resting on the burner knob.

ROMAN CANDLES

"Alex . . . you. . . ." Losing her voice, she could not finish her sentence. A rush of confused and wonderful emotions came together inside her.

Some hidden force drew them to one another. Her anxieties melted before his warmth, and everything she'd resolved about herself and her relationships with men flew out of her head. Suddenly, she was all emotion, all feeling. There was something so right in the look that passed between them—so intimate and caring—that she could not deny the sensations stirring within her.

Their lips fused and their free hands joined and clasped tightly. He drew her against him, and she was so close she could feel the powerful beating of his heart. After several minutes, Alex slowly pulled away, brushing her parted lips with his as he tried to speak.

"Maggie . . ." he whispered, "will you stay?"

Her palm in his hair, she guided his lips back to hers. Under his hand resting on the stove, her fingers turned the knob off. The blue flame was still flickering out after they shut off the kitchen light on their way to the bedroom.

Chapter 7

The sunlight filtered gently through the sheer curtains, bathing the room in a misty glow. Maggie turned in her half-sleep to face Alex. He was already awake, gazing into her face, stroking her cheek lightly with the back of his finger. Maggie parted her eyelids and looked into his soft yet intense brown eyes.

"Hi," she whispered hoarsely.

Alex smiled, then drew her close to him with his tan, muscular arm. The wisps of dark hair on his forearm tickled her side, and she was smiling widely when his lips caressed hers. That kiss lengthened and deepened as Maggie floated down deeper and deeper with him, lost in a world of ecstatic feeling. She sensed a new freedom, as if she were no longer confined by her body.

She was all feeling as Alex planted wisps of kisses on her eyes, nose and cheeks. His warm breath caressed her, waking her senses from the recesses of sleep. It hardly seemed possible she could want him again after the night they had spent together, but she did. Alex nibbled her earlobe gently and she held him tighter to her, running her hands up and down his strong back.

A gasp of pleasure escaped her lips when he touched her breast and let his fingers travel the length of her slim form, teasing and arousing her. She rolled over on top of him and pressed her lips to his, feeling his hands on her, and now she opened to him. Their limbs joined effortlessly as he entered her. They moved slowly, quietly, matching eager breaths and delicate movements. She cried out sharply once, then drifted onto a sensuous plane that left her limp and satisfied. They lay still together, body on body, for a long time.

When Maggie woke again, Alex was gone. A mass of heaped sheets and blankets marked the place where he'd been. She sat up in bed and looked around the room, blinking the sleep from her eyes.

"Alex?" she called, but the apartment was silent except for the occasional sound of a passing car outside the window. Then a church bell tolled somewhere in the distance, and Maggie remembered that it was Sunday. Yawning, she reached over to the nighttable for her wristwatch. There was a note tucked under it:

Maggie,
 Had to meet a contact in Fregene. Sorry, but it was urgent.

Love,
Alex

P.S. You're beautiful.

Maggie stared at the note and grinned. "Hurry back," she whispered.

Then she glanced down at the watch in her hand, and seeing that it read 11:20, she bolted out of bed for the shower. She had promised to meet Pippo at the Vatican at one. *Better get a move on, girl,* she thought to herself.

She immersed herself in the steaming shower, hot for once miraculously and, as she lathered her body, she thought of Alex's gentle hands covering the same areas. His touch was so special, she mused, certainly a vast improvement over Craig's big-time wrestling techniques. It hadn't really bothered her at the time that Craig was a real animal in bed—voracious and satisfying in his own way—but still basically involved in himself. His bedroom etiquette was really indicative of his selfishness, she thought. Now why hadn't she seen that sooner? Perhaps Alex's full sensuousness and ability to give was a clue to his enigmatic personality. She certainly hoped so.

ROMAN CANDLES

She stepped out of the shower and wrapped a towel around herself. She had just started to dash back to the bedroom to dress when there was a knock at the door. Somehow, the intrusion made her irrationally angry.

"Who is it?" she barked.

There was a long pause. "It is Gabriella."

What the hell is she doing here? Maggie wondered. What could she want? Then, recalling the story of her murdered fiancé, Maggie bit her lip and cut off her annoyance, feeling sorry for the other woman all over again, pardoning her rudeness of the other night.

"Just a second," she called out as she stumbled toward the door to open it.

"Hello, Maggie." Gabriella's terse words did not sound anything like a greeting. Her razor-sharp glance sliced the length of Maggie's body, settling finally on her still-wet hair. "Where is Alex?" she demanded, shrugging off her tightly-cut Persian lamb jacket and throwing it over her arm. She was wearing another incredible outfit, Maggie noted— undoubtedly something else her designer friend had concocted for her. She was dressed in a rainbow of variations on the color purple. Her skirt was a full circle of heather, plum and ecru wool with gathers around the top to emphasize her slender waist. She had on a lilac silk shirt with a shawl collar, and from the top peeked a line of lace from a matching camisole, which was violet shot through with a slightly metallic gold thread. The line of the deep V from her lavender cashmere jacket was a neat parallel to that of the blouse. A simple strand of pearls and her ever-present diamond-cluster earrings completed the look.

"Alex has gone out for a while," Maggie answered primly. "He didn't say when he'd be back." She was sort of having fun trying to ignore Gabriella's rude manner and be the perfect hostess herself. "Can I fix you some coffee?"

"I know where it is, thank you. I will make some if I want."

Maggie gave up. It was just humiliating trying to be cordial while standing in the doorway with only a towel wrapped around her. "Will you come in, Gabriella? There's a draft," she commented dryly.

Gabriella scanned the length of Maggie's body again with a

look of decided venom on her face. She stepped into the room briskly, fell into a chair and, opening her small black clutch purse, drew out a gold cigarette case. She took a long brown cigarette from the case, lit it and sent a defiant plume of smoke across the room as she stared into space.

"Make yourself comfortable." Maggie smiled sarcastically. "I'll be right with you." She marched into the bedroom, threw the towel on the bed, and grabbed Alex's terrycloth robe from the hook behind the door. She didn't stop to consider how she looked or what impression she would be giving by wearing Alex's clothing. Not consciously, anyway. She strolled back out into the living room, knotting the belt as she did so.

"Very becoming," Gabriella spat, as soon as she caught sight of Maggie's attire.

The feelings all rushed through her at once. Maggie couldn't tell exactly whether she was madder with Gabriella or with Alex, but they were running neck and neck for first place. They had both made her feel like a total jackass. There was no question in her mind now that Gabriella was a scorned lover and that Alex had been less than truthful about their relationship. Over and over, she kept picturing that blonde in Craig's bed. Tacky. To Gabriella, *she* was that blonde.

"Did you or did you not say you wanted coffee?" Maggie growled.

"No, I do not. I came to talk to Alex."

"Oh, I see."

"No, I do not think you see at all."

"Really!"

"Are you still looking for your *bastardi?* Or have you given up to return to America?"

"Not on your life. I came for a story and I'm not leaving till I get it. You see, I'm not the type to give up."

"You *giornalisti* are all alike. Insensitive, egocentric bullies. No one wants to read about *bastardi*. You are only interested in hurting people."

"*Helping*—not hurting, I assure you." She could no longer keep the snippiness out of her face, so she just stopped trying. "And maybe to your ultra-charitable way of thinking they are *bastardi*, but to me they are innocents. And they deserve understanding and justice and the opportunity to find out who they are, just like the rest of us. Haven't you ever heard the expression, 'identity crisis'?"

"You speak of justice, my friend, but you do not know the meaning of the word." Gabriella's voice was choked with feeling.

Suddenly, Maggie felt ashamed. Despite her steely disposition, it was absolutely true that no one had known injustice as well as Gabriella. One lover blown up before her eyes; the other flaunting his infidelity before her. Perhaps it was this very injustice that made Gabriella so impossible. She didn't deserve Maggie's anger and resentment. But Alex—without a doubt, Alex certainly did.

What a charmer he was! Maggie burned as she recalled him telling her that Gabriella wasn't his type, that they were just friends. So, naturally, she had trusted him. But he was no different from Craig—no, he was worse. Craig was just a spoiled, hedonistic, narcissistic idiot. Alex, on the other hand, came on like a saint, but he was a real rat under the surface. Could this be his way of getting back at her for taking his idea for the innocents story?

"I am going now." Gabriella stood up abruptly, bending over to snuff out her cigarette in the Cinzano ashtray on the coffee table, and picking up her jacket. "I will call when Alex is home."

"Gabriella, I. . . ."

"ArrivederLa." She used the formal tense—Maggie wasn't so dumb she could miss that.

Gabriella marched out the door, leaving a trail of Bal à Versailles in her wake. Maggie stood there speechless, staring at the open door. Kicking the flimsy wooden thing shut, she began to sense Alex's large, green robe enveloping her like a burning ointment, scalding her flesh.

Climbing the seemingly endless steps leading up to Saint Peter's Basilica, Maggie was glad that she was wearing her loafers. Gabriella could never hack this place in her spikes, she thought unkindly. But as she gazed back around the piazza and took in the Vatican's enormity, she wondered whether she would have been better off wearing her sneakers. Maggie faced the great row of portals of St. Peter's and was simply stunned by the detailed craftsmanship and the wealth of symbolism contained on those doors. She was desperate to take it all in, her eyes jumping from one panel to the next, spying prophets and maidens, beggars and thieves, devils and hermits, all in a dizzying montage. It was an impossible task without a guidebook or a guide. Certainly Pippo could help her appreciate these great works of art. Then Alex's self-description as a "barbarian" when it came to "art stuff" echoed back to her from the previous night. "Barbarian" was too kind, Maggie decided, with a snort of fury.

Entering the center portal, she was immediately confronted by a middle-aged man in a baggy blue suit with some kind of official badge on his lapel. He scowled at her, as he did at everyone else who walked in, and Maggie was baffled by this peculiar, cranky behavior. It was not until he stopped a young British backpacker with long, lanky blond hair and tight jeans that she realized that the man's function was to check visitors for proper attire. Perhaps it might be a good idea for her to go back to the *pensione* and change, even though it might make her a little late for her rendezvous with Pippo. Still, taking in her surroundings once more, she felt it was necessary. That deliberately casual, unsexy outfit she had chosen last night, ironically to discourage Alex's libido and help them become friendly colleagues, was inappropriate for the Vatican. She suddenly felt grimy, as if the day-old clothing shouted out her unthinking passion of the previous night. She hailed a cab, shrugging as she glanced at her watch, and gave him the address of the *pensione*. Instructing the driver to wait for her, she ran up to her room, threw off her clothes and put on the first thing she found in the wardrobe, a plaid blouse and a plain beige corduroy jumper, which she topped with her raincoat. The cabbie promptly returned her to St. Peter's when she asked, although he gave her an odd glance as she counted out the lire for the fare. He must have wondered why in heaven's name he had brought her back to her point of departure.

Apparently, this time, the inspector found her clothes as modest as she did. He looked away quickly after the perfunctory check of her skirt length, and she walked through the turnstile.

The basilica opened up before her, a gigantic space whose majesty surpassed the splendor of the riches it contained. She stood there, a little breathless, her feet stuck in one spot on the exquisite marble floor. As a child, she had been taken to St. Patrick's Cathedral on Fifth Avenue in New York. At the time, she was so awed by that church, she said afterward to everyone who would listen that she had been to God's palace. Had she seen St. Peter's back then, she might have decided that St. Patrick's was only His summer bungalow.

"It is really something, no?" Pippo's voice broke her trance.

Tearing her eyes from the heights of the rotunda, she looked at Pippo and simply nodded. She found herself unable to say anything to describe her feelings—words wouldn't have been adequate, somehow. Pippo looked ready for a business appointment. He was wearing a light gray, double-breasted suit, which she recognized as an Armani from an ad in a recent *Shout* layout. The suit had tiny, barely-perceptible dark blue nubs woven into the material. The lapels were fashionably narrow, and the jacket was cut low and loose around the waist, but trim around the chest and shoulders. The sharp crease in his trousers formed an uninterrupted line to the cuffs that broke perfectly over his pointy black Magli shoes. His shirt was snow-white, pressed and crisply starched, adorned with a narrow, red knit tie. Pippo held a navy cashmere overcoat over his arm, which was folded back on its lining to reveal a Burberry label.

"Pippo, I was afraid I wouldn't find you in here!"

"Oh, you should not to worry. I am very good at finding people. You would be surprised."

"Oh, Pippo, show me everything! I want to see it all."

"Well, as you can see, there is too much to see."

"Then show me what you think is the best."

"*Allora*, a brief tour here in the basilica first, then I will take you to my favorite place."

"Great."

They strolled down the length of the great chamber toward the ornate throne. It was an elaborate bronze structure enclosing a wooden inlaid chair. Gilded, jubilant cherubs and four clerics—two mitred, two bareheaded—joining hands adorned the throne's back.

"This is the cathedra—the throne of Saint Peter. It is said that the wooden seat was brought to Rome from France by Charles the Bold for his own coronation. Although Saint Peter never sat here, still, this is called the Seat of Peter.

ROMAN CANDLES

Whenever the pope makes an official proclamation, he makes it *ex cathedra,* from the throne. This throne."

Pippo took Maggie's arm and led her to the bronze statue of St. Peter. It was slightly larger than life-sized, and very imposing. A line of people stood with their small children, waiting to approach the statue. One by one, they lifted the children up to kiss the saint's foot.

"Here, I show you how stupid Italian people are," Pippo hissed in her ear. "Look close, you see Peter's foot has worn away from the people kissing it. In the fourteenth century, they came for miracles from God and all they got was the plague from each other! Forty years ago, during the war when malaria was epidemic, they came for miracles, and they gave themselves the malaria! They never learn, and now Peter only has one good foot. *Che stupido!*"

Maggie gave him a puzzled glance, half-shocked by his irreverence, half-intrigued by his theory of Italian society.

"Come," he said, with a sly look on his face, "I will show you the real beauty of Saint Peter's." Pippo walked her over to a far corner of the basilica, where several aging tapestries and paintings hung. In the middle of the niche was a sarcophagus with a woman's figure carved on the lid. Her frame was large, her nose bulbous, her face broad and common-looking.

"Do you know who this *bella bruta* is?"

"No." Maggie craned to get a better look at the face.

"Christina of Sweden," Pippo announced with a chuckle.

"Really? A far cry from Greta Garbo in the movie!"

"That is what everyone says. But this is how she *really* looked, you see."

"Show me your special place now, Pippo. I'm too curious to wait any longer."

"All right, *va bene*. I have had too much of the basilica, anyway. I have already brought two tours through here today. One group of Japanese, the other Americans. The Americans, they get bored very fast; they say, this is nothing like home, so what good is it? The Japanese always try to take pictures behind my back. It is forbidden, but the Japanese, they must all play with their cameras. They like better to see the sights in their photographs than to see them in real life, can you imagine?"

Maggie smiled at his caricatures of the nationalities. Pippo was so carefree, so charming, he took her mind off her problems with Alex, and she was immensely grateful for that. As they walked back toward the front portals, Maggie considered asking Pippo about Alex, his habits with women—particularly Gabriella—and his evasive personality. She wanted to confide her feelings to someone, and without Ellen or her mother around, she longed for a friendly ear to share her anger and her disappointment.

Of course, although she trusted Pippo, he was Alex's friend first, and for all she knew, they might be very close. Aside from the fact that they were both men, and therefore bound by some allegiance stronger than blood. They might even compare conquests, although she doubted that closemouthed Alex was the type to boast about the notches on his bedpost. Well, it probably would be unwise to discuss Alex with Pippo, who was such a loyal friend—God knows Alex didn't deserve such a friend. Undoubtedly, Pippo would feel compelled to defend Alex, perhaps even report Maggie's feelings back to him. No, on second thought, she wouldn't say anything.

"This is the new wing of the Vatican—the Nervi," Pippo was saying. They climbed a few steps and entered a distinctly modern, museum setting. "This is where the Vatican museums start," he told her, "but this is not what I wish to show you. We are just passing through."

As they began to walk down the long galleries, Maggie was shocked to see that the Vatican housed a great wealth of pagan statuary. At first, its presence struck her as somehow blasphemous, but as the form and grace of the countless figures of gods and goddesses started to overwhelm her, she realized that this was just another example of the Roman way—an ignorance of apparently divergent elements in preference to beauty, any beauty. In this case, it was the common beauty of classical sculpture and adoring Christian art. What is beautiful is beautiful without conditions, Maggie mused. The idea appealed to her, but she would have to get used to it—it was foreign, as was everything in this extraordinary city.

As she gazed at the severed marble heads, the limbless torsos, the crumbling cornices, and the gray stone columns held together with heavy iron bars, Maggie couldn't get this business about accepting things as they were out of her head. Gabriella's accusation of journalistic insensitivity and Mrs.

Sloan's precautions about discretion and understanding echoed back to her. Was her attitude all wrong, her feeling that she could help the innocents? Perhaps they *were* better off left alone, just as these separated limbs and heads were perfectly beautiful just as they were. She had a flashing image of herself dashing through the galleries late at night with a pot of Elmer's glue in her hand, matching Aphrodite heads with Zeus arms and recklessly pasting limbs onto torsos, producing an army of grotesque freaks.

"Here they are—all Apollos." Pippo pointed out a row of unbroken statues of the Greek god. "This must be like an American singles bar, no?" he quipped.

"Something like that," she murmured, seeing the group of marble beefcakes as some of the conceited men she had known. Now Alex was at the head of the line.

"My place is just beyond this gallery," Pippo whispered enthusiastically. "You will love it."

Passing through a high arch over which marble masks of comedy and tragedy hung, Maggie and Pippo entered a gorgeous, enclosed courtyard. The lush greenery, the sunshine and the gentle trickle of a mossy natural stone fountain was a fantastic contrast to the stark white and gray figures in the dim marble galleries. Maggie felt she had literally stepped from the theoretical intellectuality of ancient Rome and Greece to the sensuousness of the late Renaissance. The classical statues that stood in this courtyard took on a Baroque air, the conceit of the previous Apollos becoming a charming playfulness here. Of course, this would be Pippo's favorite, Maggie thought with a smile.

"This is the Cortile del Belvedere. I love this place because it is so peaceful."

"It's beyond words."

"Yes. I come here often, especially when I must think. When I have problems, I come here and miraculously, I begin to see things clearly. You know? Wrong from right? Important from not so important?"

"I understand. It's easy to see how this place really could put your mind at rest."

"Come. I want to show you my favorite masterpiece of all. It is here too."

Pippo walked to an alcove just a few yards from the fountain. He faced the interior of the arched enclosure, and a reverent expression came over his face, as if he were praying to a patron saint.

Maggie drew up next to him and was startled to see a huge statue of a man flanked by two boys, all three entwined in the coils of a monstrous, menacing snake. The painful contortions carved into their sinewy muscles and the agonizing expressions on their shocked and terrified faces made Maggie wince. It was certainly a powerful and moving creation, but it was not the kind of thing she expected to be Pippo's favorite.

"This is the magnificent Laocoön. It was sculpted by three Greek artists from Rhodes. It was found on the Esquiline and brought to the Vatican by Pope Julius the Second in the early sixteenth century. When I come to the Cortile, I always stop at this statue. I must. Always, I see something else, something new in it."

"Please, Pippo, pardon my ignorance, but what's going on here? What's the story connected with this?"

"*O, Dio!*" he whispered, surprised that she didn't know it. "Have you heard of the Trojan horse?"

"That, sure. The Greeks built a giant wooden horse and filled it with their soldiers. After they brought it to the gates of Troy in the dead of night, the Trojans took it into their fortress, thinking it was a gift from the gods. And that lack of foresight was the beginning of the end for the Trojans."

"*Sì, davvero.* But not all the Trojans were wanting the horse. This man was suspicious." Pippo pointed at the statue. "He is Laocoön, the high priest of Troy, and these are his sons. He told people to leave the horse outside the gates, that it was dangerous. But, as he warned them, a great serpent came from the sea and killed him. The goddess Athena sent the beast to punish him for interfering with Fate. After all, she liked the Greeks better. Anyway, the Trojans saw the death of Laocoön and his sons as a sign of the gods' displeasure with him, so quickly, they take the horse right in, into their gates. You know how the story ends."

Maggie nodded, staring at the figures once again with new appreciation.

"Sometimes," Pippo continued, "I come here and think Laocoön was right to warn his people, to be a martyr. Then sometimes, I come and I think he was foolish to try to challenge Fate. Perhaps his death was right. I don't think I will ever decide. Perhaps it is better that I do not choose, for

ROMAN CANDLES

then I would stop coming here." He flashed Maggie a smile tinged with irony. "And *that* would be a real tragedy!"

Maggie gazed at the terror-struck faces of Laocoön and his sons, faces that saw death coming. Then she glanced at Pippo, intrigued by his unexpected complexity, surprised that someone who appeared so frivolous had a deeper side. Obviously, there was much more to this man than she had first realized.

"Shall we go?" he asked softly. "I am beginning to get hungry."

"Oh, yes. I could go for some lunch myself."

"Good, good. But first we will go to my apartment so I can change into some less formal clothing, all right?"

"Fine." Maggie beamed.

Maggie sat on the plush, beige velvet sofa in the apartment, waiting for Pippo to change. She was absolutely dumbfounded. Crossing the Tiber from the Vatican, Maggie had been taken aback by the sudden squalor of Pippo's neighborhood, Trastevere. The strangeness of the area was particularly striking because of the strong bohemian flair that existed side by side with apparently abject poverty. Of course, all of Rome looked old, because of the official pronouncement that it was against the law to recondition the outsides of buildings, but this area was really different from any other she had yet seen. It was like putting Greenwich Village in the heart of Harlem. Also, the streets seemed so dark, the houses leaning in on one another, and there were angry-looking men of all ages wearing threadbare suits, hanging out in every other doorway. Pippo had matter-of-factly pointed out that they were all probably as shady and dangerous as they appeared. It was uncommon, he claimed, for a man in Trastevere not to have a jail record.

And yet, he stressed, this area was his favorite in the whole city. He had chosen to live here because of the exotic atmosphere, he told her. Of course, you had to be a little more careful in Trastevere, especially at night, but it was worth it for the enjoyment of this mix of humanity around you.

The contrast of Pippo's fine outfit with his neighbors' clothes began to make Maggie uneasy. He seemed so different from these people.

Pippo had become more taciturn the farther they got into

the dark narrow streets. This was an aspect of him that she had never seen. Was he embarrassed to be taking her here, Maggie wondered, despite his defense of the neighborhood? Or was he concerned for their safety? She wanted to say something to make things right, but not really knowing what was bothering Pippo, she remained silent. Quietly, she followed him up the ancient wooden staircase of his squalid apartment house, wishing there was something she could do to ease the tension of the moment.

But, when he turned the key in his lock and threw open the door, she literally gasped. It was simply the reverse image of the ghetto outside. Pippo's living room was a marvelously eclectic blend of Old World splendor and clean, modern design. A Renaissance tapestry depicting royal hunting scenes hung on the wall along with several paintings, both portraits and landscapes, that seemed like works of the Dutch masters to Maggie's untrained eye.

An impressionistic painting of a bouquet of carnations hung between the windows that looked out on the gray street below. Identical, pale pink marble pedestals stood at diagonal ends of the room. One held the marble bust of a young Greek woman, her hair tightly curled in geometrical patterns around her head; the other supported an Oriental-looking vase with an elaborate design of maroon, blue and gold adorning its exterior. These exquisite works were complemented by the distinctly Italian high tech furnishings of the room—oxblood leather and chrome Bauhaus chairs; white formica breakfront backlit with dim, twinkling bulbs; the oversized beige velvet sofa; and a square, low, ebony coffee table.

Maggie sat enthralled, unable to really take it all in. Pippo was turning out to be quite a baffling mixture, a precious alchemy that Maggie had never encountered before, in a man or a woman. The works of art looked so authentic, but Trastevere seemed so poor and downtrodden. The furnishings were so fine and Pippo's clothes were so expensive, yet he was only a tour guide. Maggie was a bit ashamed to be thinking in these terms—a person's wealth or position didn't usually impress her one way or another. But Pippo presented such dramatic contrasts, she couldn't help wondering about him.

"Now, I am ready." Pippo burst from another room, an excited smile on his face. He had changed into a pair of tight designer jeans and a salmon-colored turtleneck. The antelope suede sport coat he carried over one arm matched his suede Bally loafers. "Shall we go? As you Americans say, 'I could eat the horse.'"

"Listen, you have got to tell me about your fantastic art collection. You could open your own museum, Pippo."

"Oh, you are just being polite. These are very nice, but not great."

"And *you* are being modest. These are more than just nice. You must be a collector."

"Me? No, not at all. This is all from my uncle." He swept his hand around carelessly, indicating the objects in the room. "You see, he was a personal aide to Mussolini. These paintings, the tapestry, the vase, the bust, the Persian rug, all gifts from 'Il Duce.'" He stuck out his lower lip petulantly and knit his brows as he held up his hand in the Fascist salute, demonstrating his feelings for the Italian dictator. Maggie looked a bit uncomfortable as he held the stance for dramatic effect, and he broke into derisive laughter, breaking the mood.

"Come, before I starve," he insisted, taking her arm.

"Okay," she shrugged, sneaking a last glance at the tapestry as they left.

Pippo threw on his jacket as they walked down the steps of the apartment house, and immediately, Maggie was again struck by the contrast between Pippo's wardrobe and the dingy streets. They walked briskly to the corner and turned onto the Vicolo della Palomba. A movie marquee announcing the current feature, *Woodstock,* caught Maggie's eye.

"Wow! I can't believe that's playing here."

"Oh, yes," Pippo commented, "all the time. It is a big favorite with the young people. They show it almost constantly in Trastevere."

"Really? You know, Pippo, I was there, at the Woodstock festival."

"You? You were there?" Pippo stopped and stared at her, totally amazed. "You are a radical then!"

"Not at all. Maybe ten years ago I had radical sympathies. But as I look back, I think it was the rock-and-roll lifestyle that obsessed me. It just isn't in my character to go out on a limb for an abstract cause. You know, I'm a lot more involved with people on a one-to-one basis."

"You mean you did not fight with the police in Chicago and protest at Kent State?"

"No, I'm afraid not." She was impressed with his knowledge of American affairs. "I think I was more interested in passing poli sci at the time."

"*Che?* What is 'poli sci'?"

"Oh, sorry. Short for political science. It was my minor at Skidmore."

"You are so fascinating, Maggie. I would not think you to be interested in politics. In Italy, no one—man or woman—seems to care about politics any more. You see these people." He pointed to a group of stocky, black-shrouded women of indeterminate age waddling quickly through the streets like nervous ducks. "They say they are so proud to be Italians, proud even to be from Trastevere. They even claim a dialect all their own. But they are not ashamed to be poor, to have strikes all the time. You see how fat they are. Because they can only afford pasta and bread. Yet they are too lazy to change the political tyranny of gluttony and anarchy. They only know how to complain. Disgusting."

Pippo's tone had become so grave and disturbed, Maggie wasn't sure it would be right for her—a foreigner—to comment on this delicate matter. She chose to walk beside him quietly, giving them both time to mull over his statement.

"There is much evil in my country," he finally said.

"In every country, Pippo. Look at Watergate."

"Yes, I suppose you are right." He smiled weakly. "But what am I doing? I am ruining our evening. You are here to see *bella Roma*, and Pippo is your guide. Please, Maggie, whenever I start to sound like a *professore*, you hit me in the head like this." He jolted the side of his head with the heel of his hand, "and you say, '*Stupido, stai zitto!*'—you shut up!"

Maggie smiled warmly and took his arm in hers. "Pippo, you're very sweet."

"Umm, perhaps," he said, grinning devilishly. "This way." He guided her down the Via della Luce for a few blocks until they came to a small restaurant with a hanging sign over the doorway. It read: Gianna all'Angoletto.

When they walked in, a waiter looked up and spread out his arms congenially, indicating that they could sit anywhere they pleased in the nearly empty restaurant. It was barely six o'clock and still too early for the evening patrons.

ROMAN CANDLES

The decor was tastefully rustic with rough-hewn tables, straight-backed chairs and what looked like tall, copper milk pails holding amber fronds in all corners. They took a table in an alcove toward the back, and as soon as they were seated, the waiter rushed over with the menus.

"I know what I want," Pippo announced, leaving his menu unopened on the table.

"What?" Maggie asked eagerly, always ready for a lecture on culinary delights, particularly those she had never sampled.

"*Maialino*—sucking pig, Sardinian style."

"Hmm." Maggie scanned the menu quickly, searching for something that struck her fancy more than pork. "What's *saltimbocca?*"

"Ah, wonderful! Veal cutlets with mozzarella and prosciutto, cooked in a sauce of sage and butter. *Che meraviglia!*"

"I'll have that."

"Very good. And a bottle of nice Valpolicella."

"But of course," she agreed, with a flourish of her hand.

Pippo called the waiter back and ordered briskly, gesturing wildly as he did so. This, Maggie had observed, was part of the Roman ritual. If you wanted the entrée done rare, you lifted your fingers to the ceiling in a fluttering motion, indicating the meat shouldn't sit too long on the fire. If you wanted more bread, you waved the basket around in circles. If you were pleased with what you were eating, well, there was no telling what you might do—it all depended on the passion of the diner.

The waiter returned in a moment, apparently impressed with Pippo's hand movements, carrying their bottle of wine, which he uncorked quickly and served with great aplomb. With a curt nod and a smile, the waiter disappeared.

"You know," Maggie began, savoring the red wine slowly and intently, "I've been meaning to ask you. Here it is only a few days before Christmas, and I haven't seen any trees or lights or decorations in the store windows like back home. No carols being sung by groups of happy schoolchildren, or anything. Only a sign here and there saying *Buon Natale* and the *crèches* in front of the churches. So what gives? I would have thought that in this very Catholic country, there would be a huge fanfare."

"Exactly, you see, you say the right word—Catholic. These

religious types, they make the Italian Christmas only a family holiday. I don't know why. You can buy all of what you want for your house, the decorations and such, but you never see it in the street. Except, as you say, the *presèpio* figures, the mother and child and the wise men in the manger. The children, though, they are the wise ones. They still want their presents—the religious meaning is not so important to these innocents. Innocents—ha!" He lifted his glass ceremoniously and toasted Maggie. "To your success in finding *your* innocents."

Maggie looked down and nodded in acknowledgment, then lifted her own glass and said, "To new friends. And a happy New Year."

Pippo smiled graciously, and they drank.

"Pippo, I don't know if I should even ask you about this." Maggie studied her wineglass, avoiding Pippo's gaze, all her intentions of the morning flown out of her head. "But I don't know who else to discuss this with." She decided then she would trust him partially, with just a portion of her problem.

"Is there something wrong?"

"Well, it's Alex. I know he's your friend, but, well . . . I think he's trying to use me, if you know what I mean." She really did like this man, and his sexual presence was so unthreatening, she felt comfortable enough to share the secret.

"Alex? What do you mean?"

"Well," she took a breath. "I stayed at his place last night. This morning, when he wasn't there, Gabriella showed up and bit my head off. He told me that he and Gabriella were just friends, but it certainly doesn't seem that way, at least not the way *I* perceive it."

"And you think Alex lied to you?"

"Yes. Worse yet, I think he's trying to get back at me for taking his story. You see, the series on the innocents was originally his idea."

"Hmm, I see." Pippo brought his hand to his mouth and stroked his mustache contemplatively.

"Again, I realize he's your friend and you can tell me to shut up, but I really want to know, so I'm just going to swallow my pride and ask: Is Gabriella Alex's lover?"

Pippo shrugged and shook his head. "Honestly, Maggie, I do not think so. He has never mentioned her to me in the year that I have known him. I think I might have gotten a hint from him if it were true. Anyway, I assumed that Gabriella was *in due* with her boss, Aldo Amarone, the famous designer."

"I don't know, Pippo. I just don't want . . . I don't know what I want, I guess. I thought Alex liked me. But I'll be damned if I'm going to be one of his little bimbos," she blurted out, letting her emotion escape despite her good intentions.

"Bimbos? A curious term."

"I think you know what I mean."

"Yes, of course I do. Maggie, Alex is a very serious fellow, this I am certain of, and what you tell me does not sound like him. I do not think that he is capable of hurting a woman. He is too good, too just. Gabriella, I cannot speak for. I only met her the other evening with you. But Alex . . . no, Alex would not use anyone."

"I hope you're right." She looked dubious, and Pippo took her hand consolingly. "Do you know," he said, a slow smile spreading across his face, "that love exists only for a short moment, but life exists all around, in the air, in the food we eat, in the traffic. So!" he exclaimed as the waiter placed their entrées before them. "You see how I am, how you say, *filosofico*. And so must you be. Now, *mangia!*"

The tempting aromas temporarily placated the jealous beast in Maggie and she laughed, picking up her fork and flicking her napkin onto her lap. Pippo looked on with amusement as she dug into her veal with the gusto of a sailor just home from the sea.

Chapter 8

Sitting in Dick Ord's office in the American embassy, waiting for him to return with their coffee, Maggie examined a photograph of Jimmy Carter on the wall behind Dick's desk. The strong midmorning light cast a bright beam on a similar picture of Ronald Reagan leaning against the wall on the floor, waiting to take Jimmy's place on the wall. The juxtaposition of the two struck Maggie as wonderfully ironic, symbolic, even. She considered the possibility of writing it up as a short filler for *Shout*. But, as she was about to flip to a fresh page in her notebook to jot down her thoughts on Jimmy and Ron in Italy, she stopped herself.

Hey girl, you've got a whole series to write! Concentrate, will you? What're you fooling around with this little stuff for?

Maggie was really beginning to panic. When she woke up that morning, it wasn't Alex who was on her mind. She sat there in bed, staring at her typewriter under the brass lamp, both collecting dust waiting for some action. This was her fourth full day in Rome and she still hadn't done a thing about her story.

"Damn," she had said out loud in bed. "Let's get this show on the road."

She was sure she could get started with one good lead from Dick Ord. And after that, as one thing led to another and her momentum got going, she'd be fine. She'd better be! Mr.

Jennings's shadowy presence loomed in the back of her mind. The thought of missing her deadline, or worse, of returning to New York empty-handed and having to face Andrew Jennings, made her shiver. After all she'd gone through to get this assignment, she knew she'd be lucky to get a job writing obits in Ho-ho-kus if she blew it for *Shout*.

Just as her worst fears were beginning to sneak up on her, Dick Ord burst into the room, carrying two dripping coffee mugs in front of him.

"Oh, I'm such a slob," he said, frowning at the trail of drops he was leaving on the rug. "I'm really not a male chauvinist pig, but I do pine for the days when secretaries fetched the coffee. Not because I'm lazy or a powermonger. It's just that I'm such a mess with things like this. Look at that poor rug."

Maggie laughed politely. He seemed like a likeable guy, but why did they all feel compelled to make the obligatory reference to male chauvinism and women's lib? It was a long-dead issue in her mind, not even worthy of a joke. Well, no harm done, and probably none meant.

"Now, Maggie, what can I do for you?" he said as he handed her the coffee and took a seat behind his desk.

"Well, I guess Alex told you, I'm doing a series on the illegitimate children of American GIs. Many women all over Europe were impregnated by our soldiers during World War Two, of course. Anyhow, I want to concentrate on this area of Italy, where General Eisenhower's forces first landed in nineteen forty-four. My series is going to be a human interest follow-up as well as an historical exposé. And what I really want is to find someone who knows that his father was an American soldier. Get an in-depth interview with him, how he feels about that long-lost father, how his birth has affected his life. Perhaps, if that person is willing, I'd help him track down his natural father at the magazine's expense."

As Maggie spoke, Dick sat back in his chair, quietly listening with his arms folded, and a hard set to his mouth. The more she said, the more she noticed parallel lines creasing his high forehead.

"Well, Maggie," he said, pulling himself up to his desk, "let me preface what I'm about to say with a reminder that I represent the United States government, and therefore I cannot encourage or condone any activity that could potentially be an embarrassment to the State Department. I'm sure I don't have to tell you that you are dealing with some pretty delicate matters—people aren't going to be forthcoming with their darkest secrets."

"Yes, I realize that," Maggie murmured frostily, suspecting that this was going to be another cautionary lecture. She'd had enough of those already.

"Officially, I have to tell you not to go meddling in the affairs of Italian citizens. Don't upset anyone to the point where they end up lodging a complaint with us. Be discreet, sensitive, and stay out of trouble."

"However," an impish grin appeared on his face, "no one ever won a Pulitzer Prize by listening to a government press attaché. If you're a good investigative reporter, you're going to go poking your nose into places where you're not wanted. You'll probably ruffle a lot of feathers. *Just make sure I don't hear anything about it.* Okay?" His grin widened.

Maggie beamed at him. He was all right, after all.

"Now, let me give you some nice, safe leads that may or may not bear fruit. In all honesty, the American government never wanted to recognize this problem, in Italy or anywhere else. Whenever illegitimate children and pregnant women were reported to the embassies, the records were either swept under the carpet or torn up and thrown away. I have no statistics to offer, no names or agencies to refer you to. I suggest that you start with convents and orphanages, in the hope that you'll find someone who will talk to you openly.

"You're going to find that Italians are extremely closed-mouthed people. They keep their problems to themselves. If a girl gets into trouble, it's the family's concern—and only the family's. Frankly, I don't think you'll be able to break into a family unit to get your story. Your best bet, in my opinion, is to try to track down someone who was sent to a convent or orphanage because the mother died or was lost in the war somehow. To be blunt, people without close-knit ties will be more vulnerable to your snooping, perhaps more troubled by the uncertainty of their origins. Why don't you start off by going to the Convento di Monte Carmel on the Via Cassia? It's just north of the Villa Borghese, not far from here. The mother superior knows me, and you can mention my name. She speaks English too."

"Thank you very much." Maggie decided she really did like

ROMAN CANDLES

Dick Ord. The man was concerned with doing his job, but he was sympathetic to someone trying to do another job that might run counter to his professional considerations. "I'll go there this afternoon." She stood up and shook his hand warmly. "This is a great help, Dick." She had enough journalistic tact not to protest about his official stone-walling. The man was doing more for her than he might have, certainly.

As she started to leave, he brandished a finger at her and squinted with mock gruffness, reading her thoughts. "And, remember, whatever you do after the convent, I don't want to know anythng about it. *Capisci?*"

"Right!" Maggie gave him a curt salute and a big smile before walking across the room and closing the door behind her.

She looked down at the name and address of the convent in her notebook. *Well, it's a start,* she thought, putting the book in her bag. She was so eager to get cracking on her interview, she didn't notice Betsy sitting at her desk, staring up at her.

"It must be good." Betsy indicated the notebook sticking out of the pouch of Maggie's bag. "Whatever it is."

"Betsy! I'm sorry. I didn't see you."

"Yeah, sure. I know a spy when I see one," she jibed. "You must have wheedled the secret formula out of the boss."

"What secret formula?" Maggie asked earnestly.

"How should I know?" Betsy burst out laughing. "It's a secret."

Maggie had to chuckle, surprised to find such silliness in a place that seemed so formal. Betsy's laugh was infectious, like Ellen's back home. Well, why shouldn't there be good spirits in the Roman U.S. embassy, she thought. The fate of nations has probably been affected as much by bad jokes as by bad diplomacy.

"I hope Dick didn't discourage you too much. He's been known to bring on acute depression in eager-beaver reporters from the States."

"On the contrary. He was really helpful."

"He must like you. God, you should have been here the day Bob Lincoln, the TV reporter, came in to interview Dick about the official American policy regarding terrorist assaults on foreign executives of American companies in Europe. They almost had a fist fight."

"No kidding."

"Really." Then, in a whisper, she went on, "I think he likes to brag about it since Lincoln stormed out of here in a huff and his show never used the tape."

"I'm impressed." Maggie raised her eyebrows and nodded, always interested in good celebrity gossip.

"We still on for lunch today, Maggie?"

"We sure are."

"Shall we go somewhere grand and overthrow the autocratic rule of my diet?"

"By all means."

"Great. How about if I meet you at Otello's? It's a great big place at the foot of the Spanish Steps. Meet me there about twelve-thirty at the entrance, okay? Don't go in though. The place is so big I could waste my whole lunch break just looking for your table."

"It's a date. Otello's entrance at twelve-thirty. I'll go sit in a gorgeous piazza and start writing a few brilliant leads for my first story meanwhile."

"Terrific. See you then, Maggie."

As Maggie and Betsy followed the maître d' through the long aisles past what seemed like hundreds of tables full of beautifully-dressed people, Maggie grabbed Betsy's arm and whispered, "I guess you weren't kidding when you said Otello's was huge."

"Betsy Farrell never lies. She's with the State Department." Betsy rolled her eyes to the ceiling.

"Uh-huh," Maggie drawled, eyeing her with mock skepticism.

The maître d', a tall and painfully thin fellow with bushy black hair and eyebrows that looked like sleeping caterpillars, ceremoniously seated them. He then presented them with their menus, backing away with a sweeping bow.

"Pretty fancy for lunch," Maggie commented after he left.

"Pretty typical for Rome. Either they fall all over you trying to please, or they treat you like an unwanted guest. *Bella Roma.*"

"Sounds like you're not wild about being here."

"No, I think Rome is great, don't get me wrong. It's just

that I've been in this city over two years, and I guess I'm a little homesick. It always hits hardest around Christmas time. Oh, don't mind me—I just like to complain."

Maggie could understand Betsy's plight. She certainly wasn't unattractive, but it was clear that she was a real defeatist. Loyal and able at her work, but retiring and shy socially; the type who scares men off to protect herself from being hurt by them. Maggie was willing to bet that Betsy had had few previous dates here in Rome. She seemed to be as much in need of a friend as Maggie was.

"Listen, Maggie," Betsy said, leaning over her menu, "I've been dying to order something for lunch here, but I've albeen too self-conscious to do it alone. If I get one, will you?"

"That all depends. What is it?"

"Do you like ice cream?"

"You don't have to ask. What is it?" Maggie was practically salivating with curiosity and anticipation.

"It's called a *còppa olimpico,* a sundae with whipped cream, meringue and a big vanilla wafer on top."

"Divine. I'll take two."

"You sure now? It's enormous and, I don't have to mention, wickedly fattening. You can't eat lunch and have room for this for dessert—it's a meal in itself."

"Honey, you're looking at the original garbage pit. I can eat all day and *lose* weight from the exertion."

"I hate you."

"Stop talking and order!"

"You got it."

The maître d' raised his eyebrows when he wrote their requests down on his pad, and the two women smiled at each other conspiratorially.

"A lot of people don't understand my thing about food," Maggie confessed. "They're positive it's a cover for some deep-seated emotional problem. But I really think it's just well-developed taste buds. You know how some people have well-developed muscles? They work out, they train to get into shape."

Betsy nodded sympathetically. "Believe me, girl, if I had your figure and could keep it by eating all the time, *I'd* go into training."

They giggled together like schoolgirls—friends who had

known and accepted each other's foibles and eccentricities for years. Maggie suddenly felt that she had someone she could talk to, and that was a very welcome feeling.

"Betsy," she began slowly, "do you know Alex very well?"

"Not well enough. Some hunk, huh?"

". . . well, I guess. What do you know about his . . . love-life?"

"This doesn't exactly sound like a business interest." Betsy's playful grin faded to a look of concern.

"Only in the sense that he may be giving *me* the business." Maggie fingered her napkin, trying to fight the lump in her throat.

"Well, I have seen him at a few cocktail parties with Gabriella Sciarra, if that's what you're after."

Maggie exhaled slowly and nodded.

"I've heard . . . ah . . . they're an item." Betsy felt a bit uneasy, knowing that she was disclosing unwelcome information.

"Just what I thought," Maggie murmured evenly, though her voice sounded constricted.

"I sort of get the picture, Maggie. I mean, I don't know this for certain. I've only seen him around the office, and I don't know her at all. I could be all wrong, you know." Betsy was trying very hard to make things right, but Maggie didn't seem to be paying attention to her. She was looking through Betsy with a glassy stare.

"What is it, Maggie? What's wrong?"

"Over there." Maggie pointed.

Betsy turned around in her seat and scanned the huge dining room.

"Down there. By the curtain," Maggie murmured.

Betsy looked again. On a lower level toward the entrance, Alex and Gabriella sat at a small, secluded table. Alex was holding Gabriella's hands in his across the table. Betsy continued to stare at them with her back to Maggie, not sure what she should say.

At that moment, the waiter appeared with their sundaes, but the great proportions of ice cream and fixings were totally lost on Maggie. *Okay, kid, you knew it anyway. This is no surprise,* she told herself insistently.

"Oh, Maggie, I don't know what to say. . . ."

"I'll be okay."

Reluctantly, Betsy dug into her long-awaited treat. It struck her as inappropriately joyous fare, under the circumstances.

Maggie picked at her *còppa olimpico* in silence.

It was after three o'clock by the time Maggie found the Convento di Monte Carmel on the Via Cassia. The cab driver had been particularly unhelpful, dropping her off at a small chapel about a half-mile from her real destination. Maggie had suspected that the driver was annoyed when she first gave him the address at the Spanish Steps. Via Cassia was too far into the outskirts of Rome, and he knew he wouldn't get a return fare way out there. With a disgusted grimace and a loud sigh, he agreed to take her where she wanted to go, but when they finally turned onto the Via Cassia, he just left her at the first religious place they passed, figuring that she wouldn't know the difference. He could probably pick up a fare if he swung back through the Villa Borghese, and the sooner the better.

Just as the cab made a screeching U-turn, Maggie noticed the carved inscription over the locked chapel door: S. Vincenzo. Furious, she began yelling vehemently after the departing cabbie. Twenty yards down the road, he stopped, got out of the cab, made a few incomprehensible gestures, pointed up the road with both hands, shrugged, then got back into the cab and sped off. *What in heaven's name was that for?* she wondered, fuming.

With no buses in sight and no hope of getting another cab, Maggie started to walk. Kicking up dust as she trod along, she muttered curses at the despicable cabbie, but her mood soon turned into a brooding silence as she mulled over the treacherous Alex and his loathsome Gabriella.

I must look like a fool to men, she stewed. *Even goddam cabbies take advantage of me!*

But by the time the Convento di Monte Carmel came into view, Maggie had forced herself to put Alex out of her mind, at least temporarily. *Remember, you're supposed to be a pro*, she thought angrily, *the kind for whom work comes first. And dammit, from now on, it will.* She started to think about her approach to this mother superior she was going to see, since she had always found nuns difficult to talk to. Though raised Catholic, Maggie had attended public schools and had been taught by nuns only at the catechism classes she'd attended once a week after school. They had seemed forbidding then, and she hated admitting to herself that she still dreaded these women in black. Meeting this unknown mother superior was no small anxiety for her.

But as she approached the convent door, she thought of Mr. Jennings again. Getting an interview with a nun and requesting some straightforward information was a piece of cake compared to the prospect of facing Andrew Jennings *sans* story. Maggie took a deep breath, submerged her anxieties and rang the doorbell.

After a long, nervous moment, a tiny, elderly nun answered. Her squat form was entirely draped in her full-length, deep brown habit. The only flesh that showed were her fingers on the door and her tiny face, boxed in by her unyieldingly starched white wimple.

"*Buon giorno*," she whispered, her eyes muted and calm.

Maggie's apprehensions melted immediately, "*Buon giorno*, sister. I would like to see the mother superior, please. I am a reporter, a *giornalista*."

The little nun smiled and shrugged, almost playfully, apparently indicating that she did not understand English. She opened the door all the way and took Maggie's hand, leading her to a long wooden bench in the corridor, then motioning for her to sit.

"*Attenda, attenda*." the nun spread her fingers and motioned again for Maggie to sit and wait. Then she disappeared down a long corridor.

Maggie settled herself back on the bench that was obviously an extra or salvaged church pew, feeling totally out of place. She looked up at the opposite wall where a round fresco plaque hung, depicting Mary with the Baby Jesus. She couldn't help noticing that Jesus looked more like a fat midget than an infant in the tender young woman's arms. Even though her observation was quite accurate, she felt a bit guilty being so critical and worldly in a convent. *Well, that's the reporter in me, I guess,* she thought nervously.

The tiny nun reappeared. "*Venga, venga, per favore.*" She took Maggie's hand again and led her down the corridor to a small, sparsely-furnished office. Behind the desk sat another identically-dressed nun, somewhat younger and wearing wire-rimmed glasses. She was busy writing something down in a large ledger. On the wall behind her hung a plain wooden crucifix.

"Come in, come in, please," the second nun said flatly, looking up, then returning to her writing. "I will be finished in one minute." Maggie walked in softly on the balls of her feet, trying not to be intimidated. She sat down quietly in the long, straight-backed chair in front of the desk and waited.

"Now," the nun said suddenly, twisting the top back onto her fountain pen, "I am the mother superior. What can I do for you?" Her English was heavily accented, but perfectly grammatical.

"My name is Maggie Reardon, Reverend Mother. I'm a journalist from America; I work for the magazine *Shout.*"

The nun folded her hands delicately on top of her desk and shrugged at her lack of recognition of the name.

"I'm investigating the problem of war babies, the children of American soldiers and Italian women during World War Two. I call them the innocents."

"You are right to call them so. Yes, very good. But what can I do for you?"

"I'm trying to find one—someone who grew up knowing only that his father was an American who fought here in the war and then abandoned him. Someone who may want to locate that long-lost father."

The nun laughed mirthlessly. "Again, I must ask you, Signorina Reardon, what can I do for you?"

"Mr. Ord at the American embassy suggested that I start my investigations with the convents where orphans and unwed mothers may have been sheltered during the war. Since Mr. Ord knew you personally, he suggested that I see you." Why hadn't she mentioned their mutual acquaintance to the nun when she walked in the door? That was the first rule of interviewing, for heaven's sake!

"Oh, yes. Mr. Ord is a beautiful man. Although he is not of our faith, his wife is. She has done a great deal of volunteer work for us."

"I see, Reverend Mother. He hadn't explained the connection." Maggie hoped she sounded enthusiastic, and hoped her momentary panic hadn't shown on her face when the nun said "our faith." She wanted the woman's confidence, after all.

"As for your innocents, Signorina Reardon, I cannot help

you. To my knowledge, this convent never housed orphans or war victims. You see, until Nineteen sixty-one this was a cloistered community. We lived here alone and in silence, dedicated to our prayers. However, Pope John the Twenty-third convinced our order that community service was as important as prayer; thus, we loosened our cloister rule and opened our doors. Before that year, though, only the sisters—and an occasional priest for Mass and extreme unction—entered this convent. No one else." She shook her head slowly with an apologetic look on her face.

"Well, do you know of any convents that did take in war victims?"

"The war was a horrible, horrible event. Anyone who could spare a place on the floor or a crust of bread, shared it. I am sure that every available convent, rectory, cathedral and monastery in Italy took in people. But I am afraid I cannot give you specific names and places, for I was here during the war, praying in our chapel for salvation and an end to the fighting." The mother superior's apologetic look became grave.

Maggie sighed. This capped off a totally disappointing day. Her first lead was a great big dead end.

Seeing Maggie's distress, the nun spoke up again. "Perhaps I can be of some help. Wait one minute." She opened the top drawer of her desk and produced a black address book. Carefully, she searched for a particular name. Then, having found it, she took her fountain pen, meticulously unscrewed the top, located a scrap of paper and wrote something down. "Why don't you go to this place, *signorina?*" She handed Maggie the note, written in a wonderfully antique, looping handwriting. It said: *Orfanotròfio di S. Marco, 694 via Nomentana, Signora Trezza.*

"This woman, Signora Trezza, is the director of the orphanage—a good woman. You tell her that you have spoken to me, and she will help you if she can. Beyond this, I do not know. . . ."

Maggie smiled warmly at the nun. Being referred to a specific orphanage—instead of having to face the inevitable frustration, lack of cooperation and sore feet of the hit-and-miss telephone-book method—seemed like such a golden lead at this point she could have kissed the mother superior.

Decorum ruled, however, and Maggie took the nun's offered hand instead. "Thank you so much, Reverend Mother. You have been a great help, truly."

"I am happy for you. Now I have other duties to attend to. Please send my regards to Mr. Ord. And *buona fortuna.*"

Sitting in the worn armchair in her room at the *pensione*, Maggie held the address she had gotten from the mother superior that afternoon, examining it like a precious document or an expensive jewel. Despite all her skeptical reporter's savvy, she still thought of all the possibilities that note could hold, speculating on what it might do for her story. If only Mrs. Trezza could introduce her to an innocent, what a coup this would be! No one works that fast, not Woodward and Bernstein, not Dan Rather, nobody. "Maggie, my dear," she allowed herself the hope, "this could be paydirt. If not, she'll give you another lead, and *that* could be paydirt."

Unexpectedly, there was a knock at the door. It was past ten P.M., and none of the other guests in the *pensione* had appeared friendly enough during their brief breakfasts in the dining room together to indicate a visit might be in order. Maybe it was the manager, Ugo, informing her that she had a phonecall downstairs at the desk.

"Ugo?" she called out tentatively.

"Nope," a familiar voice came through the door. "It's me—Alex."

That creep! she thought. *He's got more nerve than brain.*

Quickly, she got up and buried her note from the mother superior in one of the travel paperbacks on the desk. She stood in the middle of the room, trying to compose herself. She swore to herself she was not going to let him think he was upsetting her.

"Come on in. It's open." Despite her efforts, the frostiness still was apparent in her voice.

Alex burst into the room, tossing his old army jacket onto the bed. "I came by to see how you were doing. Haven't changed your mind about coming back to my place?" he said hopefully.

"No."

"That's too bad." Alex whipped around and locked his arms around Maggie's waist. "The accomodations are very nice," he cooed softly in her ear.

ROMAN CANDLES

Stiff as a board in his arms, Maggie refused to give at all. "I think you'd better take your ball and go home, Alex. The game is over."

"What?" He pulled back to look at her face, still gripping her around the waist.

"Don't play dumb. It demeans us both. You were after a conquest and you made it. Now go away and leave me alone." Maggie's voice was beginning to quaver.

"Hey, hey, hey! Let's take it from the top. I must've missed something."

"I'm not fooling around, goddammit! You got me in bed. What else do you want from me, huh? You trying for two? Well, forget it. Now go away!"

"Hold it, Maggie. I don't know what's gotten into you, but I'm not leaving until I hear some explanations."

"*Explanations? Explanations!* You owe *me* the explanations, you . . . you jerk! But don't bother, if you're just going to lie to me again."

"Stop talking in riddles. I don't like blind accusations." Now Alex was getting angry.

"First you tell me that there's nothing going on between you and Gabriella. Then you tell me you need me and want me and all that junk, just to get me into bed. Then who do I see carrying on like Romeo and Juliet in Otello's today? Huh?" Maggie would not back down. Feeling perfectly justified, she would give him exactly what he deserved.

"Are you spying on me now? Just what I need—first terrorists and now you!"

"See? You've got no answer. Admit it, you're a two-timer and a liar, Alex."

"Now you listen to me," he shouted. "That woman and I are not lovers, nor have we ever been. You can believe what you damn please, but my relationship with Gabriella is purely professional. I need her for my story. And that's all!"

"Oh, don't give me that crock again! Your exciting story that's too dangerous to talk about. It's just a convenient excuse to cover your philandering! Dangerous, my foot!"

Alex's face reddened and his eyes bulged behind his glasses. "I can't believe you're this stupid! I guess you don't read the papers, do you? Look, I'll spell it all out for you. Terrorists are very scary people. I write about terrorists. If they don't like what I write, they wouldn't think twice about

127

offing me or anyone around me. The Red Brigades did blow up one newspaper editor during the Moro thing."

"We weren't talking about Aldo Moro. We were trying to shed some light on you and your faked-up stories."

"Faked-up! If you weren't such a naïve . . . dumb American, you'd get the impression that this city you've been ogling for the past few days is an armed camp. Over a million bombs were confiscated by the Italian police last year alone, and since Nineteen seventy, these guys have extorted over two hundred million dollars in ransom money. But you don't believe this, do you? This is just a fairy tale I use to cover my sexual escapades, right?

"Do you know what the Red Brigades' motto is? 'The vote doesn't work, the rifle does.' There are a hundred-fifteen known terrorist groups in Italy. Not only leftists like the Red Brigades and Prima Linea, but right-wing Fascists like Fenice, Anno Zero, Ordine Nuovo, Ordine Nero, Riscossa, Avanguardia Nazionale. . . . Oh, what's the use? You don't want to believe me."

Alex went to the window and looked out, not wanting to face Maggie. He was shaking with rage.

Maggie was quiet, not sure what to believe. "I never said your work wasn't dangerous," she said evenly. There was a long moment of silence. "I just don't like seeing the man I made love to holding hands with another woman the next afternoon."

"You don't want to understand," he muttered, still gazing out the window.

"Try me again," she said in a softer tone. "Why was she crying, Alex?"

He turned and stared at her, half-furious with Maggie's spying, half-frustrated by his inability to tell her what he felt. "I told you, she's still mourning Guido, her fiancé. She's obsessed with him, not me. From me, she wants consolation. What should I say when she cries for Guido and grabs my hand? 'Buck up, kid? Don't do that'?"

Maggie sighed. Perhaps she had jumped to conclusions again. All circumstantial evidence. *Besides,* she thought, *Alex didn't exactly pledge his undying love to me. Maybe my hopes got the better of me.*

"All right. Points well taken. Look, it . . . I'm sorry I

jumped on you like that. I don't own you and I don't want you. . . ."

"No apologies," he interrupted her. "Please, I think we've said too much already. I'd rather we just leave it alone."

They stood in the middle of the room, quiet and embarrassed, both wanting to disappear, both wanting to turn back the clock to the night before.

"The funny thing is," Alex said softly, his hands in his pockets, his head bent, "I came over here to tell you that Gabriella invited us to her mother's Christmas ball next Saturday. It's supposed to be *the* winter social event in Rome. She thought *we* might like to go. Together. She even told me to tell you that she'd call you to tell you where to go for a dress and your hair and all."

"Oh, Alex . . . I'm sorry."

"Look, I don't think we should discuss it now. Ah . . . why don't you think about it. I'll talk to you tomorrow, okay?" He picked up his jacket and went to the door. Turning back, their eyes met. "Tomorrow," he said, as if forcing himself to finalize the meeting and go.

"Okay." Maggie would not look away.

The door closed, and Maggie's brimming eyes overflowed. Her anger and doubt gave way to anguish and shame coupled with excitement and anxiety over this new problem—the *contessa's* ball.

Chapter 9

Maggie stared at the pay phone in the lobby of her *pensione* with mounting disgust as the touchy device refused to accept Pippo's number. Every time she started to dial, the phone would cut her off after the fifth digit and taunt her with a fresh dial tone. A few times, her token—the *getone*—spilled back into the coin return as if the phone just didn't want her business.

"Goddammit," she blurted out.

"*Prego, signorina.*" Ugo, the manager, came up from behind her. "I show, I show." He took the *getone* from the coin return and glanced at the telephone number in Maggie's date book. "You watch," he said knowingly. He looked at the number once more, dropped the token in the slot, then punched out the numbers as fast as he could, hurrying to beat the machine's temperamental mechanism to the draw. When the dial tone sang out in her ear, he refused to acknowledge his failure and repeated the process in the identical manner. But, again, the phone wouldn't take the number. Ugo frowned and grumbled.

An elderly gentleman in a baggy, black suit, who had been sitting in the lobby reading the newspaper, noticed Maggie's and Ugo's difficulty with the phone. He watched them for several minutes with rapt attention, holding his newspaper poised before him.

"*Attenda,*" he croaked at Ugo. Muttering and shaking his head, he put down his paper and slowly walked over to them. With no further words, he took the token from Ugo and the date book from Maggie's hand. He then carefully inserted the coins in the slot, looked at the phone number and slowly and forcefully punched out each digit. Nodding his head demonstratively with the execution of each number, the old man stopped after the fourth, held up a single finger, and looked up at Maggie and Ugo, holding his pause like a conductor at a symphony concert. Satisfied that an appropriate amount of time had elapsed, the old man continued to press out the rest of the numbers as deliberately as he had the first four.

There was a long silence. Then, as if by magic, it started to ring. The old man held up the receiver, displaying his triumph to a grateful Maggie and a sour Ugo. As the man presented the raised receiver, smiling and chortling with delight, Pippo answered.

"*Pronto.*" Maggie could hear Pippo's voice distinctly.

But, instead of answering him, the old man grimaced at the receiver like an unwanted intruder. Unwilling to speak to a stranger, the old man thrust the receiver into Ugo's hand.

"*Pronto,*" Pippo demanded.

Ugo was equally unwilling to speak, and passed the phone to Maggie like a hot potato.

"Pippo?" she said quickly, so he wouldn't hang up. "Pippo?"

Ugo and the old man both disappeared as soon as she took the phone.

"Maggie, is that you? Maggie?"

"Yes, yes—it's me."

"How are you this morning?"

"Just fine, thanks. Listen, I want to ask a favor. I hate to bother you, but do you think you could give me a lift out to an orphanage on the Via Nomentana? There's no direct bus service out there, and I've found that the cabs don't like going too far out of the center of Rome. If you have some free time, maybe tomorrow. . . ."

"I can come right now!"

"Are you sure this won't be putting you out? Please, say so. You don't have to be polite with me."

"Really, Maggie, we can go this minute if *you* are free. I have no tours scheduled for today, so I would be delighted.

ROMAN CANDLES

My business, you see, is not so jumping at this season. All the visitors, once they have seen the Vatican, they spend all their time shopping and in celebration. Besides, the Via Nomentana is not that far."

"You're a real doll, Pippo. I'll be waiting for you out in front of my *pensione*."

"A doll! Is that good?"

"Yes, yes. It means you are a wonderful person, a valuable friend."

"Okay, a doll." He chuckled. "I will be there in fifteen minutes."

By ten o'clock Maggie and Pippo were sitting on a long wooden bench in the waiting room of the offices of the Orphanage of San Marco, about to see Signora Trezza.

"Why don't you come in with me, Pippo? I'm not sure she speaks English, and you know how far my Italian will get me."

"*Certo*. I am happy to translate for you."

"Thanks."

A gray-haired woman in her sixties entered the waiting room. Her clothes were prim and simple in the extreme—a calf-length gray wool skirt and a forest-green turtleneck. The only jewelry she wore was a man's wristwatch and a heavy chain necklace holding a medallion that looked like an ancient coin. Her hair was tied back in a bun, and her eyes were obscured by her thick, black-framed glasses. As soon as Maggie saw her, she was reminded of Margaret Mead, whom she'd once interviewed for the Hartford newspaper where she'd landed her first job. This woman gave off the same aura of passion and seriousness.

"Miss Reardon," she said softly but firmly, "I am Concetta Trezza."

Maggie rose quickly and offered the woman her hand. "Thank you for seeing me, Signora Trezza. This is my friend, Pippo Geraldi."

"*Piacere*," said Pippo, shaking her hand, and she lowered her head slightly to return the greeting.

"Shall we go to my office?" She led them down a dark corridor to a small, simply-furnished office not unlike the mother superior's at the Convento di Monte Carmel. Signora Trezza dragged over a second chair before her desk for Pippo.

ROMAN CANDLES

"Now, what did you wish to see me about?" Signora Trezza said as she pulled herself up before her desk.

"I'm a reporter for *Shout* magazine in New York City," Maggie began, thinking that these introductory words were wearing a groove in her tongue. "I'm doing a story on the innocents—the children born during World War Two to American soldiers and Italian women—children who never knew their fathers. I'd like to find such a person to ask him what it was like growing up with the knowledge that his father was one of the thousands of American GIs who fought here. If he is willing, I'd like to help reunite him with his father, with the help of the magazine, of course. If not that, I'd like to ask him whatever he's willing to answer about his life and his feelings, be they positive or negative."

"I see." Signora Trezza stared at Maggie, unblinking. "And *you* are the photographer, I take it," she said to Pippo.

"No, no. Only a friend." He quickly corrected her possibly disparaging impression.

"Pippo came as my translator," Maggie said, jumping to his defense. "Just in case you didn't speak English, you see, as a precaution." Maggie began to get the feeling that this wasn't going to be an easy interview. At all costs, she had to make it clear that she did not intend to exploit her subject if she found him. The warnings of Mabel Weeks, Mrs. Sloan and Dick Ord echoed through her mind. *Be cool, don't blow it.*

"My intention, Signora Trezza, is not to expose or humiliate anyone. I am a reporter, not a judge. I'm only interested in presenting the facts. My government has never wanted to acknowledge its responsibility to these people—I'm not going to get any help with this story from them. But if I can find someone who is willing to share his feelings about being . . . a child born out of wedlock, perhaps his thought and feelings will be helpful to other people in the same position, whether as a result of war or misplaced passion or just plain accident. There shouldn't be any stigma attached to illegitimacy—that's my feeling.

"I can see by your face that you're skeptical of my motives. I swear to you, though, that my concerns are, first and foremost, for the feelings and the privacy of the innocents."

"Miss Reardon, I have no doubt that you are sincere.

However, sometimes the sincerest efforts cause the most damage."

"Pardon me for interrupting," Pippo interjected, "but sincerity in the fight for truth and justice can only hurt the ones who deserve it." Pippo's expression was oddly grim and determined.

"Perhaps, Signor Geraldi. But my concern is orphans. They suffer as children and continue to suffer as adults. They do not deserve any unnecessary pain. You say there is no longer any stigma in not having the proper name on your birth certificate," she scoffed. "Well, I beg to disagree. I have worked here for many years, and I know better than you. And frankly, the quest for journalistic truth has never been one of my concerns."

"You have every right to feel as you do, Signora Trezza," Maggie said quickly, cutting off Pippo, who looked like he was about to antagonize her further. "Orphans need your protection. If I just wanted to find the bastard child of an American soldier so I could exploit him, I would have snooped around, perhaps paid people off, and I suppose I would have found what I was after. But I did not do that because I did not want to treat these people as somebody's dirty little secret.

"Love and caring are often the deeper bases of a child's unfortunate status in the world—the relationship of two people who, at least for a short time, felt something for one another. Oh, I'm not so naïve as to think it's always that way, but even when it's just a question of two people keeping each other warm through a lonely night, that's not the child's fault. You see, I came to you hoping that you could direct me to an adult who could handle talking about his birth. I want *you* to choose the appropriate person for this project." Maggie knew that she would have to make the woman feel that she was in control to put her off the defensive. If she didn't win her confidence soon, there was no hope of having her cooperation.

"Miss Reardon, I assure you that my suspicions about you and your intentions disappeared long ago. The mother superior at Monte Carmel would never have referred you here if she thought you were unworthy. Reverend Mother is an old friend, and I trust her judgment."

ROMAN CANDLES

"Then you will help me?" Maggie asked eagerly.

"I will tell you what I know, but I am afraid that it will be less than what you may have hoped for. As you are well aware, most of the *bastardi* of the American soldiers who fought the Nazis now have families of their own. In my experience, I have never met any of these offspring from that awful time who wanted to speak of the parent who abandoned them—as your soldiers did. Indeed, this orphanage sheltered many of them during the war; however, we never made a distinction between those of American or German fathers whose mothers died or disappeared or those whose parents were married and died during the conflict. All we knew was that they were children alone in the world, children in need of food, shelter and love. At the time, we had neither the personnel nor the inclination to keep records on the kind of information you seek. Therefore, I cannot simply go to a file cabinet and offer you a list of names and addresses."

Maggie's heart sank as she listened to these words. Even Pippo seemed to look disappointed.

"But," Signora Trezza continued, "there is someone who could surely help, if you could find him. I did not know him myself, but his reputation is widespread. He is a priest who became concerned after the American and British armies landed in Anzio in January of Nineteen forty-four. He saw clearly that these soldiers would inevitably impregnate as many Italian women as the Germans and the Fascists had. I am told that he was a very practical man—he saw this simply as the price of liberation.

"This priest went to the American and British commanders on his own and told them that he would care for the *bastardi* of their soldiers if they would entrust him with supplies and food for his people. He built a warehouse in Gaeta, near his parish, and organized the town's men to guard it. He was known at the time as the savior of Gaeta, the guardian angel of all unwed mothers and *bastardi*. Occasionally, he would refer children to us whose mothers had died or disappeared.

"I wish I had met him, you know, he shared my attitude about war and what it does to people. You are too young, Miss Reardon, to understand how desperate is the fear on a night when all you hear around you are guns, and you do not know if you will live to see the next sunrise." She shook her head and looked away. "Families, most of them, they understood when their daughters' bellies began to swell. For some of them, though, the disgrace was too great. The girls were cast out. And if they were lucky, they were directed to this priest of whom I speak. He was not a young man during the war, so it is uncertain whether he is still alive. And, even if he is, there is no guarantee that he is still in Gaeta. But if you can locate him, I think he can tell you more about the innocents than anyone in Italy. His name is Padre Virgilio Antonelli."

Maggie's face brightened considerably with this piece of information. A hundred questions ran through her mind at once. How far was Gaeta? What was the name of Father Virgilio's parish? She prayed that the man was still alive. But before she could fire off her inquiries, Signora Trezza rose from her desk, indicating that the interview was over.

"Miss Reardon, I wish I could be of more help to you. What I know is very general, as you see, things you already know, no doubt. At the risk of seeming rude, I must tell you that I am very busy—this orphanage is so understaffed." She laughed, and her prim face was suddenly younger. It was the first time she had smiled. "But what orphanage is not?" she continued. "Now, my advice to you is to stop wasting time with me and find Padre Virgilio." The woman smiled warmly and reassuringly. It was just the kind of encouragement that Maggie needed.

"Thank you, Signora Trezza. I really appreciate your assistance."

"Good luck, Miss Reardon. I will look for your magazine and your article."

"I'll be sure to send you a copy when it's out. Thank you again."

"Good, good. Now if you and Signor Geraldi can find your own way out, I must leave you."

"Goodbye, Signora Trezza."

"*ArrivederLa*," Pippo called with a boyish grin as they exited from the office.

Maggie began babbling excitedly as soon as they were in the hallway and the door to Signora Trezza's office was closed behind them. "Where is Gaeta, Pippo?"

"About forty-five minutes from here. Halfway between Rome and Naples on the water. *Bella*, a quiet place."

"Hmm. Is there a bus or a train that goes there?"

"Yes, maybe. There is also a Pippo who goes there."

"Come on, Pippo. You don't have time to take me, do you?"

"Of course, remember, I am 'a doll.'"

Maggie had to laugh. "You're really something, you know that?" This man had the knack of putting her at ease—it was a geniune pleasure to be with him.

"On second thought, I have one condition before I agree to take you," he proclaimed, grinning mischievously as they started for the front door.

"What's that?"

"You must let me invite you to lunch and then show you a little bit more of Rome. You have only seen the Vatican and a few small fountains, and what will your friends say when they ask about the glories of the Eternal City? You will be, how you say, *unformed?*"

"Un*in*formed?" she prompted, smiling.

"Yes, that is it."

"Well, I don't know. I wouldn't say no to lunch, but the tour will have to be a very short one. I have a first installment to write tonight."

"All right," he said, pushing the door of the orphanage open. "You win—only a small tour. Today." He made a face at her. "But one more thing—about lunch, Maggie."

"Now what?" she asked with mock annoyance.

"You must pay. I cannot afford to get a reputation as a big spender. I will never find a rich American woman if I pay too much, not good for a gigolo. I must create the impression I am being taken care of. Do you understand?"

"I'm not sure," she said with a raised eyebrow and a skeptical grin as she climbed into Alfa Romeo.

Pippo laughed. "Is true. Believe me."

"I like this place," Pippo explained as they entered the small *trattoria* on the Via Frattina, a few blocks south of the Spanish Steps. "The food is very good, and cheap as well. See, I give you a crack with the bill. Is that right—*crack?* no, I give you a *break* with the bill," he smiled, sure of his idiom at last. "Besides, we are in a very fashionable part of Roma. Many beautiful Italian models here. And many beautiful and rich American women shopping in this neighborhood." Pippo giggled at his own ridiculousness.

"Can you spot an American when you see her?"

"I can spot her; I can smell her! You know, is very difficult. But I practice hard. Years of practice and *ecco*, I am perfect!"

Maggie shot him a skeptical glance again. He mentioned his desires for a rich American woman so often, he had to be somewhat serious about it. Normally, Maggie would have been appalled by this kind of mercenary attitude, but Pippo was so self-effacing and good-natured about his own personality flukes, she couldn't help but like him. And the fact that she was out of the running for his romantic interest because of her self-confessed lack of wealth made him all the more endearing to her. Undoubtedly, he wouldn't chase any girl who was not attached to a large and full Gucci pocketbook.

"So, what's good here?" she asked, her attention returning to important matters—food.

"Everything!"

"What's that?" she whispered, pointing to the golden-brown sandwich that a short, fat man was devouring at the table next to them.

"That is *mozzarella in carrozza*—a ham and cheese sandwich dipped in egg batter and deep-fried. But as you can see, it's very fattening. You swallow it and *guarda*, the day after, it appears again on your hips."

"I want one." Her hungry eyes were as big as her stomach.

"*Va bene*, but remember, Pippo warned you. Would you like an *acqua minerale* with that?"

Maggie wrinkled her nose at the thought of plain mineral water. "How about a coke?"

"Coca-cola? Everyone drinks this junk all the time—I do not understand it!"

"So?"

Pippo shook his head. "I can see that you are determined to ruin your figure. Well, if you insist on eating such things, why not try something new? In Italy, *aranciata* is very popular."

"Sold! I'll take one."

A waiter came over to their table and Pippo ordered as Maggie fiddled with wad of lire. Peeling off note after note just to pay for a simple lunch, she was astonished again by the

ROMAN CANDLES

inefficiency and play-money quality of this currency. You could never be a good spendthrift with this stuff, she thought, it would take you all day to pay for a single expensive item.

"What a coup, Pippo!" she said exuberantly when the waiter left them. "At least, I think I'm getting somewhere with the story. I have a feeling that Father Virgilio Antonelli will be the best source since Deep Throat."

"Deep Throat?"

"That was the title of a very popular porno movie in the early seventies. You can imagine what it was about."

Pippo nodded solemnly.

"Well, it was also the nickname that reporters Woodward and Bernstein gave to the anonymous informant who fed them secrets about the Watergate coverup."

"Fascinating! And Padre Virgilio will be Deep Throat for you?"

"I hope so . . . if he's alive and coherent."

"He will be." Pippo took her hand across the table and squeezed it reassuringly. "I know he will be."

"Thanks, Pippo." With Pippo's hand over hers, she suddenly thought of Gabriella and Alex holding hands the previous day at Otello's. Perhaps she had jumped to conclusions about Alex. Perhaps he was innocently consoling Gabriella, just as he had said he was, the way Pippo was innocently reassuring Maggie right now. But the man did have the worst track record for looking suspicious even when he wasn't guilty.

Maggie wondered suddenly if she attracted men who felt she was easy to take advantage of. Strange, how she always felt totally at ease in a professional situation—the way she'd told Jennings off, for example, when he suggested she couldn't do the job. And yet, she had so much trouble when it came to dealing with romantic problems.

"You seem far away, Maggie," Pippo interrupted her thoughts. "Are you thinking of your story? Or could you be still worried about Alex?" His face was earnest and concerned.

"You're a great mind reader. I guess Alex is sort of at the top of my list these days. I was thinking about how I had blamed him for something yesterday—something he probably didn't do. I'm a bit ashamed at my behavior."

ROMAN CANDLES

"I think I understand. I don't have to know details to see that you are very fond of Alex. You are also anxious to protect these feelings for him—*si?*—and you do not want interference from anyone else . . . maybe like Gabriella."

"Very perceptive, Pippo."

"I watch and I see, that is all. But, Maggie, I know that Alex is honorable. In the year we have been friends, he has always been a true and upstanding person, *davvero*. I know he would never hurt you intentionally."

"No, you're right. It's just that I accused him of playing up to me while he was really committed to Gabriella all the while. When he told me that he and Gabriella weren't involved romantically, I didn't want to believe him, really. But now I'm convinced that I was just flying off the handle. You know, the funny thing is, that for all her snippiness with me, she's turned out to be very generous. Gabriella invited Alex and me to her mother's Christmas ball. She didn't have to do that; she hardly knows me. I'm embarrassed now."

The waiter returned with their food: antipasto and a glass of Frascati for Pippo and a *mozzarella in carrozza* and an *aranciata* for Maggie. Forgetting her concerns in the flush of a new taste sensation, Maggie curiously took her first bite of the sandwich and her face lit up like a pinball machine. Seven huge bites later, Maggie was staring at her empty plate. Pippo had barely started his antipasto.

"Madonna mia! You must have been starved!"

Maggie nodded vigorously, with a tight-lipped grin that was about to burst into boisterous laughter.

"Maggie, you want another? Is this what you are holding in?" Pippo looked shocked.

"I can't help it. I'm hungry. I'm always hungry." Suddenly, she started chortling uncontrollably as Pippo looked at her, incredulous.

"Maggie, you are like a goat! But you say you are hungry, so. . . ." Pippo yelled to the waiter to bring Maggie another sandwich. "It is different with me," he continued. "I am a spiritualist—the food is pure sensation, every bite the most powerful aphrodiasic. So, I taste, then I am in love again. And you, you consume like one of those American cars—the gas-guzzlers, is this not the phrase?"

ROMAN CANDLES

Maggie could not stop laughing, and soon Pippo was caught up in her infectious mirth, coughing until the tears appeared in his eyes.

"You make me merry—and that is good for Christmas, yes?" he asked ingenuously.

After lunch, Pippo and Maggie strolled down Via Frattina so Maggie could do a little window-shopping. All the stores looked inviting, despite their lack of traditional Christmas decoration—the tasteful window displays of each boutique singled this out as one of Rome's ritzier neighborhoods. Dresses, leather goods, shoes, jewelry—all of Fifth Avenue quality. Maggie would have loved to go into every shop, but her promise to herself to get to work that afternoon and her concerns about her budget kept her urges under control. Still, she thought, a quick look wouldn't hurt.

"Via Frattina is one of the better places for women to shop in Rome," Pippo explained. "The *prima* street is the Via Condotti, where all the big designers are: Gucci, Pucci, Cucci, Amarone and all the others. Personally, I prefer this street, quieter, less pretentious."

Maggie was only half-listening, though, for her eye had been caught by an attractive yellow angora sweater in one shop window. It looked as soft as goosedown—a gentle lemon color that blended well with its ladylike style. The shoulders were slightly tucked, to create an adorable little-girl look, and the simple jewel neck and the cuffs were banded with an extra layer of rolled knitted fabric. Within the weave, a subtle pattern of deeper yellow chevrons ran diagonally across the bust. She was certain it would look perfect on her.

"You like?" Pippo asked, coming up behind her.

"Yes, very much," she said dreamily, fighting the temptation to go in and try it on.

"Come, I buy for you."

"No, Pippo."

"Yes, please, I want to."

"Absolutely not. You've been too kind to me already. Anyhow, the thing must be hand done. It looks like it costs a mint. Come on, let's keep going."

Maggie continued on, captivated with the array of fine lingerie and silk blouses in the next window. By the time she finally turned to look for Pippo, he was gone. She looked up and down the street, beginning to backtrack in search of him. Then, glancing into the shop with the display of the yellow sweater, she spotted him accepting a bag from a woman behind the counter.

"Pippo. . . ." she said impatiently, as he came out of the shop.

"Maggie, I did not want you to think that I am a scape-cheap."

"You mean a cheapskate."

"Yes, yes. After all, you bought the lunch. Please, I want you to have it."

Maggie dug into the bag and felt under the yellow sweater for the receipt. She pulled it out and saw the price: 48,000 lire. Quickly, she multiplied in her head. Sixty dollars!

"Are you crazy, Pippo? I knew it had to be very expensive, but I had no idea it was this costly. I can't take this from you."

"If you do not, I will be insulted." His mouth was set, his tone serious.

Maggie did not want to offend him. God knows she'd seen enough of the Italian personality to realize that hospitality was not casually offered. An invitation from Gabriella really meant something, as did this gift from Pippo. It was a similar gesture to that of making himself her personal tour guide. And, of course, his help would be invaluable in getting to Gaeta and talking to Father Virgilio.

"All right, Pippo," she shrugged happily, "you win. Thank you. You're really too good to be true." She hugged him and kissed his cheek in gratitude. "I can't tell you what it means to me to know I have a real friend."

Pippo blushed and averted his eyes.

"Now, you have to let me go. I know you're dying to show me more of Rome, but I really must get to work. The presses in New York are all set to roll, and my typewriter hasn't yet started chattering away."

"All right, you slave, you write and create the masterpiece. Tomorrow we go to Gaeta. I will pick you up at eleven o'clock, okay?"

"Fine. Pippo, you are. . . ."

"A real doll, that is right?" He laughed heartily, blushing again as Maggie left him, and then she started down Via

Frattina toward her *pensione* a few blocks away on the other side of the Spanish Steps.

The sky outside Maggie's window was a perfect midnight-blue studded with thousands of bright white stars. The scene could have been a photograph on a Christmas card. Maggie sat at her desk in her room, admiring the night. Her notes and the files she had brought from New York were spread out all over the bed and the floor. Crumpled pieces of paper were scattered around her in dizzy disarray. All that afternoon and into the early evening, Maggie had labored at distilling her notes into a solid core of background material for her first article. The information she had from Mrs. Sloan at ALMA in New York provided her with a skeleton outline on which she could fashion her story and work in her themes. But that wasn't enough. As the old saying goes: Kid, you gotta have a gimmick. So what did she have so far? Dry, legal stuff about opening files and making birth certificates available, a lot of intense feeling on both sides of the question and the fact of the difficulty of her quest for information. Now maybe *that* was interesting—Maggie's own quest to get the story, the doors slammed in her face and those that opened just a crack. Well, it was a start, at least.

Of course, that would do it. A real human-interest piece. She would have to insert herself and the story of her quest to find an innocent into the article. Father Virgilio would be her teaser. She would end this first installment with her trip to the orphanage and Signora Trezza's revelation of the guardian angel of the innocents. It was the perfect cliff-hanger. Is he still alive? If so, will he talk to Maggie Reardon? And just what did he do for the Italian children of American GIs?

Maggie tried not to congratulate herself, but she did feel that using the suspense of tracking down her story in the story itself was a minor stroke of genius. Sure, it had been done before, by Norman Mailer and Hunter Thompson, among others. But theirs were always hard-news stories—political conventions, Vietnam, Israel, the Olympics, Uganda. How much more interesting to use the technique with human-interest material. Jennings would really go for this—he was the one who kept stressing the personal angle, after all.

She sat back in her chair, watching the great night sky as she took a break. After five hours of work, she had only

ROMAN CANDLES

managed to pare down her material. Now came the hard part—putting it down on paper. The quiet of the room began to intimidate her a bit. That wonderful brass lamp threw a spotlight on her typewriter almost as if it were her opponent, standing across the ring, just waiting for her to make the first move before it came out fighting. She stared at the machine, telling herself that she was just taking a break, but knowing all the while that she was just stalling.

"Get going, girl. Stop with the procrastinating. It's not going to write by itself," she whispered.

She carefully rolled a fresh sheet of paper into the typewriter, poised her fingers over the keys and strained to think up an inspired lead.

This is the story of the Innocents. They are Innocent because they were spawned by the Guilty. And You just may be one of the guilty.

Maggie read over what she had written. "Blech!" She made a face and crossed the words out with a thick-point black felt-tip pen. She put the pen between her teeth and bit down hard as she scoured her brain for a better opening.

It's 1980. Do you know where your child is?

Maggie examined this one and rolled her eyes to the ceiling. "Too cutesie; won't work."

I came, I saw and I was curious.

"Fantastic! This one sounds like a come-on for a porno film!"

She stood up and went to the window. Leaning against the frame, she sighed despairingly. The notes always look so promising, she thought, but making them all hang together is something else again. There are so many sides to being a really good reporter. You have to have the ideas to begin with, then you've got to go around picking other people's brains, then you have to know enough to sort out the chaff from the wheat and discard phony leads and self-congratulatory interviews. And finally, after distilling the very best of your information, you have to have the skill to choose your words and your format so brilliantly that the material looks fresh and new, even when it isn't.

A sudden knock at the door startled her from her ruminations. "Must be my muse," she muttered to herself, as she went to the door. Probably Ugo coming to tell her that the typewriter was disturbing the other guests and that late evening noise was not appreciated.

"Yes, who is it?" she sang through the closed door.

"Alex." His voice sounded strong and flat in the night silence.

"Crap!" she hissed, not wanting to see anyone right now, especially not him. Hesitantly, she opened the door. "What are . . . I wasn't expecting you this late."

"I thought I said I'd be talking to you today."

"Well, yes, but. . . ."

"Oh, do you want me to go?" He looked over at the typewriter. "I see you're working."

"No, that's okay, come in. I can use a break."

Each one's awkwardness was apparent to the other. They stood staring at each other for a moment.

"I came by this morning," he explained, as he shrugged off his army jacket, "but you weren't around. Then I called about two and the manager said you were out."

"I was at an orphanage, interviewing the director for my story." She hated this kind of cautious conversation. They both knew what was going on and both had other things—honest things—to say. "Pippo came with me."

"Pippo?" His solemn tone vanished. "Why did he want to tag along?"

"The place was out on the Via Nomentana. He offered to give me a ride." She shrugged.

"If you'd like a little advice, watch out for Pippo."

Maggie looked at him curiously. She'd assumed they were good friends. "Alex, you almost sound jealous."

"Not jealous, just concerned," he said sternly. "Let's say I wonder how honorable his intentions are."

"Boy, I can't believe you're saying this. Pippo has been wonderful to me. I've never met anyone so generous and thoughtful. And as for his intentions, he makes it very plain that they are strictly mercenary when it comes to women who aren't friends. I sincerely doubt sex would ever enter the picture for Pippo unless the lady was well-endowed financially as well as physically. To me, though, he's become a good pal, and that's very different. Very precious," she added.

"Well, I can't tell you what to do. Just take what I say under advisement."

"Okay, I will." She decided against mentioning that Pippo was taking her to Gaeta the next day. As long as Alex was suspicious of the guy. Anyway, he wasn't her keeper—nor did she think much of his ability as a judge of character.

"How's the story coming?" he asked, changing the subject with a clearing of his throat.

"Oh, pretty good. I've got all my notes straightened out. Now I'm trying to think up a great opening line for my first installment. Looks like it could be an all-nighter—I have to wire the thing in tomorrow morning. What's galling is that I know exactly what I want to say, but it's just stuck."

"I know the problem." He smiled knowingly.

"Got any suggestions?"

"Usually, I just sit down and start writing. It's all crap in the beginning, but I have to get it all out of me before the good stuff finds its way out. Why not just write ten pages or so, throw out the first three, then see if you can think of a grabber to put up front."

"You're probably right. You can never be profound or gripping when you're trying too hard."

"Exactly. Look, Maggie, I can see that you want to get back to work; so I'll make it quick. I just wanted to make sure there were no hard feelings left over from yesterday. I mean, you were pretty mad and I thought, maybe you'd prefer it if I lay off. You know what I mean?"

"I jumped to conclusions, Alex, and I'm sorry I did. And no, I don't want you to go away if that's what you're asking." His honesty was so refreshing. She felt the attraction between them growing strong again.

He smiled broadly. "I'm glad to hear you say that."

"Do you still want to take me to the ball, Prince Charming?"

"More than ever." He took her in his arms and pressed her close, looking into her face for a long moment before covering her mouth with his. She accepted his embrace eagerly and drew herself up against his broad chest. Well, the guy did have some problems, but one thing she couldn't deny was that he knew where all her buttons were and just how to push them.

"Now I don't want to keep you from your article—no matter how badly I really want to stay. So . . . ah . . . I guess I'll go."

"When do you want to get together again?" she whispered, half-hoping he would keep her from her work. She could feel his hands all over her again, remembering their time in bed together.

"I'll be out of town tomorrow. How about dinner on Thursday?"

"I'll be waiting for you right here," she grinned. "You can rescue me from the jaws of work."

"By the way, if you'd like, you can send your article to the New York office with a friend of mine. It's on his way, believe it or not. I like to use him—that way all my commas are right where I want them. Prose tends to get jumbled on the Telex."

"Thanks. Where do I find him?"

"He leaves for New York tomorrow morning at eight. If you put your stuff in an envelope and address it to the *Shout* address care of Captain Pete Rogers, Pan Am, I'll have a messenger come early tomorrow morning who'll get it to him. Why don't you just leave it downstairs with the night clerk before you go to bed?"

"Great. I'll do that."

"Okay. Until Thursday."

They kissed again, both wanting to linger, both knowing better.

"Bye," she said, as he left.

Returning to her typewriter, she began to write and, surprisingly, the story started coming out immediately in a steady flow. As she typed out sentence after sentence, she began to think less and less of the task that lay ahead and more of the finished piece that was taking shape before her. Perhaps the muse had come through the door after all, she thought.

Chapter 10

At nine A.M. sharp the next morning, a loud, persistent knocking at the door woke Maggie from a deep sleep. She groaned and cursed, hoping the intrusion would just go away, but the more she ignored it, the louder it got.

"What?" she finally barked in annoyance.

"Telephone for you, Signorina Reardon. Downstairs," she heard Ugo call.

"Okay, okay. I'll be right there. Thanks, Ugo." Grimacing, she threw off her covers, wondering who the hell it could be. She felt she deserved a little more sleep—after all, she had worked until three A.M. finishing and polishing her story, then she had sealed it carefully in a manila envelope and brought it down to the front desk where she'd left it with the night clerk.

It was good, she decided after reading it over for the fourth time. Not exactly Pulitzer material, but this was just the first. The prose was clear, effective; the themes were presented in a way that really grabbed the reader. And, yes, she certainly felt after finishing it that she'd be eager for the second in the series if she were a *Shout* subscriber.

She smiled when she thought of the desk clerk's startled expression when she'd emerged from the elevator—bleary eyes, tousled hair and all—and tried to explain in her faulty Italian that a messenger would be picking up that envelope sometime after dawn. The skinny young man looked at her as though she were a ghost that had just materialized through the wall, and he seemed so frightened of her that she doubted that he even moved the package from the spot where she'd left it.

Maggie grabbed her jeans, threw on a navy crew-neck sweater and slipped into her penny loafers. If she looked frightening last night, she knew that now she probably looked worse. Descending the stairs to the lobby, she wondered who the call was from. Alex had said he'd be gone all day. Not Pippo cancelling! Please! Jennings? Oh, Lord—no! Quickly, Maggie tried to figure out what time it was in New York to decipher whether or not it conceivably could be Jennings. But her head was too fuzzy to calculate the time difference before she reached the phone.

"Hello?" she said into the receiver, her voice cracking.

"Pronto, Maggie? This is Gabriella Sciarra." She sounded more clipped and formal on the phone than she did in person.

God, what do I say to her? Maggie thought in a panic. *It's bad enough when I've had enough sleep and can sound coherent, but now!* "Hi, Gabriella. How are you this morning?" Maggie tried to sound as natural and cordial as possible.

"Fine. I have called to give you the name of my hairdresser. Aldo has also offered to fit you for a gown—at a discount, of course." There was a tense silence. "For the ball. You are still going, no?"

Gabriella's stuck-up attitude, once again, rubbed Maggie the wrong way. This is not what you need first thing in the morning after a night of struggle and creation, she almost said aloud.

"Maggie," Gabriella went on, "I'm sure your clothes are fine for New York, but this is—how shall I say?—higher style. You cannot come looking too American; you will embarrass Alex."

"Don't worry about that. I have my own people. Thanks for calling." Maggie slammed the phone onto the hook, not giving Gabriella the opportunity to reply.

"Damn snobbish, hotsy-totsy European!" she hissed. "I thought people like that only lived in the movies. You can't tell me she's not sweet on Alex."

As she turned to go back to her room, it struck her that she had neither the time nor the inclination to go out and get fitted for a dress, then spend a day in the beauty parlor. She made a sour face as she thought of facials, rollers, dryers, hairspray and all the rest. *There's nothing wrong with my hair the way it is,* she thought. *It's simple, practical; wash, dry and go.*

Then she got a mental picture of Gabriella and a ballroom full of gorgeous model-types wearing the latest fashions and the fanciest coiffures with multiple braids and chopsticks or feathers sticking out of elaborate concoctions on their heads. Her refreshing simplicity would not exactly work in that situation. She'd be the plain Jane, the wallflower, the ugly duckling. She began to ponder the notion that it would undoubtedly be easier to cancel and not go.

Then she thought of Betsy. Maybe *she* could be of some help. Maggie ran back to her room for a *getone* and Betsy's phone number at the embassy.

Sure, she figured, flying back up the stairs so she wouldn't have to wait for the gilt cage to descend, Betsy must go to a lot of these formal affairs. She must have a good hairdresser and a decent dressmaker too. God knows she couldn't afford anything like an Aldo Amarone original, no matter what kind of discount he gave her. What were designer things going for these days? She vaguely recalled some article stating that Nancy Reagan paid about $10,000 for one James Galanos—and that wasn't even a ballgown!

Surprisingly enough, it took only two tries to get her call through. The phone rang once, and Betsy picked up promptly.

"Press attaché's office. Elizabeth Farrell speaking."

"Hello, Betsy. It's Maggie."

"Hi! How're you doing?" Betsy's business tone disappeared instantly. There was a note of genuine concern in her voice.

"Pretty good. I managed to straighten things out with Alex."

"Good, great. Want to talk about it?"

"Sure, but not now. No time. What I want is some advice. Gabriella Sciarra invited me and Alex to her mother's winter ball."

"That's great! So, what's the advice you need?"

"Well, I need a dress and a do and the whole number, and I

haven't got a clue as to where to go. You have any places you could recommend?"

"Sure. I've got a magnificent hairdresser, and I know of some dressmakers who are supposed to be pretty reasonable."

"You're a savior, Betsy."

"Listen, I know. I'm a little busy myself right now. I have some personal days coming. How about if I take off work and we go shopping tomorrow?"

"Sounds good, if you really don't mind. Maybe I can wrap this up in just one day. I hate to take up your personal days, though."

"Hey, I love doing things like this. I may seem like a serious diplomatic aide, but let me loose inside a department store and the real Betsy emerges—all girl! Okay, so it's a date. I'll pick you up at your place around ten."

"Fine. See you tomorrow." Maggie hung up and sighed gratefully. Betsy was really a lovely person, she thought, feeling the warm friendliness of the other woman covering her like a blanket. Sounded like she'd rather get vicarious enjoyment out of Maggie's good times than try to find some in her own life. But there was more there beneath the surface—the woman really had that sort of caring Maggie loved in her roommate, Ellen. And she didn't have that many other friends who would be there for her if she were in a jam, or just feeling low. She and Betsy were going to be close, she knew it.

Now momentarily free from concerns about her ball preparations, Maggie began to think about the trip to see Father Virgilio—if she could find him. He was the most important man in her life right now. She ran back to her room to get ready. Pippo would arrive soon, and they had a big day ahead of them. At least, Maggie had high hopes that it would be a big day.

The drive to Gaeta was extraordinarily beautiful. Pippo had insisted on taking the scenic route, and Maggie didn't object. Driving down a small coastline road that ran parallel to the famous, ancient Via Appia, they were both delighted by the teal-blue sea on their right and the craggy foothills of the Apennines on their left. It was just after noon when they arrived in the center of Gaeta.

"My God!" Maggie's eyes were wide. "I've never seen any place this white." In fact, the town was gleaming—every building had the same white stucco exterior. The houses in the little town square sat together like close family members huddled in a tight circle.

Pippo maneuvered his car around the square, then took the right leg at a fork in the road, heading for the sea.

"Before we go to search for your priest, I must show you something very special. Gaeta is a really ancient town, the holiday retreat of the emperors. It is built on the Caves of Sperlonga, where Tiberius liked to fool around before he found Capri."

Pippo stopped the car and pointed toward the caves and the terraced houses that were carved out of the face of the cliff, running in jagged lines on levels down to the sea. "You see that?" he asked. "The old Romans built their dwellings over the caves and put in long stairways between each level and down to the water. People still live in those houses."

Maggie was awestruck by the sight. "Amazing. I thought the Pueblo Indians were the only people who built these kinds of houses. It looks so cozy—I'd love to live here."

"Many Americans do," he said with a wry smile.

"Resort town, eh?"

"No. There is an American army base here. The soldiers, they love Gaeta too. Like Miami Beach, they say." Pippo did not try to hide his disdain for the American military presence in his country.

Maggie wanted to point out that the troops were stationed here to defend Italy as part of the NATO forces, but she remained silent. She thought it wiser not to debate the issue and risk a political argument with Pippo. He had been so good to her so far, it would be stupid to stir up the waters now. If her mother had taught her one thing, it was to avoid conversations about politics or religion at all costs.

"Now, listen, my friend," she grinned, "I know you want to show me all the sights, but I do have a priest to find—remember?"

"Oh, yes, of course. *Incredible, veramente!* A beautiful woman in Gaeta who would rather find an old priest than explore the caves with a handsome fellow like me. This priest must have something. Spiritual powers, no?"

"I hope he does."

ROMAN CANDLES

"Okay, you win," he said, feigning melancholy, "we shall find the *padre* and make you happy." Pippo continued down the road until he came to a cul-de-sac where he could turn around. He gunned the Alfa back up the steep road, and Maggie's heart leapt into her throat. Why in the name of heaven these men had to drive around like they were on the home stretch of the Grand Prix was simply beyond her. It was this reckless manner of careening around streets and hills that disturbed Maggie the most about Italians. But, telling herself once again that she was the visitor and Pippo was the native, she grabbed hold of the dashboard and hoped he'd get the hint.

He didn't. He made a screeching right turn onto the main road that fishtailed the car and zoomed it forward.

"Maybe we should find a church where we can ask about Father Virgilio."

"Good idea. You are very smart." In his eagerness, he accelerated the car as he approached the center of town instead of slowing down.

As they neared the square, Maggie suddenly spotted a small American flag hanging in the window of a restaurant. "Stop!" she yelled over the racing engine's roar.

Pippo brought the car to a screeching halt. "What is it? I drive too fast?"

"Well, that too. But see that? The flag?" She pointed to the window which proudly bore the red, white and blue in full view. "Park the car. I'll buy you lunch, okay? My flag means I'm the host. And maybe we can find out something about Father Virgilio here."

As Pippo parked, Maggie felt a pang of homesickness. It surprised even her that the mere sight of the U.S. flag could touch her like that. It would be kind of nice to run into some other Americans, she mused. She hadn't really thought about the fact that part of her attachment to Alex—even to Betsy—might stem from their common nationality in a foreign land.

Together Maggie and Pippo walked into the small *ristorante* which held no more than a half-dozen tables, all covered with red and white checked tablecloths. The pale green plaster walls displayed a mishmash of framed abstract paintings that all seemed to be the creations of the same prolific but dubious talent.

ROMAN CANDLES

Looking from table to table, Maggie was a bit disappointed—the place was deserted except for one bald man with a great belly who was standing behind the bar. It was obvious that he was the proprietor from his ready smile when they entered.

"Come stanno?" he called out across the room in his low, gravelly voice.

Pippo smiled and nodded to him.

"Ask him why he has the American flag in the window," Maggie said anxiously, turning to Pippo.

"Why don't you ask me yourself, honey?" His accent was distinctly New York. The fat man bellowed with laughter as he looked at her shocked expression.

"You're American!" She couldn't believe it. His Italian accent was very convincing, but as she studied him, she saw that there was something about his face that was different, a certain chameleon-like quality that Italians just don't have.

"Angelo D'Allesio is the name." He extended his hand to her. "Formerly of Brooklyn, New York."

She took his hand and shook it heartily. "Maggie Reardon, from Manhattan, and this is Pippo Geraldi. He's a native," she added softly.

Angelo took Pippo's hand and shook it so vigorously, Maggie thought he was going to lift poor Pippo off the ground.

"Sit, sit," Angelo corraled them over toward a table. "Let me get a bottle of wine—on the house."

"You don't have to. . . ." Maggie started to protest.

"Oh, yes, I do," he boomed. "I buy for all the Americans who come in here. That way I get to drink with them and share a bit of home." He laughed with genuine delight as he ran to the bar and uncorked a bottle of red wine.

"Sounds fair enough," Maggie called after him.

Angelo trotted back to the table with the wine and three glasses. "Barbera. This stuff'll put hair on your chest—excuse the figure of speech." He filled the glasses, then lifted his and admired it briefly before he brought it to his lips as though he were kissing a baby. *"Bellissima,"* he croaked. "And Merry Christmas."

"Same to you," Maggie said, taking a sip. She was about to thank him for the wine when he abruptly stood up. "Now, Maggie, Pippo, what are ya' eatin'? The linguini with clam

155

sauce is fantastic, if I do say so myself. How's that sound?" He didn't wait for an answer, but dashed off to the kitchen to place the order with the chef.

"Very friendly," Pippo commented, as he topped off his glass. "I am glad we have found your countryman here."

"Really. Me too." Maggie nodded emphatically.

Suddenly, Angelo reappeared with a basket containing a loaf of bread. In his other hand he had a platter of green olives and provolone cheese.

"This should hold you till the linguini's ready." He plopped down the food on the table, and Maggie sighed happily as her irrepressible appetite was aroused. Somehow, just the sight of food could do it to her. She distinctly remembered the Christmas her mother took her into New York to see the tree at Rockefeller Center and the windows of F.A.O. Schwartz. In their travels, they walked past a fancy restaurant—the kind where they have all the desserts laid out on a dolly. Seeing those goodies in the window, even though she had just eaten a substantial lunch, was enough to make her stomach growl. Her mother worried about her having a tapeworm and rushed her to their family doctor, who assured her, "Mrs. Reardon, *there's* the tapeworm—it's Maggie!"

Even now, sitting in this comfortable restaurant, she felt incapable of keeping her mind on her work when there was food in the offing.

"Thank you," she managed to tell the owner before she shot an olive into her mouth. "This is very kind of you."

"*Sì, grazie,* my friend," Pippo chimed in.

"Oh, don't mention it," Angelo growled jovially.

"I must admit, I never expected to find a restaurant owner from Brooklyn in the middle of Italy." Maggie eyed him curiously through her wineglass.

"Well, I'll tell ya. I know you won't believe this, seein' I look so young," he rolled his eyes and grinned wryly, "but I first came here back in Nineteen forty-four with Ike's liberation forces. Even though the war was on and everything, I couldn't get over what a beautiful country this is—the people, the sea, the mountains, even the food tasted beautiful to me. I mean, I'd always wanted to come see the place where my papa was born, but it never really hit me that I was gonna feel so at home just as soon as I set foot in *la bella Italia*.

ROMAN CANDLES

"When I got back to the States, I promised myself that I'd come back to live here someday. Well, after twenty-seven years with the New York Fire Department, I packed up the wife and the savings and we moved. We started this place five years ago. And I'm havin' the time of my life. Got guys from the NATO base in here every weekend, havin' a ball. Plus Gaeta is like heaven. Better than Miami Beach."

Pippo shot Maggie a sidelong glance.

"But what the hell am I doing all the yakking for here? What brings you two to Gaeta?"

"Well," Maggie began, trying to extract an olive pit from her mouth as inconspicuously as possible. "I'm a magazine reporter. *Shout* magazine. Ever hear of it?"

"Sure. My wife picks it up at the PX every now and then." Angelo smiled sheepishly. "Technically, me and my family aren't supposed to be able to shop there but I do a lot of favors for the guys on the base. . . ."

Maggie waved off his explanation of the Italian way of life—you scratch my back, I'll scratch yours. "Well, I'm glad you can get it here. I'm researching a story about war babies. The illegitimate children of American soldiers conceived during World War Two. I'm trying to track down one of these people for an interview, maybe help him find his father."

"Sounds pretty heavy-duty to me, Maggie."

"It is."

"If you want my opinion, I think those guys would rather forget about their Italian mistakes. Like, at least the ones I knew during the war. Don't get me wrong, now. I'm not sayin' that our guys were animals or anything. It's just that we were kids ourselves then. I was nineteen at the time, scared shitless and horny as a crab, if you'll pardon the expression. There were days in boot camp when I'd have chased a chicken."

"Do you mind . . . ? This may seem a little out of line. May I ask you a personal question?"

"Shoot."

"Well, did *you* ever have an affair with an Italian girl during the war?"

"Of course. I was just one of the lucky ones—*we* didn't get pregnant. But there were plenty of guys who did get their girls into trouble. A real shame too."

"Do you know if it's true that the army refused to help these girls, that they didn't want to accept responsibility for these children?"

"Hey, we had a war to fight! There was no time to set up day-care centers, you know."

"Is that how the men who knew they had gotten their Italian girlfriends pregnant felt?"

"Hell, no." Angelo shook his head vehemently. "To a man, they were as guilty as all get out. Christ, sometimes the barracks began to sound like 'Dear Abby.' Especially 'cause a lot of these guys cared about the girl—it wasn't just a roll in the hay, see? A lot of them swore that when they got back they'd send part of a paycheck, no matter how small. I hope some of them did that. I had a friend tried to talk his girl into getting money somehow to come to the States, but I guess she was the sensible one—said Italy was her home first, last and always.

"But like I said, we were kids, no one was ready to be a father. For that matter, we weren't really ready to kill Nazis either. But we did both and we had to ease the pain any way we could. Guys would steal food from the mess for their girls, make them promises they knew they could never live up to just to keep them from goin' crazy, you know? Some of them didn't care—but a hell of a lot of them did."

"How about social agencies, Italian or American, like the Red Cross? Did anyone try to help these women and their children?"

"Only Father Virgilio."

Maggie drew her breath in sharply.

"Oh, I see you've heard of him. Yeah, he was the only guy who really gave a damn about the situation. See, he was a real practical guy, especially for a priest. He knew that no matter what the GIs promised, they were gonna get shipped out eventually. So he let everyone know that he would accept money and stuff from the guys for the care of their children when they were gone. He didn't condemn them or anything, you know. He just made it known that if these kids were gonna have any chance at all, they would need food, clothes, medicine and money. He would tell the guys that if they really wanted to ease their consciences, they should give him the dough so he could dole it out the right way when the time

ROMAN CANDLES

came, not leave it to the girls who might be kinda—well, maybe a little hysterical about them leaving and havin' babies when they weren't married."

"And did he do that?"

"That and more. He was known as the guardian angel of the war babies. Set up barracks and a clinic for the women whose families wouldn't have them. Had a soup kitchen too. He was quite a guy. I know for a fact that he went to see Ike himself and demanded supplies. And Ike gave him what he wanted, no questions asked."

"You said he 'was' quite a guy. Is he still alive, do you know?" Her heart refused to beat normally—it was like all the pieces of the puzzle were coming together before her eyes.

"Yeah, yeah, I think so. He must be pretty old now, though. He was well into his forties during the war."

"Is he still in Gaeta?" The excitement was evident in Maggie's voice.

"Yeah. He's at Saint Dominic's here in the village. You gonna go interview him?"

"I sure am, Angelo." She was ready to leave on the spot. "Will you tell me how to get there?"

"Sure, sure. No problem. But first you've gotta have your linguini. Poor Pippo over here hasn't said a word in ten minutes, he's so hungry."

Pippo shook his head and waved his hand, shrugging off Angelo's explanation. It was obvious to Maggie that his silence was simply due to the fact that he was rather intimidated in the substantial presence of this boisterous American restaurateur.

"Okay, Angelo, you're on."

"'Atta girl." He slapped the tabletop as he stood up to fetch their meals.

Although Maggie's mind was racing and she was itching to find Father Virgilio, the aroma wafting in from the kitchen convinced her to stay put. First, the linguini, she decided, then the directions to St. Dominic's.

The Church of San Domenico was located on a deserted road about a mile inland from the village of Gaeta. The church itself was a humble, fieldstone chapel with an adjoining stucco building—probably the rectory, Maggie assumed. The fields that surrounded the church were brown with the stalks and chaff left over from the fall harvest. With the foothills far in the background, the scene was a study in every imaginable shade of brown. It had an almost Andrew Wyeth quality to it.

"A church for the farmers," Pippo commented dryly. The remark struck Maggie as odd. Was Pippo such a cosmopolitan snob that he couldn't appreciate the beauty of this place?

"Shall we get started?" Maggie said, ignoring his evident disdain. She led the way to the rectory door.

Pippo came up from behind as Maggie took a breath and knocked on the door. No response. She knocked again, and a very young priest opened the door, wiping his hands on the long, white apron that he wore over his coarse, brown cassock. He was covered with flour.

"*Buon giorno,*" he said with a great smile. The sunlight gleamed off his rimless glasses.

"*Buon giorno,*" Maggie repeated hesitantly, still unsure of her pronunciation. "We have come to see Father Virgilio Antonelli."

The young priest looked puzzled, and holding out his hands, palms up, he shrugged and smiled again. "*Non capisco l'inglese.*"

Pippo jumped in. "*La signorina vuole sapere si qualcuno qui conosce il padre che si chiama Virgilio Antonelli.*"

"*Ah,*" the young priest nodded. "*Padre Virgilio è ammalato. È molto vecchio; purtroppo confuso.*"

Maggie turned to Pippo, anxious for his translation.

"Yes, he is here, but he is very old, senile."

"Ask him if we can see him anyway." Maggie was champing at the bit, convinced that she would be able to get something out of the old priest, somehow.

Pippo put the request to the young priest, and he seemed to protest. Pippo's tone was insistent, though, and shaking his head with resignation, the young priest finally agreed. "*Sì, sì, ma solamente un piccolo momento, va bene?*"

Smiling like a merchant who has just haggled for the price he wanted, Pippo turned to Maggie and explained the situation. "He says Padre Virgilio gets tired very easily, so we can only see him briefly. He tells me that it is very hard to have a sensible conversation with him, and he tried to discourage us. So, what did I do? I told him that Padre Virgilio married your parents and baptized you and that you just wanted to see him for a moment."

"Very clever. You'd make a good investigative reporter."

"Perhaps. Come, if the old man falls asleep, we may have to wait until tomorrow for this interview."

Maggie and Pippo followed the young priest through a series of rooms, past the kitchen where he had apparently just been kneading dough. Several large balls of it were waiting to be set in the red-hot brick oven. They went out onto the solarium in the back of the rectory.

On a daybed, smothered in his oversized cassock and covered with an old blanket, lay a tiny, wizened old man, holding a set of large, wooden rosary beads in his creased, pink hands. His low murmurs were barely audible, and the footsteps of his visitors did not disturb him at all.

"Padre, padre! Dei visitori a vederLe." The young priest gently shook Father Virgilio's shoulder, raising his voice to get his attention.

Bewildered, the old priest looked up at his young companion, not comprehending what was wanted of him. His eyes were bleary and pathetic, like an orphaned child's.

The young priest turned to Pippo and told him to speak loudly to the *padre*, who was sometimes hard of hearing. With another admonition to be brief, the young priest turned and went back to the kitchen.

Father Virgilio stared at Maggie and Pippo, obviously nervous and frightened of strangers.

"Come sta?" Pippo asked loudly and heartily, hoping to gain the old man's confidence, but his scared expression did not change.

"Let's get closer. I don't think he can see us," Maggie whispered. Pippo pulled up two chairs, and they sat together beside the bed.

"Buon giorno, padre," Maggie said tenderly, taking his hand.

The old man's mouth fell open and his eyes strained to see her better. Then he looked at Pippo, seeming to recognize him. He took Pippo's hand and mumbled some sort of greeting.

ROMAN CANDLES

Maggie and Pippo looked at each other, puzzled.

"He is confused," Pippo said softly, smiling kindly at Padre Virgilio. "He thinks we are someone else, I think."

"Try to get him to talk about the war babies and what he did for them. You know what I want to know."

"I will try, Maggie, but I do not know how successful I may be." Pippo's brows were knit in consternation.

"Go ahead," Maggie urged him, still hopeful.

Pippo started to converse with the *padre* in Italian. While Pippo spoke slowly and tentatively, the old man began to jabber on congenially, as if they were old friends. Occasionally, he would defer to Maggie and direct a comment to her, patting her hand gently, but she could only smile pleasantly at him, pretending to understand what he was talking about.

"What's going on?" she interrupted impatiently after several minutes.

Pippo finished his sentence, then quickly turned to Maggie and shrugged. "All nonsense. He is mixed up. He thinks we're . . . other people." Immediately, he turned his attention back to Father Virgilio, obviously afraid that he would drift away from the conversation if left alone for a minute.

"Do what you can," Maggie whispered to Pippo, as the priest rattled on.

Maggie began to despair. The priest grew more animated and Pippo's questions sounded more and more urgent. Damn, she thought, so close and yet so far. She honed in on the garbled words of the old priest, wondering whether she could pick up clues from his gibberish. Good leads are wherever you find them, after all.

Taking her notebook from her picketbook, she began to jot down anything she could make out from the old priest's speech. First, she tried transliterated Italian, simply writing all the sounds she heard whichever way she suspected they might be spelled. Pippo could sound them out for her later, she figured. Then she tried to hone in on individual words. He would eventually have to say something that was in her minuscule Italian lexicon.

He kept saying, *"conte e contessa,"* capping his sentences with the phrase. Frequently, he would look at Maggie when he said it. She wrote it down and underlined it. The rest, however, was just a rapid-fire blur of syllables.

ROMAN CANDLES

"Is he saying anything yet?" she whispered in Pippo's ear.

"No, Maggie. Still nonsense." His eyes, seemingly rapt with attention, did not leave Father Virgilio's face for an instant.

For five solid minutes, the priest went on and on, as Pippo just nodded his encouragement, and *conte e contessa* was the only thing that came through coherently to Maggie. As she sat trying to scheme up some way to trigger his memory, she was startled to hear the old man pause and say quite distinctly, "Lieutenant Colonel Tony Russo, *sì*, Tony Russo." He then nodded with a cryptic, almost satisfied grin, his eyes wandering to the fields outside. Then, just as suddenly, he started his non-stop chatter again.

Maggie jotted down "Lt. Col. Tony Russo," putting a question mark and an exclamation point next to the name.

As she finished writing, she heard Father Virgilio take a deep breath and, enunciating clearly, he said, "Convento San Gabriele." Quickly, she wrote that down too. The man evidently had brief moments of lucidity, after which he lost his train of thought. In a second, it was all gibberish to her again.

Pippo listened closely, his elbows on his knees, hanging on every word.

The two of them whirled around then, startled by the appearance of the young priest standing in the doorway. He had come in so silently they hadn't heard a thing. He said something in Italian, interrupting Father Virgilio, and the old priest suddenly stopped talking as the bewildered look returned to his face.

Pippo spun around in his seat. *"Sì, sì. Ora, lo lasciamo in pace."* He turned back to Maggie. "This one, he is very protective. He thinks the *padre* has had enough excitement for one day and wants us to leave."

Pippo stood up and started to say farewell to Father Virgilio. But when Maggie drew up next to Pippo, the old man leaned forward, took their hands in his and brought them together. He mumbled something in a consoling tone and held their hands firmly in a gesture of quiet strength.

"Sì, sì, padre. ArrivederLa," Pippo responded.

This gesture of calm reassurance coming from the feeble old priest seemed strange to Maggie. It should be he who got the reassurance from them. But spiritual strength sometimes is a boon, she decided. You think you're on top of things even when you aren't, if you know you have God on your side.

As they backed out of the room, Father Virgilio held that odd, kind smile on his face, even though Maggie was sure he could not see them that far away.

The young priest led them back through the rectory in silence. He opened the front door for them, then shook both their hands, displaying the same happy, open expression with which he had first greeted them.

"Thank you very much," Maggie said with an appreciative smile, although she realized he wouldn't understand her words.

"Grazie, grazie tanto, padre," Pippo said earnestly.

As they walked to Pippo's car, they both were lost in thought. At last, Maggie broke the silence.

"Could you make out anything of what he was saying, Pippo? Did any of it make sense?" She was almost pleading for a positive response.

"I'm afraid not. He went on and on about his mother and father and taking his vows. You see, he thought we were his brother and sister from so many years ago. It is a shame he is so confused. But this happens often with old people."

"What was Father Virgilio saying about a *conte* and *contessa?*" Maggie asked hopefully.

"I think he was saying that his brother and sister went to work for a royal family. But I'm not sure."

Maggie pressed on. "And what about this Lieutenant Colonel Tony Russo?"

"That is a complete mystery to me. He was talking about his brother and sister and then he began to talk about this American soldier. I am sorry I cannot tell you more. It is very sad what happens to old people, no?"

"Yes, very sad," Maggie said with a long face. She was terribly disappointed. The road to Gaeta had become a dead end. "I'm sorry I dragged you all the way out here for nothing."

"Well, you would have never known unless you came." Pippo shrugged, his tone brightening. "Anyway, the drive was beautiful, and Angelo was lots of fun." Pippo seemed to be trying to make the best of a bad situation.

"That's true. And I did get some good information about

the war-baby problem from Angelo. So I guess it wasn't a total loss."

"Of course not. Come, I think we should start back for Roma."

"Okay. Now, I guess I just go look for another lead. I really have to find someone—just one—who can speak from personal experience about being one of the innocents."

"You are splendid reporter, Maggie. You will find him."

"I certainly hope so. Or my name will be mud back at the home office."

As Pippo guided the car back onto the road and picked up speed on the way toward the coast highway, Maggie pondered what Angelo had told her, trying to figure out the best way to present him in her series.

And for the moment, anyway, she forgot about what she had written down from Father Virgilio's babbling.

Chapter 11

The next morning, Maggie opened her eyes and groaned audibly as she rolled over. She had the most awful cramps—it was as if something were squeezing all her vital organs and wouldn't let go. As she made her way down the hall to the bathroom, she recalled the fact that her period was bound to be worse after a transatlantic journey—something about the change in body chemistry, she'd heard. God, she thought, just the wrong time to have to deal with this! When she got back to her room, she fumbled through her small store of medical supplies and came up with a half-empty bottle of Midol. They never did anything but make her sleepy—still, she popped two in her mouth and then hurriedly started to dress. Betsy would be picking her up soon.

At nine o'clock sharp, there was a knock at the door.

"Come on in, Betsy," Maggie called out from the armchair where she sat almost doubled over with her nagging cramps.

"Hi, Maggie." Betsy walked in carrying her trenchcoat over her arm. She had on a pair of khaki twill slacks and a brown and white shirt jacket. The top was neat and well cut, and it skillfully downplayed Betsy's broad shoulders. "What's the matter? Why are you sitting like that? You okay?" A look of concern shaded Betsy's face.

"Just cramps, that's all. My period came early."

"Oh. You need anything?"

"No. But I would like to sit still for a minute before we get started, if you don't mind. It must be leftover jet lag—this never happens to me."

"Sure, Maggie. There's no hurry. Believe me, I understand the problem."

Betsy put her coat and pocketbook on the bed, then went over to the desk chair. She lifted a few things from the chair to make room and spotted the yellow angora sweater lying amid notes and books.

"This is lovely, Maggie." Betsy held it up to admire it. "Did you get this here?"

"Yeah. Alex's friend Pippo bought it for me—against my avid protests. I was ogling it in a shop window on the Via Frattina and he offered to buy it for me. I said no, you can't do that. After all, I only met him a few days ago. But Pippo is irrepressible. The minute I turned my back, he ran into the shop and bought it."

"It's gorgeous." Betsy sighed. "God, a present from a Roman stranger. Why doesn't this ever happen to me?"

"Well, I don't know. Unfortunately, when I got home and tried it on, I found that it didn't fit. These European sizes are really weird—the thing is marked small, but it's much too big. Maybe because it's handmade. I can't return it. That would hurt Pippo's feelings. Anyway, I don't have the receipt. Why don't you try it on? If it fits, you can have it."

"Won't Pippo be offended?"

"Only if he finds out." They both laughed, as Betsy took off her top. "I know I eat like a horse," Maggie continued, "But I'm really pretty slight. It must be these that make men think I'm bigger than I really am." She touched her sore breasts.

"How's it look?" Betsy chirped eagerly, modeling the sweater.

"Great! It's yours. Shall I wrap it up or will you wear it now?" Maggie chided.

"Very funny." Betsy pulled the sweater over her head and put it back in its bag, then dropped the bag into her canvas tote. "Thanks, Maggie, really," she said earnestly, as she buttoned up her jacket. "You sure you want to give this to me? After all, I only met *you* a few days ago."

"Yup, you're right. I just wish I didn't feel so guilty spending time shopping. I've been here a week and none of my leads have paid off. And now I've got to go find evening slippers and a bag. Who thought I'd be going to a ball when I packed for this trip?"

"Calm down. I have some black patent sandals that might do. Are you a six and a half B?"

"No, seven."

"Try them anyway. I bet they'll fit, they're just lots of straps that wind around your toes and ankles. And I've got a black clutch, not velvet, but moire. It'll do. What else?"

"You're a livesaver. Thanks."

"Now, what about your hair? You just going to wash and blow-dry like you're going to the office?"

"Why not?"

"Don't be ridiculous. They won't let you in unless you have some kind of do. And that gown deserves great hair. I know a guy at the Excelsior. I'll make an appointment for you for tomorrow afternoon. I'll call you later to tell you what time."

"Okay—I guess. How much will that cost?"

"Plenty. But you can't go back to New York without a hair-styling from Rome!"

"Hmm." Maggie wore that worried look that was all too easy to read.

"And stop fussing about your story. You'll have time. I can tell you're a genius—the words just pour out when you sit down to write. I'll pick up the gown while you're at the hairdresser's and drop it off at your *pensione*. How's that?"

"You're too much, Betsy. I think you're getting off on all these preparations."

"Absolutely. How often do I get to play fairy godmother? Now, let's go sit down somewhere. I need a drink, and I'm sure you're hungry. Then you'll have the rest of the afternoon to go back and work."

"What a manager! I should have found you years ago."

"Come on, come on. My feet hurt!"

"Damn!" Maggie repeated over and over as she stared at the hodge-podge of notes and files spread out before her on the desk. She'd been going over these stupid notes all afternoon, hoping to find some overlooked bit of information that would spark an idea. She racked her brain for a new angle for her second installment, something that would open up new possibilities for her. Now that the priest had proved a dead end, she was going to have to pull some other rabbit out of her journalistic hat.

But the more she mulled over her notes, the more evident the truth became. She had blown her wad, used all her information, and now she was up against a blank wall. Sure, she could rewrite stuff that she'd already used in the first installment, but Jennings would slash that to death, maybe even pull her off the assignment. Her only alternative was to use up a lot of shoe-leather going from orphanage to orphanage, hoping to uncover something good, somewhere.

What bothered her most was poor old Father Virgilio. She had hoped so much that he would provide her with a wealth of information, and all she'd gotten was a half-page of unconnected words and phrases. Oh, the stories he might have told if he hadn't been so old and befuddled. Feeling awful for thinking that way about a gentle, elderly person—something she herself would undoubtedly become some day—Maggie sighed. She imagined the things he had done in his long life. Did we all forget after a while? Her grandmother, as she recalled, had had an extraordinary long-term memory up to the ripe old age of ninety. She loved recounting her tales about churning butter on her father's Danbury farm and remembering the day they had their first telephone installed—the first in the neighborhood. But this amazing woman could not for the life of her recall what she'd had for breakfast or where Maggie worked. Father Virgilio evidently had the same sad mental lapses.

Unfortunately, she had already mentioned the padre, actually given him a big build-up at the end of her first article. Now she had only the stories Angelo D'Allesio had told her about Father Virgilio, and they really weren't sufficient for a whole new piece.

The solution to her dilemma was obvious. Find an innocent for an interview. But the solution was hardly as simple as it was obvious. The nuns and priests she had talked to in New York and Rome made it clear that the Catholic Church wasn't exactly eager to dig up old bones. The orphanages were in the business of protecting their wards, both present and former, not exposing them. Hospitals never give out that kind of information, she knew that from a friend of her father's who was a hospital administrator in Stamford. Then there were the government agencies—ha! Think of the bureaucratic runaround they'd give her! The situation was painfully frustrating.

But, at the moment, the only option she could think of that she hadn't yet tried were the municipal records offices. If they would show her anything—and that was a big *if*—she would have to pore over volumes and volumes of birth certificates, all of them in Italian, looking for some indication of absent or unknown fathers. And that was just the beginning. Then she would have to locate the person, tracing thirty-year-old addresses from one residence to another, hoping that the fragile chain of connections wouldn't break before she found her innocent.

This prospect of the search was bad enough, but there was also the time factor. The next issue would be put to bed on January 15th, so she had a little over three weeks to file her story. Not a lot of time for the amount of research ahead of her.

And on top of it all, her period was slowing her brain down. The discomfort was constant, just annoying enough to keep her from coming up with any brilliant notions about her work.

With one hand holding her chin, the other clutching her gut, Maggie closed her eyes, unable to read another word. But just as she was about to forget her immediate problems and let it all drift, there was a knock at the door.

"Who is it?" Her voice was weary and a bit annoyed.

"Me—Alex." He sounded sharp and eager.

Oh, hell, she thought, this was no time to entertain. She did want to see him, but she wasn't sure whether she wanted him to see her in such a state. Oh, well. . . .

"Come on in," she called out, "it's open."

Alex walked in, and to her amazement, he was all dressed up, looking gorgeous. He had on a crisp white shirt and a burnt-orange silk tie under a brown Harris tweed sportcoat, with camel wool slacks. His trenchcoat was slung over his shoulder, suspended by one finger, and he reminded her of the lovely, sexy photos that Frank Sinatra put on his albums in the fifties. "Hi, what's up?"

Too bad she was so down when he was so chipper. "Oh, nothing," she said with a small sigh.

"Uh-oh, whatsa matter?"

"Dead ends, Alex. I'm at the end of my rope with this story."

"Oh, that. Anything I can do?"

"Sure. Just find me a real, live, grown-up war baby to interview."

"Offhand, I don't know any. But maybe a candlelight dinner and a bottle of Soave will give you some new wrinkles."

"I don't know about that. I'm—what is it guys say in the locker room?—on the rag?"

"Would you rather I disappear?"

"No, no. It's just that right now it's only one more thing to screw me up."

"I think I know the feeling—about the story, that is. Sometimes a little diversion helps me put a new perspective on an article when I've been looking at it too long. Want to give it a try?"

"I dunno. . . ."

"*Tortellini* in chicken broth, veal *piccata*, *zabaglione*, *cappucinno*. . . ."

"You monster." she grinned. "You know me like a book. This is cruel and unusual punishment."

"But it works, doesn't it?" He drew closer to her and cupped his hands around her face, nuzzling her ear.

"Yeah, yeah, yeah." She threw her arms around his neck. "Ve alzo haf vays to deal mit you, mine friend." She pulled him down to her and planted a firm kiss on his mouth.

"Maybe we shouldn't eat just yet," he said, dropping his jacket.

"Sit tight, Kimosabe. I'll be right back." She ran down the hall to the bathroom, and when she came back, Alex was already undressing. He stopped and turned to face her, another warm smile spreading over his face. As she reached out for him, another cramp attacked her, making her wince.

She went to the bed and plopped herself down on the coverlet, slightly breathless. She felt cranky and crampy and just a little apprehensive about Alex and his possible reactions. Some men had some weird notions about menstruating women.

He sat beside her on the bed, then lay back against the pillows and started stroking her back. "Why don't you make yourself comfortable," he said gently. "Then we can stay here and. . . ."

"Alex," she laughed nervously, pulling away.

"Hey, come on," he said huskily.

She was quiet, just lying there, looking up at him. He leaned forward and kissed her long and lovingly, telling her it was all right. She turned her body to make it more accessible to him, and moved her hands along his back, tugging at his shirt, releasing it from his pants, sliding her hands down his back to his buttocks. She touched him all over, and then held him close while she brushed against his mouth with her own. His hands moved around her, undid the zipper of her jeans, pushed, tugged, lifted, moved away until she was pressed against him again with only her thin bikini panties between their bodies. She drew her top and bra over her head in one quick gesture. They knew each other well enough now to take time with their caresses. She moaned as he slowly ran his mouth down the curve of her slender neck and covered her nipple with his lips, sucking until it was hard.

She reached for him and their hands moved over each other's bodies until she could stand it no longer. She brought him slowly inside her, her legs encircling him, and their bodies rocked together as one. He drew out of her again, tensing and lifting himself over her, teasing her until she was desperate for the feeling of him inside her. She pulled him forward and drew him back, holding him tightly with her muscles. They both increased their movements then, she urging him without words to do the things that pleased her most, until finally, with a sigh, he fell against her.

Afterwards they slept, linked in spoon position, and when she woke some time later, she looked over at the clock and saw that it read 9:45. She slid her hands down the length of his hard body and wondered how flesh could impart such rapture, making two human beings one. He stirred and smiled, then hugged her sleepily.

She must have dozed because she felt herself come to with a jolt, the sensation of seepage between her legs palpable and not a little embarrassing.

"Hey," she whispered in Alex's ear, "don't go away." She threw on her bathrobe and, going over to her bag, she reached in and palmed a tampon. She dashed out of the room, heading back to the bathroom.

Alex yawned and swung his legs over the side of the bed, feeling lazy and happy. He looked around the room and glanced at the pile of clothes by the side of the bed, then got up and wandered over to the desk. A writer's room, he noted approvingly. There were bits of paper with notes almost everywhere he looked—the place had a sense of comfortable clutter to it. He stood and surveyed the landscape of files and notebooks and was about to go back to bed when his curiosity got the better of him.

He stood behind the desk chair and browsed over the papers in immediate view. As he had suspected, the names, places, numbers and phrases meant little to him. Every reporter develops his own code of shorthand and abbreviation, and Maggie was no different. But just as he was about to turn away, something caught his eye in one of the open notebooks.

"Lt. Col. Tony Russo?!" stood out in that jumbled army of words like a neon sign. With knit brow and set jaw, Alex picked up the book and quickly scanned the page and the one before it. Nothing else held any particular significance for him. He flipped through the notebook, reading pages at random, looking for a repetition of the name, or some explanation.

Just then the door slammed, and he whirled around to see Maggie staring at him.

"Alex! . . . What the hell are you doing?"

"Uh . . . I was . . . just curious."

"Curious? About what? I don't like anybody going through my notes—I don't know how you feel about yours."

"I wasn't exactly 'going through' them. It's just . . . well, you know."

"No, I don't know. Alex, I'm really angry. You don't even want to *talk* about your story."

"That's different. I can't talk."

"Oh, for you it's okay to clam up, but my notes are the public library." Her voice became shrill. "You sure you're not still pissed off about this being your idea for the innocents feature?"

"Don't jump to conclusions, will you? If you're accusing me of trying to sabotage you, it just isn't true. I was reading your notes because I care about you. I don't want you to blow your first big assignment. Honestly. You said you were having a hard time; I thought maybe if I took a look, I could give you some suggestions. That's the plain truth. What are you biting off my head for?"

Maggie was so angry she could only stand there glaring at him. She felt violated, and his excuse sounded pretty lame to her.

"Look, Maggie, I do care about you. But if you're going to doubt and mistrust me, I think we'd better call it quits right now."

"How can I trust you?" The calmness in her voice surprised even her. "I'm supposed to let you in on everything, and you remain the big enigma. You tell me what I'm supposed to think."

Alex exhaled, long and loud. "I don't know," he said under his breath.

There was a long, uncomfortable silence between them, as Alex stared at the floor, and Maggie refused to take her eyes from his face.

"Maybe I ought to go home," he said at last. "I was wrong to read your notes. I admit that. You have every right to be mad. I . . . I . . . I'll see you. . . ."

"No, don't," Maggie sighed, holding his arm as he tried to slip by her. "You admitted it—that's the most important thing. I guess we both have to get more out in the open, huh? Anyhow, you keep telling me I'm jumping to conclusions all the time. And maybe sometimes I'm not, but sometimes I am. It seems to me, with someone you care for, you have to give him the benefit of the doubt once in a while. Just don't do that any more, okay? It really makes me angry." She shrugged out of her robe and stood before him naked.

"Now," she went on, "if you think I'm hungry ordinarily, you should see me eat after I make love!"

"I have, remember?"

"Oh, that was nothing. This time I'm serious."

The two of them threw on their clothes hastily, and started for the restaurant.

"Yeah, but you're a woman—and a pal—that's different. So, shall we go now? I think the cramps are on a coffee break."

"Okay," Betsy laughed. *"Andiamo."*

After several hours of wandering through the exclusive boutiques on the Via Condotti, Maggie was tired, disgusted and discouraged.

"God, the hoity-toity women in these shops must think you're made of money. I could buy a car for what some of those gowns cost."

"Well, Maggie, the *contessa's* ball is a big deal. You really do have to have something special for it. That's why I figured we'd start here." Betsy frowned, feeling that she was failing Maggie in this shopping venture.

"Why do those women have to act so high and mighty? They try to make you feel like an insect. I'm used to stores where you just flip through the racks and try on what looks good. This showroom model exhibition is so embarrassing— those poor, emaciated girls waltzing around in front of us like they were auditioning for a chorus line. It's degrading—why would a woman do that for a living? And the saleswomen are worse. As if they bought little items like these every day!"

"Oh, don't let them bother you. They're all like that. They're probably all as poor as church mice themselves. Even in these fancy boutiques, the wages are terrible."

"Frankly, that doesn't make me any more sympathetic to them."

"Wait a minute! I just thought of something. Laura Ord is always telling me about the great bargains she gets on the Via Gregoriana. Come on, it's not far from here."

Betsy rushed down Via Condotti and turned the corner. A few blocks down, Via Gregoriana ran off Via Sistina. The street was lined with small boutiques and shops with dressmaker's dummies lining the windows. The decor was less spectacular and the shoppers less fashionable, but the street seemed like the kind of place where a bargain might be found.

The first two boutiques they passed had very little that Maggie felt comfortable with. She disliked beaded, clingy gowns, and she refused to try on what she told Betsy was a long disco-queen outfit, shiny and loud. Nor would she consider a fishtail skirt with a glittering bolero.

ROMAN CANDLES

"I'd feel like a stupid mermaid," she growled, fast losing hope she'd find something in time. She couldn't waste precious days on this frivolity.

"I don't know, Alex might like it." Betsy grinned. "Men get off on mermaids, you know."

"I don't think we need props," Maggie told her.

"That good, huh?"

"Better." Maggie grinned.

At another boutique, she was shown a metallic red and gold one-shoulder sheath that reminded her of Tokyo Rose and her long cigarette holders. She and Betsy were giggling when they walked out. Two doors down, they saw what looked like a tiny dressmaker's shop, no bigger than a small living room.

"Let's try this place," Betsy suggested, pushing open the door.

A middle-aged woman with soft brown hair curling about her face greeted them. She was alone in the shop. There were a few dresses, but no gowns on display.

"Mia amica ha bisogno di una veste di sera," Betsy said, then to Maggie, *sotto voce,* she added, "she's probably just a dressmaker."

The woman smiled and spoke in English. "Yes, that is correct." Betsy and Maggie looked embarrassed, but she smiled again and continued, "You are looking for a gown?"

"Yes, but not to have one made—there isn't time. It's for a very special occasion."

"I see. Was there something in particular you were looking for? I perhaps can help you. I have a gown or two that are not being taken for personal reasons. These I sell—with alterations, of course."

"Actually, it has to be quite formal, stunning, actually," Maggie explained. "I . . . it must be . . . oh, how do you say this? A knockout." Maggie was hesitant to say exactly what the occasion was, thinking that a "ball" sounded a little too fairy tale-ish.

"Will you wait?" The woman indicated two straight-backed, painted chairs.

They sat, Betsy whispering to Maggie that maybe they had just stumbled on the right place.

The woman, who introduced herself as Signora Pellini,

returned shortly with an incredible black velvet gown. It had a romantic dropped waist with gently swirling skirt that reminded Maggie of an elongated tutu. There was a soft organza overlay that made the black velvet look mysterious—as if it were covered with mist—and there were shining black beads scattered through the gauzy covering. White chiffon ruching framed the rounded neckline like a stiffened Harlequin ruff, and the white was repeated at the wrists of the long sleeves. It seemed simple in its elegance—very clean lines and perfect styling that would never go out of date.

"It is not finish, eh?" Signora Pellini indicated the hem, which was still undone. "And here," she pulled at the waist, "it is to be fitted. Do you like it?"

"It's lovely," Maggie said, wondering what it could possibly cost. "And it's for sale?"

"*Sì*. The lady who orders it has gone away. Now I must sell."

"May my friend try it on?" Betsy interjected before Maggie could say anything.

"*Sì, certo*. In here." The woman led the way to the back. A small dressing room was tucked away next to a long table on which Signora Pellini did her sewing. There were two sewing machines, and a young girl, evidently the signora's daughter from her looks, sat at one of them. Signora Pellini went with Maggie to help her put on the gown. Even without the necessary alterations, Maggie could see that it was stunning. The velvet against her skin clung and swirled, and her face above the high ruching looked like that of a Degas model.

She walked out to the front to show Betsy, who gasped in delight.

"Fantastic! It's you!"

"It is magnificent." Maggie stared at her image in the long mirror. Would Alex like her in it? She was afraid to ask what it cost and was relieved when Betsy blurted out the question that stuck in her throat.

"*Quanto?*"

The woman said five hundred dollars, and Maggie groaned out loud. Impossible. She was on a pretty tight budget, and she knew the magazine would not wire her extra money—certainly not for a personal expense.

"Too costly for me," she said reluctantly.

ROMAN CANDLES

"You no like the dress?" the woman asked.

"*Sì*. I love it, but I can't really afford it. Do you have anything else?"

The *signora* shook her head. "Not another gown. I have just a suit . . ."

"No. But thanks for letting me try it on . . ." Maggie walked back to the dressing room. She hated taking it off and ran the fabric lovingly through her fingers. She was tired of running around looking for the right gown, and she didn't have time to waste on shopping. She took off the gown and handed it reluctantly to the *signora*. She knew that whatever else she found would look chintzy after this gown. And she'd feel chintzy in it, that was the worst part of it. She half-wished she'd never seen this one.

She came out of the dressing room adjusting her bag on her shoulder. The *signora's* daughter turned and smiled at her.

"*È meravigliosa*," she said admiringly.

"Thanks, I know it's a marvelous dress, but it's too expensive for me."

The girl then spoke to her mother in rapid Italian. Maggie couldn't begin to follow their conversation, and she didn't try. She went out to the front room and sighed at Betsy.

"Guess we better move on."

"It's a shame, Maggie. That dress is you."

Just then, the *signora* called out to them and came rushing back into the room. "Would you be willing to pay three hundred and fifty American money?" she asked. She didn't exactly seem happy, and appeared to be giving in in spite of herself.

Maggie hesitated.

"Say yes," Betsy whispered. "You won't do any better."

The *signora* nodded toward the back. "My daughter wishes you to have the gown. Three hundred dollars. I can do no more than that."

"Sold!" Betsy cried out before Maggie could protest.

Maggie looked at Betsy, then at the gown in Signora Pellini's arms. "Sold," she finally confirmed with a smile of joy and relief.

"What a coup, kiddo! You did better than I ever expected," Betsy declared outside the shop after Maggie had been fitted.

"Yup, you're right. I just wish I didn't feel so guilty spending time shopping. I've been here a week and none of my leads have paid off. And now I've got to go find evening slippers and a bag. Who thought I'd be going to a ball when I packed for this trip?"

"Calm down. I have some black patent sandals that might do. Are you a six and a half B?"

"No, seven."

"Try them anyway. I bet they'll fit, they're just lots of straps that wind around your toes and ankles. And I've got a black clutch, not velvet, but moire. It'll do. What else?"

"You're a livesaver. Thanks."

"Now, what about your hair? You just going to wash and blow-dry like you're going to the office?"

"Why not?"

"Don't be ridiculous. They won't let you in unless you have some kind of do. And that gown deserves great hair. I know a guy at the Excelsior. I'll make an appointment for you for tomorrow afternoon. I'll call you later to tell you what time."

"Okay—I guess. How much will that cost?"

"Plenty. But you can't go back to New York without a hair-styling from Rome!"

"Hmm." Maggie wore that worried look that was all too easy to read.

"And stop fussing about your story. You'll have time. I can tell you're a genius—the words just pour out when you sit down to write. I'll pick up the gown while you're at the hairdresser's and drop it off at your *pensione*. How's that?"

"You're too much, Betsy. I think you're getting off on all these preparations."

"Absolutely. How often do I get to play fairy godmother? Now, let's go sit down somewhere. I need a drink, and I'm sure you're hungry. Then you'll have the rest of the afternoon to go back and work."

"What a manager! I should have found you years ago."

"Come on, come on. My feet hurt!"

"Damn!" Maggie repeated over and over as she stared at the hodge-podge of notes and files spread out before her on the desk. She'd been going over these stupid notes all afternoon, hoping to find some overlooked bit of information that would spark an idea. She racked her brain for a new angle for her second installment, something that would open up new possibilities for her. Now that the priest had proved a dead end, she was going to have to pull some other rabbit out of her journalistic hat.

But the more she mulled over her notes, the more evident the truth became. She had blown her wad, used all her information, and now she was up against a blank wall. Sure, she could rewrite stuff that she'd already used in the first installment, but Jennings would slash that to death, maybe even pull her off the assignment. Her only alternative was to use up a lot of shoe-leather going from orphanage to orphanage, hoping to uncover something good, somewhere.

What bothered her most was poor old Father Virgilio. She had hoped so much that he would provide her with a wealth of information, and all she'd gotten was a half-page of unconnected words and phrases. Oh, the stories he might have told if he hadn't been so old and befuddled. Feeling awful for thinking that way about a gentle, elderly person—something she herself would undoubtedly become some day—Maggie sighed. She imagined the things he had done in his long life. Did we all forget after a while? Her grandmother, as she recalled, had had an extraordinary long-term memory up to the ripe old age of ninety. She loved recounting her tales about churning butter on her father's Danbury farm and remembering the day they had their first telephone installed—the first in the neighborhood. But this amazing woman could not for the life of her recall what she'd had for breakfast or where Maggie worked. Father Virgilio evidently had the same sad mental lapses.

Unfortunately, she had already mentioned the padre, actually given him a big build-up at the end of her first article. Now she had only the stories Angelo D'Allesio had told her about Father Virgilio, and they really weren't sufficient for a whole new piece.

The solution to her dilemma was obvious. Find an innocent for an interview. But the solution was hardly as simple as it was obvious. The nuns and priests she had talked to in New York and Rome made it clear that the Catholic Church wasn't exactly eager to dig up old bones. The orphanages were in the business of protecting their wards, both present and former, not exposing them. Hospitals never give out that kind of information, she knew that from a friend of her father's who was a hospital administrator in Stamford. Then there were the government agencies—ha! Think of the bureaucratic runaround they'd give her! The situation was painfully frustrating.

But, at the moment, the only option she could think of that she hadn't yet tried were the municipal records offices. If they would show her anything—and that was a big *if*—she would have to pore over volumes and volumes of birth certificates, all of them in Italian, looking for some indication of absent or unknown fathers. And that was just the beginning. Then she would have to locate the person, tracing thirty-year-old addresses from one residence to another, hoping that the fragile chain of connections wouldn't break before she found her innocent.

This prospect of the search was bad enough, but there was also the time factor. The next issue would be put to bed on January 15th, so she had a little over three weeks to file her story. Not a lot of time for the amount of research ahead of her.

And on top of it all, her period was slowing her brain down. The discomfort was constant, just annoying enough to keep her from coming up with any brilliant notions about her work.

With one hand holding her chin, the other clutching her gut, Maggie closed her eyes, unable to read another word. But just as she was about to forget her immediate problems and let it all drift, there was a knock at the door.

"Who is it?" Her voice was weary and a bit annoyed.

"Me—Alex." He sounded sharp and eager.

Oh, hell, she thought, this was no time to entertain. She did want to see him, but she wasn't sure whether she wanted him to see her in such a state. Oh, well. . . .

"Come on in," she called out, "it's open."

Alex walked in, and to her amazement, he was all dressed up, looking gorgeous. He had on a crisp white shirt and a burnt-orange silk tie under a brown Harris tweed sportcoat, with camel wool slacks. His trenchcoat was slung over his shoulder, suspended by one finger, and he reminded her of the lovely, sexy photos that Frank Sinatra put on his albums in the fifties. "Hi, what's up?"

Too bad she was so down when he was so chipper. "Oh, nothing," she said with a small sigh.

"Uh-oh, whatsa matter?"

"Dead ends, Alex. I'm at the end of my rope with this story."

"Oh, that. Anything I can do?"

"Sure. Just find me a real, live, grown-up war baby to interview."

"Offhand, I don't know any. But maybe a candlelight dinner and a bottle of Soave will give you some new wrinkles."

"I don't know about that. I'm—what is it guys say in the locker room?—on the rag?"

"Would you rather I disappear?"

"No, no. It's just that right now it's only one more thing to screw me up."

"I think I know the feeling—about the story, that is. Sometimes a little diversion helps me put a new perspective on an article when I've been looking at it too long. Want to give it a try?"

"I dunno...."

"*Tortellini* in chicken broth, veal *piccata*, *zabaglione*, *cappucinno*...."

"You monster." she grinned. "You know me like a book. This is cruel and unusual punishment."

"But it works, doesn't it?" He drew closer to her and cupped his hands around her face, nuzzling her ear.

"Yeah, yeah, yeah." She threw her arms around his neck. "Ve alzo haf vays to deal mit you, mine friend." She pulled him down to her and planted a firm kiss on his mouth.

"Maybe we shouldn't eat just yet," he said, dropping his jacket.

"Sit tight, Kimosabe. I'll be right back." She ran down the hall to the bathroom, and when she came back, Alex was already undressing. He stopped and turned to face her, another warm smile spreading over his face. As she reached out for him, another cramp attacked her, making her wince.

She went to the bed and plopped herself down on the coverlet, slightly breathless. She felt cranky and crampy and just a little apprehensive about Alex and his possible reactions. Some men had some weird notions about menstruating women.

He sat beside her on the bed, then lay back against the pillows and started stroking her back. "Why don't you make yourself comfortable," he said gently. "Then we can stay here and. . . ."

"Alex," she laughed nervously, pulling away.

"Hey, come on," he said huskily.

She was quiet, just lying there, looking up at him. He leaned forward and kissed her long and lovingly, telling her it was all right. She turned her body to make it more accessible to him, and moved her hands along his back, tugging at his shirt, releasing it from his pants, sliding her hands down his back to his buttocks. She touched him all over, and then held him close while she brushed against his mouth with her own. His hands moved around her, undid the zipper of her jeans, pushed, tugged, lifted, moved away until she was pressed against him again with only her thin bikini panties between their bodies. She drew her top and bra over her head in one quick gesture. They knew each other well enough now to take time with their caresses. She moaned as he slowly ran his mouth down the curve of her slender neck and covered her nipple with his lips, sucking until it was hard.

She reached for him and their hands moved over each other's bodies until she could stand it no longer. She brought him slowly inside her, her legs encircling him, and their bodies rocked together as one. He drew out of her again, tensing and lifting himself over her, teasing her until she was desperate for the feeling of him inside her. She pulled him forward and drew him back, holding him tightly with her muscles. They both increased their movements then, she urging him without words to do the things that pleased her most, until finally, with a sigh, he fell against her.

Afterwards they slept, linked in spoon position, and when she woke some time later, she looked over at the clock and saw that it read 9:45. She slid her hands down the length of his hard body and wondered how flesh could impart such rapture, making two human beings one. He stirred and smiled, then hugged her sleepily.

She must have dozed because she felt herself come to with a jolt, the sensation of seepage between her legs palpable and not a little embarrassing.

"Hey," she whispered in Alex's ear, "don't go away." She threw on her bathrobe and, going over to her bag, she reached in and palmed a tampon. She dashed out of the room, heading back to the bathroom.

ROMAN CANDLES

Alex yawned and swung his legs over the side of the bed, feeling lazy and happy. He looked around the room and glanced at the pile of clothes by the side of the bed, then got up and wandered over to the desk. A writer's room, he noted approvingly. There were bits of paper with notes almost everywhere he looked—the place had a sense of comfortable clutter to it. He stood and surveyed the landscape of files and notebooks and was about to go back to bed when his curiosity got the better of him.

He stood behind the desk chair and browsed over the papers in immediate view. As he had suspected, the names, places, numbers and phrases meant little to him. Every reporter develops his own code of shorthand and abbreviation, and Maggie was no different. But just as he was about to turn away, something caught his eye in one of the open notebooks.

"Lt. Col. Tony Russo?!" stood out in that jumbled army of words like a neon sign. With knit brow and set jaw, Alex picked up the book and quickly scanned the page and the one before it. Nothing else held any particular significance for him. He flipped through the notebook, reading pages at random, looking for a repetition of the name, or some explanation.

Just then the door slammed, and he whirled around to see Maggie staring at him.

"Alex! . . . What the hell are you doing?"

"Uh . . . I was . . . just curious."

"Curious? About what? I don't like anybody going through my notes—I don't know how you feel about yours."

"I wasn't exactly 'going through' them. It's just . . . well, you know."

"No, I don't know. Alex, I'm really angry. You don't even want to *talk* about your story."

"That's different. I can't talk."

"Oh, for you it's okay to clam up, but my notes are the public library." Her voice became shrill. "You sure you're not still pissed off about this being your idea for the innocents feature?"

"Don't jump to conclusions, will you? If you're accusing me of trying to sabotage you, it just isn't true. I was reading your notes because I care about you. I don't want you to blow your first big assignment. Honestly. You said you were having

178

a hard time; I thought maybe if I took a look, I could give you some suggestions. That's the plain truth. What are you biting off my head for?"

Maggie was so angry she could only stand there glaring at him. She felt violated, and his excuse sounded pretty lame to her.

"Look, Maggie, I do care about you. But if you're going to doubt and mistrust me, I think we'd better call it quits right now."

"How can I trust you?" The calmness in her voice surprised even her. "I'm supposed to let you in on everything, and you remain the big enigma. You tell me what I'm supposed to think."

Alex exhaled, long and loud. "I don't know," he said under his breath.

There was a long, uncomfortable silence between them, as Alex stared at the floor, and Maggie refused to take her eyes from his face.

"Maybe I ought to go home," he said at last. "I was wrong to read your notes. I admit that. You have every right to be mad. I . . . I . . . I'll see you. . . ."

"No, don't," Maggie sighed, holding his arm as he tried to slip by her. "You admitted it—that's the most important thing. I guess we both have to get more out in the open, huh? Anyhow, you keep telling me I'm jumping to conclusions all the time. And maybe sometimes I'm not, but sometimes I am. It seems to me, with someone you care for, you have to give him the benefit of the doubt once in a while. Just don't do that any more, okay? It really makes me angry." She shrugged out of her robe and stood before him naked.

"Now," she went on, "if you think I'm hungry ordinarily, you should see me eat after I make love!"

"I have, remember?"

"Oh, that was nothing. This time I'm serious."

The two of them threw on their clothes hastily, and started for the restaurant.

Chapter 12

Alex stood in the hallway, waiting for Maggie to finish in the bathroom. His trenchcoat was slung over his shoulder again, and his shirt collar was open, his tie hanging out of his jacket pocket.

Maggie emerged from the bathroom dressed for the day. She had put on the first things she pulled out of the closet—her gray wool pleated skirt and her red turtleneck, which she'd dressed up a bit with a thin, black snakeskin belt. She gave Alex an exaggerated frown when she saw him ready to leave. "You going so soon?"

"Duty calls. Places to go, people to meet—you know the story."

"Yeah, I know." She threw her arms around him and nibbled on his lower lip seductively. "Sure you don't want to stick around just for coffee?" she offered.

"I wish I could," he moaned, "but if you keep tempting me, Jennings is going to can the two of us."

"You're right . . . dammit!"

"Where's the cub reporter off to today?" he chided her.

"Cub reporter? How'd you like to get bit by this cub reporter?" She lunged at him, baring her teeth and growling.

"All right, all right, I take it back." He cowered in jest. "Is that how you get your interviews?"

"I wish it were that easy." She sighed, thinking of the dubious work that lay ahead of her.

"Listen," he gripped her shoulders reassuringly, "I told you, don't despair. Just keep plugging and keep an open mind for a new angle. Sometimes you find gold where you'd never expect it."

"Yes, you're right. But the prospects of going through the phone directory for orphanages, then finding them and seeing someone who doesn't really want to talk to me in the first place. And the government offices—I don't even want to think about them!"

"I know, it's tough, but it's the only way."

"What about you? Where are you off to?"

Alex pursed his lips and gave her a look that meant he wished she wouldn't ask. "Maggie. . . ."

"I know, I know," she answered for him. "Hush-hush, very dangerous, terrorist killers, what I don't know won't hurt me . . . Say no more, I don't want to find out." She held up her hands as if to stop her own curiosity, but the wry grin did not fade from her face.

"Good." He kissed her deeply, drawing his hands away from her with great reluctance. "Take it easy," he said, descending the steps to the lobby, "something'll come up."

"Yeah. . . ." She sounded unconvinced.

She closed the door behind him and went to her desk, surveying the piles of notes, wondering where to start. She propped her foot up on the chair and leaned on her knee as she flipped over pages. The notebook that she had caught Alex examining was open on top of everything. She thumbed through it until she came to the page where she had scrawled Father Virgilio's disjointed words.

"Conte e contessa . . . Convento di S. Gabriele . . . Lt. Col. Tony Russo."

"Wait a minute!" she said aloud. The Convent of St. Gabriel, why not! If it was in Rome, she would start there. The padre had mentioned it, so maybe they housed innocents too. It was a shot in the dark, but . . . but where was this place? The padre lived in Gaeta—and who knew where else he'd gone during the war? There could be fifty convents with that name.

Maggie grabbed her jacket and slid the notebook into her pocketbook. If the convent wasn't too far away, she'd have plenty of time to interview someone and then make it to the Excelsior for her appointment with Betsy's hairdresser at three.

She ran down to the lobby and practically jumped on Ugo. "Ugo," she babbled at him. "I'm looking for a convent called San Gabriel. How can I go about finding it? Do you have a phone book or something?"

Without a word, he reached under his desk and pulled out the telephone directory and started to look up convents.

"Ha," Ugo declared, his ever-present cigarette flicking ashes right and left as he spoke. He turned the book around so Maggie could see the entry next to his finger.

S. Gabriele, Convento—1680 Via Aurelia: 977-1923.

Maggie quickly scribbled the address in her notebook. "Where is the Via Aurelia, Ugo? What's it near?" She could not supress her mounting excitement.

"Behind the Vatican," Ugo muttered, catching her frantic behavior.

"Thanks, Ugo, *grazie*," she shouted back to him as she ran from the *pensione* for the nearest taxi stand.

The sisters of the convent were not exactly eager to accommodate Maggie's request for an interview. After a thin, scared-looking nun refused to understand Maggie's attempts at communication in Italian, an older, burly nun appeared and sternly informed Maggie that only the mother superior could speak for the convent and that she was busy. Maggie was insistent and explained that she would wait until the mother superior was available. So she waited, sitting on a battered green vinyl couch in the mother superior's office.

Odd to sit in a convent after a night of passion in bed with a man, she thought. It made her vaguely uncomfortable, as if her sexual activities of the previous evening somehow alienated her further from these stern, silent women.

After forty-five uneasy minutes, the mother superior rushed into her office, glaring at Maggie, not even extending a greeting or an apology for the delay.

"Yes? What is it, please?" she barked in a rapid, nasal voice. She looked exactly like Charles Laughton in a habit.

"I'd like to ask you a few questions about war babies, the children of American soldiers from World War—"

"Oh, you *giornalisti!* I know nothing about such children.

Yes, of course, it is a great shame, but there were never any orphans here. Never. I told that other *giornalista* this morning, I know nothing of the innocents, nothing. Now please, signorina, I am very, very busy. I cannot waste any more time with you. Please, can you show yourself out?" The mother superior whisked out of the room before Maggie could even thank her for her trouble.

But it wasn't the mother superior's manners that bothered her right now. It was something she had said, the reference to the other *giornalista* who had come by asking about the innocents that same morning. Tears of anger and betrayal welled in her eyes as she fought back the suspicion that she desperately did not want to believe. Alex. Alex was trying to scoop her. Or sabotage her.

As she sat there dumbfounded, the evidence against Alex began to mount in her mind. Why had the nun been so nervous and belligerent? Had she been asked—or paid—not to talk? No, a nun wouldn't take a bribe, would she? But why did she answer questions that Maggie didn't even pose? She hadn't gotten far enough to ask whether war babies had ever been sheltered at this convent, yet the nun was very quick to deny that innocents were ever there. As a matter of fact, Maggie suddenly realized, the nun had used Maggie's own term—the innocents—before Maggie could open her mouth. No, not her term. Alex's term.

"That double-dealing, sneaky . . . damn him!" She still did not want to believe the possibility of what he might have done. She was simply unable to connect such a despicable, underhanded act with the tender individual she had just shared her bed with.

Why? Why would he do it? That question hounded her as she walked down the main corridor of the convent. He couldn't scoop her story. Her first installment had already gone to press, and there was no way Jennings would ever switch writers in the middle of a series. Not if she'd done her work properly. Anyway, Alex had said he wanted to help her. He had made love to her. It just didn't make any sense, none at all. What did he have to gain from doing this?

Her first impulse was to go to him, ask him, confront him and convince herself that her fears were unfounded. But then she recalled that she would have no way to go about finding him because he always refused to tell her about his "highly dangerous" work. It seemed like a marvelously convenient excuse now.

As pale as a ghost, Maggie wandered toward the front door of the convent, devastated and unsure where she should turn next.

"*Signorina?* Are you all right?" A gentle voice came out of the shadows.

"What?" Maggie was disoriented, lost in a world of her own ruminations.

"You are not well, *signorina?* Your face, so white." A young nun appeared in the vestibule. She took Maggie's hand and led her to a wooden bench, and then sat beside her. "Please, *signorina,* tell me what troubles you." The nun had a plain but endearing face with huge brown eyes that spoke of her compassion. Despite Maggie's anger and bitterness, she could not doubt the woman's sincerity.

"Thank you for asking, sister, but I don't think you can help me."

"Perhaps not, but I can see that if you do not tell someone soon, you will burst."

"You are very perceptive, but I'd. . . ." Maggie decided not to tell her about Alex and his betrayal, since she felt that a woman of the veil would not think much of problems involving sexual passion and premarital sex. However, the young woman had been so kind and open, Maggie simply couldn't clam up and refuse her sympathy. Shaking off some of the shock and hurt, she looked at the nun and thought, why not ask her about the innocents? It would temporarily take her mind off Alex, anyway.

"Well, sister, I came to talk to the mother superior. You see, I am a reporter from America. I am researching a story on war babies, specifically the illegitimate children of the American soldiers who were stationed here during World War Two. I wanted to know whether this convent sheltered such children. But your mother superior refused to talk to me."

"Really?" A look of genuine surprise came over the nun's face. She looked down the hall furtively, then stared at her toes, as if considering something.

"What is it, sister?" Maggie noticed the curious expression on the woman's face.

"I should not tell you this, *signorina*. It is only—how you say?—rumor. But I have heard this from many of the older sisters, those who were here during the war." She looked at the floor again in silence.

"Please, sister. You can tell me."

"This is just a story. Probably not true, not true at all." She paused, debating with herself. Finally, she lifted her head, folding her hands on her lap, apparently willing herself into a state of composure. "Long ago, during the war," she began, "an orphan was supposedly adopted from this *convent by a conte* and *contessa* who could not have children of their own. The baby was the child of an American, an army doctor. I do not know what had become of the mother. The American had performed some kind of favor for the *contessa*. In return that favor, she promised to find his lost *bastarda* and adopt the baby as her own. The *conte* and *contessa* found here at the convent—I do not know who brought her here. They were so deeply grateful to have found the child, they named her after the patron of the convent. It is said that she was christened 'Gabriella.'"

Maggie's jaw dropped open. "Who are the . . . ?"

"I must go now," the nun announced abruptly, disappearing down the dark corridor.

Gabriella? Could it be possible? Adopted by the Conte and Contessa Sciarra? Sitting in an enclosed stall at the beauty salon with a pink robe around her and her wet hair stringing about her face, Maggie could not stop herself from considering the complex and amazing possibility. Of course, Gabriella was a very common Italian name—it was more than likely, Maggie thought, that she was just jumping to conclusions. *Boy, you really love jigsaw puzzles,* she told herself. *You happen to know a woman named Gabriella who happens to be the daughter of nobility and suddenly you think you have the whole thing solved.* Of course, it was possible, but not really probable, that Gabriella Sciarra was the illegitimate child of an American army doctor. Lieutenant Colonel Tony Russo, right? The one Father Virgilio had mentioned.

Gabriella, an innocent! It was mind-boggling. She was

certainly about the right age. Maggie was so obsessed with the idea, she didn't even object when the hairdresser's assistant insisted on putting a rinse in her hair.

As she waited for the famous Raffaello, Betsy's hairdresser, Maggie was too preoccupied to worry about what he might do to her hair. Of all the people she could have found for her story, Gabriella was the last one she would want to ask for an interview. Maggie winced just imagining the kind of nastiness the suggestion of an interview about her questionable parentage would unleash.

Surely, Gabriella would not want the world to know that she, of all people, was a *bastarda*. The woman was so caught up in her own sense of propriety, Maggie couldn't fathom what the knowledge of her illegitimacy would do to her. Or did she know? Or was she the right Gabriella? Of course, all her mysterious leads led straight to Gabriella Sciarra—she really could be the one Father Virgilio and the young nun at the convent referred to. Maggie might actually have stumbled over her innocent, but getting her cooperation was another story entirely. It was like an awful twist of plot in a Dickens novel. No, Maggie thought on reconsideration, it was like holding a bamboo fishing pole with a shark on the other end of the line.

Suddenly, Maggie's fretting was interrupted by the entrance of the fellow who had washed her hair and a tall, thin man in skin-tight, milk-white pants and a black silk, western-cut shirt. This had to be Raffaello, she thought. Only hairdressers dress like that. The two men were quarrelling in non-stop Italian, pointing to her head and swishing strands of wet hair one way, then another. Raffaello was volatile and adamant. She managed to pick out a couple of words from his tirade: *miglioramento* and *affascinante*.

"*Per favore,* I do not want to be improved or glamorous," she insisted hotly. "All I want is a shaping, *si*? Blow dry? Nothing fancy. Do you speak English? *Inglese?*"

"*Un po',*" the young man said. Raffaello shouldered his assistant out of the way. "*Assolutamente,*" he informed her.

"All right, good. I do not want an elaborate coiffure—and please! No hairspray! A simple cut, a trim. . . ."

"It is sin to let hair sit on the head like this!" Raffaello picked up a handful of her hair, sifted it through his fingers like wet noodles. "It is *importante* to make the face shine with hair that is . . . *incantesimo*, enchantment, *si?*"

Maggie cringed. "I like to be able to do my own hair," she offered by way of explanation. Already, she was sorry she'd agreed to this. Who cared what her hair looked like anyway? Certainly she wouldn't know anyone at the ball and no one would know her. Just Gabriella—oh God, Gabriella!

"Maybe just take off a little of the length, here and here." She touched the nape of her neck, trying to make the best of the situation.

"You will allow me." Raffaello pushed aside the pesky young assistant and snapped his fingers like a surgeon. *"Fòrbici!"* he ordered. The assistant slapped a pair of scissors into his hand. Maggie wanted to jump up and run away. He caught up a handful of her hair, twisted it, pinned it to one side like a squirrel's tail and then began to snip away great swatches of her hair. He threw the scissors on the counter eventually, snapped his fingers for a brush and began pulling and tugging at the shards left on her head. She looked like a porcupine.

"Signor," she said feebly. "I don't want it cut too short. . . ."

He ignored her. She tried sliding down into the chair, but he hunched over and continued, undaunted. She closed her eyes and endured it. It would surely take her six months to grow back a decent head of hair, but she couldn't stop this madman now. Perhaps she should have gone to Gabriella's guy, after all. Better a full head of hair with clusters of ridiculous curls than this!

"Finito!" Raffaello finally announced. He reached for a hair dryer, aiming it at her head while he wielded the brush with the other hand, tugging, swirling, and pulling at what was left of her hair. *"Bella."* He stepped back to admire his work.

Maggie peered into the mirror. She was genuinely surprised that she did not resemble a fuzzy billiard ball. It was *bella*, indeed. Her hair was a soft aureole surrounding her face, giving her a pixieish look. The top was very short, pushed to one side in a graceful wave, and it tapered down in layers to the back, which still had some length to it. Soft tendrils curled around her cheeks and forehead, which softened the look. The effect was very feminine, but very modern. It was really wonderful—even her eyes looked larger.

"*Sì, bella,*" she murmured happily to Raffaello. "*Grazie.*"

While Raffaello was fussing over Maggie, adding his finishing touches, Betsy went to the seamstress shop, as promised, to pick up Maggie's gown. The mother and daughter proudly displayed the finished product, then wrapped it carefully and pinned it to a padded hanger, finally encasing it in a plastic garment bag. Betsy was genuinely pleased, and was certain Maggie would be too. She had put on her new yellow angora sweater that morning, and had to admit that she looked smashing in it—she was dying to get Maggie's reaction.

She walked the few blocks to Maggie's *pensione,* carrying the gown high, her right arm supporting it in midair.

"*Per* Maggie Reardon," she told Ugo as she walked through the door. He was at the front desk, smoking. He jerked his head up from his newspaper, as disoriented as ever.

"For Maggie Reardon," Betsy repeated. "Will you take it to her room, please? It must not get wrinkled," she declared sternly.

"*Sì, sì.* Right now." He turned and found the right key on the board, then walked around the desk and delicately took the gown from Betsy, handling it like a feeble old relative.

She waited until he disappeared into the elevator before she turned to leave.

As she descended the front steps, she was not aware of the two men standing together across the street. Snuffing out their cigarettes, they crossed over to her side and began to follow her slowly. One man was short and wore sunglasses; the other was tall for an Italian. They both wore long, dark coats and caps pulled down over their foreheads. They both had small mustaches.

As Betsy turned the corner, heading back to the embassy, the two men trotted on to catch up with her. The street was narrow and deserted, but Betsy thought nothing of it until she heard the sound of running feet behind her. Before she could even turn around, the two men had her. They grabbed her roughly by the arms, stuffed a rag in her mouth and shoved her into a nearby alley. The tall man stood behind her, pinning her arms together in his massive hands. The short man quickly looked up and down the alley, then drew a pistol from his coat pocket. He grabbed the front of her sweater, stretching it out in front of her and pulling it tight over the muzzle. He ground the knuckles of his gun hand into her left breast, then growled to her with clenched teeth in heavily accented English, "Remember this, *signorina*, remember." Three shots were fired in rapid succession, the kickback thundering through her chest, the smell of gunpowder and smoldering wool filling her nostrils. Her throat constricted and she fell to the ground in a heap, as the short man thrust the hot pistol back into his pocket and the tall man whipped the rag from her mouth and dropped her. Betsy did not hear their footsteps racing down the alleyway: she was out cold.

Maggie returned to her *pensione* that evening and was pleased to hear that Ugo had already placed the gown in her room. When she went inside, it was hanging over the door of the wardrobe, and she carefully unzipped the plastic case and lifted the layers of wrapping. Just as she remembered it, only more beautiful. Funny, she'd never had a prom dress—her circle of friends in high school thought it was absurd to spend so much money on a dance. Instead, they'd pooled their resources and mailed a check to an organization that provided medicine, food and clothing for the sick and starving of the Vietnam war. But, despite her serious interests, she allowed herself the fantasy that there might be some evening, sometime in her life, when she'd have the chance to dress up. *Well, kid, this is it,* she thought. Carefully, she unzipped the dress and placed it on the bed. Stripping down to her underwear, she slipped on the crinoline underskirt and then drew the gown over her head. She gazed into the wardrobe mirror, captivated by her new look. She was amazed—Maggie, the little brown wren, could actually look like one of the Four Hundred if she tried. The more she admired herself, the more resolved she became to confront Gabriella and request an interview. What the hell, they were both women, weren't they? Not at the ball—that would be tacky. But right after Christmas, she'd ask. She would have to make sure that Gabriella saw her at the ball, though, just so it would be clear that Maggie wasn't the plain Jane that the killer beauty might have thought she was.

She took off the gown and carefully hung it in the wardrobe. Then she looked into the mirror again, and saw her typewriter on the desk reflected behind her. She immediately thought of Alex. Had he really had the gall to go to the mother superior at the Convento di San Gabriele before her? And if he had, would he get Gabriella to shut up the way the old nun had? She hated to consider the possibility, but she was forced to. It seemed paranoid to think that someone was out to sabotage her, but the mother superior's words were just too convincing and convicting as evidence. How else would she know the term "innocent"? Why else would she have been so nasty? Maggie wanted to give Alex the benefit of the doubt, but she had to admit his record wasn't exactly clean.

She had caught him going over her notes—she had him dead to rights there. Damn, sex complicated everything. She'd always heard it was dangerous to get romantically involved with a colleague, because naturally it was harder to be professional with someone who'd shared your bed and knew your body like the back of his own hand. And knew your emotional reactions too—that was the real zinger. Alex had seen her in enough situations to get a pretty good idea of how she went about her work and her life. Well, if he was guilty, so be it. Maggie knew she was still a good enough reporter to carry on by herself, despite tampering, if indeed he had tampered. This time she would be more careful in approaching her sources. Let Gabriella sit for a while, she decided. Feel things out a little first, just to make sure Gabriella isn't scared off. Maybe let Alex sit for a while too.

She was sitting at her desk, mentally mapping out her strategy for getting Gabriella's cooperation, when suddenly there was a frantic pounding at the door.

"Who is it?" Maggie's head shot up.

"Dick Ord, Maggie." His voice sounded firm, but urgent.

"Come on in, it's open." Odd that he would be here—she wasn't even aware he knew where she was staying.

Dick burst into the room, looked at Maggie without a greeting, then scoured each corner, as if looking for someone else.

"What is it, Dick?" Maggie examined the distressed expression on his face.

"Where's Alex? I need him." He stared at her intently.

"I don't know. I haven't seen him all day. What's wrong?"

"Another terrorist prank. This time against one of us. I want to know if he's heard anything about it from one of his moles."

"What do you mean 'one of us'? Will you please tell me what's going on?"

"It was Betsy. A couple of guys dragged her into an alley and pulled a gun on her. She's okay, don't worry. They shot some holes into her sweater, not her. It seemed they just wanted to scare her. If this was an international terrorist act against a U.S. government employee, there's gonna be big trouble." He grit his teeth in fury.

"Oh, my God! Is she all right, really? How is she?" Maggie felt sick and panicky.

"Yeah, okay. Shook up and a little bruised, but she'll be fine."

"Where is she? I want to see her."

"Relax. After they released her from the hospital, I put her on a plane back to the States. Department rule—anyone involved in a violent incident gets a month's mandatory R&R at home. Now look, if you hear from Alex, please have him call me at the embassy. There'll be someone there to tell him where he can get me. You got that?"

Maggie nodded and swallowed hard. Her face was pale as Dick dashed out of the room. But why Betsy? What could they possibly want from her?

Suddenly, all of Alex's warnings came back to her. The terrorists *were* dangerous. Maybe he had been sincere about protecting her from his sources all along. But Betsy. What about Betsy? She was overwhelmed by the picture of her friend sitting numbly in an airplane seat, eyes open but blank, lost in a fit of shock. Gun shots rang out in her head, making it throb with her confusion.

"Maggie? Maggie? Hello—are you here? What is it?" Pippo poked his head through the open doorway. "Are you ill? Do you need a doctor?"

Maggie ran to him and clutched him in her distress. "Oh, Pippo, am I glad you showed up." She buried her angry, frightened tears in his shoulder.

"I am here, *certo*. I was just in the neighborhood—the man at the desk said to go up. What is wrong, *cara*?" He held her and stroked her back consolingly.

"Oh, Pippo, I don't know where to begin. The whole

day . . . Betsy was shot—almost. And Alex betrayed me . . . well, maybe he did . . . and the innocents . . . the mother superior at the convent . . . and Gabriella . . . her parents . . . the ball . . . the count and. . . ."

It was clear that she was in a bad state. "Come here, shush-shush, quiet. Lie down, lie down." Pippo led her to the bed and pulled up the desk chair for himself so that he could sit beside her. "I am here now. Tell me, tell me everything."

Nearly blinded by her rage and fear, Maggie allowed him to take control, grateful to have a friend nearby, someone she could talk to. Staring at the ceiling, she began to tell him about Betsy. Then she started in on her anxiety about Alex and her suspicions about Gabriella, all the time gripping his hand as if maintaining a lifeline with his trust.

"I see," he said when she had gotten everything out of her system and was crying quietly. "It is tragic, what has happened to your friend. The ones who did it should be shot." He shook his head in grief as if he actually knew Betsy himself. "What will you do now, Maggie? For your story, I mean?"

"Well," she sniffed back the last tears, "the magazine is put to bed on the fifteenth of every month. That gives me no more than two weeks to file my story so it can be edited, set into type and illustrated." Maggie grimaced in despair. "Is it possible that the Gabriella we know is the one I'm looking for? What do you think? And if she is—do you think I can get anything out of her and write it up in time to make the next issue?"

"I don't know, Maggie." Pippo rubbed his chin. "Frankly, I do not think that Gabriella will help you. Perhaps you should try something else while you have time. Maybe use the stories Angelo told you in Gaeta, or something."

"Maybe. . . ." she murmured, tired of talking and speculating, but unwilling to give up on Gabriella Sciarra without one good try.

Chapter 13

"Invito, per favore," one of the two poker-faced guards demanded at the entrance of the Palazzo Sciarra. The burly men made no attempt to conceal the revolvers in their belt holsters.

Alex pulled their invitation from the inside pocket of his tuxedo jacket, and the guard checked the name against his master list, which contained brief physical descriptions of the guests next to their names. The first guard then passed the invitation to his partner, who held it under a small, ultraviolet scanner. The embossed coat of arms of the Sciarra family shone in Day-Glo purple.

"Americani?" the guard muttered.

"Yes, we are the Americans," Alex enunciated in his best English, to demonstrate to the guard that he was the real Alex Parisi and not some enterprising terrorist trying to crash the party and kidnap a guest.

"Grazie," the man droned and allowed them to pass through the high arched alcove.

A magnificent pair of fifteen-foot, carved wooden doors suddenly swung open as if by pre-arranged signal, and a scarlet-frocked doorman stood before them.

"Very elaborate security system," Alex whispered to her. "The rich can't be too careful."

Maggie was too nervous to comment, and she clung to

Alex's arm. When he had come by the *pensione* to pick her up an hour earlier, she had been pacing the lobby in an anxious frenzy.

"Well, well," he had whistled as he walked through the front door. "You are spectacular."

"You too." They had stared at each other in admiration, and for a moment, Maggie's stagefright had lessened. "You know, I just wish Betsy could have seen me in my finished state. I sent her a note this morning—I feel really terrible not to have been able to see her or call her."

"Yeah, well, she'll be okay. I'll take a snapshot of you, gorgeous, and wire it to her in Danbury."

Well, she had to admit she did look extraordinary. The gown was perfect in every detail—the velvet bodice clinging to her breasts and the skirt flowing away from her slim waist in a gentle swirl. The high ruching at the neckline enhanced her face, which she had made up carefully. The look in Alex's eyes told her she had been successful in her transformation from streetwise reporter to glamor girl.

"Shall we go?" He offered her his arm.

"I love the tux," she smiled. "Just like an orchestra conductor."

"Damned monkey suit. It's rented, of course, so don't pour champagne all over me."

"I'll try." She had laughed, holding her skirts around her as she climbed into the tiny Fiat. "But I can't vouch for my behavior. I'm scared to death."

"Sweetie," he had said as they sped off, "you'll wow 'em—don't worry."

The doorman bowed down low as they entered the courtyard where a great, flood-lit fountain filled the air with the sound of gently rushing water. Three gray marble cherubs played in the spouting water, their joyous faces so realistic they looked as though they might burst into laughter at any moment.

The courtyard was lit by torches that protruded out from the walls, suspended on baroque, brass brackets. A grand staircase in a far corner of the courtyard was lined with more torches on heavy brass stanchions. At the bottom and top of the staircase stood pairs of liveried servants to indicate the way to the ball proper.

ROMAN CANDLES

"This way to the *piano nobile*," Alex said out of the side of his mouth, imitating W.C. Fields.

"The what?" Maggie was surprised to hear him joking, but figured he was probably as nervous as she was in his own way, and this was his manner of dealing with it.

"*Piano nobile*, the main floor, where the action is." He dropped the imitation as they climbed the maroon-carpeted stairs.

When they reached the top, the huge ballroom opened up before them. The lush colors and the gowns and the decor reminded Maggie of a grand Hollywood production, like the ballroom scene in *Gone With the Wind*. There was just too much to take in. Hundreds of people—men in black tie, women in exquisite designer gowns—mingled and laughed and danced, like an impressionist painting come to life.

The wall to her right was all mirrors, giving the scene a larger, more fantastic aura from the reflection of hundreds of lights sparkling off splendid jewelry. Chandeliers glittered everywhere—it was difficult to tell the real from the reflected image. The opposite wall contained tall, arcaded windows that exhibited a star-filled, blue-black night complete with a pale gold quarter-moon. It was as if someone had put in an order in advance to the heavenly lighting designer. From a rococo balcony above them, a dance band showered music down onto the ballroom floor. Maggie was disappointed with the band's Muzak-like selections. A small chamber orchestra in powdered wigs or maybe a 1920's vintage dance band with butterfly collars and slick patent-leather hair playing Cole Porter seemed more appropriate to the occasion. These musicians sounded like leftovers from Guy Lombardo's Royal Canadians.

Rows of small, gilt-painted, alternately blue and gold upholstered chairs lined every wall, and people perched on them, chatting in a variety of languages. Only the presence of the dark-suited bodyguards milling about the outskirts of the crowd kept Maggie aware of the reality hidden beneath this bubbling scene.

Alex noticed her grimacing at the bodyguards. "Whatsa matter? Don't you like the gorillas?"

"Not really."

"You know, some of them are Conte Sciarra's personal

men, some were hired just for the occasion, but a few of them came with their bosses. Some of these rich folks are so scared of being kidnapped and such they won't go anywhere without their own men. I wouldn't be surprised if they escort their ladies to the powder room."

"Are you serious?" Maggie eyed him skeptically.

"You never know with this bunch."

"What's going on over there?" Maggie indicated a raised platform opposite the band's balcony where a crowd of guests were waiting in a sprawling queue.

"That's the receiving line. You can't see it from here, but the thrones are set up there."

"Thrones?" Maggie was convinced he was putting her on.

"No kidding! The count and countess are on their thrones, receiving the new guests. Come on, let's go up and say hi to old Alfonso and Flavia."

"Flavia? Come on, Alex. Now I know you're pulling my leg. Nobody's called Flavia."

"I swear to God, that's her name. A lot of these women in Italy's hotsy-totsy old-line royalty have ancient Roman names. There must be at least a dozen Octavias here and a lot more Claudias. They identify very strongly with imperial Rome. I think they glorify that part of history because it was a time when wealth and nobility brought real power, unlike the present."

"Hmm, makes sense, I guess."

"And by the way, when you get to the count, he will take your hand and press it to his forehead. I know it sounds bizarre, but that's the way they do it here. He only kisses the hands of the women of nobility. I'm telling you now, so you won't break out laughing when he does it."

"Incredible!" she muttered.

Waiting in the receiving line, Maggie stayed close to Alex, unspeaking, still awed by the fact that she—a reporter from Wilton, Connecticut—was an invited guest in the middle of a modern European fairy tale. As they moved up in line, she spotted the *conte* and *contessa* seated on their high-backed, gilt thrones.

The *conte* was a portly man with a full head of steel-gray hair and a trim, salt-and-pepper mustache. His manner was debonair and quite sexy as he took the hands of the ladies with a sly look in his eye and bowed slightly to the men, offering a few words to each one who passed. He wore tails with a ceremonial sash of green and yellow diagonally crossing his girth.

The *contessa* sat demurely by his side, graciously bowing her head in exchange for her guests' bows, her sleepy eyelids never opening wide enough to reveal the color of her eyes. Her face was long, with a classic aquiline nose between high arched brows and a thin, Mona Lisa mouth. The closer Maggie got, the better she could see the woman. She was astounded at the absolute perfection of the *contessa*'s complexion. It was like the white marble of some of her newer statues. *Hmm,* Maggie thought, *if God did all!* Her white hair stood above her head in a soft, round, late-nineteenth-century-style pompadour, which seemed so natural Maggie could almost believe it just fell that way effortlessly.

Her dress was a brocaded masterpiece that looked like a costume from another century. The background was gold satin, and the bodice as well as the long yoke below the waist was worked with red and silver threads in elaborate swirls and curlicues. The skirt must have had fifteen yards of material in it—the dress looked like it could stand up alone if it had to. The high collar and the cuffs were banded with broad lines of the red and silver decoration. The *contessa* was crowned with a tiara of rubies and diamonds, which was complemented by an extraordinary necklace of the same jewels. The interesting thing was that the woman appeared so comfortable, as if she dressed this way every day. Maggie, for all her pleasure in her velvet gown, felt rather precarious, as if she might jar the impression of her elegance with one false move.

Standing beside her mother was Gabriella. She was simply breathtaking, wrapped in a long, tight casing of silver. The dress fit her like a pair of jeans you wore into a swimming pool and then let dry in the sun. It hugged her tall, thin form like a second skin, as did the long slim sleeves and the low-cut neck. As she turned slightly, Maggie caught the shimmer of another color under the silver, as if the material of the dress hid a black metallic weave just for accent. The dress had two high slits up the right side, without which Gabriella probably would have been immobilized all evening. Her feet, with silver-painted toenails, were perched on high silver sandals. But what was even more astounding than her dress was the bib of diamonds around her neck. They draped her olive-colored skin like a triangular collar and tied in the back under her dark hair, which was coiled and braided in an intricate manner on top of her head. Woven into her hair were strands of tiny diamonds, placed so skillfully, they seemed like a shower of brilliant raindrops at a distance.

When she spotted Alex and Maggie in line, she raised her eyebrows in recognition, unwilling to disturb the propriety of the receiving line with a smile—or God forbid—a small wave.

"There's Gabriella," Maggie pointed out to Alex.

"Oh?" Alex's brow was wrinkled, his eyes fixed on something else.

Maggie followed his gaze, and to her surprise she saw Pippo at the head of the line, now bowing to the *conte*. As he moved on to the *contessa*, bowing suavely, he leaned forward and seemed to be saying something to her. The *contessa*'s eyes flew open—she looked totally shocked. Pippo nodded to her curtly, then proceeded to Gabriella, whose previously cordial manner turned stone-cold when he offered to take her hand. Begrudgingly, she extended three fingers. When he started to lift her hand to his lips, Gabriella tensed, making it clear that any other familiarity would not be appreciated. He stood up straight, nodded sharply to her, and moved on.

Maggie turned to Alex questioningly, but his jaw was set as if he were holding down his fury.

What's Pippo doing here? Maggie wondered. He had never mentioned that he was invited to the ball. She had talked about the ball to him a couple of times and he had never said anything.

The line started to move, and within minutes, Maggie and Alex stood before the *conte* and *contessa*. And, just as Alex predicted, the *conte* took Maggie's hand and pressed her knuckles to his forehead. She tried not to giggle as they proceeded on.

"*Contessa*," Alex said, "this is Maggie Reardon, my colleague."

Maggie bowed her head. "I'm honored to be here." Maggie smiled demurely.

The *contessa* smiled back at Maggie. "Thank you for bringing Miss Reardon, Alex. Her beauty embellishes our *festa*."

ROMAN CANDLES

They moved on to Gabriella, who ignored Maggie totally and looked at Alex with an odd expression on her face.

"Later," Alex told her in a firm tone.

"Hello, Gabriella," Maggie broke in, a bit miffed at this private communication between them. She was also just a little upset about being referred to as a "colleague" instead of something more intimate.

"Yes, hello, Maggie. How are you? You are looking gorgeous tonight!" Gabriella gushed with a straight face, pouring out her meaningless niceties in a droning voice.

"Thank you. And you as well." Maggie's antagonism toward Gabriella was instantly rekindled. It was so ridiculously evident that she was still carrying the torch for Alex and made no attempt to cover it up. But what about Alex? Maggie watched him intently, but as usual he wasn't giving away a thing. As close as they had been, Maggie still felt she knew nothing about what made this man tick. Or about how he felt toward Gabriella.

"We'll talk to you later, Gabriella," Alex muttered, and moved off with Maggie as the receiving line started to back up. "How about a dance?" he asked brusquely, his mind clearly elsewhere.

"Sure," she said tersely, trying not to show that she was upset with him.

The band was playing a waltz, and to Maggie's astonishment Alex whirled her onto the parquet floor. He was an excellent dancer. She was beginning to think that his sometimes gruff manner and often slovenly dress was an intentional smokescreen. With her hand on his broad back, she let him lead her in swooping circles. He held her close and she warmed to his touch, forgetting the incident in the receiving line, feeling exhilarated and just a bit dizzy from the excitement.

"God, I've never seen so much jewelry in my life," she whispered, looking at the people dancing around the floor beside them.

"It's like a Cartier and Tiffany open house. I think it's a bit of overkill, though. You know what?"

"What?"

"You dance nice, lady," he breathed in her ear.

"You're not so bad yourself."

"That's not the only thing you do nice."

She felt herself blush, and in that instant she wished the ball and the dancers would disappear, leaving them alone. She was so moved by this man, despite her confusion about him. *I don't know*, she mused as he hugged her, *maybe my previous problems with men are what stop me from trusting Alex totally. Maybe I want to think he tampered with my work because it lets me off the hook emotionally. Maybe he and Gabriella. . . .*

"Alex," she ventured softly, deciding it was better to ask than to keep things bottled up, "what was going on up there on the line?"

"With Gabriella? She's upset about something, I don't know what." His voice sounded annoyed. "I don't know why she saves all her problems for me."

"Why were you staring at Pippo like that?"

"Pippo? Pippo must have crashed the party. Actually, that's probably what's ruffling Gabriella's feathers."

Maggie said no more, nestling her face in his shoulder. With this heavy security around it was pretty unlikely that skinny little Pippo would have crashed any gates.

By the time the waltz ended, though, Maggie had shrugged off her suspicions. She was determined to give Alex the benefit of the doubt and not jump to conclusions again.

"Hey, I'm dying of thirst, Mr. Parisi," she complained, just as the band struck up a bouncy bossa nova.

"Me too," he agreed. "Shall I find some champagne?"

"But of course."

Waiters carrying silver trays full of champagne in fine crystal were not hard to find and, as soon as Alex had captured two glasses, they found a relatively remote corner so they could sip their champagne in privacy. Maggie felt rather relieved—she dreaded being dragged around and introduced to a lot of nobility and wealthy industrialists. Alex sat her down and carefully pointed out the most interesting of the guests. There was an eighty-year-old wine magnate who insisted on trying to seduce every young woman and man who came to work for him; a *principessa* in a beaded 1930's blue crepe gown who had been a dancer in Paris; and a millionaire who had made his money on race horses and shot those poor animals who didn't make the grade for sadistic sport.

Unfortunately, no sooner had they settled in to enjoy their

ROMAN CANDLES

champagne and their gossip when Gabriella found them. She slunk up next to Alex, pulling her date along behind her. Maggie instantly recognized the internationally-renowned fashion designer, Aldo Amarone, Gabriella's boss.

Gabriella introduced Aldo to Maggie and Alex in a casual manner hardly befitting a celebrity. "Maggie, do you mind if I steal Alex for one dance? Aldo, we will be back in five minutes." Before anyone could object, Gabriella had taken Alex's hand and whisked him onto the dance floor.

As the band struggled through an awkwardly tempoed version of "The Hustle," Alex tried valiantly to gyrate and not snap his cummerbund open. Gabriella shifted her weight from one foot to the other and somehow managed to convey the impression that she was dancing gracefully without really doing anything. Maggie could see clearly that she was begging Alex for something and, frankly, she didn't care how upset Gabriella was.

"You are a *giornalista*, no?" Aldo asked, lighting up a cigarette. His question disrupted Maggie's furious glare.

"Ah . . . yes. You must excuse me, Signor Amarone, I'm a bit dazzled by all this. One doesn't go to many balls in New York."

"*Sì*. In New York you go to disco. I like New York very much. In fact, my friend Halston, who is in New York, makes me very jealous."

"Why is that?" Maggie smelled a tidbit for the "People" section of the magazine.

"Well, he is American. In America you are free to do so much. He can dance all night and be rich and famous and everybody still loves him."

"And you cannot do the same?"

"Not in Italy." He took a drag on his cigarette, then ran his hand over his short, thinning hair. "I must live like a criminal here, hiding from terrorists and robbers all the time. They do not like for people to have money. We are not safe here." He nervously adjusted the white silk scarf that he wore around his neck as an accent over his tux.

"Have you considered moving to America? Many designers really strike it rich there."

"Of course, I have thought of it," he blustered, stroking his cropped, sculpted beard. "But they hate me in America. *Women's Wear Daily*, bah! They love to write bad things about me. I am too 'formal,' too 'old-fashioned' for their tastes. They like military styles, *blue jeans.*" He said "*blue jeans*" as if it were a dirty word. "*They like Perry Ellis, they like Calvin Klein, they like Halston!*"

"I see," she said, putting on a look of concern to keep him calm, thanking God that she wasn't a fashion writer. She was curious about Amarone's relationship with Gabriella, though. Were they just business associates, or perhaps something more? Of course, Pippo had said. . . . But he might have been protecting Alex by creating a romance between Gabriella and her boss.

"What is the use to even speak of it? America *hates* me. I could never go there!" He threw up his hands in exasperation, flicking ashes onto his shoulder.

The song ended, and Gabriella promptly dragged Alex back to Maggie.

"Now I will trade you back for Aldo, Maggie," she said, with a sugary smile. "Thank you for the dance, Alex. I must go now, there are many people I am obliged to see. Please, do have a good time tonight. Come, Aldo."

Like an obedient puppy, Aldo followed her, shrugging behind her back to Maggie like a hen-pecked husband.

Maggie smiled half-heartedly after them, surveying the dance floor, although she was dying to ask Alex what was so urgent that Gabriella had to spirit him away to discuss it.

"Well, look who's here," Alex suddenly murmured in her ear.

"Maggie! Alex! Isn't this wonderful? *Bella festa!*" Pippo ran up to them, bubbling over like a champagne bottle. He kissed Maggie and shook Alex's hand vigorously.

"Hello, Pippo," Alex's voice was as cold as Gabriella's had been earlier.

Maggie was startled. *They were supposed to be friends,* she thought, *so why the attitude?*

"Maggie, are you enjoying yourself? Tell me the truth now?"

Pippo was more animated than usual, and Maggie couldn't figure out whether this was an act or genuine enthusiasm. She was dying to ask him why he hadn't told her he was invited, but, of course, in his childlike way he might have simply decided it would be fun to surprise her.

"Maggie, you must dance with me. You look so exquisite

tonight. This dress, it is the night and the sea all at once! Alex, may I?"

"It's up to Maggie," he mumbled sullenly.

"Maggie?"

"Ah . . . yes, of course, Pippo." As he led her off to the dancefloor, Alex stood immobile, a stern set to his mouth.

"I am so happy to be here, Maggie," Pippo gushed, as he drew her to him and began a simple box-step. "I cannot tell you how happy." The band swung into a foxtrot. Pippo, like Alex, was an adept dancer.

"This is really something. I didn't think this kind of royal gala still existed—except for inaugurations and coronations."

"Oh, *sì, certo*. These rich people take themselves very seriously. They must maintain a certain standard, as you can see. Like kings, like Borgias." That familiar note of sardonic criticism returned to his voice.

"Alex tells me that these royal families identify with the emperors."

"That is right. Do you see the mural there?" He indicated a huge fresco covering the wallspace next to the balcony. It depicted a middle-aged warrior carrying a naked old man and leading a naked young boy. They seemed to be in the midst of a cloud or a fog, and a beautiful maiden in billowing white robes floated above them.

"The Sciarras—like all the royal people in Italy—claim that Aeneas was their ancestor. You know, he was the Trojan warrior who was supposed to have founded Rome. In that fresco Aeneas is carrying his father Anchises and leading his son Ascanius. The woman is the goddess Venus, Aeneas' mother. She is telling him to go forth and found Rome, and she has sent this cloud to protect them."

"I'm impressed. That's quite a background. Must be kind of neat to be able to claim you were descended from a goddess."

"Don't be impressed, Maggie. All the rich people have similar pictures in their palazzos. This one is very nice because of the artist, Sebastiano Conca. But these royalty, they know nothing of art, they know only money and power. Thinking they are related to Aeneas makes them feel they deserve it."

Maggie listened to his explanation with one ear. Actually, she was not concerned with frescoes or Roman mythology;

she was worried about Alex. When she glanced back toward the area where he had been, she saw that he was gone. Something was obviously going on, but she didn't know how to find out without offending someone. She couldn't ask Pippo why Gabriella and Alex were so upset to see him there. She couldn't ask Alex why he was suddenly so cold and evasive toward his friend, yet so accommodating to Gabriella. And though she was itching to ask, she couldn't very well confront Gabriella with the question of why she was such a superlative bitch!

Then Alex appeared out of the crowd, striding toward them through the dancing couples. His mood had completely changed: he actually winked at her as he tapped Pippo on the shoulder to cut in.

"May I?"

"Alex, you scoundrel, it is cruel to take me away from this beautiful woman now." He put up a fuss with a good-natured grin on his face.

"Well, those are the breaks, my friend." Alex chuckled slightly and stepped between Pippo and Maggie.

"I will be back, Maggie. Count on that." Pippo disappeared into the crowd as Alex grabbed her and held her close.

"Phew!" she said in his ear, "I thought I'd lost you. And in this crush that would be serious."

"I was talking to Gabriella," he said calmly.

"Oh. . . ." She took a breath. "Alex . . . it could just be me, but I get the impression that something's going on here that isn't exactly kosher. Am I wrong?"

"No." His tone remained even. "Gabriella was all hot and bothered because she was convinced Pippo got in uninvited. She didn't care about him being here as much as the possibility that someone could penetrate the Sciarra security system. Well, she checked the guest list and it turned out that he was invited after all. Some relative of his is a big deal and a good friend of the *conte*. So there's Pippo's in."

"Must be his uncle, the one who was Mussolini's personal assistant."

"Ah . . . right. That's it."

Maggie wasn't entirely convinced that Alex was telling the whole truth, but she could see that the rich Italians were a peculiar, paranoid bunch, so anything was possible.

ROMAN CANDLES

"By the way," Alex's tone turned serious. "I forgot to ask you something."

"What's that?"

"Do you dip?" And not waiting for an answer, he executed a perfect dip, making the champagne and the night rush to Maggie's head.

"Oh, what an evening!" Maggie sighed with a smile, kicking off her sandals as soon as she entered her room. "I feel like Cinderella."

"Can I interest you in a pair of glass slippers?"

"Nooo. . . ." She rolled her eyes to the ceiling.

"Then how about a Veg-o-matic?" Alex pulled off his tie and opened his collar.

"Nope," she giggled.

"I've got it! A lifetime subscription to *Shout* magazine!"

"Strike three, pal!" And with that, she lunged and tackled him onto the bed, burying him in yards of black velvet and organza.

They kissed madly, rolling around on the bed despite their formal attire. Alex kicked off his shoes, then grabbed for the hook and zipper of Maggie's gown. Rather than fight him off, Maggie took the offensive, putting her arms around his waist to unbuckle his cummerbund.

"Watch it, Passion Flower!" he said. "This tux is rented, remember? How do I explain . . . ?"

She stopped his mouth with another kiss.

"Wait, just wait," he pleaded, stripping off his jacket in one movement and placing it carefully over the back of the desk chair while Maggie fumbled with her side zipper.

He came back to her, tugged on the zipper, and peeled her down to the waist like a banana.

"Hey, you! I spent a zillion dollars on this thing!" She drew away anxiously.

"What's more important to you? Money—or me?"

She reached for him and tugged at his shirttails, then pulled the shirt open in one smooth, quick move that sent shirt studs flying all over the room. Startled by the deftness of that maneuver, Alex looked down in surprise at his bare chest, and she took advantage of the pause in his attack to work on his pants button and zipper.

ROMAN CANDLES

He lunged at her and reached back for the hooks of her bra. In an instant, she lay back, panting, naked to the waist, the folds of black velvet billowing around her like the leaves of an artichoke. Laughing, she pulled the dress over her head before he could do any real damage to it, and threw it over his jacket.

Then he started on her crinoline and slip, as she finally succeeded with the button and zipper of his fly. She got his pants down to his knees, and he tripped over himself, sitting down on the edge of the bed with a jolt. He pulled his pants off hurriedly, and she undid the snaps of her bulky crinoline.

As Alex turned back for a second assault, he was startled to hear Maggie erupt into howls of laughter. The sight of this ferocious lover in his briefs and black knee socks was more than she could bear. She fell back onto the pillows, wiping the mirthful tears from her eyes, her half-slip the only article of clothing left on her.

"What's the joke?" He climbed up and lay next to her, propping himself up on one elbow.

"Those socks!" She couldn't stop laughing.

"What's wrong with them?" He pushed his glasses up on his nose, trying to fathom what she found so funny about a pair of socks.

"They're . . . they're ridiculous."

"I'll have you know that this is hosiery for black tie." He nodded sharply, to punctuate his statement.

"You mean to tell me all those men tonight were wearing them?" She pointed at his feet in disbelief.

"No doubt they were."

"Everybody?" Her voice squeaked with the effort of trying to get out a word over her giggling.

"Yes."

"Even Pippo?"

He paused. "Even Pippo, I guess." The mention of Pippo's name seemed to sober his mood suddenly.

"Sorry. I guess Pippo's on the outs with you and Gabriella."

"Well, let's just say that he's not always as wonderful as you think he is."

"But he's such a nice guy. And totally harmless, even if he does get a kick out of exploiting rich American women."

"Why are we talking about Pippo?"

ROMAN CANDLES

She rolled over and looked at him. "Beats me," she said softly.

He pulled her back on the bed and yanked off her slip. Then he began to kiss her body, starting at her neck and moving slowly down to her feet. She was shaking with excitement; she felt as though her limbs had been disconnected from her center.

At last he kissed the tip of her breast and let his mouth roam over the nipple until it was hard under his touch. She clasped his head to her and moaned. She felt drunk with passion and so wet, she hardly felt it when he entered her. They moved in a wild rhythm, and she came again and again, sobbing for more, pleading with him not to stop.

Eventually, after what seemed like hours, he shuddered against her, exhausted, and cried out, falling on top of her with a sigh as she stroked his back.

Outside Maggie's window, the pale light of morning was just beginning to illuminate the silhouette of the spires of Santa Trinità dei Monti when Alex and Maggie finally fell asleep in each other's arms.

Chapter 14

Maggie yawned, but her eyes were stuck shut. Her mouth felt sandy and her head was fuzzy. Gradually, she pried her eyes open and blinked painfully at the bright light coming through her window. She turned her head to find Alex wide awake, looking at her with a little grin on his face.

"Good morning," he said softly.

"Good morning," she whispered hoarsely. "Have you been up long?"

"A while."

"Oh. . . ."

"Just looking at you."

Maggie opened her eyes and nuzzled her head into his chest, touched by his sweetness.

"Hey," he said, "do you know what today is?"

"Uh . . . my God, it's Christmas Eve. It's Christmas Eve," she repeated with her full voice. She was suddenly awake with excitement. "What time is it? Let's go somewhere where I can get you a present!"

"You've already given me one." He smiled tenderly, his eyes crinkling with delight.

She hugged him tight. Maggie had never known any man who could say the things Alex did with such warmth and sincerity. "Alex, you're really something. You know that?"

"I know you're really something *else*."

"I guess that's why we . . . ah, work so well together." She felt slightly guilty for all the suspicious thoughts she'd harbored about Alex.

"Yes, indeed. We certainly do work well together."

They laughed and mooned, then gradually grew silent and pensive as they each filled that quiet, little room with private thoughts of Christmases past, the tiny joys, the tastes, the smells and the customs that they each longed for now. Christmas Eve in a foreign country, naked in bed in a stark, cold room—they both felt a tinge of sadness. They were homesick.

"Right now, my Aunt Rose is at the fish market," Alex began to imagine out loud. "She's buying all kinds of fish—smelts, cod, shrimp, clams, calamari. We always have fish on Christmas Eve. It's a custom."

"Christmas in Rome must be great for you then," Maggie murmured quietly, trying not to be jealous. "It must be similar to the way your family celebrates."

"No, not really. It's very different actually. Italian-Americans have their own traditions. Like we always believed in Santa Claus when I was a kid. As a matter of fact, I never knew who Befana was until I came here."

"Who's Befana?"

"She's the good witch who brings the presents to all the good Italian kids. She used to bring them on the Feast of the Epiphany, but I guess the kids here read enough magazines about American customs, and they didn't like waiting, so now it's done on Christmas Day, like at home. But this is nothing like the Christmases I remember. The tree and the cookies and pastry and shots of anisette in black coffee. All Christmas Day, relatives and friends would show up at the house with gifts. Then we'd go over to my aunt and uncle's with our presents. You'd eat so much you thought you'd burst, but the food was always so good you just had to eat more."

"Sounds terrific. So how did these particular Italian-American customs spring up?"

"Well, when my grandparents arrived in America from Naples, they were very poor and pretty disillusioned with Italy. They wanted to be Americans, though they always remained fiercely traditional and 'Italian' in some ways. Anyway, because they couldn't afford or find the foods and goods they were used to in Italy, they had to adapt to what they could get in America."

"I never thought of it that way."

"Sure. Italian-Americans are a distinct breed, all of their own. What about your family?" He moved closer and put his arm around her. "What do you usually do for Christmas?"

"Oh, it's wonderful, Alex," she said snuggling closer against him. "On Christmas Eve, my father and my brother go out for the Christmas tree while my mother and I string popcorn and cranberries. When the tree shows up, the house suddenly falls into beautiful pandemonium. I can't remember a Christmas when we weren't all wading through tangled masses of lights and garlands. My father is a perfectionist when it comes to the tree, and he insists on supervising the whole operation. Not a single ball is hung without his okay."

"Sounds like a real authoritarian."

"Oh, no, not dad. He's the biggest kid going when it comes to Christmas. I think he's so compulsive about the tree because he always wants Christmas to live up to his ideal."

"So, what do you do next?" Alex got up on one elbow, curious to hear more.

"Well, when everything is on the tree and the star has been set on top—we always save the star for last—we all sort of disappear for a while, going to our own hiding places to fetch the gifts. By ten-thirty, all the presents are under the tree. Then my parents brew up this super eggnog, while my brother and I start a fire in the living room. We sit around getting plowed, singing carols and generally acting silly until about eleven-thirty, when we bundle up and walk to midnight Mass at Saint Andrew's."

"Yeah. I always went to midnight Mass as a kid. And did you rush home afterwards to open your presents?"

"We always wanted to, but dad insisted that we wait till the next morning—give Santa Claus a chance to get there and all—but when I was small, I just couldn't wait. I remember I'd try to go to sleep, but it was useless. I'd doze for an hour, then bolt out of bed to check the sky. As soon as I decided it was light enough out, I'd rush downstairs to the tree. When I was a kid, of course, my brother and I had to wait till the next morning for the presents to show up. So, at six A.M. there I'd be, tearing into those presents like a banshee, burying my little brother in my discarded wrapping paper."

They both laughed and settled back on the pillows. They were quiet then, remembering.

"I wish I were in Wilton now," Maggie sighed. "Just for Christmas Eve. That's all."

"I know how you feel." He paused, seemingly thinking something out. "You know, I didn't tell you, but I got us tickets for midnight Mass at Santa Maria Maggiore." He grinned slyly.

"Tickets! You need tickets to go to Mass?"

"You do for this one. It's considered the connoisseurs' Mass, because it's entirely in Latin."

"I would have thought the Pope's Mass at Saint Peter's would be the place to go on Christmas Eve."

"No, no. That's such a mob scene I hear you never get to see anything."

"You know, I think I'd like the Latin Mass better, actually. I'm feeling cheerier already."

"And that's not all. The Ords are having a real American Christmas dinner at their place. Laura, Dick's wife, told me she was getting a turkey, but I think she's full of it. There are no turkeys in Europe, unless she knows something I don't. Anyway, Laura told me I could bring someone, so. . . ."

"I'd love to go, Alex." She hugged him tight. "I have a feeling this is going to be a very wonderful Christmas."

"I do too," he said, holding her close and nuzzling her hair. "Even without snow, it's gonna be just fine."

The waiter rushed up to their table, set Alex's steaming plate before him, then delicately set the copper chafing dish next to Maggie's plate and carefully ladled in half of her *zuppa di pesce*. The candlelight played off his plastered-down hair as he made sure he had served the proper number of shrimps, clams, chunks of lobster, calamari and mussels in a generous reservoir of buttery broth. Then he smiled solicitously at her, snapped up their bottle of Pinot Grigio, filled their glasses and set the bottle back on the table. As he left, he gave Maggie a sidelong glance and a seductive grin.

"What was that all about?" she whispered across the table with a grimace.

"It's called old-fashioned service. La Campana is noted for it. What it means is that all the waiters are obligated to be as flirtatious as they are efficient. I think they give them a test before they're hired."

"I'm disappointed. I thought it was love at first sight," she teased. "How's your calamari?" she asked, quickly diverting the conversation to her favorite subject.

"Good. Very tender. Usually, it's like rubber."

Maggie searched her plate for a piece of the tiny squid and popped it into her mouth. "Ummm! You're right. It's delicious."

As they dug into their meals like famished sailors, tearing off hunks of bread to sop up every last drop of sauce, Maggie and Alex noticed a middle-aged woman two tables away. She was with her husband, who seemed to be effectively ignoring her, intent upon his plate of gnocchi. Undaunted, the black-haired, wild-eyed woman raved on and on in a shrill, mounting pitch, accentuating her statements with jerky hand gestures.

"What's her problem?" Maggie asked Alex, *sotto voce*.

"She's complaining about a certain manger scene in some church." Alex paused to eavesdrop some more. "San Carlino. I don't know that one." Alex shrugged and continued to listen. "She says that it's too modern, a shame to have a *presèpio* like that. Apparently, it's a modern one with office buildings and cars and people in contemporary clothes. She says the figures are all holding protest signs that say '*Pace*' and '*Libertà*'! She's all bent out of shape because the mother and Child are hidden in a corner behind the other people. She's telling the man that it's a sin and that she's going to write to the Pope."

"Strange."

"Yeah. Nice blend of religion and politics."

They cleaned their plates, then topped off the meal with *biscotti ai pignoli*—chewy pine nut cookies—and cappuccino.

As they got up to leave, their waiter returned to help Maggie with her jacket and to wish them both a hearty *Buon Natale*.

Walking arm in arm down the Vicolo della Campana, they felt warmed and glad to be together on what they both realized could have been a very long night.

"You know, I feel very Christmasy all of a sudden," Maggie announced.

ROMAN CANDLES

"Oh, yeah? Just wait till we get into the Piazza Navona."

"Why? what's there?"

"You'll see," he said cryptically.

But before she could ask another question, she was sidetracked by a pile of rubble in the street. Articles of clothing, underwear, socks, a crutch, a pot, some tin cups, a single shoe and a deflated soccer ball lay strewn in the street, and more items flew out of an open doorway at odd intervals, adding to the motley collection. The strangest part about this was that each piece of junk was spray-painted gold.

"What the . . . ?" Maggie couldn't believe her eyes.

"Someone's jumping the gun here," Alex laughed. "They usually do this for New Year's."

"I don't get it. It looks like Santa's revenge."

"No, it's a custom. People throw their old junk and garbage into the street to rid the house of evils for the coming year."

"But why is it painted gold?"

"I give up. That's a new one on me. Come on, the Piazza Navona awaits us." Alex's cryptic grin returned.

They turned the corner and down the block was the piazza, all lit up and jammed with people. As they got closer, Maggie could see that there were dozens of vendors selling toys, jewelry, belts, hats, candy, sausage, rosaries, Christmas ornaments, candles and a thousand other things.

"Wow, what's this all about?" Maggie didn't know where to look first.

"This is the Befana market, remember the Christmas witch? Rome's version of Santaland at Macy's. But better, I think."

"It's wonderful—I feel like a kid!"

"I know, I know. Look. There's Befana herself. See?" Alex pointed toward the middle of the piazza at a figure dressed in a tattered skirt with a shawl up over her head. Her putty nose hung over her lips like an Italian hot pepper.

"However," Alex continued, "if you don't like Befana, you can have Santa Claus—actually Babbo Natale to the locals—and Rudolph the Red-Nosed Llama!" Alex pointed to a far corner and indeed there was a Santa with a long-necked, coffee-colored llama adorned with jingle bells on wide strips of red leather.

"I'm speechless." She hugged him close.

"I think they wanted a reindeer, but this is typically Italian improvisation. You know, you take what you can get here. Like . . ." he whirled her around to face him, "like you got me for Christmas."

"Well," she said softly, "I'm not interested in returning this gift."

As they strolled among the vendors, she felt like singing. The man just kept surprising her. Here she had him pegged for the heavy, no-nonsense type who wouldn't go to the john without the latest *U.S. News and World Report*, and now she found that he could be enthralled with the magic of Christmas and the childlike excitement of toys and presents. Again, she felt a pang of regret that she had doubted his word and not opened up to him sooner.

"See that black stuff on those trays?" Alex pointed to ragged black chunks of something that looked like rocks displayed on a vendor's stand. "That's kind of a traditional Christmas joke. You see, it's a candy that these kids love, but it's called *carbone*—coal. When kids are naughty, their parents tell them they better watch out or else they'll get *carbone* in their stockings."

"So that's where that comes from! And what's the stuff next to it? The one that looks like a hunk of marble with nuts in it?"

"That's *torrone*, it's hard nougat candy that they break off with a chisel and a hammer. Perugia is famous for its *torrone*, but the kind you get in Rome is okay if you like this sort of thing."

"Oh, yeah," she recalled. "There's a shop on Lexington Avenue that specializes in candy from Perugia. And what are those beads hanging above the candy?"

"Those are fava beans. People eat them like nuts. The vendors thread them and sell them by the string."

The smells of the fresh, hot candies and the sight of the children's happy faces and the colorful wares on the vendors' stands captivated Maggie as they strolled through the crowds, content just to take it all in. She lost all sense of time, and when Alex pointed out that they had to hurry if they were going to make midnight Mass, she was astounded to see that her watch read eleven-thirty.

"I'm having fun," she declared.

"Me too." He grinned and flipped a strand of hair out of her eyes.

"So let's go," she said, taking his arm. "I'm ready for the other side of Christmas."

A guard took the tickets from Alex and directed them to a young nun nearby in the vestibule, who would take them to their pew.

"It's just like going to the theater," Maggie whispered.

"In a way," Alex agreed.

The nun took them to a pew about twenty yards from the front on the right side of the church. As people filed in around them, the organ in the choir loft sang with the quiet, moving strains of a Bach prelude. Maggie turned back to see the choirboys in their red cassocks and white surplices forming ranks under the stern direction of their choirmaster. She gazed about the church, once again filled with amazement at the power and magnificence of the religious art that proliferated in Rome. The towering organ pipes and the carved oak balcony alone could be the subject of an art historian's dissertation. She glanced back again at the little boys, suffused, if only for the brief time they wore their religious uniforms, with a gorgeous, innocent quality.

Innocent, indeed. Alex and Christmas had made her forget about the innocents for a while, but her concern for her story and for them came back to her like a familiar ache. She thought of Mrs. Sloan and Signora Trezza as the choirmasters leading groups of orphans in song. Then, suddenly, she imagined old Father Virgilio at the organ, playing glorious, exalted music, his wizened, pink fingers dancing over a yellowed ivory keyboard.

"I feel a little funny going to church just on Christmas and Easter," Alex whispered to her. "It's not as though I'm exactly devout. Hardcore lapsed is more like it. But the big services are always so, so . . . I don't know how to describe it."

"I know just what you mean. I think uplifting is the only word for the feeling."

"Um," he agreed, soon lost again in his own thoughts as he studied the intricate marble carvings behind the altar.

Maggie looked along the walls where tiny alcoves dedicated

to individual saints twinkled with hundreds of flickering blue and red votive candles. Out from the shadows of one alcove stood a statue of Saint Sebastian, the martyr, graphically protrayed with arrows piercing his arms, legs and torso. Crutches supported his weary, blood-streaked form, and a small dog at his side looked at him adoringly.

As much as she tried to concentrate, her mind kept jumping to other subjects. The choirboys brought the innocents to mind, and now this statue of a martyred saint made her think of Betsy. Of course, it was absurd—Betsy was no martyr to a cause, but she been singled out for violence, for some reason. It was much more than just a sick prank. Those guys had something to say, some cause to push, some message to convey. But why Betsy? If they had a beef with the U.S. government, wouldn't it have made more sense to threaten Dick Ord? Even Dick's wife would have been a more logical choice. Maggie could not stop thinking that if Betsy hadn't been dropping off her gown at the *pensione*, the incident would never have happened.

"Would you like to look?" A voice at her side interrupted her ruminations. The man sitting next to Maggie was offering her a pair of binoculars. His rosy, round cherub's face and tiny, ice-blue eyes behind squarish, silver-framed glasses were as mirthful as old Saint Nick's, and his pronounced accent made it plain that he was not Italian.

"The ceiling mosaics," he pointed straight up, "they are magnificent, yes? I come from Amsterdam every year just for the Latin Mass and to see the mosaics."

"Thank you very much." Maggie smiled and took the binoculars. "And what is so special about these mosaics?"

"Oh, well, let me tell you." The man seemed pleased and eager to share his appreciation for the ceiling with Maggie. "These were done in the fifth century. Very simple, but very direct. Not pretty at all. Powerful, emotional. Each panel depicts an event of the Old Testament. Look for yourself. They speak for themselves."

Maggie focused the lenses and isolated the individual panels. The first one she honed in on was of Moses coming down from Mount Sinai with the Ten Commandments just as he discovered the Israelites worshiping the golden calf. His face was so wild and fierce it might easily have been that of a wolf or a mad dog, not a man at all. Moses held the stone tablets high over his head, aiming them at the idol like a guided missile.

She shifted her gaze. The next panel portrayed Abraham about to sacrifice his son Isaac at God's command. It was a disturbing representation. Maggie recalled a variety of other artistic renditions of this story, where Abraham looked fretful or forlorn, Isaac obedient, and the angel of God kind and understanding as he stilled the hand of Abraham. However, in this mosaic, Abraham's face was intent, almost driven. The angel of God looked on sternly as though checking to make sure Abraham went through with the necessary slaughter. And Isaac appeared panic-stricken, struggling in his bonds, crying out in desperation. The horror in the boy's face was vivid, graphic. The poor child knew he was about to get the knife, and was powerless to stop his own father, who was to be his executioner. Again, Maggie's mind started doing flip-flops. Why did everything seem to relate to everything else today?

She forced herself to look again. The blind, intent of Abraham's face was frightening enough, but the complacent, almost satisfied expression of the angel was the most upsetting aspect of the work.

Is that me? Maggie wondered. *Calmly looking on at other people's suffering, smugly recording the particulars of pain and injustice simply to get it on record? Why am I really chasing down the innocents? Do I honestly have an altruistic desire to reunite people? Maybe they don't want to know about one another. Maybe they want to maintain their privacy and the happiness of their lives as they now know them. Maybe the only one who really benefits from this whole damned thing is me. My series, my by-line, my career, my ego-trip, dammit! Do I really care about these people, or have I just been paying lip-service to them to ease my my own conscience?*

With a lump in her throat, she struggled to thank the congenial Dutchman as she returned his binoculars. Still wrapped up in her self-condemning thoughts, Maggie fixed her gaze on the *presèpio* just to the right of the altar. The plaster Baby Jesus lay in his crib of straw with arms outstretched.

What does a baby expect at birth anyway? Maggie asked herself. *A comfortable home, food, people who know how to give and take love. And there you have your innocent—any child abandoned to Fate takes whatever he or she can get. Any home, any parents. Look at Gabriella, my innocent.* She wondered whether her innocent, when she met her, would be as open and kind as this Baby Jesus by the altar. *Not if it really was Gabriella Sciarra,* she decided, *that was for sure.*

Damn, if it is Gabriella, there's no way I'll finish this story. How can I even approach her with her past? Maggie thought in frustration. *What right do I have even knowing about her real parents? And me of all people, the one who took Alex away from her. She'd cuss me up and down if I ever brought it up with her, and I suppose she'd have every right in the world to do it.* She didn't like the woman, but still, she felt everyone was entitled to live the kind of life they chose and bury the past if it suited them and didn't hurt anyone else. Maggie couldn't help feeling slightly guilty, knowing what she did. And, then, she felt guilty because she was really feeling sorry for herself—of all the people in the world, why did her research have to lead up to Gabriella Sciarra?

Her eyebrows were knit and she was biting her lower lip as she pondered her dilemma.

Noticing her fretful expression, Alex took her hand. "What's the matter?" he whispered.

But before she could reply, a single bell rang out and the organ rumbled forth in a fanfare as the pastor of Santa Maria Maggiore emerged from the sacristy behind the altar, followed by two other priests and four altarboys. The congregation suddenly became hushed as the pastor set down his chalice on the altar, held up his hands and blessed the altar to start the Mass.

Maggie watched him intently, trying to forget her story and Gabriella and to let the Christmas spirit wash over her for the time being.

Chapter 15

"You call *that* a turkey?" Alex laughed, pointing at the stream-lined goose roasting in the Ords' oven.

"Use your imagination, Alex," Laura Ord scolded him, with her hands on her hips and a wry note in her voice. "You know very well there are no turkeys in Italy. Isn't that so?"

"That's right. You're the one who told me that the turkey is a native American bird, Alex." Maggie copied the scolding tone of Laura's voice, and the two women laughed together.

Maggie liked Laura the moment she met her. Feeling a bit awkward about having Christmas in the home of strangers, Maggie was relieved to find that Laura was the kind of person who included you in everything, even on the first meeting. And since Laura refused to stand on any kind of formality, preferring to dole out chores to her guests, Maggie felt more like part of a family than just another dinner guest.

Laura Ord was lovely in a pale, Scandinavian way—light blonde hair, blue eyes, broad mouth—tall and athletic-looking with an enviable figure. Maggie guessed that she was in her early forties, but her open, jovial attitude made her ageless. She looked like the type who could adapt just as easily to a disco as to a sewing bee, a "good sport," as Maggie's father would have put it, someone who was game for any kind of activity. She was simply dressed in a beige, cowl-neck, lambswool sweater and a beautifully-cut brown wool skirt, her hair falling casually to her shoulders in girlish disarray. A strand of ivory beads around her neck was the only jewelry she wore.

"What's going on here?" Dick Ord asked, entering the kitchen, carrying two large glasses of eggnog.

"*Your* friend Mr. Parisi wants to know why you couldn't get him a turkey for Christmas?" Laura replied with a grin.

"I never...." Alex started.

"Well, actually I tried to have one flown in from the States, Alex," Dick interrupted earnestly. "But his wings got tired over Greenland and he couldn't make it."

"Very funny," Alex said, shaking his head as the others howled with laughter.

"Hey," Dick announced, "Tom and Alice are here. Shall we go out and do the introductions?"

"You take Alex," Laura piped up. "I need Maggie for some potato-mashing. Go on, we'll be there in ten minutes."

"Okay, boss," Dick saluted. "Come on, Alex. Tom is anxious to meet you. He's writing a book on the history of violence in Italy."

The men exited, and Maggie went right to work testing the potatoes in the boiling pot with a fork to see if they were done.

"You mash those, Maggie, while I put up the vegetables."

"Okay, you got it."

"So tell me, how's your work coming?"

"Oh, good and bad. I think I've come to an impasse."

"Really? I'm sorry to hear it. Dick told me about your topic and, frankly, I've been rooting for you from afar. I don't tell *him* that, of course—you can imagine what it's like living with the State Department—but, personally, I really hope you succeed in finding your war baby."

"Why's that, Laura?" Maggie stopped fishing potatoes out of the boiling water for a moment. "Sounds like you have some special interest."

"I do. You see, I had an uncle who got an Englishwoman pregnant during World War One." Laura offered this revelation without interrupting her work. Maggie, who was used to strong showings of emotion whenever people discussed these sensitive matters, was actually shocked by the casual way Laura mentioned her uncle's affair. "Diane—that was the Englishwoman—had a son, Harold. Well, Uncle Ben never knew about Harold—I guess Diane never wrote and told him—and he died in the early forties in a factory accident. I hardly remember Uncle Ben myself, after all I was just six or seven when he died.

"Anyway, a few years later, Harold showed up in Lancaster, Pennsylvania, where Uncle Ben's wife still lived. He found Aunt Sarah, who needless to say was a bit shocked when Harold told her who he was. Harold wanted to get married, you see, but he felt he had to find his real father first just to make sure there were no congenital diseases or anything. Aunt Sarah was very hurt that Ben hadn't even told her about his peccadillo, and she didn't even want to talk to Harold on the phone. But he was persistent, not obnoxious or anything, just determined. He rented a room in Lancaster and politely waited until she was ready to deal with him. She did come around, finally, and do you know, they became quite close. He still visits every other year or so. Sarah never considered him like a son, of course, a nephew maybe. I know in the end she was glad they had found each other.

"That's why I think your series is such a great idea. I mean, people who are caught up in this kind of situation tend to hide their feelings and, as a result, they fear what they refuse to let out in themselves. That was Aunt Sarah's problem at first. Thank God, Harold wasn't ashamed of his past or his feelings, or else he would have been too scared to even think of looking for Uncle Ben. Am I right?"

"I suppose you are." Maggie was mesmerized by her story.

"I mean, what you're doing is very good. You're exposing the irrational fears so that it may be easier for at least a few people to confront themselves and their lives. I hope your story will bring a few more Harolds out of hiding."

"I wish I could be that optimistic, Laura." Maggie frowned.

"Why do you say that?"

"Well, like I said, I've reached a dead end. I tracked down an innocent whose father was apparently an army doctor during the war. I wasn't convinced at first that I'd put the pieces of the jigsaw puzzle together properly, but the more I think about it, the more I feel certain I know this person. Odd coincidence, but there you are. The problem is that this person, who doesn't know that I know yet, is extremely hostile and uncooperative. I'm afraid that if I confront her, she'll be furious and clam up for good. It was really hard to figure out her background, and I can't imagine starting from scratch to go sleuthing out another war baby, so I'm afraid to get too close and scare this one off. But my time is running short, and I'll have to do something pretty soon. I just wish I knew how to approach her without getting her angry."

"I see your problem. Maybe you should try questioning the army doctor."

"Uh-uh. That would take about six months research—if he's still alive and if I could find him."

"How about the adoptive parents?"

"Yes, I know who they are. In fact, they're here in Rome."

"Then why not approach them first? They may not be tickled to see you, but look at Harold and Aunt Sarah. She eventually softened and overcame her fear. These people might do the same."

"You know, you may have something. It's very odd—frankly I haven't thought one bit about the adoptive parents. When I started doing my research in New York, I was indoctrinated with the party line. I mean, these days the big legal and emotional push is to get the birth parents and the children back together. But, of course . . . !" Maggie slapped her palm to the side of her head. "Naturally, the problem is bigger than that. I've been treating this like the children are the only ones who suffer, the only ones with feelings that matter. The parents, both natural and adoptive, never meant to hurt anybody. It was the war that was the real villain.

"Sure, the adoptive mother would be the perfect person to approach! The adoptive parents took the children out of love, pure and simple. And they may be more likely to agree to discuss their child—if they are approached the right way. Why didn't I think of this sooner?" She shook her head wonderingly at her own short-sightedness.

"Of course." Laura agreed. "I mean, what is a real parent anyway? A mother and a father who adopt and raise a child from infancy, sit with him when he's sick, agonize with him over his problems, watch him grow up? Why should the adoptive parent have fewer rights than the 'parent' who gave birth by accident?"

"Hmm," Maggie mused. "Do you know how this Englishwoman—Diane?—felt about her son going to look for his other family?"

"Yes. She always supported Harold in his quest to find Uncle Ben. She was never bitter about Harold's efforts to uncover old secrets, because it was what he wanted. He wasn't ashamed of being illegitimate, and it took the burden off his mother."

"Right. The adoptive parents would never think of their child as anyone's dirty little secret. I'm going to talk to my innocent's mother first thing tomorrow morning. Thanks, Laura, you don't know what a help you've been."

"Well, you're welcome. Now, if you'd just return the favor and get going on those potatoes before they're cold. . . ."

"Oh, sorry. . . ." She grabbed the masher and attacked the bowl of potatoes, adding hunks of butter and splashes of milk. A picture of the *contessa*'s face formed in her mind. Maggie prayed that she would be easier to approach one-on-one than she was on the receiving line at the ball. Anyhow, she had to be friendlier than Gabriella.

Suddenly, Alex burst back into the kitchen, his face ruddy from eggnog and the glow of the Ords' fireplace. "What's holding up the show, Laura? You've got some hungry people waiting out there."

"Calm down, boy. Have another eggnog. Maybe that'll anesthetize him," she said to Maggie.

"I heard that," he declared. "Oh, I see the problem," he sidled up to Maggie, "the potato-masher thinks she's mixing paints for Michelangelo."

"You're a real card," Maggie retorted. "You just have to be gentle to get it the way you want it sometimes." She smiled to herself as she looked down into her bowl to see the fluffy swirls forming like snow drifts.

The next day Maggie awoke feeling buoyant and optimistic. By eight o'clock she was up and dressed, thinking of the best way to bring up the matter of Gabriella's father with the *contessa*. She thought of Laura Ord and imagined how *she* might do it. Direct, cordial, but not drippy; most importantly, she would be non-judgmental. Dinner with the Ords was the best lesson Maggie could have had. Laura was a perfect example of someone who could be diplomatic, yet still get what she wanted effortlessly. She didn't take any guff, nor did she give any without provocation. She expressed her own opinions fearlessly, yet she had an open ear for everyone else's views. The woman was really admirable.

It was great the way Laura had defused a tense situation and still got her point across after dinner the day before. They had all been sitting in the living room, moaning over their full stomachs. The conversation, inevitably, had turned to terrorism, and Maggie had asked a question about the proliferation of Italian groups committed to violence.

"I don't really get it," she said. "Alex tells me every day another bunch pops up."

"Unfortunately, that's very true." Dick sighed. "The roots of anarchy in this country run very deep, but this wave began in the late sixties, when workers were being laid off right and left in the industrial triangle of Turin, Milan and Genoa. This, coupled with the youth revolts in sixty-eight, led to a lot of different people clamoring for political and economic change."

"The one I hear about all the time is the Red Brigades," Maggie commented.

Tom Vorhees laughed. "Yeah, well, only because they know how to exploit the media. The ones to watch out for in the eighties are the right-wing groups, though, not the Communist arm. The left-wing Brigades got a lot of publicity because of important figures like Renato Curcio and to an even greater extent, his wife, Margherita Cagol. They were these middle-class kids, real devout Catholics, you know? They were getting their degrees in sociology at the University of Trento when they got radicalized. I don't think they had any idea of the kind of bloodbath they were starting. Curcio got thrown in jail in Nineteen seventy-five and his wife Mara, as she was known, raided the prison with five commandos behind her and freed him. She was killed in a gun battle with police in Monferrato in the same year, and now Curcio's doing thirty-one years in the clink."

Maggie listened intently, a concerned look on her face, as Tom took a swig of brandy.

"Tom, you're not giving the real picture," Alex cut in. "The real influences were and are foreign. You know, the disgruntled Italians saw Danny the Red taking over France in Nineteen sixty-eight and the Baader-Meinhoff Gang in Germany, and they figured those guys are getting away with it, so we can too." He turned to Maggie. "I have it on good

ROMAN CANDLES

authority that ninety percent of the terrorist activity in Italy today is under foreign control. The attacks are too efficient—Italians could never manage these things so well. You know what Mussolini said: 'It's not impossible to govern Italians; it's simply useless.'" He shrugged. "The ones to watch out for now are the Fascists and the free-lancers. Like the ones who got Betsy."

"That's right," Dick said. "Since no one has taken credit for the shooting, officially we have to assume that it was an isolated incident. A robbery attempt, that's all."

"Come on, Dick, you can't bull me. I know a terrorist threat when I see one, and that had all the marks of a threat," Tom insisted.

"You're not listening to me, Tom. The embassy cannot *officially* declare war on any one of the hundreds of groups until one of them comes forward with an admission. As far as we're concerned, it's still a domestic issue. And it's not going to turn into an international incident just because you decide it should be."

"That's what's wrong with you guys from the State Department. Always talking out of both sides of your mouth and saying nothing. And who always bears the brunt of your fence-sitting? Secretaries and guards. Look what you guys got yourselves into in Iran!"

"Now let me tell you something, pal. . . ." Dick's face was flushed, when Laura put her hand on his arm and interrupted.

"You're all wet, Tom," she said firmly. "I happen to know that Betsy planned it all herself. She knew that State people get four weeks R&R whenever they're involved in a life-threatening incident. She was just tickled pink to be going home for the holidays. And at your expense too, Tom. The old taxpayer gets it in the wallet again. Huh, Tom?"

"Well, yes, but that's not the point. The U.S. government should do something, take action, show 'em we mean business."

"Not to worry, Tom," Laura went on calmly, "Betsy's been issued a tank and a license to blow any shady-looking Italian men to smithereens on sight." She winked at Maggie. "That'll fix 'em."

Everyone had to laugh at her parody of Tom's saber-rattling, and Tom could only bluster incoherently. Laura had managed to shut him up and deflect an unpleasant fight between him and Dick, yet still manage to make it clear that she thought Tom was foolish.

That's the kind of brass I need, Maggie thought, as she looked at her watch. *Still too early to call. Better go downstairs for another coffee and hold off until nine-thirty or so. If I stay here, I'll just get so nervous thinking about it, I'll end up sounding like someone trying to sell life insurance when I talk to the contessa.*

Maggie left the room and went down to the lobby, trying not to dwell on the phone call, or get her hopes up too high.

The phone rang only once after she dialed the number.

"Pronto!" a woman's voice barked.

"Ah . . . the *contessa* please." Maggie took a quick breath, prepared for some excuse or objection from the woman. Or, possibly, noncomprehension.

"Chi parla? Who . . . is . . . speak?" The voice enunciated carefully but tentatively. It sounded like this was the only phrase she knew in English. Maggie decided to take advantage of the situation.

"Tell her it is Ms. Reardon," Maggie chirped in her best imitation of a snippy Boston Brahmin.

There was silence. Then, "Uh . . . *attenda, per piacere.* . . ."

Maggie's tactic worked. The woman seemed to have been cowed by Maggie's unyielding tone in English. But would this strategy work with the next assistant to the *contessa*?

"Hello?" Another voice took the phone. "Can I help you?"

"Yes. I want to speak with the *contessa*," Maggie declared haughtily.

"Speaking."

Maggie was suddenly deflated and put on the defensive. She'd never expected it to be this easy to talk to the *contessa* herself.

"This is Maggie Reardon. I was at your ball with Alex Parisi, if you remember?"

"Yes, yes, of course I remember you. I do hope you enjoyed yourself."

"Oh, yes. I had a marvelous time. I must thank you for inviting me." Maggie stumbled over her words, taken aback by the *contessa*'s unexpected cordiality.

"Good, good. Thank you so much for calling. I trust you got our number from Gabriella."

Maggie couldn't help but wonder if the *contessa* asked this because she was so security-conscious. "From Alex, actually." She flushed on her end of the phone. In fact, she had gotten it from Alex by telling him that she wanted to call Gabriella to find out the best place in Rome to shop for shoes.

"Again, thank you for calling." It was clear that the *contessa* wanted to terminate the conversation.

"The real reason I called," Maggie broke in, "was to make an appointment to see you if that's possible. I'd like to interview you for an article I'm writing for my magazine."

If the *contessa* was at all surprised or put out, it didn't show in her voice. "Yes, of course," she agreed quickly. "Sometime in . . . let's see . . . early March. Is that good for you?" Her voice was too pleasant.

"Ah, no, not really." Maggie wasn't sure how to deal with the *contessa*'s "cooperation." "I won't be here that long, I'm afraid. Don't you think you could spare forty-five minutes sometime this week? Any time at your convenience, of course." She felt as though she were clutching at straws.

"Oh, I'm very sorry, Miss Reardon, but my schedule will not permit it. I will be very busy for the next few weeks; then we will be on vacation." The *contessa* started to brush her off again. "Perhaps when you are in Rome again, you will call and. . . ."

"*Contessa*," Maggie interrupted boldly, deciding to play her trump card, "I thought you might want to make time to discuss Tony Russo—Lieutenant Colonel Tony Russo?"

Silence.

"*Contessa?* Are you there?"

"You may come by at three this afternoon." The *contessa*'s voice was soft and resigned; the superficial cordiality was gone.

"Thank you. I will be there. . . ."

The *contessa* hung up before Maggie could finish her sentence.

A butler showed Maggie through the wide, marble corridors and brought her to what must have been one of many opulent parlors in the Palazzo Sciarra. Seated on a gold brocade sofa, the *contessa* was very still, waiting for Maggie.

She looked as though she has been sitting that way for some time. Maggie almost did not recognize her. She appeared smaller and thinner than she had seemed on her throne at the ball. Her snow-white hair was simply dressed. Only her flawless white complexion looked the same as it had at the ball. Her blue silk dress seemed frumpy, somehow, as though it were too large for her. She sat with her hands folded in her lap, looking her age at least and probably more.

"Please sit down, Miss Reardon." She spoke evenly, but her tone was weary, almost exhausted. There was a silver tea set on the coffee table in front of her, but she did not offer any to her guest. Instead, she just stared at Maggie, neither hatefully nor condemningly, just staring blankly.

"So," the *contessa* finally broke the silence, "you have discovered the truth about our family."

"Believe me, *contessa*, I did not start my research intending to impose on you or embarrass you in any way. It all happened quite by accident when I spoke to Father Virgilio Antonelli in Gaeta."

"I see." The *contessa* looked down at the surface of the coffee table, as if contemplating her next move. "Have you discussed this with Gabriella?"

"No. My research has been strictly confidential. Not even Alex knows of this." Maggie could see the torture she was going through. It would be cruel to badger and bully the *contessa* with the disjointed pieces of information she had.

But Maggie also realized that the *contessa* was no one's fool, and any show of desperation for a story or pity for Gabriella on Maggie's part would be interpreted as weakness. Maggie would have to make a strong showing, or else the *contessa* would clam up. She chose to remain terse and poker-faced, hoping to make the *contessa* try to guess just how much she knew.

"Well, perhaps it is best that you have come to me first. At least I will give you the complete and correct story about," she paused as if reconsidering, "about Doctor Russo."

Maggie nodded somberly, absolutely amazed that the *contessa* was willing to talk, and without any prodding. She had been prepared for a real battle.

"During the war," the *contessa* began, looking away, "my husband became very ill. Very ill. Spitting blood. But there were few doctors and no medicine for the people, especially for the nobility. The Fascists made everyone afraid to help us, afraid that they would be accused of something or other. Still, I begged for help for my husband. Every day I went through the streets, looking for a doctor, but no one would come.

"Then, when the Americans arrived, I had hope. One day, I found a man treating the wounded of your army. He was a lieutenant colonel and a doctor. Tony Russo." The *contessa* paused briefly, lost in her memories. "Many Italian people were there begging for help, trying to steal medicine and food. The soldiers turned them all away, told them to go to the Red Cross. But everyone knew that the Red Cross was good for nothing in Rome. So I waited. I followed Doctor Russo for many hours, until late in the evening when I came upon him standing alone by the fountain in the Piazza Colonna. He was staring into the water with tears in his eyes.

"I walked up behind him and asked him what was troubling him. He looked surprised at first to see me there, but he was off his guard, so he did not ask who I was or why I had any interest. He answered me simply—he said nothing was wrong, he was fine. I did not believe him, but I did not contradict him. Instead, I told him about the *conte* and how sick he was. He tried to avoid my request, told me that he was not permitted to treat civilians, that he would get into trouble if he did.

"Then I wept, not to make him feel sorry for me, but because I knew he was our last hope. I think I must have found him in a weak moment, because of all the people who had asked him for help, he took pity on me and stole away from his barracks to see the *conte*. By now, my husband was barely conscious because of the fever. Doctor Russo said he had pneumonia and that he would die if he did not get penicillin. The very next morning he returned at dawn with the drug. He came every day until the *conte* was well. Had it not been for Doctor Russo, I would be a widow."

The *contessa* stopped again, pouring herself some now lukewarm tea. It was as if she were stalling. She held the teacup poised at her mouth, thinking. Maggie remained silent, waiting for the *contessa* to continue.

"I . . . I was so happy to have my husband,"—the *contessa* set down her cup—"that I asked the doctor what I could do to repay him. My husband offered him anything within his power, but Doctor Russo always refused. But I would not accept his modesty, so I went to him at the army hospital.

"When I saw him, I thought again of that first night when I met him by the fountain, and I asked him why he had been crying. He was very quiet at first, then he told me his problem, relieved to share it with someone who might care. He told me that he had gotten a girl pregnant in Gaeta. Because of the war and his being a doctor, he could not stay with her. All he knew was that she was very poor and had no close relations to care for her. He was worried sick about the girl and the baby. I asked him if he would like me to find this girl and make sure that she was provided for. With tears in his eyes, he said, yes, he would like that very much.

"The American army left Rome soon after, and we never saw him again. However, I did not forget my promise. The *conte* and I went to Gaeta to find the girl, but we were told by her neighbors that she had died in childbirth. 'And what of the child?' I asked. No one was sure, but they told us to see Father Virgilio, who was the guardian angel of the war babies, they said. This priest was not hard to find. He was working in a warehouse he had set up as a clinic. Oh, I remember that day—the newborn babies all crying, the young mothers, some no more than children themselves, all of them frightened. I went over to this man, this kind priest, and I told him about Doctor Russo and the girl. He was so pleased to see our concern.

"You see, the girl was an orphan herself, so when she died, the baby had no one. The priest assured us that the baby was healthy and safe in an orphanage. He himself had been entrusted with the child, and she had been sent to a convent in Rome only weeks before. We told him of our obligation to Doctor Russo and he said we could send a contribution to the convent if we liked. The *conte* and I, we looked at each other and we did not have to say a thing. For many years, we had tried unsuccessfully to have a child of our own. We had been to many doctors, all to no avail. It was as if this baby had come to earth to be with us. We, we knew that we must adopt this child.

"We then returned to Rome and found the child at the Convento di San Gabriele. She had her mother's name then, but when we adopted Gabriella, we told the mother superior that we would christen her after the convent that had saved her for us." The *contessa*'s eyes shone with tears.

"Does Gabriella know that she's adopted?" Maggie tried her best to maintain her professional demeanor, though the *contessa*'s story had moved her deeply, and there was a lump in her throat.

"Yes. She knows."

"Has she ever been curious about her natural father? Did she ever try to find him?"

"No. I asked her this once, but she was adamant. 'No,' she said, 'you were the ones who loved me, you are my *real* parents!'"

"If I told Gabriella that my magazine could find her father, that we could unite them after all these years, do you think she would consent?" Maggie said the words hesitantly. Basically, she already knew the answer.

"You understand so little, Miss Reardon." Tears were now streaming down the *contessa*'s cheeks. "Let me tell you something. Blood is a very weak bond between parents and children. It is love, Miss Reardon, that is the stronger cement. Now, you are asking me to help you destroy the love between my daughter and my husband and myself. I hope you do not ask this of Gabriella . . . but then you are a very strong-willed woman, Miss Reardon. I see that, and *I* cannot stop you, can I?"

The *contessa* stared Maggie down unblinkingly, her eyes still moist, her emotions now held in check.

Maggie looked down at the surface of the coffee table, reconsidering.

"Thank you for your time, *contessa*," she said finally, in a quiet, faraway voice. She stood up and walked to the door. Turning back, Maggie murmured, "thank you" again, softer this time. Then, quickly, she showed herself out of the palazzo.

Chapter 16

The next morning, Maggie sat at her desk, ready to start work. Three letters had arrived in the mail that morning—one from Ellen, one from her parents, one from *Shout*—a perfect excuse for putting off her writing for a few minutes.

She read the letter from her parents first. Her mother wrote the usual gossip about people in Wilton, asked when she would be coming home and told her to be sure to stay healthy. Maggie smiled fondly as she folded the letter and put it aside.

Maggie proceeded to Ellen's letter. "I have good news and bad news for you," Ellen wrote. "The rent was raised fifteen bucks—a fuel surcharge—that's the bad news. The good news is you don't have to pay your share this month. Stan has moved in (hope you don't mind). We've set the wedding date, the Sunday after Easter, and you're invited, of course. It's going to be a *real* wedding—bridal gown, bridal bouquet, rice, the works. I know it sounds dumb for me to want this now, doesn't it? But Stan wants it, too. We know what we're getting into now, and the wedding is kind of like a blessing. Make sense?"

Maggie read the letter over a couple of times. Yes, it did make sense. More sense than the virgin bride marching down the aisle at eighteen or twenty or whatever age, hardly aware of her own womanhood before linking her life to someone else's, for however long it lasted. Ellen and Stan knew they belonged together now so the wedding was not a pagan ritual, it was a confirmation of a way of life. Maggie had never spent long hours dreaming about herself as a bride like many of her friends did. Mostly she longed to test herself as a person and an intellect in the "real" world. But now her heart was melting at the idea of a wedding with bridesmaids, a wedding cake, lots of relatives and the firm knowledge that she knew where she was going in her own way, just as Ellen did in hers.

She put aside Ellen's letter to read again later and picked up the brown envelope with the *Shout* logo on the address label. She looked at the scribbled address. It was Mabel Weeks's handwriting. Maggie opened the letter and gasped out loud as she read.

"Bravo! 'The Innocents' is a story that had to be told. Good work, Maggie, proud of you! Just to let you know that Jennings and the editorial board are thrilled with your first piece and can't wait to see the next one. Me too. I knew you could do it. Mabel."

Yeah, 'good work,' Maggie mused, happy for the praise, *but how do I follow it up?*

The *contessa*'s words had been haunting her ever since she left the palazzo. She'd been up most of the night, and at dawn she'd given up trying to sleep. She got dressed for a walk in the chilly streets and wandered lost in thought. She put herself in Gabriella's place and wondered whether she would be willing to risk her parents' love to find her "natural" father. It seemed almost blasphemous to call anything natural in such an unnatural predicament.

Maggie picked up her mother's letter and started to reread it. The knowing concern and affection implied in her words proclaimed the bond between her mother and herself louder than any media event could. There was certainly nothing in the world that could make her jeopardize that relationship. Nothing and no one. A parent's love is just too valuable.

It was then that Maggie decided to change the focus of her next article. She would take up the plight of the adoptive mother of the innocent, instead of that of the innocent herself. Although she would not mention names, the article would center on the *contessa*, not Gabriella.

She took a yellow legal pad and a black felt-tip pen from

the desk, then sat in the armchair by the window. With the pad on her knee, she started to collect her thoughts and outline the article. The exact manner in which she would present the Sciarras' story was not yet clear to her, but Maggie did have a strong feeling for how she would conclude the piece—the final theme would be that unselfish love prevails.

Maggie was sitting at her desk the next afternoon, typing furiously, when there was a knock at the door.

"Go away," she muttered under her breath, not wanting to be disturbed. "Yes. Come in. It's open," she called out.

Ugo poked his head through the door. "Telephone," he croaked.

"I'll be right down," she said, as she finished typing a sentence.

Ugo mumbled something she couldn't make out, then disappeared, leaving the door ajar.

Maggie stood up, reading the line she had just written. Then, realizing that whoever was on the phone would hang up if she didn't hurry, she tore herself away from her work and bolted down to the lobby.

"Hello?" she gasped, out of breath. "Hello? Are you there?"

"Of course I am here, Maggie. It is Pippo."

"Oh, hi, Pippo. How are you?"

"Mezzo-mezzo. I have not seen you in days, Maggie. You must have found a gigolo, *è vero?"*

"No, no, no," she laughed. "I've been cooped up here working."

"Why do you do that? You waste your time here in Rome. Why don't you come with me to Capri, eh?"

"Uh-uh. You're not going to tempt me now. My deadline is just too close for comfort."

"You hurt me, Maggie. *Dio!* I am destroyed!"

"Stop it, Pippo. I know you're not." His antics—as silly as they were—were a delightful diversion from her work.

"Then let me take you to lunch. Only for sustenance. Please! Tomorrow." He begged like a puppy.

"Tomorrow is Friday, let's see. . . . Sure, why not?" It would be good to see Pippo, she thought.

"Wonderful!" he gushed. "I will pick you up at your *pensione* at one. Is that good?"

"Fine. I'll be waiting downstairs."

"Good. Until tomorrow, *cara*," he announced with Continental panache.

"Until tomorrow," she echoed. "Ciao."

"Ciao, Maggie."

She hung up the phone and dashed right back to her typewriter. The story was hot now, and she knew she had to let it out of her right away.

Pippo patted down his hair in the mirror and adjusted his scarf just before he left his apartment. As usual, he was meticulously dressed—navy blue, double-breasted blazer; beige Cardin turtleneck; sharply-creased designer jeans; and Porsche sunglasses. A cranberry silk scarf was arranged loosely but carefully around his neck. As he rushed down to the street, the old wooden stairs of his apartment house strained under the pounding of his highheeled Bally loafers.

His Alfa was parked nearby on the Vicolo della Palomba. Pippo got in, started the engine, and immediately roared off, seemingly late for some appointment. It was five after noon.

He sped down the Via Giulia, then turned left onto Via Arenula. From here he turned into a series of narrow, winding streets and worked his way north until he passed the Palazzo Sciarra. He slowed down here and glanced casually at the scene of the Christmas ball, then accelerated again as he drove down the Via dei Fori Imperiali. Before he reached the Colosseum, he pulled over to the curb and looked at his watch: 12:17. He lit a cigarette and sat back, smoking it leisurely, eyeing the girls who passed by with obvious interest.

At 12:22, he looked at his watch again and took a last drag on his cigarette before tossing it out the window. Starting up the engine, Pippo pulled out swiftly into the brisk traffic and darted to the right in order to turn into a side street.

Again, he wove his way through a network of backstreets, until he reemerged onto the Lungotevere Avventino along the Tiber. He drove north-west, following the bend in the river, glancing at his watch every few minutes.

As he approached the Ponte Garibaldi, he slowed down and looked at his watch once more. Twelve-twenty-seven. Almost crawling now, Pippo ignored the impatient drivers

ROMAN CANDLES

behind him and stared intently at the Palazzo di Giustizia, the Italian government building across the way.

Gradually, Pippo picked up speed and returned his attention to the road. He turned left onto the Ponte Garibaldi, but when he was halfway across the bridge, he put on his directional and suddenly pulled into the slow lane. Despite the traffic, he stopped the car in the middle of the bridge. Quickly, he turned around in his seat, and over the racket of the blaring, annoyed car horns, Pippo heard the shattering explosion. A split-second after the blast, dusty clouds burst out of the demolished windows of the Palazzo di Giustizia. Pippo put the Alfa in gear and accelerated, flowing easily with the traffic. His watch said 12:30, exactly.

On the other side of the bridge, a young man in a gray tweed overcoat and worn construction boots waited on the street corner. He barely seemed to notice when the blast sounded from across the river. With his hands dug deep into his pockets, he looked preoccupied, a faraway expression on his face.

When the red Alfa pulled up to his corner, the young man calmly walked up to it, opened the door and got in. Pippo said nothing and the young man just stared straight ahead, his hands back in his pockets.

Pippo drove off, doubling back toward the bridge to drive along the west bank of the Tiber. The flashing red lights of the fire trucks, the screaming sirens and the milling crowds caught their attention as they drove along. The young man stared coldly in silence at the panic surrounding the Palazzo di Giustizia.

Pippo continued along the Tiber until he came to the Castel Sant' Angelo where he crossed the Ponte Cavour back into the eastern end of the city. They were headed for S. Trinità dei Monti and Maggie's *pensione*.

Maggie was standing on the front steps of the *pensione*, waiting for Pippo, wearing her plaid shirt and beige jumper. She pulled her raincoat closely around her as she paced the step, a bit chilled by the brisk wind. She hadn't been there more than a minute when the red Alfa Romeo pulled up to the curb.

Maggie went to the car to greet Pippo and was surprised when she saw a sullen young man in a gray overcoat emerge from the car.

ROMAN CANDLES

"Ciao," he said to Pippo flatly.

"Ciao," Pippo returned evenly.

The young man then walked away and quickly disappeared around a corner.

"Hi, Pippo. How have you been?" She got into the still warm leather passenger seat and gave Pippo a kiss on the cheek.

"Very good, Maggie. Very good. And you? Have you won the Pulitzer Prize yet?" He chuckled.

"Not yet. Soon, maybe." She was genuinely happy to see him. "How come you didn't introduce me to your friend?" Maggie jerked her thumb toward the window as if the young man were still around. "Who is he?"

"Him?" Pippo said with a broad smile. "He is my brother."

Pippo took Maggie to a noisy but friendly home-style restaurant called Da Mario, on the nearby Via della Vita. Tucked away in the back room, they drank a wonderful bottle of Est, Est, Est, a light white wine, and gossiped like old women. Maggie intentionally avoided any discussion of her work because she was so happy to be away from it for a while. Pippo did not pry, asking her neither about Alex nor her story, preferring instead to taunt her with all she had not yet seen in Rome and what golden opportunities she was giving up by secluding herself with her typewriter.

"You can write in New York," he said wagging a finger at her, "for in Rome, one must play."

Maggie gave him a shrug and tried to ignore him as she gorged on a double antipasto and a large portion of spaghetti alla carbonara, *al dente* pasta with a sauce of egg, grated cheese and *pancetta*. She couldn't decide about dessert so she had a cannoli *and* a piece of custard-rum cake. In her frantic zeal to finish the article she had been missing meals.

After lunch, Pippo left his car in front of the restaurant so he could walk her back to the *pensione*. "You are sure you will not let me tempt you, Maggie?" he asked mischievously. "I would love you to see the Castel Sant' Angelo and the Foro before you leave. We could go take them both in this afternoon, then tomorrow I can show you the Termi—the Baths of Caracalla where every summer they perform a glorious *Aïda*."

"Stop, will you please!" Maggie begged, her hands covering her ears. "I cannot be swayed. To work!" she proclaimed, running into the *pensione*. "Talk to you soon, Pippo. Thanks for lunch."

She felt refreshed, ready to work through the afternoon and into the night, without dinner if necessary, and she sat down at the typewriter with real enthusiasm.

When she finished writing inserts to plug into the weak spots in her story, she read through the rough draft and immediately started to work on the second draft. The way the article had shaped up, it was obvious that she really had used all her available material and that this would be the last part of the series. Jennings wouldn't mind that—he'd told her he wanted either two or three pieces. Anyway, if he wanted three, this article could easily be divided. She had written enough for two shorter features or one long one.

But what excited her and drove her on to finish was the perfect way it all hung together. It amazed even her that her paragraphs fit so well, forming a seamless, almost fictionlike narrative. The piece said what she wanted, she thought, and she only hoped that it would move the *Shout* readers as much as it did her.

The typewriter keys worked through the evening. The finished pages piled up on the desk, and the typewriter worked faster as Maggie became more excited and the concrete manifestation of her creativity spurred her on. Finally, around ten-thirty, after eight solid hours of work, the typing stopped. Twenty-three typewritten pages sat on the desk, face down, and Maggie lay on her back on the bed, her forearm shading her tired eyes, a gentle smile of satisfaction peeking out. Soon she dozed off, quietly overjoyed and secure in the knowledge of what she had done. She had gone out and gotten the story and written a dynamite piece of journalism. Just like she'd said she would. Only the polishing was left, she thought, as she fell into an exhausted sleep.

She had drifted off for no more than fifteen minutes when she was awakened by a knock at the door. Groggy and disoriented, she lay there, her eyes adjusting to the glare of the desk lamp with difficulty. Only half-awake, grumbling and cursing, she stumbled to the door, her jumper twisted to one side and her hair a tousled mess.

"What?" she barked as she opened the door, more to stop the knocking than to find out her visitor's identity.

"Hi." It was Alex, looking a bit bedraggled himself. "I'm not interrupting you or anything?"

"Ah . . . no, no. I just dozed off for a minute." She rubbed her eyes and yawned. "Come on in."

"Thanks." He walked in and glanced at the papers strewn about the desk and the open files on the floor. "If you're working, I'll get lost. . . ."

"No, no. I was just reading." Maggie was too exhausted, too drained to talk about her article, and she decided it would be easier to avoid the topic. And, still, somewhere in the back of her mind lurked the uncomfortable feeling that Alex still wasn't the right person to trust with confidential professional information. She couldn't let go of the remembrance of that night when she'd caught him going over her notes.

"Sit down and tell me where the hell you've been all week. I haven't seen you since Christmas." Maggie startled herself with her tone of voice—she never meant to sound so possessive.

"Bologna," he said readily, apparently oblivious to any nastiness in Maggie's question. "Chasing terrorists, of course. You know how it is, following up exhaustive leads that usually manage to net you a sentence or two that gets cut anyway back at the home office to make room for a margarine ad."

"Yeah, tell me about it," she commiserated, smiling and rubbing his weary shoulders. "What brought you back to Rome?"

"You," he stated plainly, looking a little surprised that she asked. He took her hand and drew her around the chair and into his lap. In one smooth movement, she entwined her arms around him, and they kissed long and deeply. Secure in his embrace, she felt that in a minute she might have fallen off into a dreamy, blissful slumber.

He nuzzled up to her ear and gently licked the lobe, tickling her back to full consciousness. "I came back for you," he whispered romantically, "you and the *Ordine dei Serpenti*."

"What?" she blurted out.

ROMAN CANDLES

He looked at her with an odd, pathetic smile.

"I really did miss you all week, but to be honest it was the bombing that made me rush back today."

"What bombing? What are you talking about?"

"You mean you didn't hear about it?" He looked shocked. "Another terrorist attack. This time at the Palazzo de Giustizia, a government building. Seven dead and thirty-eight hurt. The minister of transportation was killed."

Maggie inhaled sharply. "That's awful!" Suddenly, she was wide awake. She hugged him tighter, as if physically chilled by the news. "What was that you said before? *Ordine* something?"

"*Ordine dei Serpenti*, the Order of Snakes. A brand-new terrorist group in town. No one's ever heard of them before, but they're taking credit for this bombing. They haven't declared their political position yet, which is pretty odd." Alex shook his head, still dumbfounded by an event that he had seen happen so often in the past two years. "I swear, these groups grow like mushrooms."

"What did these guys want with this bombing? Money?"

"No, nothing. This was their calling card. They just want everybody to know they're here and they mean business. The kidnappings and the ransom threats will come next."

"Oh, God, it's so creepy." She shivered, a pained expression on her face.

"Yeah, but like I said, this bunch is a little different. Usually, the first thing a terrorist group does is declare its ideology. Right or left, they always want everyone to know how they intend to save Italy. Only the opportunistic freelancers dispense with the political theory. That's because they're just in it for the money. But, then, they don't go in for public bombings or fancy titles. That's the other peculiar thing about the *Ordine dei Serpenti*, their name. All the other groups have names that reflect their political or militant stance—the Red Brigades, the Front Line, the New Order, the Insurrection."

"They sound like punk-rock groups," Maggie quipped.

"Yeah, they should be so harmless. But this Order of Snakes, the name is more occult or mythic than political. I don't know, I just have a feeling there's something different—worse—about this one."

"Can we change the subject? You're scaring the hell out of me."

"Sure. How's your thing coming along?"

"Okay. Still collecting information," she lied. The new piece was still too precious to show to him. It just wasn't ready to be read yet, and she knew that if she told Alex it was just about finished, he'd want to read it right away. She was still overwhelmed by the material, still too emotional about the *contessa*'s story to put up with anyone telling her where to put her commas or that her people weren't believable. Even if the prose was faulty, she felt, the story itself was beyond criticism.

"I know I don't have to ask, but are you hungry?"

"Hmm." She grinned. "I suppose I could work up an appetite."

"Good. I'm starving, haven't eaten all day. And I don't know how I'm going to fall asleep tonight. Running around Italy chasing these weirdos gets me so hyper."

"Aw, I know you, you always fall asleep when you lie on your stomach."

"Well, I'll tell you what works better."

"What's that?"

"When I lie on *your* stomach."

She giggled. "Okay, let's do that later. Food first."

"How does *lombatina alla salvia* at La Tana del Grillo sound?"

"Sounds great—whatever it is."

"It's a veal steak in a sage sauce."

"Sounds better." She sighed.

"Then," he put his hands around her waist and drew her toward his chest," we can go to the Colosseum and chase all the cats and spoon at the moon like teenagers. Or is that moon at the spoon like teenagers?"

"Rhett Butler you're not, but you'll do." She ran her hands down his back. "Boy, will you do!" she purred in a Mae West voice.

Alex was speechless.

"C'mon, big boy, let's go before I lose my appetite."

"Oh, Maggie, Maggie, Maggie," Alex put on his best Cary Grant, "why do you torture me so?"

"Some men would die for my torture," she huffed lasciviously, still as Mae West.

ROMAN CANDLES

"Oh, my darling, torture me. Tomorrow is New Year's Eve. Let me show you Rome. The champagne, the caviar, the discos. . . ."

"Say no more, Chicolino," she quickly switched to Groucho Marx, her face lighting up behind the charade, "you've got a date."

Chapter 17

The Sunday morning church bells rang out all over the city, overlapping, singing in chorus, shouting each other down. It was a weekly ritual, a sort of holy competition in Rome. Just as American children had the Sunday comics, Roman children had bells. All morning long, on the hour and on the half-hour, some bells somewhere were tolling. There was no escape from them. Still, Maggie did not hear them.

Up at seven despite her midnight jaunt to the Colosseum, Maggie was at her desk, rereading her article, meticulously polishing her prose in the determination that she would make it so powerful and moving that no editor—not even Andrew Jennings—could bring himself to deface it with a blue pencil. Again and again, she considered and reconsidered each sentence, weighing each word for its meaning and dramatic effect. It had to be perfect, and it had to be finished today.

Alex was beginning to make things hard, and she knew she had to complete the piece soon, or he would succeed in diverting her attentions entirely. It was a struggle just to sit here alone and keep Alex out of her mind for a few hours. She was certain that after a romantic New Year's Eve celebration together, she would be hopelessly distracted, and she wanted nothing to stand between her and her work. The love of a man was certainly something she sought, but this was not the time to have to choose one's priorities between love and career. *Certainly not when you've got this deadline, Maggie, and not when you're committed to six thousand words of a piece that has already been advertised and laid out.*

Alex was fireworks, he was beautiful, breathtaking, tender—but unless she intended to write a salable article on his charms, the fact that her mind was elsewhere would cut no ice with Jennings and the editorial board. No, she couldn't risk blowing it now. The article had to be completed first, then there would be a few days left of her stay to spend with Alex, and after that. . . . She didn't want to think about that now.

The love between the doctor and the young Italian girl was never discussed with the conte and contessa. Only his tears in the dark told the contessa of his genuine concern and his passion. . . .

Maggie read the line over, considering the phrase "genuine concern and passion." Is that redundant? she wondered. Aren't concern and passion genuine by definition?

Well, what about Alex? Was he genuine in his feelings? His passion in bed was overwhelmingly exciting, and moving and tender as well. When they were alone together, he was funny and self-effacing and wonderful to be with. But when there were others around, he became aloof, almost defensive. He was so odd that way, not exactly Jekyll and Hyde, but. . . . Just the way he was, she guessed. He was too intense, too driven, to play games like balancing several lovers simultaneously. He was serious, a real professional, he didn't deceive people. If he didn't care for her, he would certainly have dropped her like a mediocre paragraph in a good story.

But was he concerned? Did he really care for her? Or was she just convenient for the moment? Craig seemed to care, but his passion was anything but genuine. Or maybe he just had a lot of genuine passion to go around. Alex seemed more mature about a relationship, but, then, they were two Americans together on foreign soil, and that might make all the difference. What would happen after she left Rome? Out of sight, out of mind? Well, if he didn't give a damn about her, he would have to be a terrific actor. He was certainly adamant about protecting her from his terrorists. Even last night at the Colosseum, when she had questioned him about the *Ordine dei Serpenti*, he had grabbed her and kissed her and said that the night was for romance, not politics. Then he had repeated his warning to her once again, "What you don't know won't hurt you." He'd promised her a big night on the town for New Year's Eve, and when she'd protested that she had nothing to wear, he assured her that no one dressed up for New Year's Eve at Jackie O's. It was the most fashionable discothèque in town, on the Via Boncompagni near the American embassy.

"After being stuffed into a monkey suit for that ball," he told her firmly, "I have no intention of glitzing up again for at least another year. And you—you'd look gorgeous in a gunny sack!"

Yes, Alex was thoughtful, Maggie mused, thinking back over his comments of the previous night. He was considerate and lovely, *but . . . but does he love me?*

Suddenly, she threw her pen down on the desk. "Goddam it, Maggie, snap out of it!" she growled. "You're wasting time, girl, and you're going to be in the doghouse if this isn't finished this afternoon."

She stood up, marched to the closet, and pulled out her mauve sweater-dress, the one she'd worn the first time she met Pippo and Gabriella. Giving it a quick once-over, she pushed her other clothes aside and hung it up again. "There!" she muttered. "It's fine. Now stop fussing and get to work!"

Marching back to her desk, she plopped herself down, picked up her pen, and scanned the top page. But that phrase stared back at her—"genuine concern and passion." Biting down on the pen, she pictured Alex's sexy but studious face. Yes, she decided, there is such a thing as *genuine* concern and passion. She sighed and blinked, then continued with her proofreading.

Jackie O's was a moderately large disco consisting of one big room with a dance floor and many smaller, quieter rooms that featured either conversation pits, pinball machines, pool tables or overstuffed, mattress-sized pillows. The blare of music poured out into the street, and it took several minutes to get accustomed to the decibel level after they walked inside. The ambiance, Maggie thought, was more like Regine's than Studio 54—classier, an older crowd, less decadent. There was no one in jeans or jogging suits, but there were no tuxedos or evening gowns, either. This lack of pretense pleased Maggie immediately—snooty disco crowds and wealthy Italians like Gabriella were not her idea of fun-people.

Maggie felt immediately at ease. She was impressed by how American the place seemed. Not American really, but more like that distinct translation Europeans always make of American style into something that *seemed* American to them. Maggie couldn't help thinking of the Italian cowboy boots she had seen in a store window—ridiculously pointy toes, almost rococo stitched patterns and three-inch stacked heels—the kind of sissy footwear that would get you tarred and feathered in Texas. It was the same way with this disco, which was obviously patterned after the disco in *Saturday Night Fever*. Everything except for the elegant manner of the doormen and the bartenders and the palatial opulence of the carpeting, the chandeliers and the burgundy-flecked wallpaper. This place had more in common with Monte Carlo or even Versailles than the ultra-modern decor of Studio 54, nor did it have the sweaty energy of Brooklyn's 2001.

"A little more civilized than most Roman discos," Alex shouted over the recorded music. "At least there are no go-go girls swinging from trapezes here."

"Where do they have that?" she yelled back.

"Around the corner at the Piper Club. It's a great big place, a real mob scene."

"I'll bet."

"What?" He tried to hear her over the noise.

She pulled him close and talked into his ear. "No use talking. Let's dance."

Alex nodded vigorously and led Maggie out onto the crowded dance floor. She found that Italian disco music and rock 'n' roll were like Italian cowboy boots; it was a good try that didn't quite make it. The songs were all very punchy and too fast, most of them riddled with weird, electronic percussion. The rock 'n' roll was also sped up, full of "yeah, yeah, yeah's" in the lyrics, sort of a throwback to the Beatles. Nevertheless, the beat was sufficient to dance to.

As far as pop dancing was concerned, Alex and Maggie were two of a kind. They both moved to the music as they saw fit, ignoring the regimented dancers around them. Alex maintained a cool sway reminiscent of some of the black

ROMAN CANDLES

Motown singers of the sixties. Maggie, who had never gone to many dances or mixers in high school or college, worked up a modified Pony with some Latin Hustle flairs. At first she was very self-conscious about her dancing, recalling the Saturday afternoons she had spent years ago studying the dancers on Dick Clark's *American Bandstand* so she wouldn't embarrass herself when she got asked out. It didn't take long, however, before she loosened up and let herself go. It felt great to dance with Alex, and the gyrations of her body offered a welcome release from the tension of putting together her article all week.

She glanced at Alex, admiring his undulating hips and halfclosed eyes. She smiled, amused by the irony of Alex Parisi in his brown Harris tweed jacket, heather wool slacks and button-down collar, looking like some assistant professor of English literature, dancing to the blaring music and flashing strobe lights in a Roman disco. The man was simply full of delightful contradictions and surprises. He defied classification, and perhaps that was one of the reasons she was falling in love with him.

As they continued to dance—now to a bouncy version of "Johnny B. Goode" sung in Italian—Maggie noticed that Alex was sneaking appreciative looks at her too. They had something good together, she mused, not to mention the mutual power of their physical chemistry. It could probably blow up a government building if let loose.

The room was packed tight, and there was still over an hour to go till the New Year. As the dance floor filled and it became impossible to execute any kind of movement whatsoever, it became clear that they had better find a drink soon or they'd never make it to a bartender.

"Let's go upstairs," Alex shouted amid the crush. "We need some champagne."

Maggie nodded her approval and clutched his hand as he plowed his way up the wide, jammed staircase. Things were getting rather wild. Maggie noticed that two young women at the top of the stairs had pulled down their sequined tube tops and were drunkenly comparing the size and shape of their breasts. Poking and touching each other's chests, they seemed like two old housewives arguing over pot roasts at the butcher shop.

ROMAN CANDLES

Maggie let Alex lead her around, since the animated madness around her was more than she could negotiate on her own. They entered a doorway and stepped down several stairs into the conversation pit. The pit was the size of a small swimming pool with beige-carpeted steps covering three sides, and a full bar built into the fourth wall. Although the music was omnipresent, it was considerably calmer here and possible to carry on a conversation. Several people seemed to be having serious discussions. In fact, one fellow in a gray business suit and an electric-blue silk shirt was reading poetry aloud from a tattered looseleaf binder. Most of the people in the pit, however, seemed to be concentrating on someone of the opposite sex, paying more attention to their curves and bulges than their words.

"This is as bad as any East Side singles bar I've been in," Maggie commented to Alex.

"Worse, I think. These people see themselves as real jet setters and free spirits. They're generally willing to do anything for a thrill. Drugs, sex in all its various permutations, shoplifting."

"I'm surprised. I'd think people would be more uptight in such a devoutly Catholic country."

"I think the Church's influence has the reverse effect on urban Italians. Many people seem to go out of their way to cheat on their spouses. The month of August is actually called Cheater's Month."

"Why?"

"That's when the men send their wives and children off to the resorts and they take the opportunity to find lovers and make whoopee."

"That's terrible!"

"But the wives supposedly do their best to pick up gigolos at the resorts."

"Delightful custom," Maggie declared as she looked at some of the randy characters around her. "Well, maybe...."

"I tell you what, though. In a country where divorce is *verboten*, you've got to settle your multiple temptations some way. Well, that's the Italian theory, anyway."

Alex directed Maggie to an open space on a step, then proceeded to the bar. He returned in ten minutes with two glasses and a bottle of Moët in a chrome bucket.

ROMAN CANDLES

"Here we go." Alex poured and handed Maggie a glass. "To good stories," he toasted.

Maggied hooked her arm around his and repeated, "To good stories," then sipped her champagne, gazing at Alex over the rim of her glass with laughing eyes. "Now my turn," she said. "To good reporters." She held up her glass with her toast.

"To good reporters," he whispered, a sly grin on his face.

The crowd was beginning to go wild, sensing that midnight was near. The music became more frantic as the minutes ticked away, and as the hour struck, a profusion of horns began to blow.

"Happy New Year," Alex screamed at her, and she responded by planting a kiss on his lips.

"You too."

"New Year's resolutions?"

"Nope, not me. Never make them."

"I'll make one."

She put her hand to his mouth. "I'm superstitious, don't tell."

"Okay." He nodded. "My secret."

They sipped champagne together, then simultaneously leaned toward each other and kissed tenderly.

"Maggie! Alex! What a surprise!" A voice pealed out of the din, startling Maggie and making Alex grit his teeth. "I cannot believe you are here!" the man yelled at them.

Maggie looked up to see Pippo dressed to the nines in a double-breasted ivory wool Armani suit, a beige shirt and a chocolate-brown tie. In one hand he held a magnum of Dom Perignon; with the other he supported a tipsy, statuesque blonde in a skintight metallic red jump suit. Her long, platinum tresses fell over her face and onto Pippo's supporting shoulder, and all that could be seen of her face were her lazily-parted, blood-red lips.

"Pippo!" Maggie blurted out, shocked by the sight of this impish fellow with his incriminating date.

"How've you been, Pippo?" Alex seemed to be trying to keep the frost out of his voice.

"Beautiful, Alex, just beautiful. Do you mind if we join you?"

"No, not at all," Maggie said quickly, curious to meet Pippo's friend.

ROMAN CANDLES

Pippo nudged the blonde and guided her to the step below Alex. "Mariscella. Mariscella! Wake up! I want you to meet some people. Mariscella!"

Mariscella snapped her head back and opened her heavily mascaraed, green-glittered eyes. She was rather eerie-looking in her Hollywood get up. *"Buon' Anno!"* she muttered, glaring at Pippo, then she immediately crumpled into a limp, drugged heap on the steps. Shimmering strands of her hair fell across Alex's shoe like stains.

"Sacro cielo!" Pippo exclaimed. "What am I going to do with you, Mariscella? You must pardon her." He turned and looked up at Maggie. "She does not know when to stop."

"Apparently," Alex groaned.

"Here, Maggie, you must have some of this." Pippo filled Maggie's glass from his bottle of Dom Perignon. "It is so much better than Moët."

Maggie thought she could see Alex's nostrils flare in annoyance.

"So, Alex, tell me," Pippo leaned back casually and faced Alex, "how is your story coming along?"

"Not bad, not bad at all. What have you been up to lately?"

"Me? Tourists and tours and then more tourists. It is a monotonous life I lead, Alex, *veramente.*" Pippo flashed a toothy grin.

"You underestimate yourself, my friend." Alex displayed a thin smile as he looked down into the glass he was rolling back and forth in the palms of his hands.

"Perhaps, perhaps."

Maggie remained silent. There was apparently more going on here than an exchange of niceties, and the undercurrents seemed rather nasty.

"And how is Signorina Sciarra, Alex?"

"Fine, I suppose. Haven't seen her since the ball."

"Oh! Of course, you were chasing the Red Brigades. I have a very poor memory." He took a long draught of champagne. "Alex, I must thank you for introducing me to Gabriella. She is someone I wanted to meet for some time."

"Really?" Alex feigned naïveté.

"You are such a joker, Alex." Pippo laughed heartily. "But even more, I should thank you for introducing me to Maggie." He gently laid his hand on Maggie's knee. "She is a brilliant *giornalista*, you know. When she is a big name, I will be proud to say that I knew her in the beginning."

Maggie quickly took Pippo's hand from her knee and held it affectionately in hers. "Thank you, Pippo." She was desperate to rejoin the conversation and break the masked tension lurking in the air. "You really are quite a tease, though. All these compliments."

"You are too modest, Maggie. I know. I tell you the truth. You will see. Listen to me."

"Okay, Pippo, you can cool it now. I'm afraid all your scintillating comments will get you nowhere. I'm taken." She let go of his hand and took Alex's.

"Ah, Maggie!" Pippo laughed, wagging a scolding finger at her. "You know me too well. You think I am the *gigolo*, and do you know what? . . . you are right," he hissed. Pippo chortled until he started to cough uncontrollably.

Alex offered a half-hearted, clipped chuckle.

With Pippo's coughing, Mariscella groaned and stirred from her nodding slumber.

"Mia bella Mariscella," Pippo sighed, shaking his head, his lips pursed. He stood up shakily, more than a bit tipsy himself. He took her limp arm and dragged her like a big rag doll. "Come, *cara mia*, I must put you someplace until you know what year it is. Please excuse us." He turned to Maggie and Alex, having propped up Mariscella on his slim shoulder. "I regret to say that I cannot spend more time with you both, but. . . ." He shrugged. *"Buon' Anno,"* he said quietly, with an impish nod.

As he struggled off with his date, climbing out of the conversation pit and stumbling out the door, Maggie noticed that Alex's eyes were glued to the departing couple. His serious, intense face puzzled her.

"Hello? Come back, Alex." She tugged at his sleeve.

"What?"

"You look upset. I wish you'd tell me. . . ."

"Hey, hey!" he exclaimed. "This is New Year's. No glum faces, no sad stories, okay? Just silliness, I insist."

And with that he drew her into an embrace that took her mind away from everything else.

The noise in the streets was maddening. Strands of firecrackers flashed and danced all over the square as fiery balls

ROMAN CANDLES

of pink, green and white sailed across the black sky. The crash and rattle of bottles, pots, drainpipes and assorted debris provided a constant undercurrent of noise as people tossed these discarded "bad luck" items out windows and doorways into the streets. Alex threw his arms around Maggie and kissed her as if he intended to go right through her. Surrounded by the blanketing racket, Maggie became lightheaded and dizzy.

Suddenly, there was a gigantic boom and fireworks burst into the night sky, lighting up the entire neighborhood. Maggie gasped and clung to Alex, who pressed her against his body and kissed her again. His body moved against hers, meeting no resistance, swaying, panting, clutching, while sharp bursts of color and light flashed all around them.

The noise at the foot of the Spanish Steps was deafening, mounting as the minutes passed. Maggie knew it was useless to shout, so she broke from his embrace instead, and pulled him by the hand.

Together they ran up the Spanish Steps, Maggie guiding Alex along until he changed the pace and decided to make a race of it. Suddenly, he surged ahead of her, bounding up two steps at a time. But Maggie was just too feisty to be undone by such a gross tactic, so she stopped to pull off her shoes. She then bounded swiftly up the stairs, lagging just a few feet behind Alex.

Maggie, once a devout jogger, and Alex, a fine swimmer, showed no sign of fatigue as they dashed tirelessly up the endless flight of steps. It was clear now that their race would not end until the leg muscles gave out. Nearing the top of the Spanish Steps and the Church of Santa Trinità dei Monti, Alex turned left and headed down an adjoining street, with Maggie close behind.

He picked up speed and gained ground here, for the cobblestone street was very rough on her stockinged feet. Despite his advantage, he still had to contend with the garbage and unwanted household items littering his path. In this respect, Maggie had the edge, since her agility allowed her to sidestep the New Year's obstacles like an all-star running back.

Forging ahead, looking back only once, Alex suddenly realized that he was running alone. He slowed to a halt and turned to see Maggie slip into a side street. Breathing heavily, he started jogging back after her, spurred on by the prospects of the end of the chase.

He rounded the corner onto Trinità dei Monti, where Maggie, now more than a half-block ahead of him, was clearly making a run for her *pensione*. Dodging pots and pans and bottles, Alex was forced to slow down to a trot as he started to become winded. Maggie bolted up the front steps of her *pensione*, as fresh as though she had just started. Alex kept a keen eye on her, but he realized at this point that she had outlasted him. Well, what the hell, she was younger.

Puffing like a steam engine, Alex trotted into the lobby and to the bottom of the stairs. However, the idea of climbing the two flights up to Maggie's room brought him to a standstill. Gasping for breath, he considered it for a moment, then walked to the elevator on sore feet and pressed the button. Ugo, who was leaning casually on his elbows on the front desk, shot a perfunctory "crazy American" look at him before returning to his bottle of wine and the stout woman who was sharing it with him.

The elevator finally arrived and Alex rode the jolting archaic vessel up to the third floor. Pushing back the birdcage door, he found his second wind and dashed to Maggie's door, which was suspiciously ajar. He pushed it open gradually, the hall light casting his elongated shadow into the darkened room. Silently, he closed the door behind him, ushering his shadow back out into the brightly-lit corridor. The only light in the room was the dim glow of the street lamps filtering in behind the half-closed shutters. An ominous lump could be discerned breathing quickly under the blankets on the bed.

Playing possum, Alex thought. He stooped down to take off his shoes, then quickly shed his jacket, tie and shirt, then carefully removed his pants, making sure his belt buckle didn't rattle or the change in his pocket jingle. On cold, bare toes, he tiptoed to the side of the bed, finding the edge of the blanket with stealthy fingers.

But before the hidden form would allow itself to be laid bare by the intruder, the blankets flew up in Alex's face and Maggie revealed herself. Her naked breasts danced as she howled with laughter. Tossing off the blanket, Alex lunged.

ROMAN CANDLES

Random patches of flesh and occasional limbs emerged from the writhing tangle of bodies. The laughter gradually subsided, and a tender quiet merged with the gray dimness. Gentle moaning and the squeak of bed springs were the only accompaniment to the indistinguishable forms, as they became one in ecstatic comfort.

Chapter 18

"Hmm," Alex growled in satisfaction as Maggie cranked open the shutters and let the sun's rays cover the bed and Alex in it.

She leapt back under the covers and snuggled up next to him as he wedged his arm under her head and draped his hand over her elbow. "Happy New Year," she whispered, licking his nipple languorously.

"Sure as hell beats what I did last New Year's," he reflected.

"What was that?"

"I covered the annual dunk of the Roman chapter of the Polar Bear Club in Lido di Roma—you know, the people who go swimming in sub-freezing weather?"

"Yeah, one of their chapters meets at Coney Island every January First, don't they?"

"Yup. Well, they do it here too, except that it was only about forty-five degrees out in Lido di Roma last year. A heat wave by Polar Bear standards, I guess."

"Sounds exciting. The kind of story you can really sink your teeth into," she kidded.

"Yeah, the best part was when this nun walked out onto the pier. She looked like she was going out to pray for the nuts in the water, then all of a sudden she dives in too, clothes and all."

261

"Incredible, only in Italy."

"That's for sure," he confirmed.

"Alex, can I ask you something?" She felt the time was right to question him.

"What?"

"What was going on between you and Pippo last night?"

"I don't know what you mean."

"Well, the two of you were as catty as old maids. I was getting scorched by the hostile vibes that were jumping back and forth between you."

"Must have been the champagne. I think you're projecting."

"No, come on, Alex. Don't play dumb. What was all that business about Gabriella?"

"Pippo's a real sycophant, a leech. He lives just to hang onto people who are richer, more famous and more talented. Gabriella's his latest fantasy." Alex made no effort to hide the venom in his voice.

Maggie became incensed hearing Alex badmouth the one who had been so helpful and kind toward her. "I don't buy that, Alex," she barked. "Pippo isn't like that. Something's going on, and you're hiding it from me."

"Hey, hey, hey, calm down, girl. Aren't you letting your emotions run away with you?"

"No, I'm not! I'm getting a little sick and tired of all these oblique, guarded references to Gabriella in my presence. I want to know why everyone's so obsessed with her!" In her blind anger she lost sight of the fact that, because of her story, Gabriella was the focus of her obsessions too.

"Look, I don't know what you're carping about, but this is a stupid argument. Let's drop it right now!" His tone silenced her, and she lay beside him feeling angry and suspicious. She stared at the ceiling and smoldered.

"Come on, Maggie." His tone softened as he tried to make up. "Let's not fight. Hey, why don't we work on your article this morning? You must be pretty close to finished. Your deadline's coming up soon, isn't it?"

"What do you care?" She was still resentful.

"Hey, Mag, it's me. I'm one of the good guys, remember?"

She remained silent, staring at the ceiling.

"Look," he continued trying to reason with her, "why

don't you let me read it over for you? I know you've been to see the *contessa*, so you must have something written."

"What?" she exploded, turning to face him with fire in her eyes. "How the hell do you know that? Have you got your goddam moles tailing me now?"

"Now, wait a minute. . . ."

"No, of course not." It suddenly dawned on her. "Gabriella. Her mother told her, and she told you. Go ahead, deny it." The hurt of betrayal constricted her voice.

"Look, you and your suspicious mind are going to get into big trouble if you don't watch out. You don't know what you're on to. You've really got to be careful not to offend high people in high places—that could get the U.S. bad marks, and *Shout* bad marks. Just let me read what you've got so far, to see if there's anything in it that'll put you in hot water."

"Not on your life, pal. You're the one who's in hot water." She bolted out of bed and threw on her robe. "I don't know if you're still trying to pilfer *my* story or you want to protect your girlfriend Gabriella. But if you're interested at all, you made a big mistake when you decided to go to bed with me, thinking I'd loosen up and talk after a little romance and a lot of good sex. You underestimate me, Alex—my professional concerns are a lot more important to me than just getting stroked. But I don't give a good goddam why you wanted to screw me up, because you're not going to. You're not going to read my piece, so forget about it."

Alex got out of bed and quickly put on his shorts and pants, while she gathered the finished pages of her story from the desk and shoved them into a copy of *Shout*. Rolling up the magazine, she thrust it into the pocket of her robe.

"Maggie, you're being unreasonable," he said placatingly, shrugging on his shirt. "Let me. . . ."

"*Get out!*" she shouted, hiding the sobs that were building within her.

"You don't. . . ."

"GET OUT!" she screamed at the top of her lungs, picking up his shoes, opening the door, and hurling them into the corridor. "NOW!" Maggie stood beside the open door, her eyes wild with hurt and tears.

Alex said nothing now, staring down at her, his eyes hard, his jaw set. He collected his jacket and tie off the armchair and his socks off the floor and walked out of the room. With all her might, she slammed the door behind him, then locked it. Throwing herself upon the disheveled bed, she sobbed into a pillow and punched madly at the mattress that was still warm with their recent intimacy.

She had been sitting in the armchair all afternoon, brooding over the recent turn of events. So upset, she had not even given a thought to food all day. She felt incapable of doing anything but rehashing the particulars of her stay in Rome and her . . . affair with Alex, searching for some clue, some sign that the whole thing was fated to fall apart. That, once again, she had been blithely oblivious to the fact that a man was doing her dirt until it was much too late.

Throwing on a dirty pair of jeans and an old green sweatshirt, she sat in that chair with her knees tucked up to her chest, gazing blankly out on the rooftops outside her window. She had to sort this mess out and put it into some kind of order in her mind, if not in her life.

It had to happen, she thought. *I was in for a fall. I must have been riding too high, couldn't maintain that kind of luck forever. First, the big break, being sent to Rome on assignment, a feature series all to myself. Ha! Maybe Jennings was right about my not being ready yet. Certainly not for this!*

I should have been suspicious of Alex from the minute I got off the plane. There was no logical reason for a hotshot like him to go for me—unless there was something else he wanted, of course. No one is that nice for nothing. Giving me his room, showing me around, taking me to the embassy. Well, he certainly was convincing, an Academy-Award performance. But what unbelievable gall! Fills me up with all that hoity-toity Christmas ball crap, Prince Charming taking Cinderella out with the debs, and all the while he's still stringing along his poor-little-rich girlfriend. And not only that, her mother is throwing the ball! Then he has the nerve to rendezvous with her there. 'Don't worry about the American,' he probably told her. 'I just have to make it look good so she won't suspect.' And, then, he has to fabricate that asinine excuse for disappearing with her, blaming Pippo for crashing the gate. And I believed him! As if Pippo could crash anything, the sweet little guy. Well, I hope he feels like a big man now, the goddam creep.

He's managed to malign Pippo, get into my pants and still end up with Gabriella.

Why did I ever get involved with him? Betsy was dying for a friend; she was the one I should have spent time with. Maybe she wouldn't have been scared half to death by those goons if I hadn't been acting like such a princess, having her deliver my gown for me. Damn! If I had shown a little more interest in her, I would have had a real friendship now, one that would have lasted. And isn't that the most important thing? Man or woman, it doesn't matter. I could never have been Alex's friend—he was just too untrustworthy—so being his lover really didn't count for much. I should have relied on my intuitive suspicions instead of always giving him the benefit of the doubt because I was infatuated. Looking at my notes after hopping out of bed with me, for pity's sake! Boy, Maggie, how much proof do you need?

She wiped away the tears that rolled down her cheeks and glanced at her desk. The loose, typed pages of her article were piled up on top of the copy of *Shout.*

I have a good mind to rip that up and start from scratch, rip Gabriella apart, give the whole story, names and all, then let her twist in the wind. See how long they keep you on the social register, cara, when they find out who you really are. Big deal, personal assistant to Aldo Amarone. You'd be lucky if you could model housecoats for Sears if Aldo knew what I knew.

But what good would that do? Not that the witch doesn't deserve to come down a few pegs. Only her mother deserves any kind of consideration. She leveled with me. When I confronted her with the facts, she owned up to them. The women went through a lot for her family. I don't want to have to live with the contessa's tears staining my future. It wouldn't be right.

No, it would be foolish to rewrite the article. Sure, she felt bitter now, but she knew that it was an excellent piece of journalism—that was what really counted. She had come to Rome to do a job, and now it was done. She hadn't come to go sightseeing or to find a man. She felt a hostile desire to sit down at the typewriter and write an exposé on that so-and-so Parisi, but she stopped herself. Who'd want to read about him? It would be a waste of her own valuable time. Anyway, her job was done, and it was time to collect her laurels, dammit!

ROMAN CANDLES

Determined to stop brooding over Alex, she got up, grabbed her article, briskly evening the pages on the desk and putting a paper clip on them. Slipping the pages back inside the magazine, she looked around the room for a good hiding place. At last, she went over to the bed and tucked the magazine between the mattress and the boxspring for safekeeping.

Off came the sweatshirt, then she dropped the jeans to her ankles, and she kicked them both into a corner. Throwing on her robe, she picked up her cosmetic bag and walked briskly to the bathroom down the hall.

Time to stop moping, she thought as she locked the door behind her, *there's a lot to be done.*

. . . The truth of the innocents is not in the pathetic eyes of the war babies seen in the old, creased, black-and-white photos taken during the war. It is not in the angry eyes of the young adults who still wear their shame and resentment like shrapnel scars. Nor is the truth of the innocents in the unknown, furtive glances of the veterans, the American GIs who must still feel the pangs of guilt, more than just now and then, because they never went back to find out.

No, these are just misleading clues to the puzzle; for the truth of the innocents is contained in the hopeful, protective, yet tentative eyes of the people who took those children in and loved them deeply. As I tracked down my innocent from World War II, I began to notice that the people I talked to each had a particular expression on their faces when I broached this difficult subject. It was almost as if their words were inconsequential compared to the messages conveyed by their eyes.

The first mother superior I contacted said she had been in a cloister during the war and therefore knew little about the innocents. Yet her eyes were blank and evasive, slightly uncomfortable. She did not want me to disturb the innocents; *they have suffered enough,* her eyes told me.

The director of the orphanage I visited seemed to be apologizing when she explained that the orphanage did not have sufficient personnel during the war to bother with keeping records about the particulars of their children. However, her eyes told me that she was actually relieved that she was unable to give me the information I sought. *If you reopen old wounds,* her eyes sighed, *it will not be with my help.*

Maggie put the phone to her other ear, then turned the page and continued reading.

The old priest, the guardian angel of the innocents, about whom I had heard so much from so many people, babbled on in the confusion of his age, conversing with phantoms of his memory. But his watery, old eyes were not senile. They shone with a lifetime's worth of love and kindness, a life that saved so many others.

The next mother superior I went to did not want to see me. She said she knew nothing about my innocents, said she didn't know what I was talking about, even though I was already certain that I had, in fact, tracked down my innocent, and that this woman, as a child, had been at her convent. The mother superior's flashing eyes shouted frantically at me, *Go away, leave her alone, go away!*

Yet these eyes told me nothing compared to the glinting tearful eyes of the *contessa*, my innocent's adoptive mother. All my research, all my interviews, and all my reading were meaningless when I looked into her eyes and read the message written there. The "facts" of this article are secondary to the feelings that underlie them. It was not until the *contessa*'s eyes showed me the reality of unselfish love, the desperation and fear of losing her child's love—the child she had adopted—the hope that all her caring would prevail over the "facts" of her daughter's parentage, that I realized what the story of the innocents was all about.

This is not the story of the individual innocent's quest to find the truth from her physical parents, who might, indeed, have been any man and woman in any country who met by accident and were together for a brief time. Rather, it is a love story, a tale of children in need of love uniting with real parents who want to love, a tale that ends with the nurturing and strengthening and preservation of genuine love.

Maggie flipped over the page and waited for a reaction from the other end of the line. For several long minutes, there was silence.

"Mabel, are you there? Mabel?"

"Yes, I'm here," she said quietly behind the crackle of the transatlantic connection.

"Well? What do you think?" Maggie demanded anxiously.

"I'm speechless."

"That bad," Maggie moaned.

"Just the opposite. I'm drained. You sucked me in and carried me along and . . . it's a very, very powerful piece, a moving piece."

"But it's too purple, right?"

"Not at all, that's what makes it so strong, your restraint. You had plenty of opportunity to gush and get flowery, but you didn't. You stuck to your facts, but you gave us the raw emotions you felt as you were tracking down that girl. A perfect blend of narrative reportage and a clear human-interest viewpoint. It's . . . it's exceptional, Maggie. You should be proud."

"Phew! Do you think the editorial board will go for it?"

"Are you kidding? If they don't, they should have their collective heads examined. When are you sending it in? I can't wait."

"I'm not sending it in."

"What?"

"I'm bringing it in. I'll take it to the office myself tomorrow afternoon."

"I thought you were scheduled to be in Rome for another ten days, at least. Aren't you supposed to be doing a third installment?"

"I had the option to do a two- or three-parter. But this says it all, as far as I'm concerned. If Jennings wants to keep it going for another issue, I can split this in two and flesh out the halves with some extra material I didn't use."

"Okay. I agree that this piece would be a tough act to follow, and I have a feeling that Jennings will feel the same way. Damn, this story would make any publisher melt, even if he didn't have a soft spot in his body. Look, when you get in tomorrow, call me first. I'll scout things out for you to see how many articles the editorial board will want. If they insist on three parts, you can stay home and work on it for a few days, so that you can hand the pieces in just the way they want it and they'll have no excuse for butchering them. You can take the ten days to polish and add stuff if you have to split it. Nobody'll have to know you're not still in Rome."

"Thanks a lot, Mabel, you're terrific. I'll call you from the airport as soon as I get in. Should be around one or two."

"Right. Take care, Maggie. You've proven yourself, kid. *Ciao!*"

"*Ciao*, Mabel."

Chapter 19

Maggie had on the identical gray-flannel slacks and faded rose turtleneck that she'd worn on the trip over. Her bags were all packed and ready to go. The night before, she had gone out to make photo copies of her article and stopped to do a little souvenir-shopping as well. One duplicate of her piece she'd inserted into her copy of *Shout* and wedged into her big valise. Maggie had put the second duplicate in an envelope and mailed it to herself at the office. The original was in her notebook in her shoulder bag. Better to be safe than sorry, she thought.

The souvenirs were all tucked away in her small valise. A wallet for her brother, carved lapis egg cups for Ellen and Stan, a leather key case for her father and a silver St. Christopher medal for her mother.

The only thing left to do was to pack the gown. Maggie went to the wardrobe where it hung pinned to its padded hanger. She pulled it out and laid it on the bed. *Beautiful,* she thought, *too bad I wasted it on him.* She sighed as she arranged the clear plastic sheath, slipping it carefully over the gown. As she touched the velvet, she thought of the ball and Alex waltzing in his tux. *I'll probably never wear this thing again,* she mused. *Wonder who I know who could use it?*

Maggie took her chenille bathrobe and fit it over the

wrapped gown for extra protection, then secured the heavy plastic wardrobe bag around it and zipped it up.

"Well, that's that," she chirped sardonically. "Three weeks in *bella Roma*. Pretty soon it'll seem like I was never here."

Stop feeling so pathetic, she scolded herself, *You're acting like an idiot. What did you expect? A Bernini fountain dedicated to your outstanding work as a reporter? Certainly not to your achievements with men! Maybe they'll erect a water-cooler somewhere for the Sap of the Year. Arrgh!*

She could not help feeling awful now, because it was like she was sneaking out of town, an unwanted guest at a grand party. Having met so many people here, it seemed really sad that she had no one to say goodbye to. Betsy was in Connecticut, Laura Ord was out, Dick Ord was in a meeting. The *contessa* surely wouldn't want to wish her *bon voyage*. She would have called Angelo D'Allesio in Gaeta if she could have remembered the name of his restaurant. *Oh, God, this was lousy!* As for Alex and his *cara* Gabriella, they could just go jump off a pier for all she cared.

But Pippo! How could I forget Pippo! You're a real piece of work, Reardon. The one who had taken her halfway across Italy just to be a nice guy, and she'd almost left the country without even a phone call.

She glanced at her watch; then, quickly, went through the wardrobe and desk drawers to make sure she hadn't left anything behind. Satisfied that all was packed, Maggie grabbed her valises, slung her flightbag over her shoulder and lugged her typewriter case to the door. She went to the bed and carefully draped the wardrobe bag over her arm.

She looked around once at the little room. *Well,* she thought, glancing at the bed, *it wasn't all bad. And someday, there will actually be a man in my life who isn't a rotten liar even if he is good in the sack.* And then she looked affectionately at the little brass lamp on the desk. Without that lamp, she might never have written a word of good prose. She was as thankful for its beneficent presence as she was for the old worn armchair and the shutters and, yes—even the bathroom down the hall.

Come on, Maggie, you really are a sentimental fool, she thought, closing the door behind her.

The birdcage elevator descended jerkily to the lobby where Ugo was leaning on the front desk, reading the morning paper. Gingerly, she trod over to him and set down her bags, then presented him with her room key.

"*Arrivederci*, Ugo."

"You go?" His eyes widened in uncustomary surprise, as if her baggage had not made her departure obvious.

"Yes, back to New York."

"Oh, that is too bad. I will miss you very much, Miss Reardon. You very good guest." He reached for the receipt pad to make out her bill.

His sudden flood of emotion caught Maggie by surprise. His I've-seen-it-all demeanor gave her the impression that he felt all guests were the same—all nuisances. Just a case of a taciturn Italian who hid his real feelings. "Thank you, Ugo. I'm going to miss Rome and your *pensione* too."

She looked at the bill and took her checkbook out of her bag. "I know it'll take some time if I just pass this on to the travel agent when I get back to the office, so I'll pay you myself—if you'll give me a copy of the bill for me to hand in with my expense report."

He smiled broadly and produced the receipt pad again. "*Certo*. For how much should I write this time?"

"What do you mean?"

"I make it for a thousand lire more on the copy. This way, you earn some money."

She laughed aloud at his desire to falsify the books on her behalf. "No, no, that's okay, Ugo. Just make it the same amount."

Ugo smiled in embarrassment and shrugged hopelessly with another of his "crazy Americans" looks.

She glanced at her watch again and fished through her bag for some lire. "Ugo, I need a token for the phone. And will you do me a favor?"

"Yes, sure, anything." He seemed very eager to please.

"Will you call me a cab so I can get to the airport?"

"No problem, no problem."

He called on his desk phone to fetch a cab, while she went to the pay phone to call Pippo. And, as if by a miracle, she managed to get her call through on the first try. It rang six times, and disappointed, Maggie was about to hang up, when she heard Pippo's voice on the other end of the line.

"*Pronto!*" he barked.

"Pippo? It's Maggie. I didn't wake you, did I?"

"Uh . . . no, no, of course not. How are you, Maggie?"

"I'm going home, Pippo. I just called to say goodbye."

"No, you are joking. You cannot leave Rome before you have seen everything!"

"I'm afraid I have to, Pippo. I'm going to miss you very much. You've been such a good friend."

"Oh, Maggie, you will break my heart this way. Can we at least have a farewell lunch today?"

"No." She sighed. "I'd love to, but I'm leaving for the airport right now. My flight leaves at eleven-ten."

"Well, then, let me come over now, yes? I will drive you."

"You don't have to do that. Anyway, I've already got a cab waiting for me here." And, in fact, the cab had just pulled up outside. Ugo was supervising the driver, who was cramming Maggie's luggage into the trunk.

"Then I will see you off at the airport. Please, I must do this for you, my friend. You see, I do not want you to forget me when you are a rich and famous *giornalista.*"

"You're a real sketch, Pippo. Okay, just a second, I'll give you my flight number." She fished through her pocketbook and came up with a small memo. "I'm taking TWA, Flight 319, leaving at eleven-ten from Gate Nine."

"TWA, Flight 319, Gate Nine, eleven-ten. *Bene!* I will find you at the gate."

"Okay, but just in case we miss each other, I want you to know that I really appreciate everything you've done for me. Without you, I would never have finished my article. Thank you, Pippo, thanks so much."

"You are very welcome, Maggie. But I must go now if I am going to make it to the airport. There are a few things I must do first."

"All right. See you later."

"Sì, magnifico. Ciao."

Maggie hung up, waved goodbye to Ugo and dashed out to her waiting cab. Now assured that she had made at least one good friend in Rome, she did not feel quite so sad about her sudden departure.

Twenty minutes later, Ugo was jolted from his newspaper, when Alex ran through the lobby and up the stairs to Maggie's room. When he got there, he found the door open, the room empty, a chambermaid stripping the bed. He raced back down to the front desk.

"Where is she?" He was frantic and out of breath.

"Who?" Ugo wore his usual bored smirk.

"Maggie Reardon. Where is she?"

"America. She go home."

"When? What flight?"

Ugo turned the page of his paper, shrugging nonchalantly.

Alex suddenly grabbed his shirtfront and pulled him halfway over the desktop. A button flew off into the air and pieces of newspaper crumpled under Ugo's weight. "Tell me!" he growled.

"I know nothing!" Ugo cringed from the man with terrified eyes. "I hear TWA, that is all. I swear, *io giuro!*"

"When did she leave?" Alex did not relax his viselike grip.

"Little while ago. Twenty minutes, no more," his voice broke as he coughed out the words.

Alex shoved him back across the desk and tore out the front door like a man possessed.

"Will that be smoking or non-smoking?"

"Non-smoking, please," Maggie replied, examining the efficient young man behind the check-in counter. His dark, handsome features were definitely Italian, but his English was flawless, without the trace of an accent, almost midwestern in its blandness.

"All right, Ms. Reardon. Now, any baggage to check?"

"Yes, these two suitcases, the flight bag, and . . . this typewriter case. That needs special attention so it won't get too bumped around, okay? And, how crushed will this get if I give it to you now?" She held up the gown in its plastic bag.

"Well, it will go on the conveyor belt, but it won't be damaged, I'm sure. If you'd prefer, however, you can carry it on, and a flight attendant will hang it for you in one of the closets."

"Hmm." She considered for a moment. It was a beautiful dress, but it reminded her of that creep she was leaving behind. "I think I'll check it with you, after all," she decided, trying to convince herself that it was the right thing to do under the circumstances.

"Fine," he confirmed, attaching a tag to the wardrobe bag, then expertly laying it on the moving conveyor belt.

ROMAN CANDLES

Maggie deliberately looked away as the gown rambled away to the loading dock. Maybe it would get rerouted to Hong Kong and she wouldn't have to see it again.

"Now, here are your baggage stubs," he said, as he counted off the five tickets like cash, "and here is your boarding pass, which you present to the flight attendant when you board the plane. Your flight will be boarding at Gate Nine in approximately twenty-five minutes. I hope you've enjoyed your stay in Rome, and have a pleasant trip." He lifted his head from his computer panel and flashed her his company smile.

"Thank you," she murmured, put off by his homogenized manner. *About as sincere as that other louse*, she thought. She glanced at her watch and looked up at a nearby television screen that gave all the arrival and departure information. Her flight was right on time—no delays posted. Now, what should she do for twenty-five minutes?

"Maggie! Maggie!" a voice shouted in the distance.

She turned around and saw Pippo in his cashmere Burberry. "Pippo! Am I glad to see you. You made it!" She left the main check-in area to greet him. He was standing several yards away, down one of the long corridors. So happy to see him, to know that she did have a friend, she threw her arms around him as soon as she reached him and embraced him enthusiastically, burying an unexpected tear of joy in his shoulder.

"Hello, Maggie," he said cheerfully, one hand around her shoulder, the other still in his coat pocket. "Please, smile, and do not scream or do anything foolish. I have a gun in my pocket."

Maggie giggled at the joke. But when she pulled away from his embrace, she saw that the bright, sympathetic expression had faded from his face. And there was, in fact, a menacing bulge in his pocket.

"This some new tour-guide tactic, Pippo?" she asked quickly. "People refuse to stay and see Rome and you pull a gun on them?" She realized her voice was shaking.

"I am sorry, Maggie." He looked odd, his eyes very intent and piercing, as though he had a slight fever.

"I . . . I don't understand. . . ." Her brows were knit in confusion and distress.

"You will." He spoke with a newly put-on smile of delight.

"Just do as I say and keep looking happy, talk to me as if we were old friends meeting after a long absence. Can you do that, Maggie?"

"Pippo, I really don't think this is funny. You're scaring me to death."

Suddenly, he jammed the barrel of the gun into her side. She felt the thick, round muzzle between her ribs. "Believe me, Maggie, this is no joke, and if you think I am bluffing, let me assure you that you would not be my first victim, not by any means. Now, if you're ready to cooperate, we will walk straight back, out the main entrance, and into the parking lot."

"Why? Where are you taking me?"

"Just a little ride. To meet some of my brothers. Now, let's go." He poked her again with the gun in his pocket, and together they began to walk off through the crowds of people rushing to find their gates or trying to locate arriving passengers, all too busy to notice the gregarious man in the expensive coat walking closely behind the stiff woman with the strained look on her face.

"Pippo?" she ventured uneasily, half-turning around. "What is this all about? Why are you kidnapping me?"

"Maggie, you are a lovely person. Really. But you are quite dense in some ways. You see only the surface of things, not what lies beneath. I thought I was such a terrible actor, but you never suspected, did you?"

"Suspected what?" Her head was beginning to throb.

"Have you heard of the *Ordine dei Serpenti?*"

Alex had mentioned that name. Yes, the new terrorist group. Not Pippo!

"You . . . a terrorist . . . ?"

"Ah, finally you catch on. A bit too late, I'm afraid."

Her throat began to burn and her stomach ached violently. She felt like throwing up. The revelation of his pretense was just as horrifying as the immediate danger she was apparently in. His glib, phony cordiality was salt in the wound.

"Yes, Maggie, I am the founder of the *Ordine dei Serpenti,*" he announced proudly.

"You? You killed all those people at the Palazzo di Giustizia? I can't believe it."

"Oh, but you must believe it. It is true."

"But, why, Pippo?"

"Some because they deserved to die, because they refused to acknowledge their own greed and incompetence in leading this country. The rest died because they were there."

His matter-of-factness as he mentioned the innocent bystanders made him doubly repellent to Maggie. The man was diabolical.

They walked through the front doors, and Pippo let her feel the gun again just as she thought she could make a run for it. He directed her across the bustling street and toward a parking lot.

"I still don't understand what you want with me." Her voice was frigid with anger and resentment.

"You, Maggie, have been most useful to us. You see, you have made it possible for me to finance the future activities of the *Ordine dei Serpenti*. Without your work, I could never have gotten the Sciarras to, let us say, *donate* to our cause. When I said you were deserving of the Pulitzer Prize, I meant it."

"You're talking in riddles. What do you mean, the Sciarras are financing you?"

"Well, I had not intended to explain my plan to you, but I believe that you do deserve to know. After all, as I said, you made it all possible." He took her arm and pointed her toward a remote, deserted end of the huge parking lot.

"Terrorism is a very messy business, Maggie. Bombings, kidnappings—sometimes they work for you, sometimes not. You get caught, shot at, blown up by your own bombs. Then, you need money for arms and materials. Unfortunately, the fact remains that you always need money to start any power venture."

"You're still talking in circles. Get to the point."

"You are right. *Certo*, I will get to the point. Anyway, you Americans have little concern for theory as far as I can tell. Well, I knew we needed money, and I knew the *conte* and *contessa* had money to give. What I was not sure about was Gabriella. For several years now, I have suspected that she was not the real daughter of the Sciarras. From my research on their family, I knew that it would be unthinkable for any actual offspring of ancient Roman nobility to become such a—a career person. And, then, Gabriella looks nothing like either of the Sciarras.

"My evidence about her birth was not strong enough to

support my suspicion, but I knew that if my assumption was correct, I could convince the *conte* and *contessa* to give me some of their great capitalist wealth. Their family is very old, very proud, the kind of family that would not want it known if their 'daughter' is really a *bastarda*. But also, and this is more important than the shame of it, under Italian law, Gabriella is not entitled to her father's fortune. Conte and Contessa Sciarra never bothered to adopt her legally. I spent days and days looking through the civil adoption records here and in Gaeta. They simply took in the child Gabriella, illegally if you will. Therefore, she is not a valid heir. Are you getting the picture, Maggie?"

"You were out to blackmail the Sciarras!"

"Preciso, sì. If they would not give us money, I would destroy their family name and make Gabriella a pauper in the process. I am not greedy like they are, however. I will only demand as much as I need. Quarter of a million dollars, no more. But I would never have been able to do it without you, Maggie."

"Because you didn't know whether Gabriella was an innocent or not until I started to pick up her trail, right?"

"Davvero. When we went to Padre Virgilio in Gaeta, I lied to you, I told you he was babbling about nothing. In fact, the old fool thought we were the young *conte* and *contessa* looking for little Gabriella. He told me what convent she was in and who her real parents were. But you were too smart for me. You wrote down words he said even though I would not translate for you. I wanted to discourage you from proceeding with your investigation. But you would not be frustrated."

"Hooray for me," she spat at him sarcastically.

"Then I tried to scare you away," he continued, "but my brothers found the wrong American. I tell them you have red hair—they shoot at a girl near your *pensione* who happens to have red hair. And who happens to be wearing the yellow sweater I bought you. I did not imagine that you would think so little of my gift as to give it away."

"You bastard . . . you goddam. . . ."

"Basta. Let me finish while we have time. After we failed to get rid of you, I knew I would have to get to the Convent of San Gabriele to confirm the matter of Gabriella's adoption. The mother superior was very helpful when I told her I was a *giornalista.* . . ."

ROMAN CANDLES

"You? It was *you* who went to the convent, not Alex!"

". . . and the mother superior was even more cooperative when I told her I would blow up her convent if she told you anything. You know, it is so amusing how people are always willing to believe you when you tell them there is a bomb someplace—even when there is no bomb."

Maggie was silent, glaring at Pippo out of the corner of her eye.

"Soon, I will be making my formal demand to Conte Sciarra, and the *Ordine dei Serpenti* will make the Red Brigades seem like the boyscouts. It is, however, unfortunate that you were such an undaunted and resourceful reporter." Pippo suddenly paused, spotting a silver Mercedes across the parking lot. He raised his arm and waved to it.

"All your good work will never see print, I'm afraid. You understand, naturally. My brothers have your luggage by now, Maggie. We must burn your story and destroy your notes. After all, if I let you expose Gabriella in your magazine, there will no longer be any little secret. And without the secret, my plan will be useless."

"Wait a minute. You don't. . . ."

The silver Mercedes suddenly pulled up beside them and the back door flew open. Two men sat in the front, one in the back. Pippo jerked Maggie's arm behind her and began to force her into the car, where a dark, burly man in the backseat grabbed her and held her firmly. He smelled of stale cigar smoke and wet wool, and she thought she would gag.

"No, Maggie, there is no time to wait now. Naturally, we must kill you. Please trust me. If you cooperate, it will be painless. If not, then. . . ."

A shot rang out, and Pippo fell to the pavement, writhing and holding his left leg. Maggie turned and looked back across the parking lot. A man was crouched down on one knee about fifty yards away, holding a rifle. Before Maggie could react, the man in the backseat yanked at her elbow and pulled her inside the car. With the door still open and Maggie's feet dangling out, the silver Mercedes screeched and tore off, leaving Pippo behind. Maggie struggled to free herself of the man's grip, hoping to be able to jump out the open door, but he was too strong for her. The two men in the front seat were yelling at each other, and the man holding Maggie cursed in low growls like a dog.

ROMAN CANDLES

"Ucciderla subito, ucciderla!" the driver barked.

"Che se la frega io? Allora, dobbiamo sfuggire!" the other man in the front spat back.

Ucciderla? Maggie thought in a panic. Kill her. Oh, my God, they're going to kill me!

Suddenly, white Fiat sedans—unmarked police cars—were everywhere, in pursuit of the Mercedes. The open spaces of the remote lot were blocked by *carabinieri*, so their only escape was back through the main road near the terminal. They would have to plow their way through the trucks, cars, cabs and pedestrians milling about the terminal.

The back door was still ajar, but Maggie's captor had a firm hold on her, one hand pinning her arm behind her, the other gripping her head by the hair.

Maggie's heart raced, wild thoughts screaming through her brain. As the car swerved and screeched around dividers and parked cars, the door swung open dangerously beside her. She was certain they would all die in a fiery crash before these men got to carry out her execution.

The driver barked and cursed with each exit he found blocked by uniformed *carabinieri*. The main road was out of the question. He accelerated the car, heading straight for the police. Shots rang out, and the Mercedes' front windshield shattered, obscuring all view with the jagged network of spiderweb cracks. The second man in the frontseat braced himself against the headrest and kicked out the glass. Violent, rushing winds threw shards of glass into Maggie's lap. The driver continued to accelerate; then, suddenly, he slammed on the brakes with both feet on the brake pedal, while he gripped the steering wheel tightly.

The tires screamed and the air inside the car was full of the smell of burning rubber. Maggie was nearly thrown from the open door as the car made a split-second 180° turn. Her guard held her tight and kept her inside. Without losing a second, the driver gunned the engine and the Mercedes shot out back into the open lot.

The engine roared angrily as they picked up speed, but before they were able to reach the open lot, two of the white Fiats converged on them, one from the right, one from the left. The terrorist in the passenger seat drew a revolver and started firing at the car on his side, but the *carabinieri* did not hesitate. Like expert stunt-car drivers, they cut off the

Mercedes, quickly wedging diagonally in front of their front wheels, touching noses, and forcing the steaming car to a halt. A third police car screamed up from behind, braking too late and ramming the rear of the Mercedes to prevent the terrorists from escaping in reverse gear.

Carabinieri in all three cars held revolvers and rifles on the Mercedes, shouting and yelling. The driver threw up his hands in surrender, and Maggie's guard loosened his grip in white-faced panic. But, instantly, the man in the passenger seat swung around and pointed his gun in Maggie's face. A shot exploded through the air, and the gun dropped from his hand, grazing Maggie's leg. One of the *carabinieri* emptied his clip into the gunman's back and head.

In the same instant, before Maggie could get a glimpse of the destroyed body and the blood, another of the *carabinieri* whipped the back door open, grabbed her violently and yanked her from the car. It all happened so quickly, Maggie only saw a blur of uniforms, guns and smashed fenders.

"Stai in giù, stai in giù!" one of the *carabinieri* ordered her, pushing her down behind a police car.

But Maggie's curiosity and reportorial instinct was greater than the terror that rushed through her chest with the speed and intensity of a dangerous narcotic. Carefully, she peered over the police car through several panes of glass. *Carabinieri* held rifles to the heads and chests of the two terrorists left alive, while, with pistols poised in their hands, two of the men disarmed and slowly extracted the terrorists from the Mercedes.

Panting frantically, Maggie still couldn't think straight. Pippo, a terrorist? All the while, using her to do his legwork. He seemed so wonderful, but . . . it was clear he had duped her, set her up with that sweater, scared the wits out of Betsy. . . . Her anger spread out and blackened her thoughts like an ink stain.

She looked up again. More *carabinieri* came running to the scene from all directions. More white cars raced up with sirens blaring and lights flashing. Then she noticed a lone, navy blue Fiat speeding up behind the late arrivals. The blue car was stopped by the *carabinieri* about thirty yards from the wrecked Mercedes, and the police kept waving the car off, obviously telling the driver to leave the area.

Maggie squinted her eyes and stared at the blue Fiat. The

driver refused to leave, though the *carabinieri* continued to wave him off, one shouting through the window, gesturing excitedly at him. Then the driver's door opened, and a man got out.

It was Alex! He started yelling at the police, insisting about something. Suddenly, the passenger door opened, and Gabriella emerged from the car. Maggie's throat constricted as her eyes filled with tears. Gabriella was attempting to bully her way through the uniformed men, gesticulating wildly, animatedly. Alex went to her side, and together they tried to get past the *carabinieri*. He seemed to be trying to make them understand something. Maggie could see Gabriella stamping her stiletto heels on the asphalt like a petulant child. She clung tightly to Alex's other arm, exhaling in annoyance as a sort of futile punctuation to Alex's argument.

No, no more! Maggie thought in panic. *I don't want to see him; I don't want to see anyone. All I want is to get out of here and go home.*

Controlling her sobs but not her tears, she took advantage of the diversion created by Alex and Gabriella, and quietly began to walk back to the terminal. No one seemed to notice her. When she reached the end of the parking lot where lines of parked cars gave her some camouflage, she glanced at her watch. Quarter-past eleven.

I can make it if I hurry.

Stealthily, she walked, then broke into a run to the terminal, racing and bumping her way through the crowds. Just before she got to the gate and the metal detector, she wiped her eyes with the back of her hand. Composing herself in line, she realized that she was still attached to the bag that clung to her shoulder like an old friend. Despite all that had happened, she had not let go of it. Or of her article. She took out a tissue, her passport, and her boarding pass. *Now, I just look like another passenger, regretfully departing from Rome,* she thought. *Who would ever know?* Pictures formed in her mind and dissolved: Pippo falling to the ground, the gunman pointing his weapon at her, Alex and Gabriella, together again.

Forcing her feet to move, she walked rapidly but steadily to her plane, refusing to let herself collapse, massaging her sore shoulder as she walked. Her plane was already boarded and just about ready to close the hatch.

"Wait! *Attenda!* Wait!" she called out, her voice cracking with sobs, desperately wanting to be on that plane.

"Okay, okay. We're waiting," a red-blazered flight attendant sang out. "Take it easy. We'll wait for you," she assured Maggie.

Maggie could not speak as she tried to swallow her sobs. She thrust her flight pass at the attendant and allowed herself to be shown to her row. When she was safely in her seat with her belt fastened, she turned toward the window and let it all out. Her tears fell freely as the still planes, fuel trucks, hangars, terminals and anonymous parking lots sped by the cabin window. The elderly woman in the seat beside her looked like she wanted to comfort Maggie, but she must have been embarrassed by the girl's passionate sobbing, and she said nothing.

Chapter 20

They love it, Maggie sighed, slumped down in the corner of her living room sofa in New York. Jennings had been raving all week. She couldn't even go to the john at the office without somebody congratulating her. She folded her arms and sank her chin into her chest with a frown. Big deal!

Somehow, after everything that had happened in Rome, being *Shout's* newest star reporter didn't mean as much as she had thought it would. Her parents had met her at the airport. She hadn't even remembered wiring them that she would be returning early. They had come to surprise her, and were they surprised when a disheveled, red-eyed Maggie stepped off the plane.

Maggie had managed to calm down during the long flight, but the sight of her mother sent her into a new fit of sobbing. A few days in Wilton with lots of tender loving care had restored her spirits and now she was back at work, business as usual.

The sight of her black velvet ballgown had almost made Maggie break down again. When it came time to return to her apartment, she had left it hanging in her closet in Wilton, telling her mother she had no storage space in the city. That wasn't quite true, but it was too painful a reminder to see every time she opened the closet.

On the coffee table before her lay a photocopy of her first

article, photocopied from the dummies. It was all laid out and set in print, illustrated with a grainy photo of an Italian war baby, a thick, white question mark superimposed over the face. This was scheduled for the next issue, the one that would hit the stands around January 20 for February. It would be all over the United States in less than three weeks; it would get to the PX in Gaeta several weeks after that and Angelo would read it. And, in Rome, perhaps even the *contessa* . . . and Gabriella. . . .

Next to these pages were other photocopied sheets—her second article, edited. There was barely a mark on any of it, a few words changed and four sentences cut in the whole thing. *Unheard of,* she thought, *I've never seen an editor accept a piece as readily as this. I just can't believe it.*

The second installment would be the lead article in the March issue. It would be laid out next week. The art director wanted to consult with her first on illustrations. *Incredible! Reporters are never supposed to have a say on illustrations!* she raged to herself. *Art directors are supposed to be pigheaded, they're supposed to do it all wrong so the writers can get pissed off! They're not supposed to treat me like this.*

An open notebook lay on the sofa beside her, with a handwritten list she had just written facing her on the open page. Maggie glared down at it.

Not only does Jennings give me a goddam promotion and a raise, but he tells me to come in next Monday with a list of ideas for future articles. He actually wants to send me out on assignment again, and right away. God, I should be happy! I should be standing on my head and spitting nickels!

She stared around the room at the furniture, the framed posters and prints on the walls. The quiet was oppressive, but the thought of turning on the TV or radio was distasteful to her. She sighed deeply.

No more Ellen. She'd be married soon—already she and Stan were setting up house. Maggie grimaced at the thought of beginning the search for a roommate. Not right away. She didn't think she could take anyone in such close quarters just yet. She could afford to pay the whole rent for a couple of months—maybe even permanently. What with the raise and everything, maybe she wouldn't need another roommate. *If I'm going to be one of those career-woman spinsters, I might as well get started. No roommates, she decided, no friends, no lovers. Cats! I need cats! About a dozen of them!*

She thought of Ellen and Stan together then, and tried not to be envious. Ellen must have gotten the last nice guy left in New York. The only men left were either gay or creeps. Ellen was one lucky lady—she'd really played her cards right. She'd never been burned by the likes of a Craig Hastings, or worse, an Alex Parisi.

Two of a kind. I can see them now, bending elbows together at some midtown watering hole and comparing notes on the bimbo! That's all I was to them. I'm sure Craig wired Alex in Italy before I got there:

BIMBO ON THE WAY. STOP. TAKE HER, SHE'S YOURS. STOP. GOOD LUCK. CRAIG.

Craig was capable of that kind of stuff, no question about it. The most bold-faced, brazen two-timer I ever met.

But Alex was worse, a lot worse. Craig was practically up-front with his cheating, his thoughtless behavior. At least, Maggie had been able to see where he was coming from. But Alex, the cunning bastard, really had her fooled. That intellectual appearance only made him look like he was above those kinds of games. She could have kicked herself—here she'd caught him red-handed in his lying; then, she'd believed the absurd excuses he'd sling at her. God, no wonder he'd treated her like a bimbo! He'd seen a golden opportunity in her and snatched it. Having her and Gabriella at the same time, even introducing them, and taking her to Gabriella's parents' home. *What crust that guy has! The ultimate male ego-trip, the ultimate conquest. What a jerk I was! What a jerk Gabriella is! At least he didn't flaunt his cheating in front of me the way he did in front of her. I just wish. . . .*

The doorbell rang, interrupting her mental tirade.

Who the hell could that be? Let it ring, I don't care. I don't want to see anyone.

It rang again.

Go away! I'm not home!

After a long pause, the bell rang again. Whoever it was leaned on the button for a prolonged, insistent ring, prompting Maggie to leap off the sofa, furious and itching to tell the bell-ringer off.

"What do you want?" she yelled into the intercom.

"Maggie? Maggie, is that you?"

It was a man's voice. "I said, what do you want?" she repeated. "Who's there?"

"Maggie, it's Alex. I want to talk to you."

She began to tremble with anger and anxiety, unable to decide whether to ignore him or tell him to go to hell. She let go of the intercom button and the sound went dead.

He rang the bell again instantly.

"Goddammit, Parisi, you've got your nerve. Why don't you get lost? Go find someone else." She didn't let him reply, but shut off the intercom and returned to the sofa, running a nervous hand through her hair.

But he kept ringing. For ten minutes he pressed the buzzer again and again at irregular intervals. Maggie remained on the sofa, smoldering, confident that she could outlast him.

But the nagging bell eventually got the better of her. She was enraged at his persistence, and in a blind fury she bolted to the intercom. "Go away!" she screeched. "JUST GO AWAY!" Against her better judgment, she pressed the listen button to see if he had left.

"Maggie, listen to me. We have to talk. . . ."

"WHY?" she cut in.

"Because I lied to you in Rome, but I have to tell you why I had to."

"Boy, you take the cake. You really think you can buffalo me again?"

"You're all wrong, Maggie. Why won't you let me explain, for God's sake?"

"You're a good actor, Alex, but not that good. Now leave me alone before I call a cop."

"You're being stubborn and unreasonable, Maggie. You sound just like Gabriella!"

That did it. He was asking for it, now. Maggie pressed the front door buzzer until her fingernail turned white. *The bastard thinks he can get away with anything? Well, I've got news for him.*

She paced the hallway in her apartment like a caged wildcat, unable to wait for his arrival. Finally, the bell rang, and she whipped the door open. Alex was clad in one of his usual rumpled collegiate outfits—wool tie undone, collar unbuttoned, his coat and jacket open sloppily, like a delinquent preppy.

"Well," she announced sarcastically, "if it isn't the American gigolo himself!"

"Look, Maggie," he began, walking into the room past her, "I wanted you to. . . ."

"Yeah." She slammed the door behind him, "I know exactly what you wanted. Now, I suppose, you think you can come flying across the ocean for some more. Well, you can just forget about that!" Her voice was high and shrill; she was straining to control her temper.

"I know you're mad," he said softly, "and you have every right to be. But only because you don't know the whole story. I came to explain—if you'll listen."

"Hang on, I'll get my boots. I hear a real snow job coming!"

Alex dug his hands deep into his coat pockets and sat down on the edge of the sofa. He sighed and started to speak in a low voice. "I did lie to you. I admit it. But I had to. For your protection and mine."

"Oh, come off it, Alex. Can't you be more original than . . . ?"

"Hear me out!" he barked sharply. "I was the man in the middle between Gabriella and Pippo. I was in a dangerous position and I wanted to keep you out of it. But you still managed to get yourself in a terrorist shootout. Just what I was afraid of. You're lucky I tipped off the *carabinieri* when I did, or the magazine would be running your obit now."

"What are you talking about?"

"Let me start from the beginning. When I was researching the Aldo Moro story, I met Pippo. He was part of the Red Brigades then, but he was disillusioned with them. So, for a price, he gave me information, introduced me to the right people who could give me more information. One day, about a year ago, I met him at Tre Scalini, the place in the Piazza Navona where we had the *tartuffi*, remember?"

"Oh . . . yes, sure, I remember."

"After he walked away from the table, Gabriella just walked up to me and sat down. I had no idea who she was, but she knew all about me and my work for *Shout*. There were tears in her eyes but she looked very determined. She asked me to help her find the terrorists who killed her fiancé. I told you about that."

"Yeah."

"Well, Gabriella said that she saw a man hanging around on the street just before her fiancé's car blew up. She swore that the man she saw that night was Pippo. After that, she happened to see me and Pippo together having dinner in some restaurant, and she started following me. When she found out who I was, she asked for my help in nailing Pippo for the murder."

Maggie sat quietly in a chair opposite the sofa, looking skeptical and uncomfortable.

"Well, Pippo was my best contact. I wasn't about to risk losing him just to do her a favor. But, then, she made me an offer. If I helped her get Pippo, she said she would get me an exclusive, in-depth interview with her parents for my article on the plight of the besieged royalty in Rome. It was a hard offer to pass up, since rich Italians uniformly avoid the press like the plague, and the Sciarras had already turned down Mike Wallace and Oriana Fallaci. So I agreed to help her even though I wasn't sure whether Pippo really had anything to do with her lover's assassination, or if she was just out for revenge. What I didn't know was that Pippo was using me to get close to Gabriella and the Sciarras because. . . ."

"Because he wanted to blackmail the Sciarras with the truth about Gabriella's birth," Maggie finished his thought.

"Hey, you know more than I suspected." Alex was surprised.

"Sure, Pippo used me to do his research. I tracked down the particulars of Gabriella's past for him. That's why he wanted to kill me. If I published my story—which he assumed named names—he wouldn't have been able to shake down the Sciarras."

"And that's why I was so crazy to see your article on New Year's Day. I knew you were getting in deeper and deeper. I was hoping to convince you to leave Rome that morning. But you got mad and threw me out first."

She was quiet for a moment. "You were just looking out for me," she murmured at last.

"Of course. You were doing your research too well. I didn't want you to get hurt because of it. See, after the *Ordine dei*

Serpenti declared themselves with the bombing at the Palazzo di Giustizia, I was convinced that this was Pippo's new gang. One of my other moles told me that Pippo left the Red Brigades because he was sick of life on the lam, hiding out in cheap apartments and so on. It was known that he had champagne tastes. I learned that he had assembled a small gang who were in it simply for the money; the politics was just a cover for them. The *Ordine dei Serpenti* came off too apolitical, too obtuse to be really interested in changing the country. I knew that Pippo's group was about ready to strike."

"He did think of himself as a real *bon vivant*," Maggie confirmed. "That art work all over his apartment, those clothes...."

"All ill-gotten gains. The art was all ripped off or extorted, some pieces were from the Nazi treasury of stolen works of art. God only knows how he got them."

"And the name! It all makes sense!" It suddenly dawned on Maggie. "The Order of Snakes—of course!"

"What? Tell me."

"When Pippo took me to the Vatican, he showed me what he said was his favorite art work, the Laocöon. The sculpture of the high priest of Troy and his sons being murdered by this huge snake. The high priest was warning the Trojans about the Trojan horse, but the gods wanted to stop him from interfering with Fate by telling the truth, so they sent the snake to silence him. Pippo obviously identified with the snake snuffing out the good guys."

"That's interesting. You're probably right."

"So, is that why you suddenly got testy with Pippo around Christmas?"

"Yeah. It was getting harder and harder to play both ends against the middle, and the more I saw him sidling up to you, the angrier I got. You didn't know it, but he really upset the ball."

"Because Gabriella thought he crashed it?"

"No, actually, she invited him herself. She was so anxious to nail him, she didn't want him out of her grasp for too long. But when he had the nerve to go right up to the *contessa* in the receiving line and tell her that he knew all about Gabriella, previewing his blackmail plot, he got everyone crazy."

"With all those guards around? Why didn't they just take him there?"

"Pippo was clever, always stayed in the thick of the crowd. He said that if anyone tried to grab him, he'd spill the beans and embarrass the Sciarras at their big clambake. He had them right where he wanted them."

"And he looked so . . . so harmless."

"Harmless my foot. He was getting more dangerous by the day. You saw how arrogant he was on New Year's Eve at Jackie O's. He had the goods on Gabriella, so he didn't need me anymore. I also suspected that he knew that I knew about his new gang. I figured he was either going to rub me out or threaten to kidnap you, so I'd keep quiet. You still trusted him, so you would have been easy pickings for him."

"Why didn't you tell me all this?"

"Perhaps I should have, but I was convinced that you were better off staying ignorant. I wasn't sure how you'd react, or if you'd try to confront Pippo with my suspicions."

"Do I look that dumb?"

"Face it, he had you charmed. I was the one who looked villainous and untrustworthy, I knew that. You would have certainly wanted to give Pippo the benefit of the doubt over the guy who had been evasive with you all along."

"Well, I guess so," she had to admit. "But why did you demand to read my article? And why the hell were you going through my notes?"

Alex sighed, looking somewhat guilty. "I'm sorry about that, really. There was something I had to find out, and I didn't know how else to do it. I never intended to read your notes until I happened to glance at your open notebook and saw that you had Lieutenant Colonel Tony Russo written down. I became very curious. You see, I knew that Gabriella was adopted and I had to know if this was really her father. She didn't like to talk about her real parents, so of course I couldn't ask her if Tony Russo was her father."

"No, I suppose you couldn't. But I still don't get it. Why should you care who her real father was?"

"Remember I once told you that I had an uncle who was an army doctor?"

"Tony Russo?"

"That's right. My good ole Uncle Tony—may he rest in peace—was Gabriella's natural father. That's why I was so crazy about reading your piece. I was dying to know what you'd found out."

"Oh, my God! That means you and Gabriella . . . ?"

". . . are first cousins." He beat her to the punch.

"And I thought you two were. . . ."

"Never were and never will be. It only looked that way."

"I'm curious. Did Uncle Tony ever try to locate his daughter?"

"Not to my knowledge. I always thought he was a nice guy, but you never know what goes through someone's mind. I don't think he ever told anyone in the family about her."

"God, and what I thought about her! She's really been through a lot. I wish I'd had some inkling sooner. I mean, frankly, I don't think I would have liked her any better, but I would have understood how she got to be the way she is."

"Yeah, well, I think she's beginning to come around now and get over the past. She was quite relieved to know that Uncle Tony was no longer alive. She was always afraid her real father would show up like a ghost from the past. And it seems that she and her boss Aldo are getting tight. I wouldn't be surprised if they tied the knot in the near future."

"And what about Pippo?"

"In prison nursing his leg wound. Next month, he goes on trial in Turin for the murder of Gabriella's fiancé, then he'll have to face charges for the murders at the Palazzo di Giustizia bombing. I don't think he'll have to worry about paying rent for quite a while—if ever."

"God! I still can't get over it; he really had me fooled." She shook her head in disbelief.

"Maggie . . . ?" Alex stared at the rug, then looked up at her with uneasy eyes. "Are you still angry with me?" he asked tentatively.

"Uh . . . I guess not. I mean, you did lie to me, and you did make me feel like you were trying to sabotage my work, but I suppose you were just trying to protect me."

"That's right. You know, after you left, I did a little research into the innocents myself. There are a lot of possibilities with that topic. I mean, your series is great. I read it at the office yesterday. It's beautifully-written, that goes without saying, but it also makes some really important points; it has enormous ramifications for all kinds of people. There's a lot more that could be done with it, I think."

"Oh," she murmured distantly, "what do you want to do with it?"

"I'm thinking about a documentary film. I've done some dabbling in filmmaking in the past, and I've got a friend who owns his own production company in California. He's been bugging me for years to do something with him. I thought that maybe you'd like to collaborate with me. I mean, this is your topic—I couldn't take it away from you, and I'd really like to have the chance to work with you on something. Maybe you'd let me buy you dinner and we can talk it over." Alex seemed uncustomarily nervous, like a kid asking a girl to the prom.

"I don't know, Alex. . . ."

"Come on, Maggie, don't play hard to get." He stood up and went to her, taking her hands. "You know I came here to win you back. I love you. Don't make it difficult."

"Hmm. . . ." She had a sly grin on her face. "I'm not so sure about all this."

"Maggie? Don't you feel well? I'm offering you a meal! I've never seen you refuse food!"

"Well, frankly, Alex . . ." She stood and entwined her arms around his neck, ". . . I'm not hungry right now." She kissed him. He embraced her, his mouth covering hers. They parted after several minutes, and he gazed deep into her eyes.

The sly grin still on her face, she peeled Alex's coat off his shoulders, then undid his tie. She took his hand and led him toward the bedroom, walking backwards so she could face him.

She smiled. "I think we should take a meeting on this. . . ."

Dear Reader:

Would you take a few moments to fill out this questionnaire and mail it to:

Richard Gallen Books/Questionnaire
8-10 West 36th St., New York, N.Y. 10018

1. What rating would you give *Roman Candles?*
   ☐ excellent ☐ very good ☐ fair ☐ poor

2. What prompted you to buy this book? ☐ title
   ☐ front cover ☐ back cover ☐ friend's recommendation ☐ other (please specify) _____

3. Check off the elements you liked best:
   ☐ hero ☐ heroine ☐ other characters ☐ story
   ☐ setting ☐ ending ☐ love scenes

4. Were the love scenes ☐ too explicit
   ☐ not explicit enough ☐ just right

5. Any additional comments about the book?
   _____

6. Would you recommend this book to friends?
   ☐ yes ☐ no

7. Have you read other Richard Gallen romances? ☐ yes ☐ no

8. Do you plan to buy other Richard Gallen romances? ☐ yes ☐ no

9. What kind of romances do you enjoy reading?
   ☐ historical romance ☐ contemporary romance
   ☐ Regency romance ☐ light modern romance
   ☐ Gothic romance

10. Please check your general age group:
    ☐ under 25 ☐ 25-35 ☐ 35-45 ☐ 45-55 ☐ over 55

11. If you would like to receive a romance newsletter please fill in your name and address:

    _____
    _____
    _____

You Have a Rendezvous with Richard Gallen Books...

EVERY MONTH!

Visit worlds of romance and passion in the distant past and the exciting present, words of danger and desire, intrigue and ecstasy—in breathtaking novels from romantic fiction's finest writers.

Now you can order the Richard Gallen books you might have missed!

These great contemporary romances...

____	**DREAMTIDE** by Katherine Kent	41783/$2.75
____	**HIGH FASHION** by Victoria Kelrich	43164/$2.75
____	**THE GOLDEN SKY** by Kristin James	42773/$2.75
____	**THE SUN DANCERS** by Barbara Faith	41784/$2.75

Continued next page

...and These Thrilling Historical Romances.

____ **SWEET NEMESIS**
by Lynn Erickson 83524/$2.50

____ **SILVER LADY**
by Nancy Morse 83504/$2.50

____ **SAVAGE FANCY**
by Kathryn Gorsha Theils 83561/$2.50

____ **THIS REBEL HUNGER**
by Lynn LeMon 83560/$2.50

____ **FAN THE WANTON FLAME**
by Clarissa Ross 83446/$2.50

____ **A FEAST OF PASSIONS**
by Carol Norris 83332/$2.50

____ **THE MOONKISSED**
by Barbara Faith 83331/$2.50

____ **SOME DISTANT SHORE**
by Margaret Pemberton 42772/$2.75

____ **THE FROST AND THE FLAME**
by Drusilla Campbell 83366/$2.50

____ **THE VELVET PROMISE**
by Jude Deveraux 41785/$2.75

____ **CARAVAN OF DESIRE**
by Elizabeth Shelley 83681/$2.50

____ **TOMORROW AND FOREVER**
by Maude B. Johnson 83636/$2.50

POCKET BOOKS/RICHARD GALLEN PUBLICATIONS
Department RG
1230 Avenue of the Americas
New York, N.Y. 10020

Please send me the books I have checked above. I am enclosing $_____
(please add 50¢ to cover postage and handling for each order, N.Y.S. and N.Y.C. residents please add appropriate sales tax). Send check or money order—no cash or C.O.Ds please. Allow up to six weeks for delivery.

NAME_____

ADDRESS_____

CITY_____ STATE/ZIP_____